LOVE WAITS

RAIN TRUEAX

The Civil War has just come to an agonizing end-- corruption with its destructive divisiveness has spread to far off Oregon

Belle Stevens Morgan has led an adventurous life, far from her beloved family. On assignment in Oregon to investigate counterfeiting, she is posing as a governess in the employ of a wealthy and ruthless man. Lies are her stock in trade.
Captain Rand Phillips is asked to take on one of his most dangerous assignments regarding an attempt to start a new rebellion, with the Civil War barely over and the country still in turmoil. The biggest danger of all, however, may be to his heart as he sees the woman Belle.

When two warriors meet, with secrets between them, danger is bound to be in the mix.
Sometimes to win, one must risk it all.

Bounds for the Hills
is an original work of Rain Trueax.

ISBN: 978-1-943537-05-1
Paper Back Edition

Prepared and presented by:

Seven Oaks
Monmouth, Or.

Sign up for new release notifications at http://raintrueax.blogspot.com

Personal Contact and Rights Agreements write to: raintrueax@gmail.com

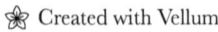 Created with Vellum

CHAPTER 1

1867, middle of September
—Oregon Outback

As the stage wound its way down the dusty and uneven road heading toward the Deschutes River, Belle Stevens Morgan asked herself, for the hundredth time-- why am I here? There were so many better places to be than a road so rough that her kidneys were being jarred, a road heading into country with an Indian war raging.

She imagined herself back in Chicago at one of the finest restaurants. She'd have been wearing a black gown of the finest silk, off her shoulders enough to scandalize. The food would be the best money could buy with servers hurrying from table to table to keep the patrons happy. Oh and then, instead of stale biscuits, there'd have been that café with the Bavarian pastries. Her mouth watered. Why the hell had she left? Oh, she knew. She just needed to remind herself why it had been wise to take this particular job with all its complications.

The bumpy road sent her leaning into the peddler who was already trying to find any excuse to grope her. She stiffly pulled herself away as she seriously considered giving him a punch that he wouldn't wake up from for enough hours to get them to their first stage stop. She calculated where she'd strike and just how hard. He smiled at her until he saw the expression on her face and quickly turned to look out the window.

Delicately she put a handkerchief over her mouth, wondering if anybody in the stage, other than she and her charges, had had a bath in the last month. Scratch that—last year. In close quarters, the stench was overwhelming.

With nothing else to do, she began to run through what lay ahead. Her employer, William Forester, had gone ahead in his private coach insisting he must travel faster for important and unnamed business meetings that simply could not wait. She wished she'd had more time to find out what else was in that high sprung coach with the eight powerful horses. All that just for him? Not possible.

Thanks to the secrets she knew he harbored, it would take his family three full days to travel the nearly two hundred miles from The Dalles to Canyon City. A trip he had likely made in a day and a half. Actually, even more amazing to her was that he even wanted his children to come to Canyon City or that he had bothered with a governess. That man had secrets-- none of which boded well for his offspring. She snuggled Jessica closer to her as the five-year old slept. Despite the elaborate home that Forester claimed awaited them, she pitied his children. Oh, he gave them all the luxuries anyone could desire—all but time with their father, who had bigger fish to fry. The question of exactly what those fish were, she was here to find out.

She felt certain that any evidence to prove what he was involved in had gone on that private coach. Why Pinkerton hadn't wanted him arrested with it while in The Dalles—that was another mystery. She knew Alan well enough, after working for him for four years, to realize he kept secrets close to his vest. He had not told her everything. She had a mission, but she didn't know how far it might go.

Jeremy's eyes popped open, and he looked at her with all the wisdom of a nine-year old. When she smiled back, he closed his eyes quickly. Across from her, he was wedged uncomfortably between a plump woman, with a flower and feather strewn hat, and what she judged to be a mine owner. Sitting just beyond him was a heavily made up young woman who smiled now and again at all the men in the coach. Her profession wasn't hard to guess. On the other side of Jessica was a slick looking, even handsome man, maybe late twenties, broadcloth jacket of good cut, tightly set lips, and he had no interest in talking or looking at any of them.

"You all right, Miss?" the miner asked gesturing with his chin toward the peddler, as she pushed back the pervert's hand with no small gentleness-- bending his finger until he winced. She'd have put Jessica between them except she didn't figure he was the discriminating type. The little girl would get the same treatment. The next time his hand landed on her thigh, she'd break that finger.

"I can deal with it," she said, adding, "and it's Mrs."

"Where is your husband?" the plump woman asked, again adjusting her hat.

She managed a sad smile. "Died in the War."

"Which side?" the peddler asked.

She gave him a look designed to kill. "Dead is dead."

He then turned to look out the window at the barren ground over which they were passing. If any of the country since they had left The Dalles had been pretty, she'd not have seen it, given the uncomfortable ride. There would be eight relay stations to change horses. Their two nights on the road would be in stage stations or camping, depending on which made travelers feel safer. She had been assured she and the children would have accommodations in the buildings, but the thought of the unclean bodies, who had likely been on those cots, had her believing outside might be better and safer.

Between depredations of Indians and outlaws, this was not a safe stage route. Before she had taken this assignment, she researched the region for any potential dangers. The Paiute, Shoshoni, Bannocks were seeking to reclaim their native lands and many were no longer interested in treaties likely to be broken. Add to that, the stage route was regularly preyed upon by outlaws, who found stealing gold more profitable than digging it from the ground. Boomtowns weren't noted for safety or longevity for those who hoped to find their fortunes and too often found a place in boot hill.

Belle wasn't after a fortune. She glanced out the window at the sky, which now appeared to be threatening. She was after truth, which was a bit of an irony considering. She was carrying with her so many lies that she felt a need also to run those through her mind to keep straight.

Her biggest lie, but easiest to remember was her name. Although Belle Morgan still sounded strange, that necessary lie had begun enough years earlier to make it easiest to remember. To hire women to work for the Pinkertons, Alan was culturally sophisticated for his time. He recognized the places women could investigate where a man never could. He did not hire unmarried women.

In 1861, Belle had looked up the records for war deaths and became the widow of a young man killed at one of the skirmishes that had no name. The no name part was important; so that she never had to remember details or take the risk of coming across someone who had been at Bull Run or all the other battles that early in the war took so many lives. She had to have a real name. The Pinkertons would check. They wouldn't go too far though with their research. Just enough to be sure it was possible. Alan saw the value in hiring beautiful women.

The rest of the lies came from her real reason for coming to Canyon City. Working for Alan had led to interesting assignments, many during the war. Her education had helped her adapt herself to this persona as a governess. It wouldn't be hard to teach small ones what they needed to know. What would be hard was not falling in love with these poor little waifs. Small children were a tender spot for her, but this time she had to toughen her heart. What she was about to do in going to the gold camp in the middle of nowhere was prove their father was a master counterfeiter. That would leave them not only motherless but also fatherless.

When she had learned where this would require her traveling, she'd had concerns beyond the dangers of the job itself. Part of it involved her family but an even bigger concern involved a man.

Just thinking about Randall Phillips made her angry. She had been such a naïve girl when she had thrown herself at him, already a tested soldier. He had held her off as if she was a child. Certainly, at nearly seventeen she had been young. It had taken her years, to realize how young she had been. She sighed as she stared blankly out the window.

With the Civil War behind him, she knew Captain Phillips was in the region, to which she traveled. The reason she knew made her even angrier with herself. Ten years had passed. Had she learned nothing?

She always knew where he was. Fool. She knew more about the battles he had fought in the Civil War than about her supposed husband's. Maybe she should have used them for Private Morgan, except she couldn't bear to do that given the unfortunate end of that *husband*.

After the war ended, Rand had been on the Plains fighting Indians before he was sent to Oregon to be part of ending the Indian war known by some as the Snake Conflict. Although Camp Watson wasn't that many miles from Canyon City, she felt she'd be unlikely to run into him. He was likely out in the field most of the time. She wouldn't let herself think about the danger that meant. His life had always been dangerous.

Unfortunately, Rand wasn't the only potential complication. She had family along the north fork of the John Day River. Farther away than Camp Watson, still, they might have more reason to spend time in Canyon City.

Hopefully, no one would think to inquire about her maiden name; but if they did, she had prepared a lie. She would say she and her family were estranged, hadn't talked in years. Whatever she did, she would not let them become entangled in her work.

Being a Pinkerton had made her good at lying and cautious of giving enough details that the lies could be ferreted out. She carried appropriate papers, of course, forged, but a wily counter agent could find they were based on fiction and dead people-- leaving her a potential dead person herself. No negative thinking, Belle, she demanded of herself. Be positive.

She hated how a long stage ride left way too much time for thinking. As bouncy as it was, no way could she read. All she was left with were memories and thinking. With relief, out the window she saw that they had reached the Deschutes River.

"You folks need to take a little walk around, stretch your legs and then walk across the bridge," the stage driver suggested as the guard opened the door, pulled out the step and helped the ladies and children down.

When Belle looked out at the rickety bridge, she realized taking weight off the coach might've been a factor on having them walk over it.

"I need to find a bush," the older lady said as she headed downstream a bit.

"Watch out for rattlers, ma'am," the guard said as he handed down Jessica. "I'd beat the bushes for ya," he suggested to Belle, with the kind of smile she was used to receiving from men.

"I can handle it myself," she said as she led her two charges downstream as the coach moved onto the bridge. She hoped it wouldn't be swept away before they got their chance to cross. Maybe she should have suggested they go first. Too late now.

The river rushed through the rock chute setting up small falls and rapids. No place to fall in. She wished again that Jeremy would stay closer. Her demanding he do it would more than likely send him rushing to the bank. He had a stubbornness that clearly was his way to get attention. It also might get him killed.

By the time they reached the thick bushes along the bank, the heavyset woman was coming out. "Nothing in there," she said. "By the way, my name is Miranda Campbell."

"I'm Belle Morgan. She is Jessica and he is Jeremy Forester."

"You their step mama?" the nosy woman asked with the kind of smile that probably got her snoopiness a pass from most people.

"Governess." Belle helped Jessica with her slips and pantaloons, but Jeremy took care of himself then headed back toward the passengers waiting on the bank watching the coach now mid-river as it lurched across.

"Jeremy, wait for us," she yelled but the boy ignored her. That one had a lot of anger as he was likely more aware of the neglect of his father than Jessica.

"He's got a stubborn head on those little shoulders," Miranda observed.

Belle nodded, took care of her own needs, grateful that Miranda waited with Jessica.

"I'm meeting my husband in Canyon City," Miranda said as the three walked.

"Have you been there before?" Belle asked feeling more predisposed toward her with the way she had looked after Jessica.

"No, that man, he's always off somewhere. We were in Oregon City when he heard about the gold strikes in California. That didn't pan out. Figured it wouldn't, and I stayed where I was because I was working in the restaurant there, and you don't give up good jobs like that to run off after a scalawag."

She wondered then if Miranda might know her mother or stepfather when he had been sheriff there. With a bit of luck, at least not well. "But you came this time."

"Yes, he said he has a real claim and enough gold in it to set us up back in Portland when he gets it all. I figured I better go before a floozy like that one on the stage takes him for all he's got—which ain't been much." She smiled.

As they reached the bridge, the coach had finished crossing, and they followed the guard as he led them to the right places to walk. When Jessica got frightened of the distance between the boards, no amount of reassurance would comfort her that she couldn't possibly fall through them, and Belle picked her up.

"She's heavy for you, ma'am," the man she had dubbed a miner said. "My name is James Williams. I'd be happy to carry the little one on across. "I got a small one like her myself."

"Thank you, Mr. Williams. That is very generous of you, but I can carry her just fine." She watched the spaces between the boards and kept a steady pace, happy that she regularly did exercises to keep her muscles in shape for whatever they might be called upon to do. She was however relieved when she touched solid ground and could set Jessica down.

"Time for a water break," the driver said as he tapped the barrel in back and filled cups for each of them. "It's about an hour before we reach our first night stop. Hope you folks are enjoying the trip so far."

Belle nearly smiled thinking he had to be joking. But then what would a man say who was taking a load of passengers into wild country where they could be attacked at any time. She wondered how many of the passengers understood exactly how dangerous this stage road could be. She made sure the children had their cups and then sipped from her own studying the others on the stage. She wondered how much help any would be if they did run into trouble.

The slick dressed man who had remained silent stepped forward. Belle saw for the first time that he carried a revolver on his hip. "Can I rent a horse there to finish out the journey faster?" he asked with a distinct southern drawl.

"Not likely but you can ask. Ma and Pa Jamison just took it over and still trying to get it stocked." He chuckled. "Make that keep it stocked. The Injuns love to steal mules or horses. Ol' Paulina might be dead but plenty still out there raiding and burnin'." He took a chaw. "Should've got yourself a horse in The Dalles."

The man snorted. "The military commandeered every decent looking animal. I didn't need a mount going lame part way there." He stared into the distance as the driver spit at his feet.

"Then you're stuck with me until we get to Canyon City. With gold, you likely can buy a good horse there, Mr. Hoyt."

"Gold, huh? No taking federal dollars there?"

"Not sayin' nobody would. Jest it's a gold camp. You ever been in one of them?" the guard asked, having listened to their conversation. "Man, that country's gone gold crazy. Ain't nobody goin' there that ain't looking for diggin' it or..." He chuckled. "Stealin' it."

"What's your hurry anyway?" the driver asked. "I'll get you there two nights and two more days."

Hoyt sighed and stared into the distance. "I was supposed to meet someone but missed them in The Dalles."

"Better hope yore friend's got gold then or a horse, cuz you ain't likely to find neither you being a Southerner," the guard said with disdain.

The man smiled faintly. "Did I say it was a friend?"

"Reckon you didn't. Well might be good if it was-- as a southerner you'll need one."

"Nobody digging gold there fought for the South?" he asked as he drew a fine cigar from his vest and bit off the tip before lighting it behind his cupped hands.

"Them what was don't go talkin' about it." The guard chuckled.

"Wal, one does," the driver said. "Jed Hardman walks tall and proud wherever he goes. You know him?"

"Might've heard the name. Having a southern accent doesn't mean a man fought for the South," Hoyt said. "Virginia split in the middle over partition."

"You a Virginian then?" the guard asked with a tad more friendliness.

"I didn't say that either."

"So what's the name of this friend of yours what ain't a friend?" the driver asked. "Might be as we know him."

When Belle heard William Forester's name, she studied the stranger with more interest. Handsome face, but she felt an instinctive distrust of him. "I am Colonel Forester's governess. These are his children," she said. "Pity you missed him in The Dalles."

The stranger for the first time looked at her. "I was to meet him there."

"He hurried ahead on personal business," she said meeting his gaze.

"Of what sort?" the man asked.

She gave a laugh. "I am the governess for his children, not his personal secretary, Mr. Hoyt."

He smiled as he blew smoke out away from her. "Dylan."

"Mrs. Morgan," she responded, sure now she didn't trust him.

Belle heard the sound of gunshots from what she saw ahead had to be the station where they were supposed to find shelter. It looked like Ma and Pa Jamison were facing problems of their own. She lifted her skirt and unfastened the derringer strapped to her thigh, ignoring the attempt by the peddler to see more of her leg.

"Injuns?" Miranda asked with fear in her voice. "Shouldn't we turn around?" The slick dressed man pulled his Colt and moved to where he could look out the window. The heavily made up woman also brought a small revolver from her small valise and checked its load as though she knew how to do it. Probably she did. Of the adults, only the peddler and Miranda appeared to be unarmed.

"I would like Jeremy over here with Jessica," she requested and the adults did some shuffling. She sheltered the children with her body on one side and the peddler's on the other. There would be no point in her shooting out the window. This gun would not reach far. It was deadly if the attackers got close.

The stage driver did not slow the stage but ran them full speed toward the stone building. If the Indians were surprised by their arrival, they quickly adapted and began shooting toward the stage as well as the building. Miranda screamed with fear, which led to Jessica crying.

Belle heard the guard shooting and then the stage slammed to a halt inside the corral and the driver was leaping down, opening the door and helping them toward the building with the stage to shelter them as much as possible. Hoyt was the last one inside, slamming the door and throwing the bolt.

The children huddled into a corner with Jeremy now reassuring his sister. Miranda Campbell put her arms around them both. Belle went to one of the shuttered windows. Outside, through the dust, she saw seven, maybe eight Indians racing toward the corral. They'd be after the stage's relief horses. Maybe leave if they got them-- or would they.

"You know how to shoot, Miss?" the man she knew had to be Pa Jamison asked.

"Very well but this peashooter doesn't have much range."

He handed her a rifle. She smiled and moved to the window where she would have a chance at hitting something that counted. It was then she heard the sound of more horses coming fast. Were the Indians being reinforced? They wouldn't be surviving this attack if that was the case, stone building or not.

The shots increased. The Indians whirled to meet the new charge before they headed their ponies north and out of the small valley. It was then that Belle realized the new arrivals were wearing uniforms. The cavalry had arrived.

Pa Jamison opened the front door with a big grin as the soldiers hauled their mounts to a halt. "You got here in the nick of time," Pa said with a laugh.

A tall man, covered with dust and looking totally worn stepped from his saddle, took off his hat and hit it on his thigh to knock the dust from it as he walked toward Pa. Belle knew his rugged features even with the bearded stubble on his square jaw. Rand Phillips.

CHAPTER 2

"We have been chasing them the last five days," Rand said reaching for his bandana to wipe sweat from his forehead. "Wish we'd caught up with them sooner. Anybody hurt here?"

"Would'a been us all if you hadn't shewed up, Captain. Sure am glad to see ya."

Rand turned to his corporal, "Muldoon, look for any survivors, take prisoners if there are any. Arrange a burial detail." He could see at least four Walpapi bodies on the ground and wanted to be sure that they were not capable of doing more damage.

"Stage passengers all right?" He looked toward the building.

Pa Jamison looked back in the door. "Everybody all right in there, Ma?"

"Just skeered is all," she hollered back. "Tell the captain, I just got to make a few more biscuits, plenty of stew, if him and his men want to eat with us."

Rand considered that. He'd like to have continued following the hostiles. They were Northern Paiute and had already killed one lone traveler and stolen horses from two outlying ranches. Still, he had to consider the safety of the passengers. The bunch he'd been following weren't the only ones out there.

"Yes, we'd appreciate that," he said making the decision to see this stage through the worst of the country. When they reached the second overnight stop, they'd be safer, and he could resume his hunt for the Paiutes.

He looked then back to the house and saw her for the first time.

She was older, even more beautiful if that was possible, but he had no doubt who she was. Before he could say anything, she said, "Captain, you have blood on your shirt. Are you wounded?"

He looked down at his side. It was sore but had bled little. "Just a gouge. It happened yesterday. Doesn't amount to much," he said accepting by the coolness of her expression that she didn't want him to acknowledge that he knew her.

"I think it should be looked at. If the driver doesn't mind, I have some supplies in my bags on the stage. Are any of your men in need of medical care?"

"Grayson got a scratch across his forehead but otherwise, no."

The driver retrieved her bag, and she delved into it pulling out a small sack. "I saw a well out back, come with me," she said. "By the way, my name is Mrs. Morgan."

"Captain Phillips," he answered. He turned back toward Sergeant Smith. "Get the horses unsaddled and put out a watch." He followed her, wondering if she would admit she knew him once they were alone.

At the well, she brought up a bucket and then turned back to him. "Take off your shirt," she said with a faint smile.

"You are pretty pushy for a woman just went through an Indian attack," he observed as he pushed his suspenders off his shoulder and began unbuttoning his blouse.

She gave him a saucy smile. "And you don't look sufficiently surprised to see me here."

"Should I be?"

When he slid the shirt off, he looked down at the angry scrape in his side. He'd dodged a bullet with that one as it could have been a whole lot worse.

She moved over to feel around the wound and then reached for a carbolic acid bottle.

"That necessary?" he asked having had experience with wounds enough to know how much it would hurt.

She had a small cloth dipped in water and used it to wash away the dried blood from his side. "Why didn't you have this treated?" she asked with a tart tone.

"The surgeon general was busy at the moment."

"Smart ass."

"I was chasing Paiutes, which took priority-- Little Hand's band. They don't wait around for afternoon tea. I either stayed with him or gave up and let him do what he would. Good thing I listened to my instincts."

She smiled up at him. "Perhaps, and we are fortunate also, but this has infected." She pressed against the center of the long gouge, and he winced. He looked down and realized she was right.

"Open it then."

She drew a small blade from her bag. "It was sterile," she said taking it from a sheath.

"Carbolic should make sure of that."

She nodded. A moment later, he hissed as she opened the pocket of puss and pushed out what she could before using the carbolic.

"Damn, that hurt."

"Less than if it had formed an abscess and gone internal."

"You know quite a lot about wounds for a lady wearing such a pretty traveling suit."

She grinned again meeting his gaze before getting back to her task. "You like my suit?"

"Do your folks know you are here?"

"No."

"And you don't want them to?"

"You are more insightful than I remembered."

"So you do remember?"

She took a salve from her bag and applied it over the wound, which was now just barely seeping fluids and blood. "I remember."

"Why the Morgan?"

"I'm a widow. Of course."

He didn't like that much, but it was his own doing. "Your parents know about that?"

"You are a nosy man and as pushy as I remember."

He smiled at that. "No new husband on the way?"

"Not yet. I am going to Canyon City as a governess for Mr. Forester's two children."

"Is he a prospect for the next man to change your name?" He didn't know why he said that. It revealed far more than he wanted.

"Who knows? Maybe." She cut off a length of surgical tape to secure a cotton pad over the infected part of his wound. She stood back then to survey her handiwork. "You look tired, Rand."

He nodded. "Five days trailing right behind them can do that. They can go night and day when required. They stole fresh horses once that we didn't."

"And now you can't go after them because of me." It wasn't a question.

"I already made that decision before I saw you," he retorted.

"Us."

"There are things more important than getting one band. I'd like to have them, of course, but we did kill four of them here. There will be another day."

"When you might be killed as well as them."

"It's a soldier's life. I've been lucky so far."

She looked at his torso as he pulled back on his shirt. "I see the scars to say that's not totally so."

"Belle, I could be dead. I call that lucky."

She smiled. "All right. I cede that."

"I have to see to my men but can we talk later?"

"It's best we don't, and please, if you see my family, don't tell them I'm here. I will let them know eventually."

"I won't lie if they should ask."

"I don't expect you to lie, but they have no reason to ask for now anyway."

"The last I heard you were in New York City."

"Ah, well, obviously, I am not." She smiled. Repackaging her supplies, she walked from him.

As Rand got his men settled for the night, he thought back on the strangeness of finding the only woman he had ever loved right in his path. Not that it mattered. When she had been seventeen, it had been irresponsible and impossible, and it was no less so now. He was a career soldier and had little chance of surviving to be an old man. Even if he did, he'd have no fortune to give a woman like her the life that other men could offer.

He thought then about how beautiful she was. She'd been a pretty girl, but as a woman with sculpted cheekbones, big blue eyes, that blonde hair piled high, even with lengths straggling out after all she'd been through, she was enough to set any man back on his heels. She was a lady through and through. Her mother would be proud if she saw her.

But Belle was right. It was better they not talk. He wasn't a man to fight lost causes. He laughed at himself then. On the other hand...

Canyon City

The handsome young lieutenant tucked in his shirt and reached for his jacket.

"That's mine," William Forester said with a smile.

"I am sorry, sir, but it's mine."

"Was."

The young man stopped and looked at him. "Why would you want it?"

Forester's smile increased. "It doesn't matter. I do and that's that." Oh, he was such a handsome young man but so naive. He liked them that way—for a while.

"Are you angry at me for something?"

"Disappointed might be a better word."

"I've given you all I know about the patrols. I've done my best." He again reached for his jacket. Forester stopped the supple, young fingers, took hold of the jacket and threw it behind his desk chair. He saw the debate on the officer's face before he realized he had no choice. "They will make me buy a replacement."

"Your problem." He gave him the hard look he knew intimidated many men. He wanted him intimidated. "And your best wasn't good enough." He liked to see those cool blue eyes look down. The best control over people was dominance. He knew all about how to do that.

"He is not an easy man to second guess. He operates fast and that makes it hard to give you information in time."

"That's your problem. You do like the gifts you receive."

"You know I do."

"There must be an accounting."

"He's my superior. I don't give him orders."

"Perhaps we need a man there, easier to deal with. An accident would take care of the problem."

"You aren't expecting me to..." He again looked away. He was in too deep now to have a choice. "I have to get back."

"So go."

The younger man sighed. "You sure about the jacket? I can't see what it will do for you."

"It's not your business why I want it. Let's just say it's the price for failure." He smirked as he again saw the young officer turn away.

"I thought I had been of value to you."

"Some, but not enough. You can do more. You know to whom you owe your first allegiance, don't you?"

The young man nodded. The knock at the door ended what he might have argued next as Harold Moriarty walked in.

Forester felt disgusted at how Harold had let himself go. Bald wasn't his fault, but fat was. He admired physical beauty. Harold had once had it himself. No longer.

"Good afternoon, Harold," he said.

The lieutenant edged toward the door with one last look at where his jacket lay out of reach. "I must go. They will be expecting me," he said without ever looking at Moriarty.

"You need to distract and keep the captain out of our way. If you don't, he will have to be removed."

"What do you mean?"

"You know what I mean. Now get out of here. Close the door as you go." When he heard the door shut, he smiled as Harold went to the sideboard and poured himself a whiskey before sitting across from him.

"I am surprised you want a murder," he said as he sipped the hard liquor. Harold believed he was his partner. Forester liked it that way. No man was really his partner. He ran the show, but he ran it by forcing his will on those who otherwise would never get anywhere with their plans. Sometimes he used greed as he had with Harold. His skill was in knowing his subjects

"Only if I have to. I am still hopeful the captain can be bought or otherwise persuaded." He smiled and steepled his fingers. "However, sometimes it's how it must be. I am above all a practical man."

"It's just a small camp, not a lot of soldiers. Aren't you making too much out of his importance?" Harold watched him over the rim of his glass.

"One leads to others."

"Have you directly tried to bribe him?"

"Of course not. I don't know him well enough to know his weaknesses. Perhaps I need to do that." He had only seen the captain once. Tall, slim of build, probably muscular, he had ridden through Canyon City with a patrol. One might have expected him to stop at the bar. Did the man have no thirsts? His failure to linger infuriated Forester. If he had directly spoken to him, he'd better know how to deal with the unpredictable barrier to his goals. He didn't need to tell that to Harold though. He would deal with the captain in his own way. Everyone had a weakness. He just needed to find his.

"When do your children get here?"

"Two days."

"I'm surprised you want them here."

Forester shrugged as he lit a cigar. "They make good cover. I am going to become an important man in Oregon. Besides, I am quite attracted to their governess."

"I thought your interests went other ways," Moriarty said with a smile.

15

"They go toward beauty of all sorts, my friend." He used the term loosely. He had no friends either.

"And she is pretty?"

"Beautiful."

"So you intend to court her?"

"Perhaps. I will decide that when I spend more time with her."

Moriarty shook his head. "Just out of curiosity... Do you have anyone you respect, Will?"

"Come, come. Don't you know I respect you." He smiled. Of course, Harold had been right. He did respect no other person. They were all to be used. He was the only one who understood his aims and knew how to get what he wanted. Someday the world would be grateful for what he brought to it—order and a system that worked as it should.

"I know you use me as you do the others. That's all right with me though. I know you for what you are."

Forester lit a cigar. "And that would be?"

"Totally ruthless."

Forester chuckled and blew out the smoke. "A nice compliment. Doesn't it worry you to work with me?"

"No, because we are two of a kind. And if you ever try to pull on me what you do on the others, I'll kill you."

"If you can." Forester wasn't worried. He could use Moriarty. When that changed, he'd get rid of him before he ever knew he had a risk. His ability to read people was his greatest talent.

Cuddled together with Jessica on one side and Jeremy on the other, Belle lay awake staring up at the moon overhead It was a crescent and seemed so close. She had tried to sleep. It was impossible knowing he was so near. Sleeping just beyond the station perhaps in a tent or would he be out in the open staring up at the night sky, hearing the same owl in the distance.

My God, he had gotten handsome. She had last seen him at twenty-five and he'd been handsome but not more than a youth. Now ten years later, his face had hardened with a toughness that had only begun to show back then. His hair was dark, thick and a little longer than regulation probably favored. Then he had taken off his shirt and she had had to resist a groan. No man's body could be more beautiful sculpted than Rand Phillip's. The scars on his shoulder and arm told her as much about his life as his words. A soldier's life. Once she had thought she wanted to marry a man living that life. Now she wasn't so sure. It was best they not talk. There wasn't anything they could say that could change reality. Two different people from different worlds.

"Belle?"

She was surprised to hear Jeremy's small voice. "What?" she asked stroking his hair.

"You had a gun today."

"Well, yes."

"And then you took care of that soldier who had been hurt."

"Yes, I did that too."

"You know a lot of things."

She smiled as she reached over to brush the hair off his forehead. "A few."

"Could you teach me things?"

She felt a flush of warmth. She had not intended to love these two children, but the months she had spent as their governess, it had happened. "I could if your father didn't mind."

"He doesn't care what I do." His voice was not sad or even mad. It was just a stated fact. Sadly, he was right. William Forester did not appear to love his children. Why then had he wanted them to come to Canyon City? Perhaps part of his ruse. She didn't hate him. She didn't care enough about him to hate him. Disdain rather suited what she felt for such a cold man.

"Yes, Jeremy, I could teach you those things along with literature, history, and mathematics."

"Jer."

"Jer?"

"I'd rather you called me Jer. It's what my friends called me back when he let me go to school."

She felt a kindred sadness for Jeremy. She had left home earlier than many, but in her case, it was by choice. Jeremy had been pushed into boarding schools and now disrupted from them by this journey to Canyon City with no clear idea why he was wanted there. "I will do that, Jer," she said. "Now sleep. It'll be a long day tomorrow."

The little boy closed his eyes and soon she felt he was asleep. When she heard a step at her side from the direction of the station, she reached for her derringer.

"It's just me." The slender woman lay down on the porch on the other side of Jessica.

"All right." She released the weapon and pushed down her skirt.

"You don't like me much, and I wouldn't have disturbed you, but it stunk to high heaven in there. That peddler, he snored so loud, I couldn't sleep."

"I don't own the porch," Belle whispered. The woman settled down with a blanket she had brought. "And I have no reason to like or dislike you."

"Most women don't like women in my trade."

Belle smiled. "You consider it a trade?"

"Sure is. Gotta know what you're doin'. For some there ain't a lot of options for making a living. I don't have no fancy education like you. Can't go teachin' children what I don't know myself."

"I'm Belle Morgan."

"Annie Jessup."

"You think it will be good for you in Canyon City?"

"Where there's gold, it has the chance of me gettin' some." Annie suppressed a little giggle.

"I guess."

"That captain, the man you took care of, he was a mighty good looking fella."

"I suppose."

"You know his name?"

"Why?"

"Just curious. Don't see men that handsome often. Tall too. Wonder if he's tall everywhere." Annie giggled again.

Belle felt irritated but suppressed it. "I believe his name is Captain Phillips."

"I'll remember that." A new note was in Annie's voice—a hardening. "I hear there's a fort not far from Canyon City. Watson or some such. Maybe soldiers get to town."

"Not a lot of money with most soldiers," Belle observed.

"A man like that one, I'd do for free."

"You can always offer."

"Nah, he wouldn't touch a woman like me. Got class written all over him." She ran her fingers over Jessica's red hair. "She's sure a sweet little thing. Hope she never gets into... ah never mind."

"It's never too late to learn things and change a life path," Belle said feeling sympathy for a woman some referred to as soiled doves.

"It can be. Things can happen that make a woman... not have a choice."

"Nonsense. It's all in what you want. You can find other ways if you wish to anyway."

"I had my way paid here by Rance Dickinson. Got to work in his crib to pay it back."

"How much money?" Belle knew she was being a fool to ask. What this girl did was none of her business. She'd already chosen her world. Why feel sorry for her.

Annie went up on one elbow to look at Belle. "Why would you even ask? Maybe I am just playing you."

"That's possible."

"God, you seem like a simpleton to even suggest such a thing."

Belle suppressed her own laugh. "And you just forgot you don't have any education."

Annie laid back with a reluctant smile that showed teeth with the glow of the moonlight. "All right, so maybe it pays to be a little stupid and not know much."

"How long have you been in the trade? And your calling it that was my first clue that you weren't all you portrayed yourself to be."

Annie chuckled. "Do you know Han Jei?"

Belle felt a surge of her own concern. She didn't know him but her mother had written of him. "Not really. Chinese gentleman, of course."

"I worked with him and Bernice McDowell in Portland. It was a high class operation, and I was there two years."

"Why leave it?"

"Several reasons. My brother was killed in The Dalles—shot in the back, murdered in cold blood. He'd been helping me out financially. I'd love to take care of the stiff who did it. And I don't mean service him. Anyway, after he was dead, it got dicey to stay in Portland. The whole power structure on the waterfront shifted when the man who kept the operation safe and profitable was killed. Jei had gone. Bernice too. I didn't know who'd be taking over... I told you too much, didn't I?" Belle could hear the smile in her voice.

"It means little to me."

"I heard there was a lot of money being made in Canyon City. And Dickinson didn't pay my way. I just said that as part of... Well, you know."

Belle considered what she could say without giving herself away. "I have heard Canyon City is also a very dangerous place to be."

"So why are you going there with these two adorable children?"

"It's my job, and it's where their father, Mr. Forester, wants them to be."

"It doesn't seem he's showing very good judgment, but then what do I know about being a father or a mother."

"It is normal for a father to want his children with him especially with their mother dead."

"She's dead?"

The tone in Annie's voice had again changed, and Belle wondered what that had meant. Clearly, this woman had her own secrets. For her own reasons, she had opted to reveal something of herself to Belle. The question was why. Until she had the answer to that, she'd be cautious around her. She remembered the woman also carried a gun that she had been prepared to use.

"We should try to sleep," Belle said to end a conversation she did not want. "It could be a hard day tomorrow." She wondered if she could but whether she did or not, she didn't want to talk to Annie Jessup again, at least not until she had a chance to find out a bit more about her. Something was very odd there.

In the morning, Belle had slept as well as she could have expected and had the children at the table for the breakfast Ma Jamison was preparing. "You like hotcakes?" Ma asked.

"They're all right," Jeremy said without much enthusiasm.

"I have some apples too." She was frying bacon and added more strips to a plate in the center of a big wooden table. The peddler, miner, and Mrs. Campbell quickly filled their plates. Hoyt, the man Belle now took to be a gambler was smoking, standing in the back door. He had watched Annie return from the outhouse. Belle didn't like the look in his eyes. Opportunist at best and at worst, she didn't want to think.

"You folks be ready in half an hour," the driver said as he entered sitting across from the children. "The captain said him and his men'll ride with us as far as Fossil and maybe some beyond to see us past more risk of Injun attacks. Ya got any more of that syrup, Ma?"

"You need to eat more than that," Belle pointed to Jessica's barely touched pancake.

"I don't like it."

"You'll be hungry later."

Jessica stuck out her lip.

"Tell ya what," Ma said, going over to her cupboard. "I made some biscuits for later. Maybe take a few of them with you for the little ones so's they won't be hungry later."

Belle smiled appreciatively and wrapped them in a small cloth before putting them in her valise. She sipped her coffee and ate two strips of bacon. When she heard the sound of boots and spurs on the wooden front porch, she resisted the urge to look up.

"I am leaving eight troopers to ride with the stage," Rand told the driver. "Two will follow by a few hundred feet. I'll be scouting ahead with two more. I don't look for trouble, but if something should happen that we don't find first, fire two quick shots, and I'll double back fast."

The driver nodded and smiled. "I appreciate you staying with as far at least as Fossil."

"Or beyond if I have reason to think you will be having trouble. We'll turn back then and see if we can catch up with the hostiles."

"Sorry we took ya out of yore way, Captain," the driver said.

"It's our job to protect citizens not just go after Paiutes. I'm glad you didn't end up with any casualties."

"You got any spare horses?" Hoyt asked Pa Jamison when he came in from outside.

"Not to sell you," the hostler said. "Between the stages, military loads and private parties, we are short ourselves."

Hoyt sighed and then looked at the captain. "How about you?"

Rand laughed. "You must be joking. We nearly ran our horses into the ground. Sorry, but if you hoped to get a mount, your best bet is Shaniko, but not sure you'll find any there either. Traveling is a risky business, and horses are stolen as often as the hostiles can find them."

Hoyt looked irritated but said nothing more as he walked out front. Jeremy had finished off his second hotcake and was asking for another.

"You have a hearty appetite, sir," Rand said as he sat across from the boy and accepted a cup of coffee from Ma Jamison.

"Would you like some yourself, Captain?" Ma asked.

He shook his head. "I ate two hours ago with my men, had a ride around beyond just to be sure nothing was there to cause trouble." He then looked toward Belle. When his gaze met hers, she felt the heat all the way to her toes. "How did you sleep, Mrs. Morgan?" he asked sipping the hot brew and watching her over the rim of his cup.

"Quite well, thank you, Sir."

"Captain," the peddler asked, "how long before you get these redskins back on the reservations where they belong?"

Rand shifted his gaze to him, his expression hardening. "You have suggestions as to how we do that, I assume?"

"Well, more troopers would be a good start."

"And willing to pay more taxes to cover that?"

"Well..."

"The Civil War took a lot of the nation's funds. Last winter I had to buy food for my men from my own funds. Forts like The Dalles have been shut down due to cost saving. I think you need to write Washington and suggest higher taxes."

"Not saying that's a good idea."

"Then perhaps you need to be grateful there are horse soldiers out here willing to live on nothing, ride all day, and then get shot at for their troubles. Without what we have now, this would be a hundred times worse."

"Have you shot some Indians?" Jeremy asked his eyes looking bright with curiosity.

Rand turned back to the child, and his expression softened. "I've done what I had to do but never with pleasure, son."

A soldier appeared at the door, "Captain, Carmody is back with a report."

"Excuse me." He rose, finishing off his coffee with a swig and stalking out the door.

Belle refilled her own coffee cup, got Jessica to drink a little milk, felt of her forehead and was relieved this wasn't a fever. This was so hard on a child, but then she remembered her own trip west with the wagon train. She had been older but still a child. Life was hard. She would do what she could for these two, while she had them under her wing.

Annie was sitting next to Jessica and brushed out her hair with her fingers. "Such pretty red hair. Did you get that from your mama, Jessica?"

The little girl looked down at the table without answering.

"We never knew our mother," Jeremy said. "Well I did but don't remember much about her. She wasn't around a lot and then when Jessica was born, she was gone."

"I am sorry."

Jeremy shrugged with an expression on his face far too old for his years.

Belle was grateful that Annie didn't try to pry further. She was convinced there was a reason for her question, a reason for the game she was playing. She would find out what it was. She wondered if Jessup was her real name. If it was, she'd know more when she got a chance to send some messages.

CHAPTER 3

A t first light, Rand walked to his horse where Carmody awaited. "They went northwest. Just guessing, sir, but I think heading toward Tygh Valley where they are likely to find horses again."

Cursing, Rand rolled a cigarette as he tried to think what they needed to do. His squad was too small to divide. If he left the stage, they were likely to be attacked where there was no shelter. No, with small children and women, he had to stay with the stage. Even his small force would discourage any attack—at least as things stood.

"We don't have any choice, Corporal. We'll have to see the stage through. You take Sischy and follow about a mile or two behind." He looked toward the other men listening. "I'll ride point with Muldoon. Smith, you and the rest stay with the stage. Any trouble and you all know the drill."

They nodded.

"Mount up."

The stage driver was helping the passengers back into the stage. Rand rode to where the Jamisons were watching. "Don't go out when you don't have to. I'll be sure you get new supplies as soon as possible."

He had been heading to The Dalles before he'd been distracted by the war party. It hadn't been a major deterrent. No, that was the stage which was taking him totally out of his way. No choice for that.

The Colonel wouldn't like his not being there by Monday, but he would have to understand. What the secretive meeting had been about still had him wondering or would have if he had not been too busy to try to work it through. Bad news had a way of coming fast enough regardless of worrying ahead of time.

He nudged his horse with his spurs and got a burst of speed he was sure the gelding didn't want to give. A mile or two ahead would be sufficient to warn the others if Carmody had been wrong about the destination of the Paiutes.

As he rode, he tried to avoid thinking about the other complication that had reentered his life. What was Belle doing in Oregon without wanting her mother to know? She was an adult but still the family had all been so close. Had something gone wrong that he didn't know?

Although there were times he didn't like being a soldier, mostly the life suited him. He had gone from West Point straight into the fray with only rare breaks since. He remembered how much he had had to learn when he first got to Oregon. It had been Adam Stone, Belle's stepfather, who had taught him most of what kept him alive through one battle after another. West Point knew little about actual Indian fighting. Adam had been an expert, and he revered the man.

At one time Belle had resented her mother remarrying after her father's death, but he thought she'd gotten past that. He doubted very much Martha had been told about the marriage and Belle's loss of a husband. No, something was going on, but it wasn't his business. He had enough trouble handling what was.

After a miserable trip along the rough stage road, Belle felt relief when she saw ahead Canyon City. Rand had left them thirty miles back where the area was settled and traveled enough that he regarded it as safe. They had had no second chance to talk, for which she felt relief.

He had looked exhausted as he had waved them on and then set off with his men back the way they had come. She wished she had had the right to tell him to rest first; but he'd denied her that when she was barely seventeen. He didn't look anymore inclined to give it to her ten years later. Not that she would give him the chance. She had grown up and wasn't about to play the fool again for any man.

Canyon City wasn't big by Eastern standards, but it had 10,000 residents due to the gold strike. Buildings has sprung up fast. Along with them had come the wildness of any boomtown. It would be safer than the stage road. Of course, that depended on how it all went with William Forester.

At the stage office, a driver for Forester-- James Dunham, a thin older man who smiled pleasantly, met her and the children. "I'm to take you to your home," he said as he began to put their bags into the back of a fine looking buggy with seating for at least four.

"Is he there?" she asked as she helped Jessica and Jer into the backseat and then stepped up herself.

"Don't know about that, ma'am. He don't tell me what he's doing. Just what he wants done."

Before he could pull out, Hoyt came up. "I was to meet Mr. Forester in The Dalles but was delayed, and he had gone. Can I ride with you to his home and perhaps meet him there?"

Dunham rubbed the side of his nose as he considered. "Suppose it can't hurt nothing. But if he wants you gone, you can walk back." He gestured to the seat beside him.

"Fine."

The home was on the hill above the town and a fine structure by any standard—boomtown or not. Two stories with pillars along the front to make sure any who saw it knew it to be that of a successful man.

When they drove up, smiling broadly, a dark-skinned woman came out to welcome and usher them inside as the driver carried in their bags. "I am Sally Hansen. Please call me Sally," the woman said. "I am so glad to see you all here, safe and sound. There is so much talk about Indian trouble on the road that I did worry." No plural. Interesting.

"Thank you for your concern." Belle smiled and took the woman's hand.

The main hall was polished dark wood, its floors covered with what looked to be quality Persian carpets. Through double doors to the parlor, she saw a large Batik of storks above a marble fireplace, gilded candlesticks, purple brocade coverings on the sofas and chairs. Forester's home could be that of any wealthy man in any major city— a true showplace, but for what?

"Mr. Forester won't be back for several hours," Sally said. "You folks hungry?"

"In a bit," Belle said. "Could we see our rooms?"

"Of course," she turned to the driver. "Please take their bags to their rooms." Belle was led up the stairs to a lovely bedroom at the back of the hall. The children's rooms were on either side of hers with connecting doors. She glanced out her large window to see a large spreading oak just beyond. Perfect.

"We'll be down in a few moments," she told Sally. "I'd like to unpack the children's things first." Having their clothing and toys again accessible might make this transition easier for them. Their father having greeted them might have helped also.

When she had finished, leaving her own bags for later, she washed their faces and then her own with the scented water on the dressers. She did not change from her traveling suit. Its heavy fabric made her derringer less noticeable.

Back downstairs, she saw Dylan Hoyt drinking some beverage and looking edgy. An officious looking gentleman came from the back. "My name is Jenks, Miss."

"It's Mrs. Morgan and glad to meet you, Mr. Jenks."

"Just Jenks, Ma'am. Would you like a glass of sherry?"

She didn't, but she nodded. With her first sip, she recognized it as a very fine vintage. But of course, what else would William Forester have.

"I would like another glass if you don't mind," Hoyt asked. He was clearly in a foul mood, a mood that was not improved when the children came bouncing into the room, looking around with excitement and no longer appearing tired from their trip.

"Dinner will be at eight. May I get you anything else for now, Mrs. Morgan?" Jenks asked.

"The children probably would like milk, if you have it, and something to eat. It's been awhile since we had a meal."

"Of course." He smiled then at the children. "Come with me. I do believe Miss Sally said there were some fresh baked cookies."

When they were again alone, Hoyt moved from his chair to the window to look out at the grass. Belle had noted when they arrived it was brown with the late season but cut to resemble a lawn. Everything to impress. She settled herself onto one of the Victorian chairs and watched the man pace. She wondered what role he played in Forester's operations. The legal or illegal side? She knew, just on instinct, which one she believed.

"Mr. Hoyt, what exactly do you do for Mr. Forester?" she asked deciding bluntness might get her more information than going for chitchat, which clearly Hoyt was in no mood for anyway.

"Is that your business?" he asked in a derisive tone.

"I was trying to be polite."

"Don't."

At that, the door opened and William Forester walked through with three men Belle didn't remember from California or The Dalles. He smiled broadly when he saw her. "Ah my beautiful governess. How was your journey down? I was so sorry I could not wait to take you with me," he said with that drawl she found hard to place but then everything about William was hard to place. He was smooth featured, handsome enough, she supposed in a cultured way, and of medium height. He would be non-descript in a crowd other than the fine and often colorful clothing he favored.

"It was fine. The children were tired, of course."

"Ah yes, my children. Where are they?"

"Something to eat in the kitchen."

"Excellent." He looked then at Hoyt. His expression hardened. "You were supposed to be in The Dalles."

"I was delayed. I tried to buy a horse but that was impossible, and so I was forced to take the first stage."

"Fortunate for us," Belle inserted. "We were attacked by Paiutes at the Jamison station. Mr. Hoyt was quite handy with his gun."

Forester smiled then. "Oh well, then good. Perhaps all is well." He looked back at the three men who had entered with him. One was tall, one short and the other stocky of build. None had a look she would trust, and Forester did not offer their names.

"Take Dylan down to the hotel, get him a room, and I'll talk to him in the morning," Forester ordered with a dismissive tone to his voice.

If Hoyt was disappointed in not being invited to dine at Forester's home, he didn't argue as he left with the three men.

"And how are my children?" Forester asked when they were alone as he poured himself a brandy and seated himself on the sofa.

"They are bright, intelligent and sweet. I have enjoyed my time getting to know them better. They were frightened, of course, by the attack, but seemed to handle the shock well. They are, of course, happy to be here."

She didn't add how much better it would have been if it had been their father shepherding them through hostile territory. Even had she not known Forester was likely a counterfeiter, maybe worse, she would have found his behavior odd to entrust his precious children to a woman he'd hired only six months earlier.

"I thought you'd be the perfect governess to bring out their best traits. I knew it the moment I saw you." He smiled then with a certain look in his eyes. In the past, he hadn't given her any clue he was interested in more from her than being his children's governess—so the look surprised her. She had no interest in him at all and was in no mood to be molested. If she intended to stay long enough to satisfy Alan's requirements for this job, she would have to be very careful. Killing her employer wasn't going to help her get the needed evidence especially if the counterfeiting involved more than Forester himself.

The children burst into the parlor all smiles and cookie crumbs until they saw their father and stopped short of approaching him. "And how are you, Jeremy and Jessica?" he asked without rising from the sofa or putting out his arms.

"Fine," Jeremy answered for them both.

"Good. I am sure you need an early dinner and bed after such an arduous journey," Forester said with a coolness that at one time would have surprised Belle.

"I would actually love that also," Belle said. "I will bathe them after they have eaten, and if you wouldn't mind, I'd prefer to eat with them tonight."

If he was let down, he hid it and nodded. "Of course. I will see you in the morning then. I suppose I should go down and talk to Mr. Hoyt after all." And with a nod to his children, he was out the door.

Sally had prepared chicken and mashed potatoes for the children, which suited Belle perfectly. She felt starved and even took a second helping of chicken, which clearly pleased the cook. "Would you like me to help you get the children ready for bed, Mrs. Morgan?" Sally asked when the children had also polished off a small piece of apple pie.

"Thanks so much for offering but I can manage."

An hour later, the children were in bed as was Belle. She had looked to see if her door had a lock. It did not. But since she had connecting doors to both children's rooms, she left them open, which was fortunate when Jessica began to whimper. She carried her into her room. Cuddling together, they both slept soundly.

With morning, she woke and tried to think how she would get the information that she needed regarding Forester's activities in Canyon City. It would be wise to spend a few days simply getting the children their lessons before she started looking through the house. She doubted anyway that he'd risk having the large presses in his home. Where would they be? He had offices downtown. She would start there.

Like a bad penny she could not lose, she thought about Rand, about touching him to tend his wound, what it might have been like to touch him in other ways. She forced the thoughts from her. He wasn't hers. He would never be hers. She had a job to do. Two jobs really because the children had become one whether they had originally been simply covers. Now she wanted to do the best she could for them and that included teaching them, especially Jer, some survival skills. She knew things that would be useful, skills such as those her father and then stepfather had taught her.

Thinking of Adam made her think then of her mother. She wanted to see her. She wondered what her home on the John Day ranch looked like. Adam had built it near her sister, Raine's home. They had a closer relationship than she had ever managed with either sister or her mother. She loved them, but she had wanted to go out into the world, to explore, to have adventures. Well she had had that. But what she had missed on the way was family. Was it too late for that someday?

By the time Rand arrived in The Dalles, he and his men were near exhausted. He wanted a barber, bath, and to sleep twenty-four hours. He wasn't sure how fast he would get either since he was two days late for the important meeting Colonel Schaeffer had set up for him. He dismissed his troop and told them to meet him at the supply depot by noon the following day. Then he headed for offices down near the waterfront.

Brushing the dust off his hat and jacket, he walked in, told the orderly who he was, and asked for Schaeffer.

"He'll be glad to see you, Captain," the man said. "You look like you've had a hard go of it, sir."

"You might say that." He slumped into a chair to wait.

When Schaeffer walked out, Rand got to his feet to salute and greet him. "Sorry for the delay," he said. "I ran into obstacles."

"Knowing you, I understand they were necessary. Come on back. Let me get you some coffee."

"That would be very welcome, sir," Rand said as he followed him into a tidy office overlooking the Columbia River.

Schaeffer waved Rand to a chair and poured him coffee before sitting behind his desk. "I am sure you wondered why this meeting here and not at Camp Watson."

"I wondered why it was at all to be honest."

Schaeffer grinned. "Captain, get something to eat, clean up, and come back in three hours. I have someone I want you to meet."

Three hours later, Rand was back in the office, not having eaten, but having bathed and shaved.

Schaffer said, "There were reasons for the meeting to be here. We did not want it to get out that he was here." He opened a connecting door, and a man walked through wearing a suit. Rand didn't know him, but he did recognize authority when he saw it.

"Rand, this is Undersecretary Mason Williams. I am sure you are familiar with the attempt to impeach President Johnson over his trying to remove Secretary Stanton and replace him with Ulysses S. Grant. Much of the current political turmoil is due to the Reconstruction Act and its repercussions on the North and the South."

Rand nodded. The attempt at impeachment had narrowly failed. The government was in some chaos as was much of the country after four long, bloody years of fighting a devastating war.

"Secretary Williams is here because there is yet another problem that has been growing, one which could endanger the unity of our nation, which we are only slowly rebuilding."

Williams took a cup of coffee and nodded. "Colonel Schaeffer has a great deal of faith in you, Captain Phillips."

"I appreciate that, sir." He waited for an explanation, as he had no idea what might be endangering national unity way out in Oregon. Surely, the Indian uprising, difficult as that was proving to be, wasn't sufficient for that.

"Here's the long and short of it," Williams said. "When the War ended, what didn't end was the desire of some to break away from the Union. There have been several plots uncovered and likely there are more who would love to do such a thing. What we have found is one of them seems a bit more apt to succeed because of the power and money behind it. With the dissatisfaction and the constant desire by some to rule over others, we are seeing a possible resurrection that would begin here in Oregon."

"East of the Cascades?"

"Yes."

"Pardon me for saying this, sir, but that seems unlikely. It's a lightly populated area. Yes, Canyon City has about 10,000 living there now, but it's a boomtown, which will be gone about as fast as the gold is."

"It is an area rich in gold though at the moment. And gold is what the Union is shy of and what it takes to begin a movement. There is something more though operating here, and it's a master counterfeiter. He has been buying up arms with phony money. The false denominations work two ways to sow dissatisfaction and insecurity. When people realize they have been cheated, they lose faith in the government to protect them. The arms that are being stored somewhere are another threat."

"I don't quite see how I'd fit into this. I am responsible for keeping settlers and travelers safe, for eventually getting the Northern Paiute, Western Shoshone, and the Bannocks onto reservations. That's not going well enough for me to think I could be helpful-- unless you were pulling me from that mission." He didn't like that idea at all. It had been hard dirty work, but he knew more about that then possibly ferreting out rebels. Damn, he'd had enough of that.

"We still need you there. One of the things we want is for you to visit Jed Hardman. Ideally on your way back from here."

"Sir?" He even more didn't like that idea.

"Rand, he is loyal so far as we know, but he is a southerner, and fought for the South. You can find out if he knows more since you are a friend."

Now he knew he didn't want any part of this. "I wouldn't go so far as to say we are friends. I know him and have been there. He's an honorable man, as far as I know. If he was plotting something, what would make him tell me anyway?"

"For you to go there will enable you to inform him what's going on."

"You'd want me to tell him?"

"If you determine he's loyal. If other southerners are visiting him, you might collect names."

"I am no spy, sir."

"You won't do it?" Schaeffer looked disappointed.

"I won't betray friendship. I suspect you know Adam Stone is a close friend of mine. He lives on the John Day Ranch with Hardman."

"You might though be willing to ferret out someone ready to break apart this country?" Schaeffer asked.

"Is there more to this request then?" He felt sure there had to be more.

"We have at least one traitor at Watson and maybe more. I am sure you would consider that your duty?"

"How do you know one is stationed there?"

"The bandits have known too much for there to not be a source, a source that has a way to know what's going on and is delivering messages to someone who then can conduct raids," Schaeffer said. "Remember when the South surrendered, some of the men took on other names and rejoined the Army. You probably know who they are."

"You are distrusting Southerners? There are reasons besides growing up in the South for a man to be interested in an insurrection."

"There are indeed. You can find out who makes frequent personal visits to Canyon City. If he is betraying his country, he is also betraying the military."

Rand considered that. "Who do you believe then is in Canyon City and behind all this?"

"We have no proof. That is hopefully being gathered, but we believe the leader is William Forester."

He didn't like hearing that. "I know of him but have not met him. What makes you believe it's him?"

"He has the connections. Counterfeit bills have been passed many places he has been. We also believe that the large purchases of armaments were connected to his travels."

"That's not evidence."

"No, it's possibly coincidence. It's why we need more."

"It won't be easy to get proof on a man like him. He has a lot of ways to put out underlings instead of himself."

Rand had helped break an earlier gang that involved a traitor in the military. He now saw it likely was a factor in what they wanted now, besides his knowing Hardman. He didn't like any part of it. He didn't even more like that Belle had gone to work for Forester. How much did she know or suspect the kind of man he was? In no way could he believe she would be involved in any plot to tear the nation apart—not for love nor money.

"We can tell you this-- there is a Pinkerton on the job. And although we do not have an official spy agency, we have sent in a man who has proven competent in spying during the Civil War."

"Am I to know who either of these men are, and will I be expected to contact them?" Rand had already decided he would take the assignment, short of spying on Hardman. If he had a traitor in his unit, he needed to know it. He didn't want another rebellion to lead to another war.

With Belle working for Forester, he had a personal reason to do what he could to assure her safety. She presented a personal complication in stopping at the Hardman ranch. He didn't want to have to hide his knowledge of her marriage and current abode. Maybe they already knew though. It'd been six months since he'd stopped by. He walked to the window staring out at the Columbia.

"Yes, you will need to know who they are. And one more thing, Rand."

He turned back. "Your brother was befriended by Forester before he left San Francisco. I don't know how involved he is with the cause. He had not been working for him that we knew, but Jason left The Dalles this morning on the stage for Canyon City."

Hellfire. He hadn't seen his younger brother in years. Their father had found Rand to be a disappointment for reasons Rand never quite understood. Jason had continued to live with him. It didn't make sense though that he would befriend someone like William Forester. For what purpose?

"How loyal do you consider your father to be?" Williams asked watching his face.

He turned to stare back at the Secretary. "He was a well decorated general before he retired. As far as I know has always served with honor. Why would you ask such a thing?"

"Since his retirement, General Phillips has had some... friendships that have been regarded as questionable—one of which had been with Forester. I realize that alone doesn't mean much. Often powerful men are attracted to each other."

Rand tried to think what he knew. He'd never heard the name William Forester before the man arrived in Canyon City. "Perhaps you know that I am not close to my family, but last I knew, my father was in Maryland."

"They were both in San Francisco up until last week. Our sources there lost connection with your father. It's uncertain where he is now."

"He and Jason were together?" At one time, his father had been estranged from both his sons. Had that changed?

"Yes, in San Francisco," Williams said. "How they left there is a bit of a mystery. Jason left a clear trail north. Your father signed out of his hotel, and disappeared."

"No train or ship tickets?"

"Nor renting a driver."

"Could he have died?" He should have cared more than he realized he did.

"Although we don't believe that to be the case, we don't know. We need more information than we have and you seem to have the best chance to get that."

"Will you take the assignment, Captain?" Schaeffer added.

Reluctantly, Rand nodded. "I don't know how effective I can be though."

"We know the caliber of man you are, Captain. I am confident you will do your best," Schaeffer said. "I have a dossier for you to study on Forester to learn what you can. Burn it when you finish. Take a few days here in town before you head out. You look exhausted."

"If any names stand out for you," Williams added, "please file a report before you go. But from this time on, be careful how you contact us. Leave no clues that you are looking into this as it could be very dangerous for you-- at least until you know who not to trust at your back."

Rand nodded as he already began thinking about the man at his fort who might be a traitor. "Off hand, I can't think of any of my men, who seem likely, but I will be looking at them a little more closely when I get back."

"I hope you understand my eagerness for you to find out who it might be," Schaeffer said. "Make it your first priority before you contact either agent at Canyon City. I don't have to tell you how careful you must be regarding all of this."

"Yes."

"My concern for you is having someone in the fort who might prove dangerous to you. I like you, Rand, and don't want you having an accident while out on a patrol. Remember anyone willing to risk the hangman's noose as a traitor, will be willing to kill to protect their cause and themselves. Until you know who it is, any chance they find you are investigating this will be deadly to you."

"And my contacts should I need to get information to you or from them?"

"Dylan Hoyt is our man. Belle Morgan is the Pinkerton."

Rand hoped his mouth hadn't dropped open at hearing her name. He'd met Hoyt, of course, heading south, but hadn't paid him much mind. He had seemed just another gambler. Spy material? That is something he'd never have guessed. Belle even less so. God, what a reckless thing for her to do.

"You know Mrs. Morgan, I believe," Schaeffer said studying Rand's face.

Grateful for the many years he had had to hide his emotions, Rand nodded. "And her family, of course."

"Alan said she did not want them to know what she's doing. She is a competent agent with a great deal of experience. Don't let her beauty fool you."

Rand clenched his jaw. No, he'd not let that happen... again.

CHAPTER 4

Taking one hand of each of her charges, Belle walked into the woods behind their home. She had had worn her own jacket and dressed them warmly as the early morning air was still a bit frosty. She had told Sally where they would be but did not expect their father to be home before they returned or to care even if he did. He'd shown little interest in anything his children did and only asked that they be kept out of his way. His business had apparently grown increasingly intense. She wished she had a way to pry into it, but the opportunity had not yet arisen. In the meantime, she would enjoy the children.

"Hear that?" she asked them, stopping so they could listen.

"A bird," Jer suggested.

Jessica made a clicking sound. "I can talk to it," she said smiling and then giggling.

"You can. It's not a bird but a big gray squirrel and does not like us walking here. Can you see where he is?"

The two peered into the woods trying to see from where the sound was coming. Jessica shook her head. Belle then pointed to the branch about forty feet up in a tree two trees over to their left.

"I see it now. Bushy tail," Jer observed.

She nodded. "He's fat too. Look at his cheeks full of pine nuts probably where he'll be taking them to store for winter."

"I'd call him Bill," Jessica suggested as she looked from Belle back to the squirrel.

"You could also call him dinner if you were lost in the woods and had to find food. He is in the family Sciuridae, a small rodent."

"He'd be too fast to catch," Jer said wisely, as the little animal jumped from one branch to another.

"There are ways to catch something without being fast." She brought out a long piece of cord. "You can make a trap but there is something else the squirrel might do for you besides providing meat or using his fur for warmth."

"What?" both children asked at once.

"Watch where he goes and find his stash. There will be plenty of nuts in it, maybe other things you could eat. He likely, at this elevation, has pulled out his fur to insulate it."

"But then what would Bill eat or do?" Jessica asked with concern. "If we took his home?"

Belle smiled. "You would only do that if you really, really needed to live and had nothing else you could find. There are many things you can eat in the forest, and it's good to learn what they are... and also what not to eat. Some plants are poisons."

She took them further into the woods, not so far from the home but pointing out plants she remembered from her own lessons. If she ever had a home of her own, not something that appeared likely anytime soon, she'd grow herbs like her mother had for healing. In the forests though were plants that could be used in an extreme situation —the kind where no one ever wants to find themselves.

"Do you have a gun again?" Jeremy asked looking toward her leg.

"Why do you ask?"

"Well if you did, you could shoot the squirrel."

Jessica's face grew pained.

"I would only do that if we needed the food, Jer. We don't ever kill for fun, do we?"

Now it was his turn to get a somber face. "I'd like to have a gun," he said finally.

"To protect yourself?" she asked, curious how much the little boy understood regarding his father's doings and all the men who showed up at the home unexpectedly.

His expression was fierce. "And my sister and you. I wouldn't let someone I loved be hurt if I had a gun."

"When you are old enough, you can probably have one, but that's something it takes time to be old enough to safely handle and to have the wisdom to know when to use it."

"I'll grow up fast!"

"But wait until you are told it's safe. Guns can kill by accident too. If you see a gun, don't touch it."

"Why not?" He had a stubborn look.

"Would you want to kill me or Jessica?"

"No."

"Accidents happen with guns when people don't know how to use them safely."

"All right." He sucked in a breath. "I won't touch one without permission."

"Good. Did you know that guns have a kind of kick. You fire them and they bounce back against your hand. That can become dangerous if you aren't prepared for it."

"I'll be prepared."

"Someday, you will be, but until such times, there are things you can learn that might save your life and Jessica's. Like how not to get lost."

The children looked around at the woods, which now totally enclosed them. "Which way is north?" Belle asked them.

"What's north?" Jessica asked turning in a circle.

"It's a direction, stupid," Jer sneered.

"It isn't nice to call anybody stupid," Belle corrected. "Jessica did something very wise by asking."

Jessica stuck out her tongue at Jer. "What was wise?" he asked.

"When you don't know something, ask. Now finding north when you are in the woods can be difficult. Sometimes you can tell by moss." She pointed to the trees. "In some places, moss only grows on one side of the tree. That will be where it got the least sun—the north. If though you can go until you find the sunshine, then your shadow can help you because with each season it will be in a different place. Learn the seasons and your shadow and you can always find north."

"What good does north do us?" Jer asked with definite interest.

"In this part of the country, the big rivers go first west and then north. If you go far enough north, you will find the biggest of the rivers, the Columbia. It goes to the west and the ocean. Follow it and you will find towns. You need a map and to learn how to read it."

Jer looked concerned. "We don't have maps."

"You do now. When we were in The Dalles, I purchased you each a map of this area. They are at home today, but you will have it and need to spend time studying it. I also have something else for you, when you don't have sunshine to help you." She reached into the pocket of her skirt and brought out two small compasses. "Learn to use these, and they will always tell you true north."

Both children eagerly grabbed the compasses that Belle had also purchased when they had been in The Dalles. "I will keep it safe," Jer said looking at his and how the needle moved.

She showed them how a compass worked. "Now with maps, you can find your way if you need to."

"You won't help us?" Jessica asked, her lips puckering.

"Of course, I will-- when I am there; but you need to know for times you might not be with me. With a compass and a map, you can set a course to return home or to some other safe destination."

She remembered how resentful she had been when Adam had first given her such a compass and explained what she had just told the children. What would she need with such knowledge? She intended to go to big cities and stay there. She smiled at her own youthful rebellion. It made it easy to understand Jeremy.

Jessica hugged Belle around the legs. "I luv you, Belle."

"And I love you both," she said scooping the reluctant Jeremy into a group hug. "Now let's find our way back to the house. I think it's about lunchtime."

"Thank you for remembering about teaching us," Jer said as they walked onto the dried up lawn.

"I was fortunate to have those who taught me. It's my turn," she said thinking of how many there had been. She had left those people behind for excitement. She realized how much she missed the warmth of family. When this was over, when William Forester was where he belonged, she would spend time with them. Her family was her true north. She suddenly realized that her need for them had grown greater than for any excitement.

Uncertain if he could even trust the men with whom he had just ridden into battle, Rand called Sergeant Smith to him at the supply depot.

"I won't be going south with you right now. I am giving you written orders for Murphy, instructions for getting the camp ready for winter. This is a list of what I want done. I'll be back in a week or less." He handed the sergeant the paper.

"Shall I tell the lieutenants why?" Smith asked folding them and putting them in his jacket pocket.

"Just that I am on a small vacation."

"They might not like that."

Rand smiled. "I don't ask them to like it. It's their job and yours to make sure we have a supply of wood for the winter. No patrols until I get back."

"Shouldn't you at least take the corporal with you?" Smith's expression showed clear disapproval.

"Quit dawdling. You will have one night on the trail. Get." The sergeant gave him one last look but left without further argument.

Rand left two days later, dressed in civilian clothing, a rough cotton shirt, dark pants, a holster tied down on his thigh, and a hat slung low over his forehead. He brought enough food for a few days in the wilderness, his uniform neatly folded in one of the saddlebags as he rode southeast, cutting across country as he remembered doing several years before. Among the military mounts, he had found a nice buckskin gelding. Riding out reminded him how much he had once enjoyed pleasure riding with a good horse and how little time he'd had to do it. Every ride he had taken for years had been toward a battle, to kill, or avoid being killed. What kind of life was that?

He had studied the dossier on Forester but found little to help him before he burned it. He kept trying to remember if any of the names were connected to his father, but nothing came to him. Memorizing the names, he would ask Hardman when he arrived at the ranch.

Once upon a time, Rand had seen himself as a man who set himself to a task and didn't try to avoid the unpleasant aspects of it. Early in his life, with a disapproving father, he had learned it didn't pay to think too deeply as to the why of things. Live in the moment. Do his duty. Don't look too far down the road as the path might end very abruptly. He had seen that happen for too many men not to know life was not promised. He hadn't worried about it. Tomorrow took care of itself.

Now, he was troubled that he was beginning to second-guess his choices. A man in his world could not afford that weakness. He was grateful for this break to get his head together, for the chance to visit the Hardman ranch, to have time with people he respected, and who he was confident that he could trust. He'd do no spying there but alerting Hardman to what was going on was something he owed the family.

The rolling hills out of The Dalles made for easy riding. It was a region where, with the small farms and town so close, had little risk of Indians hiding in an arroyo to attack. He had chosen not to take the major stage route, not only to avoid other people, but also for the freedom of cutting across country.

Past the hills, his mount climbed into juniper and sage country. Rocky bluffs were dark against the skyline. In the distance, he saw clouds building up. It was past the usual time for thunderstorms—still a storm looked probable. For the night, he headed for a canyon above any possible flash floods but also with shelter just in case the sky did break loose. Unsaddling the gelding, he rubbed him down before hobbling him near the small stream with grass to eat.

After a simple supper of canned beans, he took a flask of whiskey from a saddlebag and leaning against his saddle, took a few sips before he rolled a cigarette. His rifle was at his side, but he didn't feel concern that he'd need it. That might come when he got higher in the pines and farther south.

He liked Belle's family. Evidently more than she did. He would have spent more time with them but for several reasons. One was the job he held. He had responsibility for a wide swath of territory. The other was not to hear what Belle was doing.

Except, how much of anything she'd written had been the truth? He didn't think for a moment they knew about her Pinkerton work. Why had she lied? Was it to protect them with a comfortable illusion where the reality would have worried them? Why hadn't she told them of her marriage and being widowed?

Those were questions he'd not likely soon know the answers. He hoped she didn't arise in the conversation. He wasn't going to lie to her family. He wouldn't tell them though if he could avoid it. Making her work more dangerous or pulling them into it wouldn't help anybody.

As the darkness grew more intense, his own fire long gone, Rand lay back in his blankets, with the saddle as his pillow. Memories flashed through his mind of how it had been with Belle when he'd first met her. He had come to visit her family, to stay with Adam and Martha Stone. He hadn't expected Martha's youngest daughter to be there.

At almost seventeen Belle had had an innocence and yet sassy wisdom that had astounded him and attracted him more than he'd expected. He'd known no one like her. She was fresh and enjoyed so much of life. Already she'd traveled some and even lived in San Francisco for a time. It made her seem older than she was. When she began to flirt with him, he at first didn't know if she understood what she was doing. Then he had seen in her eyes that she knew exactly, if she didn't know where it would take her.

He had been astonishingly attracted, which he found hard to believe since she had seemed such a girl. And yet, she'd been a girl with sweet, very kissable lips and those beautiful blue eyes that seemed to see right through him. She was Adam's stepdaughter, and there was no way he would betray a trust to the man who had saved his life more than once. In addition, career soldiers had little time in their life for women or family.

Then came the evening when Belle had made it clear what she wanted. She had come to where he was sitting on a swinging bench that Adam had made under a big maple tree.

"You smoking out here all by yourself?" she had asked.

"It's a nice night for it." Adam and Martha had put their baby to bed and the house was quiet.

She had moved to sit beside him, letting him swing them both. "You are leaving tomorrow, aren't you?" she asked with a tone to her voice that had made him uneasy.

"Orders."

"When will you be back?"

"That's hard to say. I'm heading to Arizona Territory."

"So far?"

He had nodded. "Fort Buchanan, to be exact at the head of Sonoita Creek, or so I have been told. It's near the border." He had been talking to avoid having her say something he didn't want to hear.

"To fight."

"To protect but sometimes that means fighting. Cochise is not willing to go to the reservation and that means innocents pay the price —on both sides."

She had remained silent; then before he knew it, she had moved and was on his lap, her arms around his neck. As she had bent toward him, he had known what she wanted. He wanted it too, but somebody had to be the grown up. He couldn't take what was likely her first kiss this way. He had a career to build. She had a life to make. This was the wrong time for them both. He blocked her with his hand, feeling her soft lips against his palm. He felt the touch still as he thought about that moment, and the choice he had made for them both. True, there were girls who married as young as Belle, but she could have had so much more.

"It isn't the right time for this, for you," he had said as he had gently lifted her from him to put her back on her side of the bench. He had risen to avoid being tempted to overrule his own common-sense. He saw her tears glittering in the moonlight. "Someday you will know I was right," he had said and walked away without looking back.

He knew he had been right—in his head. In his heart though, he had looked back a hundred times. He had realized what a precious gift a woman like her would have been to him. Except a soldier's life didn't make a good one for women. Even at twenty-five, he had seen that.

Left behind or coming along from difficult post to difficult post. Never a real home. Belle could do better.

Except now, he wondered. She had found love again, but he never had. He'd been so strong that day. He wondered what he had lost by saying no to what they both had wanted.

Then even more, he wondered what had led her to choose being an agent for the Pinkertons. Perhaps it had been her husband's work, and she'd carried on after he died or was that killed?

For a man who prided himself in doing little deep thinking beyond what was required, he couldn't stop himself from second-guessing his actions, hers, and that didn't even get into the concern regarding what his father and brother might be doing. Were they involved in some kind of crazy conspiracy? He hadn't met Forester, but from the sounds of it, the man was a borderline lunatic.

Finally, he slept, with dreams filled with violence strangely mixed with eroticism. He was relieved in the morning to wake without remembering any details.

Late afternoon found him riding into the lower pasture below the Hardman Ranch. Rand had babied his gelding on the ride with walking and riding. He had known he could need the option of moving fast. Even this close to the ranch, there were no givens. When he heard the motion to his right, he pulled his horse to a halt.

"Almost shot ya, Captain," George Kalama said stepping out from behind a large boulder.

"You shooting all strangers these days?" he asked as Joe Kalama also stepped forward both brothers holding rifles but not pointed at him.

"Depends on who they be," Joe said smoking a cigarette. "You quit the army?"

He shook his head and hooking his knee over the pommel of his saddle, rolled a cigarette. "This is a friendly visit. Not too many of them these days?"

"Boss just likes to get a warning and that's why we're out. You'd never seen us if we hadn't recognized you," George said.

Rand lit his cigarette and took a deep draw blowing out the smoke with satisfaction. "Where's he at?"

"He was helping Kane put up their cabin but said something about checking the far canyon for a few animals we been missing. Not sure where he is by now."

"Matt has come too?"

"Got the whole lot of them here now, that's what I heard the boss say, well maybe minus one. He'll have that one too afore it's finished. His missus calls him the laird. She's got good reason for that." Joe chuckled.

"I need to talk to him."

"Whether he be at the headquarters or in the hills, he'll see you coming." He laughed again. "Not much gets by him. If he's still at the new cabin, it's only a few hundred feet from the one for the Stones. Got the whole place outfitted like a stockade. Ready for what comes."

"They won't shoot first and ask questions later?" he joked only half teasing. He didn't blame Hardman from being antsy about what was coming in Eastern Oregon. It was a dangerous time from every direction.

"Nah, the fact that we didn't shoot would mean you're okay. See ya later, Cap."

Rand dropped his leg down and gave the gelding a nudge in the side. He was glad to hear Hardman was taking nothing for granted regarding strangers.

As he entered the large meadow, the lodge-like dwelling loomed at the top of the hill. Now there were two more large cabins as well as two smaller ones. The largest of the new dwelling had walls raised but was not yet roofed. A log fence provided a barrier on two sides and with the cliff behind, it was a defensible position.

When he saw Hardman coming down a ladder, He rode toward him. Beyond him nailing a timber was a tall, muscular blond man. He had met Matthew Kane years before. He still looked formidable and capable of standing up to any challenge.

Hardman walked to him as Rand dismounted. He stretched out his hand with a friendly smile. "Been awhile, Captain."

Rand nodded. "Been busy."

"And now no uniform. You quit the blue coats?" He grinned.

"Not yet."

"Pleasure or business?"

"A little of both." Matthew Kane walked up also to shake his hand. "Always use a good man with a hammer," he said with a grin. "You a good man with a hammer, Captain?"

"You are pushing it-- starting late in the season to get your cabin up," Rand said.

"Most likely they'll be spending this winter in the lodge," Jed acknowledged. "Plenty of room."

"That where the ladies are? I hadn't heard Kanes were joining you."

"Not just them." Rand looked toward the doorway and saw two old men walking toward them. Jack Grimes and...

"Well, I'll be damned," Rand said heading for the white bearded man. "How the hell are you?"

"Better everyday. This is good country, like the air and the work," St. Louis Jones said with a big grin under his beard.

"I didn't realize the two of you knew each other," Jed said.

"It was a lot of years ago." Rand smiled and shook the still strong hand. "Back then I was a shave tail and he was in Oregon City homesteading. Couldn't stay away from trouble, I guess."

St. Louis chuckled. "Couldn't let my whole family go off without me. And you ain't no shave tail no more."

"No, I've learned a few things since those days."

"I can tell. Glad to see you, Rand."

"I guess you know it's going to be rough going here for a few years."

"Yep. Boring back in Oregon City." He grinned more broadly.

"Jack," Jed said looking at his old hired man, "go tell the gals who's here, if they haven't seen. Then take a break. You look beat."

Jack managed a smile. "I am that. Glad to see ya, Cap. Talk to you later." He ambled toward the main house.

"All right," Jed said, "have a seat." He pointed to a rough hewn bench where there was room for the four of them to sit. He and Rand rolled and lit cigarettes. "Let's hear the bad news."

"Where is Adam?" Rand asked as he took a long draw on his.

"He took grandson and son hunting. Should be back in an hour or so."

"My news doesn't require immediate action, and if you don't mind, I'd like to explain it to you when Adam is here too. In the meantime, it happens I am, surprisingly for a military man, handy with a hammer," he rose with the cigarette dangling from his lip.

"Wal, if there's no news for now, you young whippersnappers may not need a break," St. Louis said, "but I can use one too. I'll I think I'll head on up to the house and see if I can wrangle myself some tea."

"I am glad you are here, St. Louis," Rand said. "The more white hair to offer wisdom, the better."

"You think do ya?" He chuckled and followed Jack up the rise to the house.

As Rand worked with Matt and Jed, he felt a lessening of his tension. Solid, real work, something where death wasn't staring at him from all the hidden places, felt good. Lately his life held little opportunity for real accomplishments. He'd take advantage of the opportunity when he found it. Nothing else looked promising.

Belle found an excuse that enabled her to walk to what served as Canyon City's main street. She needed thread and needle to repair a rip in one of her slips. Sally Hansen had been happy to watch the children. As it stood, Belle had no idea where William Forester was. If she ran into him while she scouted the locale, she would offer her excuses, not the real ones, of course.

Rather than first heading for the store, she found the stable.

"Can I help ya, Miss?" the hostler asked as she entered the dim interior.

"I hope so. I am Mrs. Morgan. I want to purchase a horse."

He looked at her again. "For yoreself?"

"Yes, I consider riding good exercise and would like to keep up my skills while here. Do you have an animal, which might suit?"

"You a good rider, ma'am?"

"I consider myself to be."

"Ride with one of them sidesaddles. We ain't got none of those less'n you got yore own."

"Given the rough conditions here, I'd want to buy a regular saddle."

He looked a little scandalized. He'd have been even more if he'd seen her riding bareback, flying across the land. Riding had been her pleasure but also potentially could be a future need. She wanted her own horse should that situation arise. She was operating with instinct to believe it would.

"Wal, I got a nice little filly ya might like." He led her to the corral and showed her an old nag with swayback.

She laughed. "You must take me for a fool," she said. "If that's all you have, I'll have to look elsewhere."

He smiled at her with a little more respect. "Wal, I got a gelding if ya was thinking that'd do."

"Let me see him."

At a corral to the left of the stables was a fine looking Morgan. She was surprised to see such an impressive animal. "What's his name?" she asked as she moved into the corral and felt of his legs, ran her hands along his back, and lifted his hooves to check for problems. He was a strong animal, his brown coat smooth. He showed good care.

"Sammy. Just got him four days ago. Fella had enough of Canyon City. Didn't get his fortune and wasn't gonna ride off with Injuns everywhere."

"How much do you want for him?" she asked running her hand along his neck.

"Ya don't want to ride him first?"

She had looked into the gelding's eyes and felt they had a meeting of the minds. "I do need a saddle and tack and will, of course, be stabling him here for when I am not able to ride. So let's talk dollars."

Nothing was cheap in Canyon City, but she worked out a price she felt was fair for saddle, tack and such a strong animal. She surprised the hostler by reaching into her small purse and paying him the full amount in federal dollars as well as for the first month's board in advance. "Take good care of him for me. I'll be back to ride him as soon as I can."

Leaving the stable, she saw Dylan Hoyt walking toward her. He smiled with more friendliness than he'd shown on the stage. Apparently, his business was going well with Forester. "I am surprised to see you here," he said as he turned to walk with her toward the general store."

"I am entitled to time off on occasion, Mr. Hoyt."

"And when you do, you like to spend it at a stable? You are a most unusual woman, Mrs. Morgan."

"I will take that as a compliment."

"If you were wise, Mrs. Morgan, you would head back to Portland or whatever big city you came from." His tone was dictatorial and superior.

"Is there a reason for that, sir?"

"Experience."

"I have a job here. I like working with children and have become very fond of my charges. I would not leave them without an instructor."

He gave a small smile before he turned and left her. She didn't trust the handsome man. He said things that were bland, except, she felt they had hidden meanings. He could not know who she was. What job did he have with Forester? It appeared she was not about to learn that from him.

CHAPTER 5

When Rand saw Adam ride in with two boys and a string of turkeys hanging from his saddle, he climbed down the ladder and walked to greet him. The bows and quivers of arrows on their backs explained why no shots had been heard.

"Good with a bow too, I see," he said as Adam took him into a bear hug that lifted him off his feet.

Adam laughed. "Comes in handy and sometimes a lot better than a gun that scares off the rest of the game. Eli and Rufus are getting pretty good at using theirs."

Adam's son, Eli, was growing tall. He'd be a big man like his father with the same coal black hair. Rufus, Matt's son, three years younger, was visibly excited. "I almost got one too. Just missed by this much." He held his fingers a few inches apart. He was blond like his father with the same sturdy build.

"Take them up to your Mama, and tell St. Louis how you did," Adam told youths. As the two boys ran off, he turned back to Rand. "So what's up? Not that I'm not always glad to see you. You don't usually come alone and especially without a uniform. I don't suppose I can hope you finally got smart and left the military."

"I'll be putting the uniform back on when I ride out." He grinned.

"Let's lay off for the rest of the afternoon," Jed suggested. "Thanks to Rand, we got more done today than I was expecting."

"You don't have to convince me," Matt said.

"I'd like to talk to you all including St. Louis, now that I know he's here, but without everybody if we can manage it," Rand said as he went down to the corrals with Adam and helped him unsaddle the horses.

"You sound serious," Adam said as they walked back to the Hardman house.

"Are Bernice and Han Jei still here?"

"They left two months ago for Baker City. Does this involve them?"

"Probably not."

As they reached the big open front porch, Jed said, "After we clean up, I have a good bottle of bourbon I've been meaning to open. Sound good?"

Toddy came out from the house. "Me and Josh too?" Behind him was Jed's half-brother, Josh—his father's child but born of a colored serving girl. Rand had heard the story of how he'd been raised as an equal son to the other Hardmans after his mother died in childbirth. There would not be two closer brothers. Josh looked depressed, but he supposed that related to the dangerous situation or was something more going on?

"Sure... better yet, I'll get two bottles." Before they could enter the house, two dogs and the women erupted along with two little girls. Raine, as beautiful as ever, threw her arms around Rand. "You scalawag. Why haven't you been to see us sooner?" She looked at her husband, Jed, and winked.

"Playing around, of course-- chasing Paiutes, Shoshone and Arapaho, when they aren't chasing us," he said with laugh as Martha also gave him a hug.

"No excuse, not any at all," she said with a laugh. "You remember my younger sister, Amy?"

"We met years back. Looks like her mama." He looked at Martha and knew it was true. "You have just gotten more beautiful. Hell, you have all gotten prettier. What's in that water here, Jed?"

"Try it and find out," Jed said with a crooked grin.

"Our son, Jesse is taking a nap," Raine said. "I can hardly wait for you to meet him too. Of course, babies at six months don't take too well to strangers usually." She laughed.

"I won't take offense if he cries when I look at him."

Fifteen minutes later, the women were back inside working on supper. The men sat on the wooden chairs on the porch enjoying the beginning of evening settling in with the sound of birds along with a rustling of the leaves as the breeze picked up. Inside Rand could hear children playing some sort of game and laughing.

"Figger it'll be a late winter?" St. Louis asked reaching down to pet Deucy who had come to lie at his feet. "I ain't yet used to how it is this side of the Cascades."

"Maybe. It's warmer than usual for October," Jed said as he took a sip of whiskey.

"I figure I'm doing my part," Rand said. "I told the men to gather up a huge pile of firewood—high as the fort wall on the west. That's what they're doing while I take a little vacation."

"That go over well with them?" Matt asked sipping his whiskey.

"About like you'd figure. But with these bars come some privileges." Drawbacks too. "This is fine Bourbon, Jed."

"Glad you like it. You are staying for a few days." It wasn't a question. One thing Rand had observed about Jed Hardman-- he came from southern wealth, fought for the South, and was used to giving orders that were obeyed. He wasn't called the laird without reason.

"I'd like that," he said not eager to go on. The things that awaited him were less and less appealing. Being with these warm and laughing people felt good and right. He only wished Belle felt that way.

"Amy, Matt and their kids are in the left wing where you were before. You can have Jei's room if you like."

"I was disappointed he wasn't still here."

Josh had been standing back in the darkness, only listening, but now he spoke up. "He had his reasons."

"None of my business," he said.

"No, but it's no secret. Bernice lost the baby, our baby. She went into a depression, wanted to leave, to get out of here, and Jei said he'd take her East to where she could get settled. He'll probably be back someday."

"Oh." He wondered if there were words to say. Words he should have thought of saying. Sorry didn't seem to cut it for the loss of a baby.

Jed rose and poured more whiskey into each of their glasses except for Matt and St. Louis who put their hands over theirs. Before Rand could decide whether this was the right time to broach his reason for being there, they were called in for supper.

An hour and a half later, a delicious roast having been devoured, Jed said that the ladies should give them a chance to discuss business. They gave only mild protests as Martha walked home with Eli. Amy put her three small ones and herself to bed in their wing, and Raine took Jesse to their bedroom to feed and then put into his crib.

Rand walked to the edge of the porch to stand beside Adam. "This is a beautiful place," he said. Birds swooped low over the meadow looking for their last meal of the day. In the distance, he could hear a coyote, then a wolf. Ace and Deucy lifted their heads to listen but they didn't bark. Well-trained dogs.

At any military post, with a hundred or more men around him, he only heard silence when out on patrol. Even then, he wasn't alone. He was never alone or without accountability.

"It will also be peaceful some day," Adam added. "I wish you'd join us in the operation. With the land I bought and what Matt and St. Louis added, we are going to change its brand. It'll be the John Day Ranch. It'll be a big spread with cattle, logging, even fruit trees and vegetables. Just got to get this Indian business behind us."

"That's not a minor thing," Rand said as St. Louis came to stand with them.

"It could be the country will see a lot more of that before it's over," the older man said

"It will with death and destruction on both sides, but it will be settled—just not as soon as anybody would wish."

"This will be a good place to live," Adam said. "I wish you'd think on it."

"I will." He realized to his surprise that he actually would. "You sure Jed would be open to me coming in. He kind of likes to run things."

He heard laughter from behind him, and the step he recognized as the southerner's. "Who said I won't be?"

"You now have five strong headed men here—not to mention equally determined women. I know how it works with the military. Someone has to be boss," Rand said. "Who's it going to be?"

Josh had come out to join them and chuckled. "You thinking my brother have to be boss. Why he's gentle as a lamb."

"We've been working on listening to each other," Jed said. "Each of us has one area we know best. A family doesn't need a dictatorship." Jed moved to sit on one of the wooden chairs and lit a cigar. "We are stronger together. Even our children are learning to use weapons and fight. It's what it will take to hold a land like this in a time like this. You would be an asset if you decided you wanted to join us. I understand you may feel your duty calls you other ways, of course, but what Adam said, I also would welcome. Your deciding to become one of us would make success here on the North Fork more likely."

Matt settled into another chair, his long length sprawled out. "So now tell us what you came for," he said.

Rand smiled considering how to approach this without making one of these men angry. "St. Louis, does your name mean you were born in Missouri?"

"I was."

"That state was a border state and very divided in the war."

"The war's over," Jed said.

"Is it?"

"All right, what is this about?"

"In answer to your question," St. Louis said, "I was long gone when the war broke out. Most of my family though fought for the north."

"Most?"

"I had a brother who went for the gray. I had five brothers when the war broke out. Ended up with two by the end. I never seen much sense to wars."

"It seems there are some who don't want feel wars are bad. They haven't given up," Rand said.

"You are going to tell us who," Jed said.

"Do any of you know William Forester?"

"I'd recognize him on the street," Jed said. "Came from out of nowhere less than a year ago. Built a house bigger than anybody's-- on the hill above Canyon City. Went off for some months. Seems I heard he is back now. A man like that stands out when he's got a big black, sprung coach and equally expensive horses to pull it."

"Last week I was asked to come to The Dalles and take on assignment which involves him. The evidence is pretty clear. He is a counterfeiter."

"I figured he was shady but didn't imagine that one," Jed said taking a drag on his cigar. "Why hasn't he been arrested if there is proof of this?"

"And why would he come here? Wouldn't San Francisco or Portland make more sense for putting out phony bills?" Adam asked. "Why Canyon City?"

Rand rose and walked to the edge of the porch before looking back. "From what I read in a file on him, he was there. I should add that Mason Williams is the man I talked to in The Dalles."

"An under secretary or something?" Jed asked.

"You are up on your politics," Rand said with a smile.

"I've learned it matters."

"Counterfeiting is not all he is about. He has formed a group and centered it in Canyon City."

"I'd like to better understand what you are saying. Just a country boy here," Matt said with the look in his eyes that told Rand he was no country boy.

"Here's what I was told," Rand said. "The goal of this group is threefold. One is to cause Americans to lose faith in federal dollars by flooding businesses with counterfeit. Secondly, Forester has been buying arms—a lot of them and shipping them to Canyon City."

"Was he a southern sympathizer? I don't recall hearing him serving in the military on either side," Jed said.

"They believe this is not about the South rising again. It is however, about using the resentment that is still festering over the war. It's about chaos. With chaos, there is a need for someone to bring order. That would be a militia."

"There was one over here during the war, The Oregon Company or something like that, but it disbanded. The men went home when the Federals arrived," Adam said.

"The question is why start a rebellion over here? The middle of nowhere," St. Louis said, his expression turning thoughtful.

"Gold. Where there is wealth, a lot of drifters come along-- many who might be easily stirred up.

"That does fit Canyon City," Jed said.

"It does."

"Phony money and real gold." Jed poured himself another shot of whiskey.

Rand nodded. "They think that he's looking for those angry at the North, which would in the beginning be Southerners. If you have noticed, Washington has had its share of corruption lately, and it's not just those in the South, who are angry right now. Add to it those who want power or money. So I am to look for disenfranchised men who will be drawn to his cause."

"Am I under suspicion?" Jed watched Rand through the smoke of his cigar.

"The Colonel wanted me to assure him that you are a loyalist."

Jed rose and stalked to the opposite edge of the porch staring out into the darkness, the mountains only dimly outlined in the far distance. "I am not a loyalist to anything except my own land and people. I though would not support in anyway a rebellion or insurrection if that's what this is about."

Rand nodded. "Have you had anyone coming around to try to talk about such?"

"Not to me. I can talk to Jack as he gets to town more than me. You know I still have some property in the South. I've tried to sell it all but some has been hard to get a good price considering the way the carpetbaggers are trying to milk every asset and dollar from the southern states."

"Well, there's more to it than just Forester," Rand said. "And it's not just riffraff. My brother apparently is on his way to Canyon City. Probably there now to meet with Forester. To add to it, my father was in San Francisco recently when he apparently disappeared. Williams didn't say but it seemed obvious he believes the general is involved in some way and coming here or working for the cause at least."

"So," Adam said sipping his whiskey, his expression contemplative, "their belief that your family is involved, why they wanted you?"

"Part of it. Remember, this is a combination of talk, the counterfeit money, and rifles purchased in various locations with the belief they are now here. It is putting together a lot of things with no proof for any of it."

Jed rubbed the back of his neck. "Damn, as if we didn't have enough trouble here with Indians and bandits." He growled before he sighed. "So what can I do to help?"

"Dang, this is getting' to be more interestin' here than I figgered," St. Louis said with a grin.

"What do you want from us?" Adam added with Matt and St. Louis nodding.

"Keep your ears open. If you go to Canyon City, be aware of anyone approaches you and begins to hint at something. Out here— just be ready."

"That last part we already had down," Jed said.

"They expect you to find the proof for them." Adam said without a question.

"They hope at least, with one addition. I have to find a traitor or maybe more than one at Watson."

Matt whistled before he rolled and lit another cigarette. "You do have your hands full. So is this all secret or can we tell our wives?"

Rand laughed. "Could you keep it from them?"

"Not if we have a choice," Jed said with an answering chuckle.

"What about Toddy?" Jed asked. His hired man had gone to bed early. "I wonder if I should encourage him to go back to Portland for awhile. Actually, it might not be a bad idea for the family to go with him and stay in Raine's home there for the winter. This could be a hard one."

"I don't know him. Can you trust him?"

"I believe so."

"To share this with him, you need to be sure." Rand knew if it leaked out, his life would be the one most at risk.

"How do you feel about it possibly involving your father and brother?" Matt asked in a contemplative tone.

"Like someone stuck a knife in my gut. We weren't close. That's obvious but I still... hate to think either would be involved in something like this."

"You know how little use I have for the military," Adam said, "but it's hard to imagine a general risking his whole reputation, not to mention his life, for a wild plot like this sounds."

"Might be more likely to work than you'd think," St. Louis said as he stared off toward the mountains. "Lots of things been done unfair to this or that one. Folks can get easily riled in such times."

"I have no idea about my family's loyalties—neither of them. What I do know of my father wasn't especially good," Rand said. "But I would also not have believed he'd become a traitor to his country."

Adam's smile was crooked. "Being a father is not an easy job." He poured himself another shot of whiskey.

"Not having been one," Rand said, "I can't speak from that end. Generals tend to be gone a lot. When he was there, he had high expectations. My mother died when I was quite young. He remarried and had a second son. I had thought perhaps one more to his liking than I ever was. Now I wonder about the brother I barely knew." Suddenly another shot of whiskey sounded good to him too. He downed it in a swallow.

"How old are you, Rand?" Adam asked.

"Old enough to know better," he said with a bitter laugh.

"Seriously how many years? When's your birthday? Friends should know things like that."

Oh, they should, should they? When is your birthday, old man? Or do you have one like ordinary mortals?" He chuckled finally feeling in a better mood. Maybe the whiskey had helped or was it just being with these men, men with no ulterior motives, and who he could trust. That wasn't something he had often in his life these days—even before being asked to turn spy.

"I have one," Adam said with a smirk. "You figured I was hatched out on the prairie?"

"Or in a cave," Jed agreed laughing.

"July 31, 1825 in Indiana in case you needed birthplace for an investigation."

Rand laughed. "Oh yeah, like I'll remember that."

"Want me to write mine down?" Jed asked. "More likely to need it."

"Look, I did not come here to gather information or investigate anybody. Mostly they wanted you to know what's going on. Something might come along that would seem innocuous otherwise but now you'd see what was meant."

"How old are you, Rand?" Adam repeated.

"Too old if you count experiences. If it's by years, I'll be thirty-six in January—if I live that long."

"You a pessimist, Yank?" Jed asked.

"Lately."

"Resign," Adam said. "I have told you that more times than I can count. How many wars do you need?"

Rand rolled another cigarette and took a long draw before blowing out the smoke and watching it curl upward toward the star-strewn sky. "I can't quit until this one is settled."

"Isn't there always one more for a career soldier?" St. Louis asked without a smile.

There was truth in that. "What would I do if I quit?" he asked finally studying the glowing tip of his cigarette. "All I know is organizing men and fighting battles. Being a warrior doesn't have much of a career path outside of the military one."

"Could come in handy these days keeping a ranch operating," Jed said as he lit another cigar.

"You have enough on this place as it is." Rand wondered if that had been an offer.

"Not so. We need a community. Ten thousand more acres is available to the east of my place. With that, we could run a sawmill, orchards, cattle, maybe even a vineyard. The hills here are rich in minerals, not gold but others that would surprise you what they could produce—once we are past the Indian problem."

Rand considered before he answered. "I think we are facing years before that's settled."

"And you want to be fighting through all of it?" Adam asked.

"I didn't say that." He looked over at Jed. "Did you hope when this current conflict is over, it's done with Indian troubles and will be safe in your hills?"

Jed smiled. "I quit counting on safe some years back."

"Good, because I think there will be more than ten years before you can hope to have it here. And even then that just means the Paiute, Bannock, Snake, Umatilla, Cayuse and Walla Walla will be satisfied to stop fighting us and each other. For at least ten years, you can look for sporadic and undependable attacks. Your place will be hit. It's becoming a far more attractive target."

"Which is why I still run longhorns, and why I built what amounts to a fort."

Rand nodded approvingly. "It was smart. I wish I could be more optimistic but..."

"The tribes are fighting for their existence as they have always known it to be, fighting for their lives," Adam finished.

"And so are we," Jed added.

Canyon City

William Forester read the note and then called for Dunham to come into his office.

"Yes sir," the man said.

"I am going to need Beckham and Nash. Bring them to me."

Dunham hurried away to do his bidding. Forester poured himself a whiskey as he considered what he could do. A traitor had to be not only killed but punished. He grinned as he thought about the many ways that could be done. What he liked best was knowing that person would have no clue of their danger. To see them naive and finally recognizing their options were gone, that was his delight. He loved to see fear.

He sipped the fine liquor as he considered how he would do it. Torture for certain but maybe more. The traitor was so attractive. The very idea of power over that beautiful body made him hot with wanting.

"You want me?" Beckham said as he entered the room.

"Have a drink, Jack."

Beckham looked surprised, but he eagerly took the whiskey. Finer than any he could ever afford.

"Where is George?"

"Last I saw at the saloon."

"I need you both for a special assignment. There will be a reward attached."

"I can't do it alone?"

"Possibly but it's more certain of success with two of you. It has to be done quickly and subtly. I have been betrayed." He told Beckham the name of the miscreant and felt some satisfaction at his surprise.

"You are sure?"

"I am. I want him in secure bonds and you know the house we use."

"The same one?" Beckham asked.

Forester worked to control his temper. He still needed Beckham and would have to overlook his stupidity. "Yes, the same one."

"Right away then?"

"You will need Nash to make sure there is no resistance. I will meet you there just after dark."

When Beckham swigged the rest of his whiskey and headed out, Forester considered the steps he had taken to date. He would let no one stand in his way. His counterfeit operating wasn't about attaining riches. What was money? All he had done to this point had one purpose and that was to give him power. The same was true on the guns he'd bought and in some cases distributed. All of it was just a beginning and the real time of risk was now at hand. He would let no one stand in his way.

He had to end the life of the traitor—of course after getting everything the miscreant knew. He wanted to see fear in those beautiful eyes. Then horror when his victim understood his helplessness and that there would be no escape. He felt hot just thinking of the pleasures that lay ahead—for him, of course, not for that worthless excrement.

What more could he ask from a day. He liked games. He liked them very much. Sometimes they led to information he could use. That part though didn't matter. Today would be a very good day—for him. For the rubbish, it would be a bad day. Perhaps, depending on how it all went, more than one, and then would come the last day. He smiled.

CHAPTER 6

With morning, Rand was feeling a mix of emotions. He sat in the large kitchen, sipping coffee, listening to the men discuss the work ahead, and watching the women as they fried bacon and eggs. He was torn as to what he wanted to do next. He should get back to Watson except what awaited him there?

He still had not decided on whether the family had the right to know where Belle was. Fairest might be to give her a chance to tell them before he did. What was fair to both the mother and the daughter? Once she knew where Belle was, even without knowing what she was doing, she would worry. Saying nothing was likely best. He would though find a time to tell Belle what she needed to do.

"You look troubled, Captain," Raine said as she refilled his coffee cup and sat across from him.

He let out a little laugh. "I've had better times."

"Stay here awhile. Do some fishing. Forget the world and then when you go back, it'll all be better." She put her hand on Rand's. "The river always makes it better."

"And if you stay an extra couple of days," Jed said from across the table, "I'll give you a look at that land upriver, show you what I am thinking. If you decide it's not for you, that's fine, but it's pretty country. You'll enjoy the ride either way."

Rand smiled. He should get back. He didn't want to get back. "All right, thank you. I'd like a day more here."

"Salmon are in the river," Raine said. "If you two go for a ride, be back by late afternoon. Maybe we can catch some for dinner."

"Sounds like a plan."

An hour later, Jed, Matt and Rand rode up the river. Adam and St. Louis stayed back to keep an eye on the place with Josh but also to get the fishing gear ready. "I am interested in what's up here too," Matt drawled as he studied the hills, riding with the ease of a man comfortable in the saddle but also one familiar with dangers in his surroundings. They rode heavily armed with cartridge belts, revolvers and good rifles.

"It's a nice piece of land," Jed said. "I'd buy it myself except I don't want more land than I can manage. I think I have pretty much got that now at least until our son grows up some." He grinned.

"From where do the Shoshone come when they ride through?" Rand asked.

"There is a trail that goes to the headwaters. Some of it is pretty rough. I've thought of taking a herd that way to Baker City as a way to avoid most of the hostile action. Eventually I will have to do a drive, as we will have to remove stock or they will graze the place down too far. In this kind of country, doing that would be the end of ranching."

The hills were rugged with canyons, creeks, and tall pines as the river moved between rapids and pools. It was beautiful country—with colorful cliffs and interesting rock formations, even grassy meadows. Being a rancher, however, hadn't ever been something Rand had seen for himself. Still, if he left the military, when this campaign was over, what exactly would he do? As it stood, he had no better ideas.

Belle got her charges in bed, but then told Sally she was going for a little walk.

"It's gonna be dark soon. Aint you afraid to go out at night, Miss? Lots of troubles happen at night."

"I like the night. It's actually safer if you know what you're doing."

"Not real safe, ma'am," Sally said with concern.

"I won't go far. I can take care of myself though." She had dressed in a dark brown dress, bonnet that covered her hair, and a black coat. She had debated but not taken a weapon. She didn't intend to get beyond the most traveled roads. "Would you like to come with me and let Jenks stay with the children?" she asked to defray any suspicion if Sally felt it necessary to inform Forester of her plans.

"Not me at night. No way, but I got work to do anyway. Thanks for asking. I'll just keep an eye on the little ones." She set about kneading dough for the next day's bread.

Outside, Belle walked quickly. She intended to check out access to two buildings, ones Forester might be using for a printing press. She had been to the newspaper office, one likely spot, but it wasn't being done there. Not unless that building had a cellar, which had seemed unlikely given its proximity to Canyon Creek.

As she neared the first of the buildings, she heard voices. Not wanting to be seen, she moved back into the shadow of a narrow alley.

"Been looking for you all day. The boss wants to see you," a man's voice said. She could not see his face but had heard that voice speaking with William Forester.

"And he sent you?" The other voice was that of Dylan Hoyt.

"To be sure you came."

"I have no reason not to go with you. You didn't need to pull the knife. He could have sent a message."

"Didn't know where you was," another man said.

"Put your hands behind your back." The voice she recognized ordered. She heard the sound of a brief scuffle.

"God, you didn't have to tie me up. I am not resisting."

"It's how he wanted you to come."

"This is ridiculous." She heard then the men shoving the now bound Hoyt ahead of them. She moved to where she could see them head down the street. Hoyt had been kidnapped on what she deemed a public street. Others had to have seen. Sally had been right about the danger in this town where no one would help anyone else. Was that fear, lack of concern, or were they together in whatever was going on here?

She debated what she could do about it. Hoyt was no friend of hers. She had no idea for what purpose they had grabbed him off the street. If she let them know she'd seen, would she end up also bound? She had no weapon. Interference wouldn't have been smart even if she had. Hoyt had put up little resistance. Perhaps this wasn't a serious matter. Going back to the house for her gun wasn't an option, not if she wanted to find out where they were taking him.

The men's pace was quick, and then they turned off the street to a house a hundred feet back. She dodged into the shadows beside a shrub as she saw that the home had more men around it. Whatever was going on, she could not get close enough to find out. She moved farther into the bushes and sat on the cold ground to watch for who entered or left. She needed names. Possibly she'd have a chance to talk to Hoyt later.

Nothing happened for longer than she had expected. It was at least two hours, maybe more when two men emerged from the house. It took a second for her to realize a third was being dragged between them. Although his jacket was gone and she couldn't see his face, she felt certain the third man was Hoyt. What happened to him?

She followed at a safe distance still uncertain what she was seeing. She dared not risk following closely enough to hear their conversation. She caught only a laugh, a muffled groan, and one word-- traitor.

By the creek, the men headed up a trail where she dared not follow. Had Hoyt been beaten as a lesson but for what? Should she have stayed watching the house? It would have been useful to know that Forester had been there. She could not do two things. She used her instincts and waited in the shadows.

Five minutes later, the two men came back down the trail. The third was no longer with them. She waited long enough for them to have disappeared before heading up the trail grateful there was enough moonlight to show the way and hopefully avoid tripping. She was taking a risk but if Hoyt had been beaten, he might need help. She vowed never again go out at night without a weapon. She stopped when she saw the figure of a man lying on his stomach, his arm in the slow moving creek.

She knelt and turned him over. His wrists were no longer bound for an obvious reason. He was dead. A gory wound to his throat told how he had met his end. Blood still seeped from the wound to join the pool under his body. He'd been murdered where he lay.

There was worse if anything can be worse than death. Gruesome swellings and cuts marred the body of the previously handsome gambler. His shirt hung open. Cut marks surrounded his nipples. She felt shock not just at seeing sudden death but her realization that he had been tortured. She looked into his staring eyes and resisted the temptation to close them.

She needed to get away from the body, but took time to check his pockets. No wallet. Perhaps they hoped this would look like a robbery. A small piece of paper was in a side pocket. She took it and a key and chain. She left a small compass as she restored his body to the position in which she had found it. She knelt by the stream and carefully washed any blood from her hands.

Rapidly she walked back toward the Forester home trying to still her breathing. She was no stranger to death, but the times she had seen it, there had not also been signs of torture. Someone wanted to either punish Hoyt or... get information from him. She had no way to know who or why. Did the kidnappers work for William? If so, was he the one who wanted Hoyt dead or was it someone else? Finally—traitor to what or who?

She doubted that the key would give her a clue but maybe the paper might. At the house, she decided not to take the key inside. It would be hard to come up with a reason for having it if her things were routinely being searched—as she knew was highly possible. She secured the key chain under loose dirt near the foundation where she could easily find it. It was then that she realized there was an unusually solid and deep foundation to the mansion. There was one obvious explanation for concrete going so far down-- a basement. She knew where all the doors in the house led, had checked closets for any hidden accesses. This has be a secret door, most likely reached from a panel and hidden lever. It seemed she had been looking too far away for the presses.

In the house, she quickly changed from her dirty dress into a fresh lavender gown. The piece of paper offered nothing more than the words—I love you. It looked like in a woman's handwriting, but it was not signed. So, Dylan had had a lady friend. She refolded it put it in her dress pocket and went then back to the kitchen to offer her help to Sally, who was still working.

"You have a nice walk, ma'am?" Sally asked as she pumped water and then put a pan on the stove to make tea.

"Please call me Belle, and yes, it was lovely out." She put on a smile that required some work. "I needed to stretch my legs and clear my head. There was enough moonlight that I went farther than I had intended."

"When the moon comes out, so do the goblins," Sally said with a little laugh that didn't sound amused.

"If one worried about such," Belle said smiling.

"Nope. I don't neither. I do understand a body wanting to clear her head. The goings on here can make a head spin for sure. Coming and going. Coming and going."

If Belle had been a less experienced agent, she might have asked what Sally meant, but she understood how sometimes such questions were put out as traps. She had no reason to trust or distrust Sally, but she did need to be careful of everybody.

"Children do keep me busy. They can be a handful," she said as she accepted her tea. "Do you have any of your own?" Sally was old enough to have grown children.

"Nah, never had a man I'd want to trust being a father. Men, they are plumb bad news as daddies. I guess you didn't have any with your husband."

"No, we were not so blessed," Belle said. Where she had never minded telling lies as part of her work, it was beginning to bother her more each day. It sometimes left her wondering who and what she was.

The door opened as William Forester walked through with a big smile as he looked at Belle. "May I talk to you a moment?" he asked as he poured himself a generous glass of brandy. He was clearly in a very nearly jubilant mood. If he had been involved with Dylan Hoyt's murder, it had not disturbed him.

"Of course, sir," she said without a good feeling at being alone with the man. For all his suave manners and good looks, she knew him to be a counterfeiter. Was he also something far worse? The boss had to be William. How ruthless was he? She smiled. She'd better be good at her game or she'd end up like Hoyt. Sally handed her a teacup, and she followed William to the parlor. She sat on a straight chair and watched as he moved to the sofa. She looked at his hands but saw no bruised knuckles. Perhaps William had had nothing to do with Hoyt's violent death. The men who had taken him could have lied.

"Are you enjoying working for me?" he asked as he sipped the brandy.

"Your children are delightful, eager to learn and very sweet." She sipped her tea.

"Really?" He smiled. "Would you like some brandy, Belle?"

"No thank you. I sleep better with tea before bed." Especially when she needed a clear head.

"My main reason for wanting to talk to you was an invitation. I am hosting a very special dinner and ball Saturday night, with the more important citizens of Canyon City. I would like you attend as my guest."

Unexpected but perhaps it should not have been. "Certainly, as your employee, of course, I would be delighted." She needed constantly to establish distance between Forester and herself. Loath though she was to be close to him, she could not refuse such an invitation. Besides, it was her job to investigate. At what sounded like a large and important gathering, she would have a chance to see who his friends were, possibly his cohorts.

"Do you have the proper gown for such an affair?" he asked. "I mean did you bring such with you?"

"How formal will it be?"

"As much as Canyon City can provide. It will be held at our largest hall. I don't suppose it will match the balls you are familiar with in Chicago or New York, but it will be as exciting an event as Canyon

City can provide. Well, as gold can provide." His smile seemed smarmy to her but then perhaps it was because of what she knew about him more that what it really showed. She worked to school her features.

"I believe I have a dress that will be appropriate."

"Good. You will be gorgeous, I am certain. I will be proud to have you on my arm."

"Thank you."

"I also wanted to let you alert you to the news that we will be having a preeminent guest arriving Thursday. I hope you will like him. I will, of course, want the children on their best behavior."

"I am sure they will be. Of course, they are children."

"Of course."

"Do I know your guest?" Fortunately, her identity as a Pinkerton was neatly buried under many appropriate activities. It was unlikely his guest would know anything that would threaten her cover.

"I am not sure. You were both in Chicago and New York City but not perhaps at the same time. It is General Abraham Phillips. He is retired now but has many powerful friends."

She worked to school her features. "I am not familiar with the name." Actually, she was but as a governess, she should not be.

"Before the war, the general lived in Virginia, which as you know led to many divided loyalties. From the time of his graduation from West Point, he had risen up the ranks with every expectation of becoming even Secretary of War. Unfortunately, when the war began, he was pushed aside by younger and showier soldiers. You know the type. He is, however, an excellent example of the best our nation produces."

"Was he in the Confederacy?"

"He fought for the North."

"I just realized that the name is familiar. The officer who saved us at the Jamison stage shop was a Captain Phillips. Might they be related?"

He smiled. "That would be his son. An invitation has been sent to him at Camp Watson. General Phillips has another son already in town, Jason. He was never in the military. A very handsome lad."

This was getting more and more complex. What would Rand's family be doing out here? "Of course, I would like to meet him also. I barely know the captain. We only talked in passing that day."

"Jason actually will not be a guest here as the general will. He's staying at the Elkhorn Hotel. He is, however, in my employ."

"I look forward to meeting him." She tried to remember what she knew about Rand's younger brother. Very little. Fortunately, on her earlier assignments, she was certain she had met neither.

"Jason is your age. He will join us for dinner Thursday night. You might find you have much in common."

"Friends are always nice."

"Belle, come and sit beside me. I am straining my voice to talk to you so far away and that chair doesn't look comfortable. The sofa is much more." He patted the spot beside him. The look in his eyes told her that sitting beside him would not be wise. Still she did not wish to offend him unless it was essential to her safety.

"Mr. Forester..."

He interrupted. "William."

She licked her lips forcing a shy look onto her face. "I have very firm rules regarding friendships with any gentlemen for whom I am working, sir. I hope you respect that."

"And just sitting beside me would break those rules?"

She sighed. "It has proven to be so in the past."

He smiled and nodded. "All right, I do respect that. While you are working for me, you said?"

"Yes."

"I'll have to see if I can do something about that." His smile was confident.

If she had been the shy inexperienced woman she was portraying, a widow, but one who had little idea how to handle a mature, powerful man, she knew this could turn ugly. Well it might anyway. It was one reason she had wanted a horse and had begun to accumulate supplies--just in case. If it turned ugly with William Forester, she would have to leave town and not wait for a stage. She wasn't about to end up like Dylan Hoyt.

She smiled and rose. "I am quite tired tonight. I look forward to meeting the general and his son. Of course, also the ball. It sounds very exciting."

"Do you dance, Belle?"

"I have been known to."

"Would that also be against the rules with an employer?"

"Of course not." With that, she left the room and walked up the stairs. In her room, she pushed a chair against the door not that she thought Forester would try to rape her—at least not with an important guest soon to arrive.

She was usually good at reading men's personalities. Forester's manner indicated seduction. His first attempt at it with her. Something about it didn't ring true. With his handsome features and suave ways, he was likely used to getting what he wanted. Did he really want her though? He acted like it but...

Lying under her covers, she considered what she had to do. There had to be a way to access the hidden basement from the house. The obvious answer had to be a panel that served also as a door. In that hidden room, she'd find the proof of Forester's counterfeiting. Proof of his ordering Hoyt's murder wasn't as easu to attain if it was even possible. Counterfeiting was enough to satisfy her assignment. She no longer cared who was working with him. Perhaps if Forester was arrested, he'd be willing to reveal that information for a lighter sentence.

Closing her eyes, she was maddened to see a tall cavalry officer appear in her imagination. She could see him striding across the hard land to the stage stop, whipping off his hat, and knocking the dust from it. Then that faint smile when she told him she wanted to treat his wound.

She wondered if he had continued to take care of it. Where was he? Would he come to the ball? How would seeing his father affect him? She remembered their relationship had not been good. Rand had looked so tired... Her thoughts went in circles.

Ridiculous. She could not keep fantasizing about a man who was only part of her past—a very small part. She needed to get a long way from him. It had to be the proximity that was making this all happen. It was time to find the proof she needed and get out of Canyon City. She wanted to see her mother, sisters, their husbands, meet their children. Then perhaps another case from Alan, one a long, long way from Oregon.

She worked to keep from her the vision of Dylan Hoyt's dead body. The poor man. What had he done to lead to his horrible end? Thinking of the violence that was around this house, this town, she thought of the Forester children. Tears seeped past her lids as she remembered how rejected Jeremy had felt at his father's lack of caring for him. Jessica, poor baby, she needed love so much. But what could she really do about them? They were not hers. She had never to forget that. She had a job to do. When she finished her assignment, she would have to forget everything that was here in Oregon. Every single thing.

Late Wednesday evening, Rand rode into Camp Watson and

dismounted in front of his quarters. Private Smith came to take his mount. There were many Smiths in the military after the War.

"Rub him down good," he said as he handed over the reins. "He's had a long, hard ride."

"Yes, sir."

Entering his room, he moved to the small stove and looked around for kindling. It was getting considerably cooler. Lt. Murphy came through the door behind him. "What can I do for you, Rand?" he asked as he handed him a hot cup of coffee.

Rand sat at his desk, sipped the coffee and looked at the stack of reports. "No further attacks, Pat?"

"There are some complaints regarding stock being stolen. Nothing that required action."

"How'd the wood gathering go?" He saw no kindling by his stove but that didn't tell him much.

"We have a good supply." Murphy pointed to an envelope on his desk. "This arrived for you morning by special courier. It looked important."

When Rand opened it, he groaned.

"Bad news?" Murphy asked.

Rand took out the makings for a cigarette. "You might say. My father and brother are in Canyon City."

"Doesn't that come under the category of good news?" Murphy dropped into one of the wooden chairs in front of Rand's desk.

"Depends on the father." He lit the cigarette, taking a long draw and staring at the glowing end.

"Ah."

He looked toward the door where Corporal Muldoon awaited orders. "Find Lockwood and ask him to join us."

In less than five minutes, his other lieutenant was sitting beside Murphy. "It seems I am being called to Canyon City Saturday night, which means of necessity, I will again be leaving the management of this fort to you and the fighting of the Indians to other troops." He drew on the cigarette trying to fight back the feeling of bitterness that seemed to be swallowing him.

"What will you want us to do?" Lockwood asked.

"Drill the men. Keep them from buying so much liquor at the Suttler's that they get drunk regularly. None of this is good news to me, gentlemen. But it is unfortunately not a choice."

"Who will you take with you?" Murphy asked.

"This is a social occasion." He knew his voice sounded angry and worked to moderate it. None of this was their fault. "I won't be needing anyone."

"Under the circumstances, I think you should take at least a squad, Rand," Murphy said. "Speaking as your friend, of course, not your subordinate."

"I don't want to have them in Canyon City looking for trouble when I'm not in any position to keep an eye on them. It seems William Forester is holding a ball. His invitation was only for me or I'd invite one of you to join me."

"Won't a ball be a pleasant amusement?" Lockwood asked.

Rand let out the smoke. "Not in this case, Jim. Damn." If Belle was not included, it might be easier, but he had little hope that would be the case. Forester had to have hired her as an ornament. He would want her there and on his arm.

"You could have me go with a squad and I'd keep an eye on them," Lockwood said.

"No."

"But, sir, we should be going out on patrol," Lockwood said. "It's not really possible to keep one hundred men from getting themselves into fights when they don't have enough to do."

"I will ride there Saturday morning and come back that night if possible or at the least early Sunday morning. After that, we will be back on a regular schedule for patrols. I am sorry, gentleman but this event is not an option for me nor are my orders negotiable."

The two lieutenants rose and left with Lockwood surly and Murphy his usual easygoing self. As he smoked, Rand considered Lockwood's attitude. Was that a clue that the man was his traitor— that he was so eager to go to Canyon City? It didn't have to be a lieutenant. It might be one of the sergeants, even a private. Someone though was reporting the activities. He had to find out who. He went to the door.

"Corporal, assemble the men. I need to speak to them."

Once again, Muldoon was quick to the task. A good man. That didn't mean he wasn't also a traitor. Rand put on a fresh jacket, adjusted his hat and headed out to explain the events of the next few days.

As he came into the sunlight, he saw them gathering, the lines forming. One hundred troopers. They were at least adequate on horseback, some real horsemen. In leadership, there were five sergeants and two lieutenants. He had a responsibility to lead them all in ways that enabled them to fulfill their purpose and stay alive. The fort was a small community and at its head was its captain or colonel.

His experience in war yielded some wisdom, but the reality was fate stepped in more times than he cared to count. He could not guarantee they would all survive their enlistment.

With the men lined up in front of him, he cleared his throat. "It's been a hard year, men. It isn't likely immediately to get easier. We have ahead another winter, with limited supplies."

"We appreciate the captain," one of the men said and the others yelled their approval.

Rand nodded. "And I appreciate you and how hard this job is. I know you depend on me as I do on you. Although it might seem your gathering of wood has not been much of a war effort, I know what the winters are like here. Thirty of you have not been here for a winter and do not realize how isolating it can be. It might seem the wood gathering is only about heat, but it also serves to build muscles. It will be your task for the next week. Clearing the woods back from the camp has other advantages in terms of making hostile attacks more difficult. The fact that they do not generally attack forts or camps, does not mean they cannot gather sufficient numbers to do so.

"When I am back from Canyon City, we will resume patrols. Our engagements with the hostiles so often seem running battles and skirmishes. We might all like to see it otherwise, but as the tribes fight is how we must fight also. Sometimes it seems we see little progress, but we will win. Our cause is a necessary one. For now, that is all."

The men saluted and returned to their barracks. If this was to be a hard winter, they would be glad of the heat. For now, it would also serve to keep them occupied and out of trouble—he hoped. Damn, he wished he had something to keep himself occupied. Dress uniform had been requested. He'd have to figure out where in the hell his was and get it pressed.

CHAPTER 7

Taking the children for afternoon jaunts into the nearby forest had become part of their schooling. Belle was not sure for what she was preparing them. Perhaps it was like her stores of supplies and a horse, all of which she might suddenly need to access.

"I want to go camping," Jeremy said as Jessica bounced alongside them.

"What do you know about camping, Jer?" she asked.

"Tent, right? Sleeping in it. Killing game to eat. And a fire to cook it."

"Hunting is more than killing. It requires stealth. Do you know what that word means?"

Jessica shook her head. Jeremy said, "Sneaky."

She smiled. "A bit more than that. Stealth is being quiet, moving fast when required, and observing always what is around you. It is especially about being quiet."

"I could do that," Jessica said.

"You are never quiet," Jeremy said with the superiority Belle remembered from her older sisters when they wanted to subdue her high spirits.

"Camping can require that word as well as wisdom as to where it's wise to camp."

"Is camping dangerous?" Jessica asked with some concern now in her voice.

"It actually can be."

"Great. I would like dangerous." Jeremy looked down on his small sister. "I'd protect you, Jess."

The little girl smiled. "Then I will go camping with you."

"Maybe sometime we can get permission to do that," Belle said considering that this conversation made no sense. For what did she think she was preparing the children?

"Do you have clothing that lets you play in the woods and stay warm?" she asked thinking she had only seen the ones for their daily use. Hardly fit for venturing out at night and sleeping away from a house.

Jeremy shook his head. "Just school clothes."

Belle considered that. She would have to make sure they had such. If they only wore them when not around their father, she could take them farther out into the woods and teach them more about what lurked there. Hopefully, without frightening Jessica too much or exciting Jeremy such that he went out on his own. Adam had taught her so much about woods craft—once she had gotten past being mad at him for marrying her mother. She liked the idea of passing that information onto these children.

She had been a governess for a brief time before, and it had always been part of an assignment. She almost forgot it was a job when she was with these two. She liked being with them and for once feeling no intrigue. She could be herself with no role to play because she was their teacher.

She had never thought of having children, but if she ever had wanted them, Jessica and Jeremy would have been a perfect fit. She stopped their walk and gave them each big hugs, which this time Jeremy didn't even resist.

Entering the house, the children ran ahead with their usual excitement after a time outdoors, only to be stopped by their father's sharp voice. "Behave like ladies and gentlemen," he instructed and then looked up at Belle. She looked as little like a governess as probably it was possible with leaves in her hair, some dirt on her hands from digging in it to reveal the layers and a very plain dress.

"General Phillips," William said with an apologetic tone. "You will not believe my children are generally well behaved, not running around like little hooligans, and my governess can look quite respectable herself." His smile was tight.

Belle looked beyond him to see the older gentleman, rising from a chair. He wore a formal uniform that marked him as a general, retired or not. She recognized some of Rand's features. He was several inches shorter than Rand but did hold himself proudly. He had the same lanky build, even in what had to be his mid 50s. His hair had turned a becoming shade of silver and a large mustache covered his upper lip. His smile was forced. She wondered what the two had been discussing when interrupted.

"You are teaching them about the wilderness," the general said.

"Biology and even history are best taught outdoors," she said, removing her shawl.

"Children, will you go to the kitchen for some milk and a biscuit," William said dismissing them without even using their names.

"I'll just change and be back down if you wish," Belle said.

William smiled. "No, come in as you are. Would you like something to drink? A brandy perhaps?"

"Tea could be nice if you have it," she said. While William ordered the waiting Jenks to get that for her, she settled into the chair across from the general. "Are you enjoying your visit to Oregon?" she asked with a smile.

"It is rugged, of course, but very beautiful. I saw fascinating rock formations as we arrived. My driver was well informed as to the fossils that have been found. Even with the Indian trouble, we did make a bit of a detour. Very captivating area."

"I'd love to take the children there, but it's not really safe for them as it stands."

The general snorted. "The military, as usual, has dropped the ball in making the savages return to their reservations."

"One of them was much appreciated by me," Belle said as Sally emerged from the kitchen with a teapot and cups. "I was saved on my way here by an officer, whom I believe is your son."

"I did hear of that. I would say more, but it's not really my place," the general said with almost a sneer.

William poured more brandy into his glass and the general's. "I think you will find Canyon City to be a pleasant surprise. I invited Jason to dine with us tonight."

"I suppose Randall was too busy." The general gave a little laugh that didn't sound amused.

"It is a ways to come. I did send a message to Camp Watson requesting his presence at the ball on Saturday. I am sure you will see him then."

The general looked back at Belle. "You will be there also, I hope, Mrs. Morgan."

She nodded. "I am looking forward to it." She wasn't but that was the expected lie. She was good at expected lies. The whole idea of investigating this unsavory plot to ruin the Federal currency, with who knew what intentions behind it, was making her hate the very idea of being a Pinkerton. For the first time in her life, she wished she were just a governess. She looked down, sipping her tea.

The knock at the door came and Jenks soon invited a young man into the parlor. "Hello, Father," he said as he looked with curiosity at Belle.

"This is my son, Jason," the general said. "Jason, this is Mrs. Morgan. Belle, I hope to her friends, of which we shall be among." His smile seemed sincere, at least for wanting the friendship if not the rest.

Smooth with the words. His son, his other son, could have bene-fited from some of that or then again maybe she preferred Rand outspoken and without that level of finesse.

Jason came as a surprise as he sat beside his father. Instead of Rand's rugged features, his strong nose and jaw, Jason had a soft face, smooth features, perhaps more like his mother, who she knew nothing about. She decided to be blunt, after all, what was she supposed to know? "Is your wife also in Oregon, General Phillips?" she asked knowing she at least had not made the journey to Canyon City.

"My mother prefers San Francisco to Oregon," Jason said with a twinge of disgust.

"It is a very nice city." Belle took a sip of her tea and looked down wishing she was back in the woods.

"I hear you met my brother," Jason asked and when she looked up, he was studying her.

"You might call it met. He was leading a unit or whatever you call a group of soldiers." She smiled, as she knew very well what it was called, but a governess should not. "They saved our lives, I am sure."

"How noble."

"It seemed so at the time to those of us on the stage which included, of course, the Forester children."

"Oh yes," the general said, "Randall does have gumption if nothing else." He snorted.

She was now with three men she disliked. What sort of career had she chosen? It was supposed to be one of adventure and doing some-thing to make the country safer for citizens. Except it was turning sour. She wondered then if Jason was involved with William's unsavory dealings with counterfeiting. How much did the general know of any of it? Even more—was the counterfeiting part of something else—

something where murder was necessary? She forced a smile onto her face.

"I really would like to change and clean up before dinner," she said as she rose.

"Of course. Don't take long though. It should be ready in fifteen minutes," William said as he again refilled the glasses of the others.

By the time Belle returned, wearing a long-sleeved white blouse with a dark blue skirt, her hair more tidily on top of her head, Jenks was coming in from the kitchen. "Dinner is served."

"I hope the children are being fed in the kitchen," William said. Jenks nodded. Belle barely resisted the frown. Although it was common for children not to dine with prominent families, she remembered how different it had been at her mother's tables with all generations gathering and laughter as much a part of the meals as conversation. She had no right to find fault with what William chose to do with his children, but more and more, she pitied them.

At the long table, with candles already lit, Jason was the one to hold her chair, and he then sat beside her. "Do you like being a governess?" he asked probably as the only thing he could think of to say.

"Very much when it is for children like Jeremy and Jessica. They are so intelligent, amazingly quick to put things together."

"I hope you are not teaching them political or cultural views that I might not agree with," William said, smiling. The smile didn't reach his eyes.

"You and I did agree on the curriculum before I arrived. I brought the right books. The only real addition is teaching them an hour or two a day outdoors when the weather makes it possible."

"I don't suppose that could hurt." William didn't sound convinced.

Belle was convinced of one thing. She was in for a long boring evening—none of which would get her any closer to answers or how to get into what she was convinced was a secret room under the house. As things stood, she wasn't sure when she'd get that opportunity.

Staring up at the dark sky, Rand stood on the porch in front of his quarters smoking what he planned to be his last cigarette of the day. He had worked as hard a day as he could-- hoping to be so exhausted that sleep would come easily. Besides ordering the men to practice defensive and offensive fighting without a weapon, where he took an active role, he had also gone out twice on wood cutting expeditions, working alongside them. He knew some thought officers should remain apart from their men, but he had never operated that way. He didn't treat them as friends. He treated them as equals with a critical difference-- he made the decisions.

"You ready for that shindig tomorrow night, Captain?" Muldoon asked as he joined him.

"If having my uniform pressed means ready, uh huh." Rand drew in the smoke wishing it gave him more pleasure.

"I wish you was takin' me," Muldoon said as he asked permission and then rolled his own cigarette.

"It just is how it has to be." With no idea who the traitor was within his organization, bringing even a squad with him would leave someone able to deliver information, not to mention others of the men getting into trouble. Canyon City made that all too easy. "I've ridden the road by myself before. Men ride it all the time without escorts," he said when it was obvious Muldoon wanted an answer.

"I just worry about ya, Cap. I ain't had a better officer to serve under. Don't want to go breaking in someone new." They both laughed.

"How was your family?" Muldoon asked him. They hadn't really talked since Rand had returned.

"I don't have family there if you meant at the John Day Ranch."

"Seem like it though, or did the time we was there."

"Yes, they seem like it." More than his own. He wondered what his brother was like as a man. The last time he had seen Jason, had been before the war began. He had taken a short side trip before reporting for duty and facing a war that offered him no further breaks, not even when later he had been wounded. What had been happening on the warfront had mattered too much to the nation for him to take time off —short of being ready for the casket—which a time or two had seemed possible.

Jason had been an angry young man who had just been rejected again by West Point—a failure that was not helped by the war beginning. It had also been a time of stress and irony for Rand. Many of the West Point graduates headed to the South and a fight against the very men they had been taught alongside. Although by that time Rand had experienced war, he also had been tense. He had tried to be friendly to his brother but was met with bare civility. Jason had not volunteered for service and said if they didn't want him at West Point, they could do without him. Rand had never been told if Jason had been drafted; but if he had, his father might well have bought him out.

As for Rand's time with his father, he had only drawn him into the library, puffed himself up as he sat at his desk before he told Rand he hoped he would not sully the proud military name of the Phillips. Rand had ground his teeth to resist replying, as he would have preferred. He didn't want to leave for war with bitter words, but he had none that would be healing either. Nor did his father offer them.

Now he would face them both and worse, more than likely, Belle Morgan. Every time he thought of Belle having been married, he felt fury at himself—even knowing that his choice had been the right one. He didn't want to think of her with another man. Yet what else could he have expected would happen? She was too beautiful to have stayed a single lady.

"Something worryin' ya, Cap?" Muldoon asked. "Seems ya ain't been right since ya got back."

Rand blew out the smoke and stared into the distance. "Just not looking forward to a formal ball is all."

"Don't blame ya on that one."

Of course, it was only one of many things on his mind. It was high on the list. He'd been to his share of the affairs, often when serving at bigger forts where a single officer, who could dance, was in much demand. He'd never been much for the formalities. Maybe the whole military life was wearing thin for him. He was tired of giving and following orders. His experience at the John Day River ranch made him again want to be with friends, not subordinates who had to ask permission to smoke, where protocol controlled everything.

Belle adjusted her skirts over the bouffant slips as she looked at her image in the mirror. Off white and gold patterns, a tight bodice and waist, with a skirt that took up half the space in front of that mirror. She had decided to leave her hair down with a flower at her ear to pin back some of its weight.

Staring at herself in the mirror, she tried to work through what the evening would hold. She had a responsibility to assess William's possible associates. If he had a group who were helping pass counterfeit bills, she might have names in what otherwise would seem an innocent social event.

General Phillips had her mystified as to exactly what he was doing in this out of the way place. He had been very polite to her but seemingly distant from Jason, who clearly wanted his approval. He gave away none of who he was-- beyond a constant smile. She was unsure if he was part of the counterfeiting or someone William hoped to use in other ways.

Walking down the stairs, making sure she held her skirt up enough that she didn't trip on it, she heard Jessica's oohh, from the hall. "You are so beautiful," the little girl rhapsodized.

She smiled and saw that Jeremy was also watching her. "much pretty ." His tone was without emotion. Whatever he felt would be hidden when he was anywhere near his father.

"I wish we could go," Jessica said with a sigh.

"It's a big people thing," Jeremy said with a dismissal of her foolishness.

"You'd be bored," Sally told them. "And you look right pretty, ma'am."

At the bottom of the stairs, she twirled her full skirts for them. "It's not particularly comfortable, but it is a pretty gown." She had packed it only on the off chance it would be needed. She didn't mind wearing fancy clothing once in a while-- although these days it was a case of less than more.

William came out from the parlor. "You did indeed have a dress to make a man proud to be your escort," he said with a pleased smile. He lifted his glass to her.

"I hope this skirt will fit in your buggy," she said as she wondered how much he had been drinking. She had not seen him drunk, but he seemed to be slightly slurring his words. She hoped this evening would not end badly. Her derringer was strapped to her thigh. She hoped she'd not need to use it.

James Dunham tapped on the door. As it opened, the blast of cool air reminded Belle to collect her shawl. Outside the sky was beginning to cloud up. "Hope it won't rain," William said as he helped her down the steps and into the buggy.

"Looks like'n it might—if'n it don't snow," Dunham said as he clicked his tongue to get the team to start.

"Isn't it early for snow?" she asked thinking she knew almost nothing about this country for weather.

"Ya never know when it's here," Dunham responded.

"Where is the general?" Belle asked surprised he was not coming with them.

"He wanted to meet his son at the Elkhorn and go with him." William said. "We will meet them there, of course."

Perfect. Riding in a coach with William Forester where it was impossible to avoid his sitting next to her. She only hoped he would be a gentleman. If not, she might be out of this job sooner than she wished. Alan would understand. He didn't expect his agents to be assaulted. Belle was not about to let that happen nor start down any road where rape was likely to be the destination.

Fortunately, William was not in a talkative or flirtatious mood, and they arrived at the large hall with no untoward movements on his part. Carriages were arriving and disembarking with ladies in beautiful gowns and gentlemen in fine suits. Definitely an impressive event for Canyon City.

Once she and William were inside, he left her by the refreshment table as he went looking for the general. The band that would be playing had gathered on a stage and were tuning their instruments before beginning to play patriotic tunes with enthusiasm.

The room had been decorated with colorful streamers, making it look exceptional and again patriotic. To one side were a series of long tables with chairs. The room was large enough to provide sufficient space for dancing. She looked toward where William had gone. She hoped to identify some of his friends, or would that be cohorts.

"Glad to see you again, Belle," a familiar voice said. She turned and saw Miranda Campbell.

"I might say the same thing, Miranda. I am happy to have at least one person I know here."

"Not like I know anybody either. Nothing would do but Mr. Campbell demanded we had to come once the invite arrived. Josiah didn't even mind having to buy me a dress. You look right pretty, I might add."

Miranda had chosen a dress of many ruffles and frills in a bright pink color. "As do you," she said with a smile. One thing about Miranda, she had her own unique style and confidence in herself.

"I hope you will come visit me," Miranda said. "My house is the first one off the main street, right after you cross the creek and to the east. You cannot miss it, kind of a pretty shade of green. A nice home. Best I ever had to be honest."

"Then it seems that his mining did pan out," Belle said hopefully hiding her shock. She knew the address-- the one Hoyt was forced to enter before being murdered. She would consider what that meant later.

"So he claims." Miranda gave a little laugh. "Wal, I'll be hornswoggled if it ain't that handsome captain. My, ain't he a fine figure of a man in his dress uniform." Belle resisted turning, but it took all her control. "I think he's coming our way," Miranda whispered.

Then Belle knew he was beside them. "Good evening ladies." the deep voice said, freeing Belle to turn and look up into his eyes.

"Captain," she said, "I didn't know if you'd be here tonight."

"You didn't?" His voice was tight like his smile.

"I met your father and brother. Your father is staying with Mr. Forester."

Before he could answer, Miranda said, "Josiah is beckoning me over to meet someone. Glad to see you both again."

Then they were alone. Or as alone as someone could be in a large hall with over a hundred guests milling around. "You look very beautiful, Belle," he said, not taking his gaze from her.

She smiled. "So do you."

"I don't have cause to wear this uniform often."

"And a sword."

"Part of the dress code. Although in battle, it can become a lifesaver when a rifle jams or can't be reloaded fast enough."

"You've used it in combat."

"I have. I see your frown. Don't worry. I have cleaned it after each such battle." This time she thought his smile was a teasing one.

"You are a good soldier."

"Is there such a thing?" The smile turned cynical.

"Of course there is or you'd not still be one, would you?"

He shrugged. She looked up then to see William, General Phillips and Jason approach them. Rand's eyes grew cold though the smile was still faintly there.

"I hear I owe you my governess and children's safety, Captain. I am grateful," William said.

"Your governess and Mr. Hoyt were also part of what kept them safe," Rand said as he nodded to acknowledge his father and brother's hello.

"Sad about Mr. Hoyt," William said. "He was killed in a robbery just a few days ago. Tragic thing. Such an enterprising young man."

Belle looked at William's face wondering if she saw any cynicism. She knew by now that he was good at schooling his features.

"That is sad," Rand said, his face giving away none of what he was thinking.

"How have you been, son?" General Phillips said.

"Busy."

"Not having much success with catching the savages then." The general's smile looked satisfied

"For now, there are not deciding moments in a war such as this one. It is mostly one skirmish after another. Not one winner take all battle. Fighting that kind of war doesn't suit the Indian's way." Rand was not smiling.

"And they control the war then, not you."

"You might say… for now anyway."

"I am famished," she said hoping to provide a diversion.

"Ah yes", William said, watching Rand with more interest than Belle would have expected, "and dinner is being put on the table as we speak. I hope you all will dine with me at the head table. I will enjoy hearing more of this conversation—on wars from men who have fought them." The general coughed but said nothing more.

At the table, Belle was seated between the general and his younger son. She watched Rand when she could. Much of the conversation was directed at him-- designed to put him on the defensive. He looked much like a cougar treed by dogs. She had seen it happen once, and it wasn't pretty how the dogs tore at the more powerful cat.

The sarcastic jibes didn't come just from Rand's father and brother but surprisingly were fed also by William. Rand responded as little as possible. She recognized the political game he had to play to avoid making an enemy of a powerful man, who could lodge complaints making his work more difficult.

She did what she could to divert the baiting, but it wasn't easy. The general obviously found great delight in thrusting barbs at his oldest son. She wondered what had made this his primary interest when he should have been proud of the man Rand was. Instead, it was like William with his son Jeremy.

Having had a diverse life of her own, where she had seen more than she probably should have, she recognized animal behavior in both these fathers. It was similar to what old bulls would do, whether in a cattle herd or with elk. The old wanted to be sure the young bull never took over the herd. She resisted an instinctive shudder as she recalled how far old bulls sometimes went to keep their power. It wasn't always enough to drive out the young bull. Sometimes it was to the death.

CHAPTER 8

When they had finished eating, William moved to the stage with a huge smile. He held out his hands and as the room quieted, he spoke. "And now, I hope we will all join in dancing to the wonderful music provided by our small but wonderful orchestra. Will the beautiful Belle Morgan help me to lead off the dance with a piece only recently written by Johann Straus, The Blue Danube Waltz? Fortunately our musicians have proven adept at learning and playing it, bringing to it their own bit of magic."

He stepped from the stage and held out his hand to Belle. "I hope you do know how to waltz."

"A little late to ask me that now." She smiled and stepped into his arms. Instantly, she was caught in the wonder of waltzing around a large room, whirling to the music, and an inner feeling that was building within. The music and dance increased a certainty she had felt the moment she had seen Rand again. She wanted to be in only one man's arms. Would he even ask her to dance?

The answer came before the next waltz began as Rand came up to her and without asking, swirled her around the room. She looked up and their gazes met. Her breath came faster as he tightened his arms around her. Before the dance could end or someone else cut in, he had waltzed her out of the room to a balcony she had not realized was at the far end of the building. Outside the air was warmer than she had expected given how it had been earlier. Or was it her own body heat that had grown to where outside air was meaningless.

"I thought it was cold earlier," she said seeking something safe to say, "and now it's warm."

"It is unpredictable in October," he agreed with that deep voice that she had not heard in so many years and yet seemed so familiar as if she'd heard it all her life. The sky overhead was full of stars. His arm was still around her as he walked her to the far end of the patio.

Before she could say a word, he lifted her chin. She understood then what he was going to do. She wanted it more than anything she ever remembered as she lifted a little to meet his lips as they descended. His lips were hard and firm as they claimed hers, his arms tightening around her waist. Instinctively, she opened her mouth as his tongue pushed against her lips. The shock was when it then moved within. The sensations seemed to go all the way to her toes. She yielded to the kiss, now using her own tongue to meet his. She had never been kissed that way. She wanted him in a way she'd never known.

The risk of such a passionate kiss in a public place should have stopped her, but it didn't. She could only think how she wanted him holding her in his arms and didn't want him ever to let go. He released her and stepped back, his eyes intensely scanned over her face.

He looked a little shocked himself at the kiss, at what had happened between them. Nothing had changed in the years since he had denied her the kiss she had wanted. When another couple entered the balcony, she pulled Rand farther into the darkness.

"We have to go back," he said, but he made no move to do so.

"I know." She did know, but she didn't want to go anywhere she could not go with him.

"You need to visit your family on the John Day River for a week or two," he said.

"What?" The world came crashing in.

"You should let them know you are here but better yet, visit them." She felt irritation at the authoritarian tone to his voice. "I was there last week."

Apparently, nothing had changed in his way of deciding everything for them. "Did you tell them I was here?"

"No."

"Thank you."

"They are anxious to see you. I..." He hesitated and didn't finish his sentence. If he had even intended to, Jason's appearance on the terrace stopped him.

"I was hoping to dance with Belle," Jason said with a sound of annoyance in his voice.

"Of course," she said as she took his hand and followed him back into the room not looking back.

Rand moved to the low wall that surrounded the terrace and sat on it as he rolled and lit a cigarette. He tried to steady his breathing. He had not intended to kiss Belle. Having her so close had overcome his sense of what was wise. Whatever willpower he had exerted ten years before, now it was gone. If he was near her, he would want her in his arms. Hell. This was pure craziness. It no more worked for them today than it had back then.

It was only then that he realized his father had followed Jason and had been watching him. He met the old man's gaze knowing nothing had changed if he had ever expected it would.

His father moved to where he was sitting and took a cigar from his pocket, lighting it. "So you like that girl, do you?" he asked without looking at Rand.

"She's pretty enough." He wasn't about to give his father any information at all. "What are you doing here?" he asked instead. "This doesn't seem like your kind of town."

"I was invited by William, of course. He offered Jason a job when we were in San Francisco. I didn't have much else to do. Retirement is boring in case you didn't know."

"You could find a new job." He took a long draw on the cigarette.

"I could but nothing has come up. There is not much need for an ex-general." His father chuckled.

"You're good at managing people." He knew that wasn't so much a compliment as a complaint. He had seen how Belle had reacted to his comment on visiting her family, by the way she had stiffened. He supposed he had gotten too used to issuing orders. It went with the territory.

"I was not so good at it with you. You left home as soon as you could."

"As you wanted me to do."

His father smoked without answering. "After I lost your mother, I lost my moorings for a while. Then I remarried. That didn't go so well either." He gave a strange little laugh.

Rand was surprised at the confidences. What was this about? It didn't make much sense. "I'm sorry," he said finally, drawing again on the cigarette and wishing for a whiskey.

"What say we get out of here? Find somewhere we can get a drink," his father suggested with another laugh.

None of this was fitting what he expected from his father and then he realized it was about Belle. His father wanted Belle for Jason. They were of an age. A woman like Belle would be what any man would want for his daughter-in-law. He didn't care who Rand was with but evidently he did Jason. He had followed his younger son here. Whatever hope he had, had for Rand, he maybe had pinned onto Jason.

"I am afraid I need to stay longer," he said grinding out his cigarette in the sand pot provided for it. "Thanks for the offer though." He smiled, didn't wait for his father's response, and walked back into the room looking for Belle. It wasn't hard to see her blonde head as she was being whirled around the room by a man he didn't know. God, she was gorgeous. The smile on her face, that beautiful long hair, the body that even under that evening gown was obviously all a man could ever want. Before he could decide what to do about her, William Forester had come to stand beside him.

"She is beautiful," Forester said with a smile.

"Agreed."

"Like a porcelain doll."

Rand looked over at him with surprise. A toy was hardly the way he saw Belle. He looked back at the dance floor to see Jason cut in on Belle's partner and then whirl her off. "My brother is working for you, I hear," Rand said.

"Yes."

"Doing what?"

Forester chuckled. "Whatever I tell him."

"I am not very familiar with what you do, Mr. Forester."

"Please make it William, and I'd like to call you Rand."

"No problem."

Forester put his hand on Rand's arm. "You are a fine looking man, but I suppose you have been told that by many," Forester said, applying a little pressure to his bicep.

Rand looked down and saw a familiar expression on the man's face. For the first time, he understood what Forester wanted. He smelled alcohol on his breath. He moved a little to the side and Forester quickly released his arm.

It wasn't the first time Rand had been propositioned by a man— some far less subtle than this one had been. It surprised him though that it would happen here in such a public place or was that what had been meant by that look? He looked back, saw the sly smile. Exactly what was Forester's game.

"I hope you will have lunch with us tomorrow," Forester said.

"I'm sorry, but I will be on the road to the fort quite early." He'd leave with first light. For the first time he considered where he would stay.

"The hotel is full, I'm afraid, thanks to my event," Forester said, reading Rand's thoughts more than made him comfortable. "Why don't you spend the night at my home." At Rand's look, he laughed. "I have guestrooms, of course. Your father is there tonight. Come on and spend the night."

"I'd have to leave with first light," Rand said tempted. Maybe in Forester's home, he'd find out something to help Colonel Schaeffer and get that quest behind him. He had not seen Forester talking to anyone enough to assess any kind of conspiracy. On the other hand, he'd been so distracted by Belle that he hadn't paid the attention he should have.

"That would not be a problem. I have a cook who is up quite early. She can fix you something in the morning when everyone else is still sleeping."

"All right. I need to arrange at the stable for my horse."

"I have a fine facility to the left of my home as you come up the drive."

"All right."

"We shall see you later then."

Rand looked back out but this time Belle was walking toward him, no partner at her side. "I believe you owe me another dance, Captain," she said smiling faintly at Forester as she reached for Rand's hand.

"I do?" he asked as the melody this time was slower and gave them more time to talk. He realized then that it was a song he'd heard only a time or two. *Beautiful Dreamer*, one of Stephen Foster's ballads, was perhaps his last song. It was both sad and haunting. The first time he had heard it, he thought of Belle, the desire to find her, and the hopelessness of it.

"You know you do," she said as she looked up with a smile.

"You have forgiven me then?"

"For what? Rejecting me when I was almost seventeen?"

He couldn't resist the laugh. "I wasn't thinking quite that far back. No, I was thinking just now, trying to tell you what to do. I am used to giving orders, I'm afraid."

She laughed then. "I should have expected it. Perhaps I am also used to giving orders."

"To your husband?"

She dipped her head not looking at him. "As a governess," she said finally her head now against his chest.

"Ah, of course. I had forgotten that you teach."

"Among other things."

When the music stopped, another man came to claim Belle. She was definitely the belle of this ball. No woman could touch her for beauty but more than that, her vibrant spirit.

"Now, don't forget," she said before she left him, "the last dance is mine."

He bowed his head and smiled. He forced himself to look away from her. From then on he forced his concentration on locating and not losing track of Forester. The man seemed to drift from group to group but not long with any. If this gathering had an ulterior purpose, it was more likely establishing him as a power in the community than it was plotting with a subversive group.

He had nearly forgotten the ball would end, and Belle would return but then there she was. "This song was requested for you specifically, Captain Phillips," she said with a smile as she put her hand out to him.

When he heard it start up, he understood why, Garryowen, the fighting song of many a soldier. Some regarded it as an ending song as well. He swept her into his arms and began the quickstep that was best danced to it. They spun around the dance floor, this time with no chance to talk. He realized as they danced that others had stepped aside. They were in the center of the floor and then they were the only dancers. When the music ended, the others applauded and Belle laughed.

"You look a little stunned." she said as they left the floor.

"Custer has claimed that for the Seventh Cavalry."

"Does that mean no one else may claim it?"

"No, but do you know it's a drinking song?"

"Actually no... but I did know about Custer. Miles Koegh actually claimed it first."

"How did you know that?"

She smiled. "Well, don't tell anyone but I did happen to have met General Custer once."

"Ah."

"You know him too, then and it's why you said ahhh."

He smiled. "Only on an acquaintance level. He is known as a lady's man."

"Really? I thought his wife was delightful."

"Did you know them through your husband?"

"Please, I'd rather not talk about that." Then they were with Forester, the general, and Jason.

86

"Jason," Forester said, "will you make arrangements for the captain's horse to be taken to my stable and then readied in the morning before first light."

Jason looked stunned. "Why?"

"Because the captain is to be my guest tonight. I would like him to ride back to the house with us."

Jason looked displeased but had no choice but to agree. When Belle was handed her wrap, Rand put it around her shoulders before anyone else could. He felt caught in a web but was unsure how to extract himself or even if he wanted to do so.

When he thought about Belle as an agent, thought of what had happened the other agent, Dylan Hoyt, he wanted her out of this town, away from Forester. She did not look as though she'd be easily budged. He supposed he could have told her he knew why she was here. He had not had time, and now he felt it was probably wisest. He couldn't help her. He hoped she understood all Forester was up to. He would have no opportunity to ask her. He would have to trust Pinkertons would not have sent her here if she wasn't experienced enough to handle herself.

Belle had been surprised to learn that Rand would be staying at the Forester house, but it made sense if he didn't want to ride home late at night or sleep on the ground.

She was upset with herself for giving away that she had known Custer and Elizabeth. It was a bit better than she had admitted. It had related to a job in Texas, one that hadn't taken long, but she had come across them in the process and found them a delightful couple. Custer was a bit wild and perhaps reckless, but she believed Elizabeth grounded him.

While it was true that Custer was a lady's man, paying lavish compliments to her, since they had been made openly in front of his wife, who hadn't seemed to mind, Belle hadn't been concerned. What did concern her was that she had given away her knowing the Custers at all. She was falling down on her needs as an agent, and if she wasn't careful, she would give away all her secrets to Rand.

The ride back to the house was brief. She had been put on the other side of the general. Rand had ridden up front with the driver. At the house, Forester suggested a brandy before bed. This time she didn't turn down the liquor. She was so stirred that sleep would be hard to find.

It hadn't been the hours of dancing but had been being so near to

Rand, to have been in his arms. The kiss left her with a heady feeling, which was hard to define except it was all about him. Knowing he would be under the same roof for the first time in all those years left her feeling short of breath.

The general sat on the sofa and again Belle took the straight chair. Rand settled into one like it across the room. "You really have to go back tomorrow?" Forester asked him as he handed them each a glass of brandy.

"We have to go out on patrols which have been put off too long."

"Any definite direction?" the general asked with at least the sound of interest.

"As I said before, where they are is not where they were. We go out based on reports. The last one didn't tell me much, but the next one might."

"Rather hopeless then."

"Tell us about what's going on," Forester said. "We read the papers, but they get so little real news or they distort it."

"On my last report, Crook was at Fort Harney. He has been going out and staying there, with supplies sent to him. It enables a faster reaction to any attacks or reported camps. We might try something like that up here although admittedly the greatest predations have come from south of us."

"You really think this might be winding down?" Forester asked. "I'd like to hear that as it'd make the mining and shipments much safer, of course."

"Probably for the winter anyway. Maybe settled by next summer... for a time."

"For a time?"

"I think it'll be a matter of years. Harsh weather provides only a hiatus until it starts again. They keep trying to get the Modocs to go onto a reservation with the Klamaths. They are bitter enemies. The Modocs being a smaller tribe will not stay. Farther north, I am not convinced the Umatillas and Cayuse will stay on their reservations."

"So how much longer can we expect these attacks?" Forester asked as he watched Rand almost raptly. Any over indulgence of alcohol appeared to have vanished from his demeanor.

"It's a guess but-- ten years to see all hostilities ended, and the tribes convinced they cannot win."

"Treaties?"

"Treaties are made when one side is convinced they have lost. The tribes here have not reached that point. Not yet."

"Disappointing. Will you be stationed here all that time then?"

"That's not totally my decision. Watson will stay open as long as there are hostilities nearby. If that settles down I'll probably be called to the south."

Belle didn't like hearing that, but then what could she expect? She sipped her brandy sure that sleep would not easily find her, not with Rand so close and so far.

An hour later as she lay in her bed, she tried to think what she could do to change the dynamics between her and Rand. Nothing. There was nothing. She had to find the counterfeiting plates. She had to finish this assignment, and then she would leave Oregon. It was the logical thing to do. Except she was in no mood to be logical.

If she hadn't known how stupid and reckless it would have been, she'd have gone to his room and had it out with him. She couldn't do that. Besides, he'd likely push her away again. They had flirted before when she had been not quite a woman. When it had come time to take it to another level, he had backed away. Likely, he'd do it again. He was a career soldier and appeared in no mood to change that. Fine, she could handle not being with him. She had done it for ten years. What she could not handle was another rejection. She would just let it be. It was for the best.

CHAPTER 9

With morning light barely coming over the distant Blue Mountains to the east, Rand rode west. True to Forester's word, his cook had been up when he had come downstairs and fixed him a breakfast.

"You gotta eat a hearty meal, Captain Phillips," the woman said and sent him off with biscuits in a small bag. His horse had been waiting out front. The gelding was as eager as he to get out of town. He felt frustrated as he rode considering how little he had learned by putting himself out to go to an event that he had been convinced would be hard on him and had proven to be just that.

The road between Canyon City and the Camp was traveled a fair amount and often by heavy wagons. It skirted the John Day River as well as an assortment of creeks. As he neared Fort creek, which flowed past the Camp, he saw the first unshod pony tracks. Five horses and moving fast from the way they were stretched out.

They looked to be heading north up the John Day River. He nudged the gelding with his spurs and got to the fort at a run. Jumping off, he threw the reins over the hitching post and yelled for the duty guard. "Saddle me Blue and wake up Sergeant Smith. Tell him to get his squad on their horses."

He went to his quarters and quickly changed into garb more suitable for riding through the brush. Maybe this time they would have a chance to catch this band before they hit someone else. North there weren't any ranches or communities until closer to Monument.

Five minutes later, he had pulled on his campaign hat and was riding out of the fort with a squad. As they rode, he told Smith what he had seen. "You think we can catch 'em?" the sergeant asked.

"If I didn't, I wouldn't start out." Or maybe he would since he had a need to work off the tension that had built from his frustrating and frankly fruitless trip to Canyon City. More accurately, that had begun with The Dalles. He didn't want to be a spy. He didn't want to attempt to sort out bad guys from good unless it was in battle.

Six miles up the canyon, he saw riders ahead. They were traveling at a good clip but weren't yet concerned at anyone following them. This road was not the main route north anymore. Using his spurs, he urged his gelding onto a faster pace. By the time the Indians recognized someone was following them, they opted to stop rather than try to outrun the fresher horses.

"Hey boss," the apparent leader said, "whatcha doin' followin' us?"

"You Warm Springs?" he asked as he recognized one of the men. The two hanging back though did not look like they were from the same tribe.

"Yeah, I'm Charlie Kalama. Been down scoutin' near Fort Harney for Crook. He wanted different tribe." He sneered. "We're on our way home."

"This seems out of your way."

"Got two brothers workin' a ranch up on the North Fork. Thought we'd stop by."

Rand eased back on his saddle. "Who are those two?" he asked gesturing toward the ones trying not to be seen.

"Picked up on the way. Said they wanted to get out of the trouble. Goin' back with us."

He considered that. "All right, but don't go dragging your feet doing it. The wrong gang might see you and not ask questions."

"Gotcha."

As they rode off, Smith said, "Who were the other two?"

"Looked like Northern Paiute. What did you think?"

"That's what I figured."

"They might have had enough of fighting."

"Maybe." Neither of them were totally convinced, but for now, they had no reason not to let them go. It wasn't like Rand wanted two prisoners with no idea what to do with them. Perhaps the two were just tired of fighting. Hopefully, Paulina's remaining followers weren't hooking up with the wrong side of this war. With the old chief killed by civilians in one of those unlucky coincidences in the spring, it was difficult to know where Paulina's band would go without their wily old leader. A reservation seemed least likely.

The squad rode back to Watson slower and feeling more depressed. Rand felt tired, but the last thing he wanted to do was to stay in the Camp. For the next week, he planned to send out various squads including himself and do reconnoitering. He would make their presence felt. The small ranches nearby usually were the first to find out when their horses or mules were stolen, their steers butchered or driven off. Waiting for a report didn't tend to find the thieves or the stock. He needed to follow Crook's example and spend more time in the field.

For the week after the ball, Belle kept a low profile, working with the children, but constantly keeping her eyes open for an entry to what she felt convinced had to be an underground room. Surprising her, the general had not left the Forester home. Once she had come in from a walk with the children to hear voices raised, but as soon as they realized she had returned, Forester and he stopped talking.

Finally, she decided the only possible solution to getting what she needed would be to pretend to go to bed, before heading back outside with her dark pants, boots, coat, and revolver to see what she could observe. It had more danger, but she was tired of waiting around. She had no real way to receive instructions or forward information to the Pinkertons, since any communication could be monitored. If she didn't want to surrender the assignment, she was on her own.

After dinner, she yawned and said she intended to retire when the children did. William seemed fine with that. Since the ball, he had in no way suggested he wanted to further their relationship. Whenever Jason had visited, he had tried to engage her in conversations but it didn't take much to discourage him.

Quickly changing her garments for those that would let her move more freely, she plumped pillows where her body would have been. Tucking her hair into a dark hat, she shoved a revolver into her belt and let herself out onto the porch roof. She took hold of one of the largest of the oak branches and using it, in moments was on the ground. It'd be equally easy to get back up when she was ready. She was a lot more athletic and kept in better shape than Forester would ever guess. Before she could decide where to go next, she saw Jason entering the front door. Where had he been? She moved around the house to squat below the window in the parlor. Inside she heard the general greet his son. "What are you doing back?" he asked with irritation in his voice.

"Will asked me to be here," Jason said. She could hear him walk to the sideboard and pour himself what sounded like a generous portion of liquor.

"For what?" The disdain was obvious in the general's voice.

"For whatever I wanted," Forester's voice came from the doorway. "Pour me a whiskey too, son."

"I need to leave," the general said. "I am due back in Portland. If I leave too late, the weather will make future travel more difficult."

"And so you want to run?" Forester had an amused sound to his voice.

"It is not running. I simply don't like how this is going."

"You signed up."

"I signed nothing. I have no purpose in being here. Winter setting in at this elevation won't be good for my rheumatism."

"I need you for a job. Only you can do it. Then if you still want to go... well that's your choice."

"You know how I feel about that. I told you."

"I also told you how it will be. There is no other answer."

"It's too dangerous. Too many ways it can involve me."

"The whole thing already does." Forester laughed. "Campbell and Moriarty will be here soon. Just relax. Our plans are proceeding as scheduled."

"I don't see anything happening that gets us closer to the results you promised me in San Francisco."

"More than you know is happening." When she heard new steps and more men entering the room, there was the sliding of a door. It had to be the panel that led to the lower level. In moments, the room was silent. No one had walked out the door to the hall. She was frustrated that she could no longer hear what they were saying.

On the other hand, she now knew that the decorative wooden panel in the parlor was the entrance to the probably location of the counterfeiting operation. She was unsure when she could investigate that further. For now, she had to get back to her bedroom.

Before she could climb back up the tree, she heard footsteps and ran lightly into the nearby woods grateful the moon was not yet up. Although she could not make out their features, she thought she recognized one of the men as someone she had earlier seen in the house. There were four of them moving rapidly, not talking, and with a clear destination.

Keeping well back, she followed. There was a shed not far beyond the house, and the four disappeared into it. When they emerged, they carried two long boxes—heavy enough to take two to carry each. She waited in the woods. When it was safe, she went to the shed and determined it had no lock. It would be something to check during daylight. Maybe a little game of hide and seek with the children. Perhaps anything it had been used for had been removed, but she would definitely look.

Half an hour later, she was in her room, quickly throwing her rustic garb under the bed before she pulled on a nightgown. She considering what she had learned. The boxes were too big for counterfeiting plates. Too heavy for counterfeit money. They were the right size for Remington or Henry rifles. Why though would they be stored there and where were they being taken?

She had another concern. Had the arriving Campbell been Josiah, Miranda's husband? In a town the size of Canyon City, there could be several Campbells, but that couple had been invited to the ball. That made it more than likely that he was connected to William Forester. She decided a social call on Miranda was in order. She might find out a bit more from the talkative lady and not give away her reasons for wanting to know.

Then, as happened so often before she fell asleep, she thought of Rand. Worse than the memories were the dreams, that filled her nights. As a young man, he had stolen her heart. She realized she had never gotten it back. Foolishness or not, she could not get him out of her mind. She never had been able to erase his image. Worse, the mature man was far more attractive now. She wondered when she would see him again.

Maybe if she got her assignment in Canyon City finished, she could go see her mother and find a way to draw Rand there. He liked her family. She realized she did too, and for the first time began to think that she might never want to do another assignment for Alan. She just had to get this one finished... and not end up like Dylan Hoyt.

With morning, Belle had her opportunity to visit Miranda when Sally offered to watch the children while they did their penmanship assignments. "I do need to buy a few things and would like to visit a friend from the stage ride down," she told her. "I should be back in an hour or so."

"No problem, ma'am. I like the little rascals." She grinned at them.

To avoid standing out, as she knew her blonde hair often did, Belle changed into her unadorned, brown dress and used a plain bonnet to tuck her hair up inside, adding a coat because the air was beginning to cool. She took her purse and enough money for the purchases she planned to make.

Her first stop was at the mercantile, pleased at all the supplies they had. She took a basket, found candy sticks for the children, dried food that would be lightweight but offer substantial nourishment. Coffee, two small pots, utensils, three little plates, and an oilcloth for wrapping a box of matches. Wandering around she looked at the ropes. It was hard to imagine a need for rope, but Adam had said there always was one. She bought a small spool of half-inch rope and a spool of heavy twine. Two wool blankets, several soft towels, and a tarp went onto the pile, as she tried to remember what else she might need.

When she put her selections on the counter, the female clerk looked at them with interest. "You going on a trip, ma'am?" she asked. "You know we still have Indian trouble around here."

"No trip," she said finding the lying bothering her more than usual. "I teach the Forester children and find teaching biology means more to children with practical examples." She added a small whiskey bottle and a can of beans.

When the clerk looked at the whiskey, she said, "Sometimes the children do tax me."

The lady chuckled. "I had six of my own and do understand. You need any opium?"

"No, but..." She looked beyond her and saw the rifles on the rack. "Oh, I see you have a Henry lever action here."

"You know your guns." The clerk had a curious note to her voice.

"I have heard of this one. My grandfather might like it. I've been told they are excellent weapons. May I see it?"

The woman handed it to her, and Belle brought it to her shoulder, checked the action and said, "I could use a scabbard for him too. The old gentleman does love good leather." The woman smiled and handed her a finely tooled scabbard.

"He will love this," she said as she slid the rifle into the scabbard. She added several boxes of cartridges, a generous sized saddlebag but had the gun and scabbard wrapped. When the order had been tallied, she was glad she had brought two hundred dollars with her. She didn't want any of this put on Forester's credit even though he had approved her use of it.

"Where is the post office?" she asked to deflect any suspicion if this woman also worked for Forester as so many seemed to do in Canyon City. From there, the walk to Miranda's home was not far. She stopped at the stable first. "I bought a few gifts,' she told the hostler as he came out. "I am not sure when I will want to mail them, might I keep them here until I can arrange for that?"

He nodded and pointed her toward a large box. "That one's empty. Surprised I ain't seen ya here to ride yore hoss."

"It's been difficult to find time away from the children, but I still plan on doing it. Mr. Forester has been quite busy though and unable to accompany me."

"Understand that. Your booty will be safe here until ya need it." She looked up and met his gaze. She wondered how much he understood of what she planned. She hoped his curiosity would not lead to examining her purchases. She was unsure how much longer she could safely remain in Canyon City. She had a bad feeling but could not put her finger on what exactly it meant. She had no right to take the children, but it was also on her mind. She didn't want to leave them if she had to leave suddenly.

She had barely knocked on Miranda's door when it was opened, and she was pulled inside. "I am so glad to see you, Belle," the woman said as she led her back to a tidy kitchen. "A cup of tea?"

"I'd love it. I was happy to see you at the ball but just haven't had a lot of time away from the children." She looked around but saw no clue that violence had ever happened in this home. Yet, she knew it had. Did Miranda also know?

"You were a sight for sore eyes, I can tell you. I haven't made friends here yet. Not working doesn't have me out much. I went to church but folks there didn't seem real friendly."

"You aren't happy here then?"

Miranda poured her tea. "Josiah is gone a lot. Big doings. Mysterious even."

"His claim perhaps?" She sipped the tea and took a scone that Miranda offered.

"I am not sure what he does, but he's making money so I guess it's all right." Her voice sounded jumpy.

"The scone is delicious, Miranda. Did you make it?"

She nodded. "I am a good cook if nothing else."

"I am sorry to hear you aren't happier."

"It's lonely is all. I started a quilt, and it's helped some."

"You seem to have the domestic skills all women want."

Miranda smiled. "I suppose it's all been a substitute for having wee ones. Did you ever want children, Belle?"

"I suppose someday. I enjoy working with them. Of course, that is why I also haven't gotten out much either."

"I expect a lot come in and out of the Forester house. He seems to be cock of the walk here."

"Had you met him before the ball?"

"No. I think though Josiah had."

"He has apparently gained a lot of power for only having arrived this month."

"He was here earlier and directed the house being built."

"I didn't realize that. I only began to work for him six months before we came here. Perhaps I told you that. He's accomplished a great deal in a short time."

"His partner has been here all along, setting things up."

That was a surprise. "I didn't realize he had a partner."

"Harold Moriarty. I am not sure that it's like written down or something, but they both have been here to talk to Josiah." She sighed. "Want me to get out of the room when they come too. I don't like Mr. Moriarty's looks either. I guess I should not have said that."

"I won't tell Mr. Forester, of course. I do not think I have met him. Was he at the Forester ball?"

"I didn't see him there that night. He travels a great deal."

Belle spent a few more minutes to be polite and then made her excuses. Miranda insisted on sending scones with her for the children. As Belle walked back to the Forester home, she thought about what a nice lady Miranda was, but what a complex situation. What was really going on here? She saw no evidence for any businesses Forester might run. Why had he hired all the men? They weren't being paid in phony bills. True there was gold in Canyon City, but wouldn't there be better places to disperse counterfeit dollars than the middle of Oregon with an Indian war raging?

Just past the stable, she saw a woman walking toward her and realized with surprise that she knew her. As they came abreast, she stopped. "Hello, Miss Jessup," she said with a smile.

"Didn't figure to run into you again," Annie Jessup said but she also smiled. "How is the teaching business going?"

"A delight when it involves children like Jeremy and Jessica. How have you been?"

"I'm thinking on leaving soon, maybe heading for Baker City or Boise."

"Not as lucrative here as you expected? I'd have thought all these miners would be flush with cash."

"It's more than that. Did you hear what happened to Dylan?"

She had not expected that. "Is that Mr. Hoyt?"

Annie nodded.

"Something about a robbery?"

"He was murdered." She drew in a long breath and tears ran down her cheeks. Belle remembered the brief note Dylan had carried when he was killed. Had Annie written it?

"I've been so busy with the children but now I remember. Horrible, but such could happen anywhere. Just bad luck." Sounding dumb usually got her more information than giving away any of what she herself knew.

"Not like this." Annie looked away and then back. "If you were smart, you'd find a different job somewhere else."

"Why?"

"I like you, Mrs. Morgan but I can't say more."

"Remember, you are to call me Belle. I would not tell anyone anything to get you trouble. I hope you know that. I just would wonder why you would suggest I should leave a good job."

Annie considered a long moment. "Is it good?"

"It's teaching children. I like that part."

"I remember them being sweet children. Jessica is so pretty."

"She is. They are both quite intelligent."

She could see Annie considering before she spoke. "But consider who you are working for."

"I don't have much to do with Mr. Forester."

"You are lucky then." Annie looked around nervously. "Look, I should not have said anything." She started to move past, but Belle put out her hand to stop her.

"Please, if it's not safe for me, then it would not be for the children. You remembered how sweet they are. What do you know?"

"I know I should not have told you as much as I did."

Belle managed a smile. "All right. I thank you for wanting to be a friend."

Annie sucked in and then let out a breath. "He's a mean man who takes pleasure in hurting people. He is a sadist who hides it until someone is weakened. Just don't be weak around him... I should not have said anything. I just have to get out of here. Sorry for saying what I did."

"Of course, I won't repeat it. I wish you luck, Annie. I hope the next place you stay will be better for you."

"Me too."

"Do you need some money? I could help you if..."

"No, money isn't my problem, but thank you for offering."

And with that, she was gone. It was only then that Belle saw the hostler had been watching them from the stable. She decided she better put out a few more false trails and crossed the road to him.

"I was thinking I could ride Sammy in two days, if you could arrange for that, say at ten on Friday."

"I'm uneasy about ya riding alone, ma'am."

"If Mr. Forester is too busy to ride with me, I will ask him to arrange for an escort from one of his men. Sammy does need the exercise."

His expression looked relieved but then again concerned. "I saw ya talkin' to that whore."

Belle forced a smile. "She was on the stage with me, and we went through a terrible trial together with an Indian attack. It tends to provide a bond. She might be a lady of the night, but she was very brave that day."

"Oh, I figured there must be a reason for it."

"I will send word tomorrow on whether I can arrange the ride." She walked to Sammy's paddock and when he came to her, she rubbed his nose. "You want to go for a ride?" she asked the horse who seemed responsive to her voice.

"He could do with the exercise for sure."

"Could you move my saddle and tack to the fence above my box now?"

"Sure can. It'll be ready whenever you are."

"Good."

As she walked back to the house, she felt even more concern for the children. A man who liked to inflict pain might consider them prime targets when he had no others. What could she do about it though? If she had to go, taking them would be regarded as kidnapping. Leaving them though... how could she leave them?

One thing she could do was find enough evidence to put Mr. Forester in prison. At this point, not just based on what Annie had said, but her own instincts, no father was better than the one they had.

She had to find a way to get into that underground room and do it when she was not going to be caught. She would engage the children in a game of hide and seek outside with the nice afternoon. Then she'd know what was in that shed if anything was left. She was relatively sure it had held rifles-- but for what purpose?

Forester closed the heavy door to his den to give himself privacy with General Phillips and Jason. He poured each a snifter of brandy. "It is time for you to give me the help I need, general," he said as he settled back on the settee.

"I've told you I don't want to do it."

"I didn't pay your expenses to come here without some expectations."

The general looked down. "I see."

"I need to *talk* to your son." He swirled the liquor in the glass before he took a sip.

"You don't mean me?" Jason asked as he rose and paced before sitting back.

Forester snorted. "I don't need help to talk to you."

"What do you need with Randall?" the general asked. Forester saw the fear on his face. How did such a weak man ever become a general?

"Do you no longer believe in a higher purpose? In fixing the ills of our nation? In gaining power in your life to make a difference?" He avoided snickering. It wasn't easy as he saw the general's sick expression.

"Do you mean to hurt him? I would rather not be involved."

"How ridiculous. Why would I hurt him? He will respond to his father. It will be a friendly conversation, of course."

There was a long silence. "I don't want to go to prison."

Figures that'd be his concern, the selfish old bastard. "No one will know you had anything to do with it. Besides, I just need to get him away from the fort where we won't be interrupted." He could have just ordered the captain killed by a sniper. After he had been rejected by him at the ball, he wanted something more.

"Just talk?"

Forester smiled. He glanced over at Jason and saw he knew there would be more than talk. It wasn't as though he cared. Jason had long ago made it clear that he hated his older brother. He would not care what was done to him—probably would enjoy it.

"Of course. He can cooperate and then I would let him go." Another lie. The handsome captain would not walk away from this. The general knew it also. He just wanted the lie to salve his conscience.

"He won't come at my request," the general whispered.

"You will go to prison for what I already have on you. You helped me pass those bills, found arms merchants. None of that needs to come out." The general paled. He knew he had him. "Cooperate with me and you will grow in power." That, of course, would not happen. He would have the general killed. No other action would secure his own situation. Once he didn't need him, an accident or possibly a drug overdose. Many things could give him what he needed. There was only one thing the general could do for him. When that happened, he was useless or worse with the nervous fear he exhibited.

He looked then at Jason, wondering how much he could trust him. Not much was his guess. No, they'd both have to die in various ways that didn't connect to him.

The general finally nodded. "What must I do?"

He put fine paper and a pen on the desk. "Write what I tell you."

CHAPTER 10

After a week of hard drills and several forays out to look for tracks or signs of trouble, Rand felt the men were feeling better about themselves. He knew he was as he fell into his cot or bedroll, tired enough to sleep. He would be glad to spend this night in his own quarters. The reports from the south had indicated activity was mostly happening down that way with Crook. It might drive action his way. With winter soon to settle in, it might all be quiet until spring.

On his desk was an envelope. Lt. Lockwood came in behind him. "It came this morning by special courier again. Looks like another from Forester."

He looked at the handwriting. "No, this one is from my father." It was no more welcome. It was even less when he opened it.

'My son, I need to talk to you privately. I have come to distrust Mr. Forester, and I fear what he's doing to your brother, Jason. Please come to meet me. I found a house I can use privately to discuss what I have learned is going on here. You need to know but please, for my sake, tell no one. Thursday night at seven, please meet me at 31 Cactus Street. I can explain more of this mess then. Please come. I need you. Your father, Abraham Phillips.' A small, hand drawn map was below the signature.

He smiled with what he knew was cynicism as he set the letter on his desk. The formal signature fit his father. But asking for help did not. What the hell was going on with the old man? He rolled a cigarette. Lockwood watched him but said nothing until he had lit it. "It was bad news, I see."

"Complicated. Ask Murphy to join us please."

As he smoked, he tried to decide the right course to take. Was this the answer to the secret assignment? Just as likely, it could be a trap. He had no reason to trust his father; yet what he said fit what Rand believed to be going on.

When Murphy arrived, Rand said, "I will have to go to Canyon City tomorrow afternoon. Murphy, you will be in charge of the camp while I am gone."

"Going alone again?" Lockwood asked with disapproval in his voice.

"I'm afraid it has to be that way. This is personal business."

"I think you should take me, and leave Jim here to watch over the camp," Pat said.

"Not this time. One more thing. In an hour, I will have a letter that will have to go to Colonel Schaeffer in The Dalles. I want that sent with Corporal Muldoon and Private Carmody."

"The mails aren't good enough?" Again, it was Lockwood finding fault.

"Not for this one. All right, gentlemen. I need to write that message. In the morning, we will drill again. Dismissed for now." Neither of them were pleased with his order.

Maybe if he was fortunate, this would be the break they needed. If not, it could turn ugly. He sat at the desk writing the missive to the colonel explaining what he was doing and sealing with it the letter from his father.

If this was a trap, it might yet serve to catch the conspirators. Sad that it might involve his father, but at this point, he had no way to know it did. Maybe his father had realized what was going on and wanted to stop it. Maybe. But why alone? One definite fact, if he came with a squad or platoon, he'd learn nothing.

He walked outside to stand on the porch. The moon was almost full. There was a name for full moons but he couldn't remember what it was for October and then he did. This was the Hunter's Moon.

Riding into Canyon City just before dark, he headed down the main road until he saw the designated side road. The house looked dark, but if his father didn't want to be seen, that would make sense. He dismounted, tying the reins to Blue to the post and stepped onto the porch. He loosened his revolver in the holster and then knocked.

The door was opened by a woman, whose face he remembered

from Forester's ball. "I am Mrs. Campbell," she said. "My husband said to come in. He'll be right out." She looked disturbed but perhaps having such a meeting made her nervous.

"And the general?" He stepped inside the house and saw that it wasn't as dark as it had appeared from outside. A single candle was on a side table. He looked beyond the woman as his father stepped through the door to what he could see was the kitchen.

"Hello son," he said.

When Rand stepped forward, he heard a step behind him, and something hard was jabbed against his back. From the other end of the darkened parlor, a man moved. His shotgun was pointed at Rand's belly.

"What is this?" He knew and tried to think what he could do about any of it just this side of getting shot.

William Forester came to stand beside his father. "Don't make a move toward your gun, and this doesn't have to turn messy."

"What do you want?" With two guns trained on him, he had no chance to get out his own weapon and make any kind of stand.

"Just some questions. It doesn't have to be unpleasant for you. One way or the other though, you will give me answers. Remove your jacket. I want to assure myself and my men that you have no other weapons."

Shrugging out of his jacket, letting it fall to the ground, he heard movement on his other side. So, there were two men behind him. One again had the barrel of a gun pressed hard against his spine as the other lifted his revolver from its holster.

"Your methodology doesn't strike me as friendly," he said.

"I didn't promise friendly," Forester said with a smirk.

The man with the shotgun moved forward with another man beside him. So five, if he counted Forester. From the look on his father's face, he wasn't a factor beyond the bait to get him there.

"Come into the kitchen where we can talk civilly."

Rand let out a snort, but he moved across the room debating whether a quick death was his best option. Was there any chance he could he talk his way out of this? Would Forester really kill a United States military officer?

At the doorway, he saw three other men in the room. One was not a stranger-- his brother. A family reunion... of sorts.

"You are showing good judgment so far, Captain," Forester said as he watched him from across the room. "I hope that will continue. Put your hands behind your back."

He could try to fight them, but he wouldn't win and would likely end up dead. Being dead seemed the likeliest end anyway. He slammed an elbow backward into the man with the gun, knocking the pistol to the side. Before he had a chance to grab the gun, the others were on him. Someone shoved him hard, and he was thrown to the ground, on his belly with his hands quickly roped together behind his back. Rough hands jerked him to his feet.

"That was foolish, Captain," Forester said. "I thought you a more intelligent man than that."

From the darkened parlor, he heard a woman's cry and then a man say, "Miranda, shut your trap. Get in your damned room. Don't ya say nothing about what ya seen."

They shoved him to a chair whose back was against the table. Forester moved forward to stand in front of him. "Ah Rand, this is far more pleasant for me than our last meeting."

He sucked in a breath. "You don't take no well, I guess."

Forester laughed. "I am not used to the word."

"I did as you demanded," his father interrupted. "May I go?" His voice sounded old and weak.

"Of course. Have a good evening. Far better than our captain will be having, of course." The laugh was nerve-wracking.

"I'd like to stay," Jason said-- not hard to understand why. Any questions he'd had about his brother were answered.

"Of course," Forester said. A door closed.

"What is this about?" he asked trying to delay but unsure what good it could do. He began to pick at the knots that held his wrists together. When he felt some give, it was an encouragement although against at least seven men, not a lot.

Forester took hold of his head and forced his chin up. "Answers, of course. This really doesn't have to be unpleasant. I only wanted you tied up to ensure you were listening."

He gave a snort of disbelief.

"Captain, you can cooperate or not, but it will go better for you if you do."

"You won't get away with this."

Forester laughed. "I won't? Well, we'll see about that. My dear boy, I'm not an unreasonable man. If you give me the answers I need, you won't even have a bad evening." He watched as Forester put on thin leather gloves. "I need names, Rand, if I may call you Rand. You have them. I will before this evening is over. I guarantee you that."

The slaps were hard and knocked his head first one way and then the other. The pain wasn't so bad. The humiliation was worse. He damned himself for coming to this house without an escort, for wanting to trust his father, for agreeing to take on Schaeffer's assignment. He was going to pay for all his mistakes. Forester stepped back and one of his men took over slamming his fist into Rand's jaw and then his belly. He was rocked in the chair, as pain went through his body, and air whooshed from his lungs with a rush.

"Who did you talk to in The Dalles? You see I do know you went there and were given an assignment." Forester again stood in front of him before he reached out and grabbed hold of the front of Rand's shirt. Yanking hard, he ripped the buttons off as he bared his chest, shoving the fabric off his shoulders.

"You really are a sick bastard," he said as he saw how the man's eyes avidly moved down his chest and then back to his face.

"It isn't as though I want to hurt you. It is really a crime to damage such a beautiful specimen, but alas I have to do what I have to do."

"You mean what you get off on doing."

"That too." Forester took out a knife. He moved back closer to Rand's chair and pushed his knees apart. He pressed the tip of the knife against Rand's right breast. "This is a sensitive part of a human's anatomy. Many don't realize how sensitive especially to pain." He turned the blade to where it cut a shallow slice around the nipple.

Rand clenched his jaw. He wouldn't give the son of a bitch any more satisfaction than he had to.

"The last time we were together, you rejected me." Forester made another shallow cut across his chest. It bled but only a little. It wasn't intended to do serious damage-- yet. "You had the power that night. I have it tonight." He put the knife back into its sheathe and again took Rand's chin in his hand. "You could learn to please me. I might even let you go-- if you proved amiable. I can be quite generous to my pets."

"I was a dead man once I walked through that door. You think I don't know that?" He felt more give in the knot and pulled on it.

"That might be true or not, but there are many ways to die." He slapped Rand hard across his right and then left cheek.

Rand realized his brother had moved to where he would have a better view. "You are a fool, Jason," he said when he could talk levelly. "You stick with this twisted bastard, and you will end up dead."

Jason giggled. "Not as soon as you though."

"Now, now, Captain, I will have those answers," Forester said. "Everyone breaks and will talk when it reaches a level they can no longer bear. Spare yourself that unpleasantness." He ran his gloved fingers lightly over Rand's cheek, pinching hard before he slammed a fist in his belly. "Come. Tell me who else is investigating me. You know the names. I will have them sooner or later."

Sucking in a breath, Rand said, "You talk enough for both of us."

"I know you were in The Dalles and received orders that I am sure regarded me. Who was it? How much do they know or suspect?" He yanked on Rand's hair forcing his head up to where he was forced to look into Forester's eyes. "Come, boy. I could make your last hours pleasant. I know how to do that." His smile turned seductive. "Just tell me who you talked to and what they wanted. How much do they already know? Who else is investigating me here in Canyon City?"

When Rand said nothing, the gloved fist was slammed against his jaw nearly throwing him out of the chair until he was yanked back to it. He spit blood onto the floor. He had the knot loose. He held the rope in place. He wasn't likely to get out of this alive, but he could inflict some pain on at least Forester before he was killed.

"When in agony, the kind of agony most cannot imagine feeling, humans will tell everything they know. Dylan Hoyt did. It earned him a merciful death-- finally."

"Sorry he met that end, but he means nothing to me."

"He was a spy for the military. You do know him because you are too. You were doubtless working together."

Rand snorted. "We were huh? Then you don't need me, do you?"

"I do though. He didn't have the full picture. He knew you were sent to The Dalles but not who you met nor all they knew." Rand felt some relief at that. It meant Forester still didn't know a Pinkerton was here.

"I want the head of it and the network. I want who you work with and talked to about this."

"Sorry."

"He won't break, William," a voice he'd not yet heard said.

"Of course he will, Harold. They all break."

Forester grabbed his hair and yanked it viciously as he came right into Rand's face, almost touching him with his own. "I will have my answers. You have come to the end of your life, Captain. You can give me what I want, all of it, and it will be easy. You can deny me, and it will be hard. That is your only choice." The hand again went out as almost a caress at Rand's throat before it tightened, taking away his breath.

When he was again aware, Forester leaned forward and whispered in his ear. "If you were nice to me, you know this wouldn't have to go this way." He ran his hand along Rand's shoulder down his arm. He grabbed Rand's jaw, yanking his head up, and planted a kiss on his lips. "You owed me that one from the ball."

For Rand, hearing his brother giggle was the last straw. He lunged forward and with his freed right hand, slammed a solid punch into Forester's face, sending him flying. He turned to hit the man to his left. He tried to dodge the one approaching from his right, but was hit hard on his head. He turned to block another blow, but the next one drove him to his knees before the world disappeared in a final blinding pain.

The knock at the door startled Belle. William had gone out. The children were in bed. She had expected Jenks to get it, but when he didn't, she put aside her book and opened it to see a crying Miranda Campbell.

"Come in," she said taking the woman's arm and pulling her into the parlor and the sofa. "What on earth happened?"

"I didn't know where else to go. My husband has gone mad. He's..." She sobbed again.

"Calm down. Do you want some water?"

Miranda shook her head. "I need you to help me get away."

"Tell me what happened."

"They took him. The captain. They... I think they are going to kill him. I know I'll be next. I don't know what to do."

"Calm down. What captain?" She knew and felt her own level of panic rising.

"He saved us. I wish I could have saved him, but they told me I had to open the door and not warn him. They... They have him Miss. They will kill him and me next."

"When did this happen?"

"Just now."

"Where?" She forced her voice to sound calm as she remembered Hoyt's dead eyes. Please God, not Rand.

"My home. My husband has been working with... Mr. Forester. They are... I don't know what have been doing." She looked around nervously. "At first I thought it was good that the general was involved. Then... er uh is the general here?"

"Not at the moment."

Her face was consumed with fear. "Then he could come, and he'd tell Mr. Forester I'm here. He'd tell my husband. Please, Belle. Please help me get away. I should have never come to this hellhole. I should have never trusted Josiah to do anything right." She sobbed again.

"All right. I will help you. Go outside, Miranda. Stay by that large pine tree. Keep quiet. Don't make a sound. I will be with you as soon as I change."

As she ran up the stairs, she wished she could tell Sally she was leaving, say goodbye to the children. None of it was possible. In her room, she threw off her slips and dress before changing into heavy pants, a shirt, coat, and a scarf. She tucked her pants into boots. Using a pin, she knotted her hair on top of her head and pulled on her big slouch hat. Back at her dresser, she pulled out the third drawer and turned it over. She had used surgical tape to secure the rest of her money—federal currency and a small sack of gold coins. She shoved that into her coat pocket. In the other pocket went her compass.

Next stop was the nightstand first to retrieve her folding knife, which went into her pocket. Pulling the stand out from the wall, she picked up her six-shot, Army Colt revolver, shoved it into its holster, and belted it around her waist. One quick check told her it was loaded and ready for use.

Quietly opening her window, she slid out. She was leaving everything she owned. She would not be returning. Down by the pine, Miranda was crying. At least she had had sense enough to wait. Belle handed her five twenty dollar bills.

"What is this for?" Miranda asked as she closed her hand around it.

"It will get you wherever you want to go. Head for the stage office and get a ticket on the first stage out. I'd suggest you not wait for it there. Hide until the stage is here. Don't go back to your house for anything. Do you understand?"

Miranda nodded. "You will come with me?"

She shook her head. "No. Don't talk to anyone, Miranda. Don't trust anyone. Just go."

Forester wrenched Rand's head up, but he was still out. Furious, he slammed his fist into Beckham's jaw. "You were not supposed to kill him."

"I didn't think I hit him that hard."

"Twice," Harold said. "The first blow stunned him. You added to it."

"Sorry," Beckham said without sounding sufficiently sorry to Forester's thinking.

"Is he dead?" Jason asked but showed no sign of caring.

"Not yet." Forester cursed and again yanked on Rand's hair. Clearly he was not going to regain consciousness anytime soon, if ever. He had not gotten what he wanted from him. He had been savoring all that would mean. He had been cheated. He wanted to kill the man who had denied him those pleasures.

"I have bad news, Colonel," Campbell said as he entered the kitchen.

"What else can go wrong," he groaned.

"My wife is gone."

"I thought you watched the door and kept her here." He barely restrained himself from hitting the man.

"She must have gone out her window. I never thought she'd do that."

"You fool. Go find her. When you do, you know what to do." He gave Campbell a vicious slap before the man ran out of the house.

He turned back to look at Phillips' body lying motionless on the floor. He'd never get anything from him for a long while if ever. All right, he just had to get rid of the evidence. If Miranda went to the law, he had to get the captain out of here. He studied the slumped body and then turned to Beckham.

"Tie his hands together again. This time, do it right! Then, you and Nash secure him over his horse."

"The creek."

"No, can't repeat that. Besides, best if this looks like an Indian killing. Take him to the side road that goes north. When you get him there, drag him to a tree, tie him to it, like they would, slit his throat, and scalp him. He'll just be another victim of the savages."

"Just us? That's dangerous out that way."

Forester sneered. "It's dangerous here. Quit wasting time."

The two ran out of the house.

Forester looked down at the unconscious man as he waited for his men to return. He felt so furious that he kicked him in the side. He had wanted to torture him, strip him of everything, and then take him against his will. Damn that man. He toyed with killing him anyway. What satisfaction would that yield when his victim didn't know, when he couldn't see the fear and desperation in his eyes?

"You could hide him in the cellar for now," Jason suggested. Obviously he cared not at all that his brother was about to be murdered. In many ways, that pleased Forester.

"No, there is no time now for anything but to remove him." The longer he waited, the more he seethed. Then he had a happy thought. Maybe Phillips would regain consciousness on the way, would know what was being done to him. He tilted up his head and lifted an eyelid. He was still out and maybe would never come to.

He felt like killing Beckham for the pleasure he had denied him. He looked up then at Jason, who would have to do. Since Jason liked what he would do to him, it wouldn't be the same, but it was as close as he'd get to satisfaction given the failure of the night. Where the hell were those useless fools?

Belle hoped Miranda was smart enough to get out of town, but she was no longer her problem. She headed for the stable. The moment she had been expecting had come-- but it wasn't supposed to be like this. She would go to where they held Rand and kill whoever held him. First, she needed Sammy and the supplies she had stored. Once she had Rand, and by God, she would get him, they would have to leave fast. She was glad Sammy was a big enough horse to carry two —at least for a while.

As she saddled him, she saw three horses being ridden past. She ran to the big doors. One horse had a long, unmoving body thrown across a saddle. It was on a lead line. She understood then that she didn't need to go to the house. She needed to follow. If Rand was dead and they were taking his body to bury him, the two with him would also be dead men.

She stopped at the box where she had the Henry and shoved it into her scabbard, securing it to the saddle before she put her foot in the stirrup and mounted Sammy. It would have been good if she'd had more chance to get to know the gelding, but she trusted he would come through for her.

At a distance, stopping now and then, she followed the three horses. This full moon was an intense one and seemed to light up the ground. All she had to do was keep close enough to be sure they didn't turn up a road she didn't know. At the crossroads, they headed west.

She couldn't make plans for what she would do because it would all depend on what they did. If these were the same men who had killed Hoyt, when they stopped, the risk to Rand would demand acting fast and without hesitation.

The men trotted their mounts a few times but mostly walked them. They were in no hurry. The horror of the miles they covered was how it left her mind free to wander, to remember what it had felt to have his strong shoulders under her fingers, and even more when he had kissed her.

There had been a time that her memories of Rand were of a young cavalry officer, how he had come to their home and charmed her with his smiles and stories of West Point or the mistakes he'd made that were humorous. She had never laughed so much or been so taken. Then he had gone out of her life with a complete rejection. She had been unable to forget him. The memories had come at the most inopportune times.

Now it had changed. She saw a mature man, dusty and striding to the stage station after galloping and shooting into an attacking horde of Indians. She saw him in full dress uniform and sweeping her out onto the dance floor, kissing her, and then disappearing again.

None of those images was the man ahead, helpless for the moment, needing her succor. She would not let herself think of him dead. If she imagined that, she'd lose all ability to function.

With a full moon, it made it easy to keep them in view and yet hang back. Then she thought she lost them only to realize they had turned up a side road that headed to the north and the hills. In case there were other Y's in the road, she needed to stay closer. They were going slowly enough, as though looking for a place, that she dismounted and wet forward on foot, leading Sammy. She took her Henry from the scabbard and levered a shell into the chamber.

As she walked, sometimes dodging toward the junipers, a life or death situation waited ahead. Two men, perhaps even these two, had slit Hoyt's throat. If Rand was still alive, that might be the plan here. She had to stay close.

Tying Sammy's reins to a juniper just off the trail, she went forward. The men were talking. Near now, she could make out their words.

"This is far enough, George. Damn it all. We want him found."

"All right. Get him off the horse."

They dismounted and one of them untied some ropes and then pulled the long body from the saddle. They dragged him to a tree where they wound the length of rope around his torso to secure him in a half sitting position.

"We could just leave him here. He ain't goin' nowhere."

"You heard what he said. Dead."

"Hell, I ain't got a knife on me. You do it."

She saw the glint of moonlight on the other man's knife as he walked toward Rand. Bringing her rifle to her shoulder, she sighted on his back and pulled the trigger. She didn't wait to see if it had been a killing shot as she quickly levered in the next cartridge and aimed at the second man who was reaching for his gun. That one she shot right between the eyes. Two of the horses shied at the shots and smell of blood, but the third stayed by Rand. She waited, watching for movement, before she went forward to be sure both were dead. Reluctantly, she felt for pulses. These at least would slit no more throats.

She moved then to where Rand was slumped against the tree. She felt of his neck and nearly groaned with relief at the strong pulse. She dug into her pocket for her knife and sliced through the rope around his chest, lowered him to the ground, and turned him enough to free his hands.

Kneeling at his side, she tried to assess his injuries. By the last of the moonlight, she could see blood in his hair, bruises and cuts on his chest. He was breathing but showed no other signs of life. To give him warmth, she pulled his shirt up, onto his shoulders, looked for buttons that weren't there.

She went for her canteen and again knelt at Rand's side. "Rand, I'm here. You're safe now." She only hoped that was true. He lay as if dead. She might have thought he was if not for the steady breathing. She cupped a little water in her hand and smoothed it over his face. No movement. No recognition. The blood in his hair was not new. None of his injuries, with the exception of to his skull, appeared life threatening.

She forced herself to think. The first priority had to be getting as far from the corpses as possible. Two of the horses had run off. The horse that remained had to be Rand's, trained in battle to stay with his master and used to blood. She ran back to where she had left Sammy and brought him up trying him to a nearby juniper.

Grateful for the lessons from her stepfather, she looked through the nearby trees. Helped by the sun beginning to rise in the east, she finally found several cottonwood saplings that looked strong enough. It took some time to saw through two sufficiently that she could break them off. Using a tarp, rope and cord from her supplies, she rigged a primitive travois.

Before securing it to his horse, she dragged Rand onto it, tying cord under his arms to hold him in place. She brushed her fingers again over his face, fighting back tears. However serious his injuries, they had to find a sanctuary. There was no time to waste, but she took time to tuck a blanket around Rand's shoulders to give him as much warmth as possible. It was all she could do for the shock to his body.

Leading the two horses, she headed north, grateful she had studied the map of the terrain between them and her family's ranch. For a while, they would stay on this narrow trace, but what they really needed was a hiding place with water.

Two hundred feet up, she secured the horses and went back to brush out their tracks. She could only hope when the bodies were discovered, those coming would assume it was Indians and not look further. If whoever came was from Forester, they would know there should have been a third body. Possibly, she should have partially scalped the two men. She couldn't bring herself to do it. Once though, she had not imagined she would shoot two men as mercilessly and rapidly as she had.

'If you pull a gun, be prepared to use it.' She remembered Adam's words. She had so little understanding that day that his demand she not hesitate would help her when she came to that deadly choice.

The narrow trail followed a small creek. Once in a while she looked back at Rand. He hadn't moved or even groaned. When the trail forked, she took the right to get them higher into the hills. She nearly screamed when a rabbit ran across in front of the horses. "Get hold of yourself, girl," she demanded.

Between her map and the compass, she knew she could find the Hardman ranch if Rand stayed unconscious. Not right away though. She and the horses needed rest. They all needed a secure place to camp for the day. Once hidden away, she could see about Rand's wounds. She forced away fear of how badly hurt he might be. Head injuries were unpredictable. He might never wake up.

Miles went by. When an antelope looked up and bounded off, she had calmed enough to appreciate its beauty. She was beyond panic and just determined to do what needed to be done.

Finally, she saw a possible hiding place. A small creek came down from the hills and seemed to lead back to a slit in the ridge, a small canyon. The sun was fully up. They needed to get off any well-used trails. There might even be a cave.

There was no cave, but it was a box canyon and did have a spring bubbling out of the rocks with a small pool. When she stopped, Rand's horse stood to let her untie the travois and lower it to the ground. She was too tired to unsaddle both horses, but she did it anyway. She looped her rope loosely around both their heads. Rand's horse would keep Sammy near. Finally, she went back to the animal trail she had followed up and did her best to again brush out their tracks.

Back with Rand, she laid her Henry beside him as she studied the blood on his head. Dried, no fresh bleeding. She felt for swelling—two lumps, one at the base of his neck. She wished for her mother's healing knowledge. She would have to go with what she remembered.

From her pack, she found clean cloths and a small whiskey bottle.

In the spring, she wetted the cloth. At his side again, carefully she washed the blood away from the wounds in his hair. She felt along the hair for cracks in his skull. If there had been any, he was going to die, but it all felt smooth. It was likely a concussion. Only when he woke would she know how bad that was. She could not even think of the possibility that he would not wake.

She talked as she worked, enjoying touching him even in such desperate straits. When she poured alcohol on the shallow wounds in his chest, she felt him jerk and then his eyes opened. "What the hell," he said reaching up and touching his head. "How..."

"Lie still and let me finish."

For the first time he looked at her with awareness and then at his surroundings. "Where are we?"

"I am not totally sure. There are mountains to the north of the John Day River. We are somewhere along a ridge between them." She went for her canteen and lifted his head for him to drink.

"God, I don't remember..." He frowned then and groaned as she let his head back down. "How do I come to be here?"

She fought back tears. "I found you and brought you here."

He groaned as he tried to sit up. She pushed him back. "Rand, lie still. You've been hurt. With you waking and being able to communicate, you don't have serious brain injury. I was afraid you'd lose what little sense you had." She smiled. Their situation was still dire, but they were together. He sounded lucid. Suddenly nothing seemed that dire-- not if they could face it together.

Except, they weren't really together. He hadn't wanted her before. Probably he still didn't. Even that didn't matter. He was alive. And not that long ago, she hadn't been at all sure he was going to end up alive. Her own situation hadn't looked that promising. She had failed in her mission in Canyon City. She had left behind two children that she loved, with a man she knew to be a monster. She had killed two men, shot one in the back. Despite it all, she was alive and so was Rand.

"I should be dead," he said with a grimace.

"There is still time for that eventuality," she said with a smile. "We're not out of this yet."

"Tell me what happened."

She tried to think how to tell him. Her exhaustion was making it impossible to find the words. "I am too exhausted to make sense. Try to sleep. I'll try to tell you what I know when we wake up. For now, it's enough we are in a safe place, isn't it?"

A heavy tiredness seemed to be sapping her strength. She had pressed herself beyond what she had believed she had been capable of doing. She felt a mix of pride and horror at what she'd gone through, what he had.

He frowned then as he looked above them to the canyon walls, then to the two horses. She saw the confusion in his eyes, but he didn't argue and held out his hand to her. She lay beside him, curling against his side and felt oblivion take her.

CHAPTER 11

It was past noon, from what Rand could tell by the position of the sun, when he woke again. He remembered lashing out at Forester, a blinding pain and then nothing until he awakened with Belle tending his wounds. He hurt, but more disturbing was not knowing what had been done to him when he was unconscious.

"How are you feeling?" she asked, as she reached over to stroke his hair back from his temple, one of the few places he didn't hurt.

"Lucky to be alive. I wasn't supposed to be."

She sat up. "Can you drink?"

He nodded and took the canteen from her, levering himself up on an elbow to drink.

"I have some biscuits."

"My mouth feels too cut up to eat but thanks."

"I have some dehydrated food, a can of beans, coffee, flour, oil, not sure what I can do with it all. Dare we have a fire?"

He considered. How far off a trail were they? "Safer not to during daylight where smoke could be seen." He managed to sit up. He felt another victory when he got to his feet without fainting.

"Don't push it, big guy," she said as she went to the bushes to take care of her bodily needs while he did the same on the other side of the small canyon.

Rand was having a hard time getting past his shock at where he found himself. He had gone from death to life. Just to watch her, see her beauty as she ate a biscuit, handed him the canteen, rose to move the horses, had him as stunned as earlier the barrel of a gun had done —just in a different way. He wanted to pull her into his arms. He forced the desire away. He had to get his mind around what had happened, where they were, how she came to be with him.

"Now tell me what happened," he said when she sat across from him. "The last I remember I was in a kitchen in Canyon City. Then the lights went out."

"Assuming we both make it out of this, you will owe your life to Miranda Campbell. She came to the Forester house to find me. She was frightened out of her wits as she told me what happened."

"The general had sent me a letter that he needed me to come to what I guess was her home. I wasn't totally naive as to the risk of trusting him, but... I had an assignment here as I know you did."

"You knew that?"

He nodded. "Dylan Hoyt was also looking for the same answers. Forester must've figured that out and had him murdered about like he had in mind for me." He shrugged resisting a groan. He seemed to hurt at any movement. "When they told me in The Dalles that you were a Pinkerton, I admit I felt sick. You kept that from your family, didn't you?"

"That bothers you."

"You have a pretty wonderful family. I hope you know that." He thought about his own family. A father who had betrayed him, a brother who wanted to watch him being tortured.

"I do know it. I didn't tell them because I was trying to protect them and yes, myself. I began working for Alan in '62. It's safer when an agent takes on different identities, that they aren't in touch with family. Besides, there seemed no need. I wrote but never letting them know from where or what I was doing. Pinkertons make that easy.

"Of course, when I came here, I knew they were nearby. I did plan to contact them when this was over, but it was best they not know while I was doing my job. It was a risk, of course with them so close. I counted on moving in different circles."

"They love you."

"I know. I am glad you didn't tell them what you had learned."

"If they had asked, I wouldn't have lied. They had no reason to ask."

"I am glad. It's safer for them that way."

"I doubt that, not as it stands."

She cocked her head to study him. "Why would you say that?"

"First, tell me how you came to save my life."

"Once I got to Canyon City and realized what kind of man

118

Forester was, that's when I began putting together my own escape plan. I bought a horse supposedly for pleasure riding. That's Sammy. I also gathered some supplies, whatever I could without creating suspicion. I stowed those at the stable. I had a feeling I'd have to leave fast at some point." She smiled up at him. "I didn't expect though what actually happened."

He let out a breath. "I don't suppose the supplies included the makings for a cigarette."

"Sorry. I never took up that particular habit. To be honest, I was more likely expecting my traveling companions might have been Jessica and Jeremy."

"Forester's children."

"Yes."

"Oh well, it's an unhealthy habit but I could use one about now. My own were in my jacket which he took." He pulled his shirt as closed as it could get with no buttons. "He's perverted in his tastes to say the least."

"Yes, the very least."

"Did he ever try to attack you?"

"He hinted but respected my letting him know I didn't get involved with employers... or maybe he was planning something else." She let out a breath. "I am not sure what he does go for."

"Yeah there is that. I suspect controlling and hurting people is his main interest."

Sitting cross-legged on the ground, she watched him. "You should wrap that blanket around your shoulders. Even Indian summer can be a cold at this elevation. And then I'd like to hear what you know about William."

He nodded and took her suggestion, then lowered himself to sit with a big boulder at his back. "After I left your stage that day, I headed to The Dalles. I had been asked to meet with Colonel Schaeffer. When I got there, it also involved Undersecretary of War Mason Williams. They laid out what they wanted."

"Williams has the ear of the President."

He stared into the distance. "So it would seem. Their belief was that Forester is involved in more than counterfeiting. The military had sent Hoyt to Canyon City hoping he'd get proof of a possible insurrection."

"I came across part of that story... the last part."

"What do you mean?"

"I was out looking around town, hoping at that point to find the presses. I saw two men grab Hoyt off the street. He didn't resist or maybe he knew it'd do no good. They tied him and took him to the same house they took you. I stayed back, watched, and when they dragged him out several hours later, I followed at a distance. I had gone out without a gun and don't know what I could have done even if I'd had one, but I just thought they had beaten him as a traitor and were dragging him off the street." She shuddered.

"Evidently he told them all he knew. It's probably how they were sure of my assignment," Rand said not liking thinking about her being that close to danger. He supposed that was a foolish concern. He was still used to thinking of her as a pampered belle and instead, she was a small warrior.

"After they came back down the trail," she said, "I went up it. I realized too late that they had taken him up there to slit his throat. They had taken his identification and any money he had to make it look like a robbery. The thing was... he'd been tortured."

"What they planned for me," he said. "When I was knocked out, it ended his games." Knowing Forester's desire to control people, my being knocked cold saved me from worse, maybe much worse.

"He's a horrible man."

"It wasn't just Forester... or my father leading me into a trap..." He stopped and let out a breath. "Jason was there."

"Oh my God."

"You are the only reason I am alive. That much is clear. I'd have just been another Indian victim if they'd had their way. They had no other reason for taking me out of town. How did you get me away from them?" He knew he wouldn't like hearing it but he had to know it all.

"I was getting my gear together to go to the Campbell house, when I saw two men ride past the stable with another slung over a horse. It was just a guess but based on what happened to Dylan. I followed but stayed far enough back. They weren't looking for someone to follow. They seemed to have a place they wanted to use. When they turned off the main road and the trail narrowed, I followed on foot. I saw them tie you to a small tree and then one approached you with a knife."

She stopped, but he waited. She needed to get it out.

"I shot him in the back and the other between the eyes before he could get his gun out. I killed them both."

He closed his eyes at the knowledge of what she'd had to do. He put out his arms, and she came into them. He cradled her against him. "I am so sorry," he whispered against her hair.

He could hear the tears in her voice, feel them against his chest. "I worked for Alan for five years and never imagined... never saw anything like what has been happening in Canyon City. I had seen war, investigated greedy men. I had no idea how decadent a man would be until I got here. After finding Hoyt's body, all I could think was finding the location of the plates and getting out of there. Indirectly his death helped me do that."

"How?"

"I went through his pockets to see if anything was left. I found a key and ring. I had no idea what it was to but couldn't keep them in my room as I assumed it was being checked. I buried them along the foundation of the house. It's when I realized there was a basement under the house and there had to be a secret entrance from inside. I knew then it was where the plates were."

"You are such a brave girl."

She pushed herself back and looked at him. "I am not a girl, Rand."

He laughed, grimacing as it still hurt. "No, you are not."

"I just wanted this past me."

"Would you have then gone to see your mother, your sisters?"

She sniffled but smiled. "You may not believe this, but you did not need to issue that order."

"I saw how well that went over."

"I guess it's a bad habit you've acquired. Probably due to being a captain."

"We likely have that in common—being in charge. Except, this thing is like nothing I've ever known either. I've been a soldier now for too many years, but this was the worst I've been through, the closest I've come to death. I was a fool to go alone but wanting it to be over was why I did it. I knew what kind of man he was... to a degree anyway. I was worried about you working for a man like that, even worse to realize you were also investigating him." Again, he wished for a cigarette. "I'm just glad Hoyt didn't know about a Pinkerton being on the job. If he had told Forester that, he might well have figured out who it was."

She nodded. "William would have had no reluctance at hurting or killing me if it gained him anything. I ran into Annie Jessup in town this week. She had been on the stage with me. She warned me about Forester and his cruelty. She was leaving. I believe she was a special friend to Hoyt. She told me I should go. At that point, I didn't want to leave without the plates and the children."

"His children?"

"They are wonderful, sweet, bright, and so deprived of love. You saw them at the stage stop."

He nodded. "And now you're worried what he might do to them."

"Originally I had thought I might take them with me, kidnap them basically, but this all happened so fast, I had no choice but to go with my instincts."

"Jesus Christ."

"I had planned to take you to the ranch for Mama to heal if you didn't regain consciousness first. Now, I guess, we need to figure out what we do next."

"The big question I have right now is how many men he has with him. A few hired men but how many have fallen in with starting an insurrection?"

"I don't know. I didn't know he was planning that. Do you think the ball had some of them? We know Mr. Campbell was one, and I think there is a partner, Harold Moriarty."

"The recent shipment to Canyon City, on that fast coach had to be arms. He's been buying them for his war and there is reason to believe some have found their way into Indian hands."

"The printing press was already here?"

"I think it had to be."

"On one of my nighttime ventures, I came across a shed behind the house. Four men carried out two crates that looked the right size for rifles. I hadn't had a chance to go back and investigate that either." She rose and walked to the other side of the small clearing and then looked back. "I failed in my assignment."

"Doesn't seem that way to me. You found out more than I did. There is one more thing they told me in The Dalles. I have a traitor at Watson. I still don't know who." He stood up and then felt a wave of dizziness that had him leaning back against the boulder to stay upright. She was instantly at his side and eased him back to the blanket.

"You need to sleep and eat when we can start a fire."

"They might show up here. I don't have a gun."

"I have the Henry and a Colt." She patted the gun on her hip. We'll hear them coming if they do. Maybe though they will just assume the Indians got those two if they do find the bodies."

"Maybe." He needed to think, but his thoughts were muddled. He wasn't sure what they should do, but he knew one thing. He could afford no more mistakes—nor misplaced trusts. She was too precious to risk. "I need to know you are somewhere safe."

She lay beside him on the blanket and cuddled against his side.

"You pushed me away once before, Rand. If you do it again, it will be forever."

He didn't pretend he didn't know what she meant. "How could we ever work it out between us?"

"I don't know."

"It's not safe here for you."

"I am not the one who nearly got killed."

She had him there. He needed sleep. He needed his head to stop hurting so much that it made clear thinking impossible. He wasn't sure how long they could safely stay where they were but for the moment, this was the best place for them.

She ran her finger over his nose, down his lips and chin. "You were so beautiful at the ball. I'd never seen your dress uniform."

He smiled. It was getting easier. "Men aren't beautiful."

"You were that night."

"Not as beautiful as you."

As beautiful as she had been that night, as he looked at her, he knew she was more so now with the smudge of dirt on her cheek, her blonde hair straggling out of a bun, and her beautiful blue eyes looking tired. As much as he had thought he loved her, he had had no clue how much more was possible. When this was over, he would... He stopped, unable to think what might be possible. Closing his eyes, almost instantly he was lost to sleep.

With the sun setting, Belle gathered dead branches to build a small fire. They needed coffee and something to eat. The dehydrated food would be at least nutritional. She pulled the small pan from the saddlebags and with water from the spring, she set coffee and what would be the stew on rocks and lit the fire.

"You were well prepared," he said as he fed the flames more twigs.

"Not enough for long, but it shouldn't take us long to get to the ranch from here.

"I've been thinking. I should take you to the ranch, but I need to head for Watson right afterward."

She felt a chill. "You said someone was a traitor there."

He nodded. "But it's also where I have troops. I will take a platoon and head right back to Canyon City. Forester won't be expecting that this soon. Since you found out where the plates and guns are, I need to retrieve them."

"Then I will go too. I can also get the children, and we won't go to the ranch first. We can't waste time-- as soon as you are in condition to ride." She stood up with her hands on her hips. For her, how he handled this would determine if they were to have a future.

He studied her and she could see his indecision. "I admit I have a weakness. I can't stand to have anything happen to you," he said finally.

The coffee was perking and the small pan was beginning to simmer nicely. She waited. "You know who I am, who I have been."

"Who you want to be," he added.

"Maybe... but I do not want a man who treats me as the weak link in a chain."

He let out a breath. She could see he didn't like it. Finally, he said, "I can't deny that you've proven you can handle things better than me."

"I wasn't a target and that helped. It is also neither here nor there. You can't go right away. Give yourself a day here and then we'll both ride to Watson. I know I can be an asset when you go to Canyon City. I want to get those children away from their warped father. They are more likely to go with me than if you come in with your troopers and try to force them."

He considered that. She could see the wheels turning. She moved to him and slid her arms around his waist. "You rejected me once before."

"It wasn't because I wanted to." His arms closed around her. "The timing was all wrong."

"How is it now?"

He bent and kissed her hair. "Lousy. About as bad as it gets." He lifted her chin and brought his lips down on hers. The kiss was sweet. It might not have lasted long if she hadn't opened her mouth and delved her tongue into his. As he responded, she felt the kiss all the way through her body. His hands stroked down her back, cupping her buttocks and bringing her hard against him.

The smell of the food stopped her. "We better eat," she said regretfully. "I hope you can now."

He felt of his mouth with his tongue. "If it's soft enough."

He hunkered down by the small fire and took a bite of the stew, which wasn't that bad compared to Army rations on a march. Eating, he thought of the kind of woman who had thought ahead enough to have a horse and supplies ready for a quick getaway.

He'd have shaken his head if he hadn't known how much it would hurt. Belle had seemed always so stylish. Even as little more than a girl, she'd already been to San Francisco and had an air about her of sophistication. The impressions had been even stronger at the ball when he had her in his arms but knew she would never be his. She wasn't the kind of woman to follow the guidon.

She was a lady who belonged on Boston's Beacon Hill. Except there was the memory of her at the stage stop, ready to fight off Indians and then bandage his wound. As he watched her hungrily eating from the tin plate, squatting on the other side of the fire, she seemed at ease out here in the wilderness where, at any moment, they could be attacked by Indians or Foresters' men. She showed no fear. She had killed two men and gotten him out of the mess into which his own foolishness had landed him.

So, who the hell was she? Finished with his meal, he wanted a cigarette... and even more to make love to the beautiful creature who he realized he had never known.

"You are thinking hard," she said as she took his tin plate and using some of the water she had heated, washed up.

"I am." He forced his mind to more immediate concerns. He only wished he was more himself. His head still hurt, he was not steady on his feet, and his thinking was less than clear. Was that the blows he'd taken or just being with her. He had to get on top of this. "You know when those horses get back to town, someone is likely to come checking. What are the odds they will know right where to find them, that they had been told where to take me?"

She thought about that. "They did seem to be coming directly there. No hesitation but not in a big hurry either. After I got you, I tried to brush out our tracks but only for a few hundred feet."

"How did you ever get me on the horse?" He wished he remembered more of what happened.

"I didn't. I rigged a travois."

He stared at her again feeling flummoxed. If he had seen her as too much a girl back in Oregon City, now he wondered if he was enough of a man for the woman she had become. What kind of man must her husband have been?

"Do you want me to keep watch while you sleep?" she asked as she came to sit beside him and handed him the small flask of whiskey. "This might help."

He smiled but shook his head. "Tempting but I need as clear a head as I can manage." She reached over and handed him her Henry. "Do you want this or would you prefer the Colt?" It was still buckled around her waist.

"God, who are you?" he asked taking neither.

She smiled then. The light was beginning to fade but the moon was rising throwing a silvery light onto her face. "I am still that girl," she said finally as she ran her fingers over his jaw. "And you need a shave."

"I can do that when we get to Watson."

"What do you think is the safest way to do that? If we ride back down past the men I killed, we are more likely to be found."

"From my best guess as to where we are, we will have to head north and then west. We'll hit the road south of Monument."

"I don't know this country."

He gave a little laugh. "Damn for a woman who doesn't, you did pretty well."

She held out a small compass. "I had this and knew where the Hardman ranch lay—approximately anyway, from Mama's letters."

"You did good. Better than I deserved."

"Quit saying that. You might convince me."

He gave a little laugh.

"So the route we need to take, what will that be like?"

"Rough. It's the only safe way to go as things stand. The hills are steep. We'll need to walk our horses past part of it. It goes into what are some unusual, very colorful canyons, pretty actually, blue rocks, like a grotto. From there though, it'll be easy back to Watson. We are less likely to run into Forester's men that way. We'll go in the morning."

"You still aren't yourself."

He knew that. He also knew that they had to stay out of Forester's range until he was. "We'll take it slow," he said finally.

"I know you aren't feeling well," she said again stroking his cheek. "You need to sleep."

"So do you. We'll put out the fire and sleep down near the horses. I wake up quick when there is a sound. We need to both sleep tonight."

"Curled together," she said with a suggestive smile that he could recognize even in the moonlight.

"It won't be easy," he said as he bent to kiss her forehead. "But I'll struggle with it."

As they lay on one blanket with the other over them, she whispered, "How do you do it?"

"Do what?"

"Kill. You have killed haven't you? Does it give you nightmares?" She ran her fingers through his chest hair making him almost forget the question.

"Yes, I've killed." A lot, if he stopped to think about. "Most though were in war or a battle, and it's different than what you had to do. I only killed one man that way. And yes, it bothered me."

"I had to do it. I knew I did, or they'd have killed you."

"I know."

"Can you tell me about the one you killed?"

He didn't like thinking about that any more than he knew she did, but maybe it would help her. "I did it for the same reason you did. To save someone's life. I had gone to one of The Dalles least savory bars to arrest a corrupt officer. When I got there, I saw I hadn't brought enough men. Lieutenant Montgomery had met up with the man who he had been working for, Russell Grayson."

"I think Mama wrote me some of this."

"Your stepfather, brother-in-law, and a man you don't know, Han Jei, had come in right after me. They were after Grayson because of his attempts to kill Jed. The place, mostly filled with Grayson's men erupted. I then shot Montgomery. Maybe Adam did too."

"And he's the man you meant?"

He shook his head. "No. I considered that a battle. There was a lot of shooting. Anybody could have ended up dead."

"Self-defense."

"Yes. When you have something like that, you go get a drink, after you clean up the mess anyway. After working through the legalities with the local sheriff, we all went to a better quality bar. I had a shot of whiskey. Jed had been wounded in the earlier shooting and was leaving early to rest before heading back to his ranch. I was thinking I needed to write a report and went a minute or two after him. A man called Bill Jessup, who had been working for Jed at one time, had then been working for Grayson. He was preparing to shoot Jed in the back. I could have said something and maybe ended up with Jed being shot anyway. I made one of those decisions, you can't afford to second guess later. I killed Jessup."

"Oh." She was quiet for a moment. "I heard something about that but from Annie."

"Annie?"

"Bill Jessup was her brother. She wanted to kill whoever killed him."

He smiled. "Welcome to the club. It didn't feel good when I did it, but I honestly believe anything else would have had Jed dead. It sounds like you faced the same quandary."

"Adam had given me advice to not bring up a gun if I didn't intend to use it. It helped me and at the moment I didn't stop to think about guilt."

"Sometimes you can't. I am sorry she lost her brother that way."

"She was still angry at the man who did it. She did not though say if she knew his name. Maybe she will forget about it once she gets out of Oregon. You don't need more holding grudges against you." He smiled and kissed her temple before falling asleep.

CHAPTER 12

She moved her fingers lightly to touch his nipple, avoiding where he'd been cut. He felt his body beginning to tighten and rise to her touch. "You better stop that," he said.

He could hear the smile in her voice. "Rand, does that mean you feel some... er desire from my doing this?" She ran her fingers down his belly to the edge of his pants. He sucked in a breath.

"You are a tease."

"You can't believe all the things I am thinking about right now. Maybe I should show you." She moved over his chest and took the nipple in her mouth.

He got harder. "And maybe you shouldn't."

"Not good to put things off. Sometimes the right time never comes." Now her fingers were delving below his belt. He gritted his teeth as he felt her nearing where she'd find how much effect she was having on him.

He had to break this mood. This wasn't the right time for them-- if there ever was to be a right time. He wasn't sure about that either. "I suppose you learned a lot from your husband." He thought reminding her of her dead husband would make her sad or maybe even guilty and she would... It didn't work as she moved her fingers farther down to what was straining against his pants.

"Oh him," she said with a little laugh. "He wouldn't mind."

"Most husbands would." He removed her hand.

He felt her smile against his shoulder where she had pulled the shirt away and moved to kiss him. His whole body felt on fire for what she would do next. Sleeping together was going eventually to make resistance useless. He wanted it as much as she apparently did. He was trapped as much as he had been with Forester except this time the bonds were sweet and tender, but maybe no less wrong for them both.

She went up on one elbow to study his face in the moonlight. "Does it bother you that I was married? That there was another man?"

"It was my own doing."

She smiled then and sat up. "You're right. It was your fault."

"What are you doing?"

"Just unbuttoning my shirt. It's not comfortable to sleep in. You do want me to be comfortable, don't you?"

"God." He sucked in a breath. Before he could say more or even decide what he was going to do, he heard the sound of horses coming from the north on the trail below them.

"Maybe they will go past," he whispered. From the sounds of it, they were Indian ponies as he didn't hear the sound of metal against rocks. There was no creak of a saddle. Maybe five of them.

She offered him the Henry, and he shook his head. Better she have it. She'd proven to be good with it. He pointed to the Colt and she handed that to him. They sat then without moving. If the Indians heard their horses, they would come up the trail to check. There would be no choice but to fight.

Five minutes passed and finally he felt confident the horses had gone on past. They were not looking for tracks evidently and made enough of their own noise that they weren't listening for what should not have been in this little box canyon.

"That was too close," he whispered still listening.

"Indians?"

"Most likely Northern Paiute. They're what we mostly see in this region. On their way south where more of the battles are being fought."

He drew her back down on the blanket. "Let's postpone the talk we started for when we are somewhere safer."

She kissed his chin. "Talk?"

"Among other things." He drew her against him and in a few moments knew she had fallen asleep. She'd been through so much. He guessed working as a Pinkerton had gotten her as used to living with stress, as his being in the cavalry had for him. He tried to think if they could really make it work. That is if she wanted more than a romp in the blankets. He wondered if she still loved her husband, and on that, he also fell asleep.

With morning, they drank coffee and ate biscuits before saddling their horses. First, he headed them to the south and then west to the main northly road. "About five canyons up, keep your eyes open for a narrow trace that doesn't look like much but leads down and out to the west, through the blue basin."

"Is that its name or what it looks like?"

"I don't know that it has a name. It's geologically interesting with layers of rock in all different types and shapes. It's a steep canyon with loose, shale like rock in layers. There are colors I haven't seen anywhere else. It's like a moonscape or something from another planet. Only thing that grows there is along the little creek that runs through it."

She felt uneasy at the prospect and finally decided to admit it. "I am good at riding but not so much with steep heights."

"When we get to that, I'll lead the horses down. You will walk behind. If you find it necessary, you can use the three point method."

"What's that?"

"Feet and butt."

"Do the horses slip?"

"They have four legs, so less, but they can. I have confidence in Blue but don't know your horse."

"So it's dangerous to lead them down." It was not a question.

"Safer than the other options." She didn't like the sound of that. "I would not choose to take you this way at all, Belle, but it will be safer than any alternative I can think of if you are determined to go with me to Watson."

"I am and to Canyon City."

"You know I'd rather you didn't."

"I know. You don't think I am strong or tough."

"I know you aren't, but you are smart enough, and we can work it out one way or another."

"It is pretty up here. The trees are taller again."

"That will change as we get to the basin."

"And you've been there."

"Mostly through it, but I've heard about it also. Are you familiar with Charles Darwin?"

"He devised a theory of evolving animals, that each change as they have different environmental or catastrophic events."

"Right. I ran into a Rev. Condon. He was looking for evidence that would prove that right here in Oregon. He first got to what he calls fossil beds in 1861. He was anxious to talk to anybody who had been there and when he could get there, he came to see for himself. Fossil evidence could prove Darwin's theory. There is evidently such in the blue basin and other places where the mineral content protected them."

"You are interested in such?" She sounded surprised.

"I am not going out digging there if that's what you are asking, but yes, I find it interesting. Mammoths or sabertooths, species of animals we have never seen. Condon has done a lot of digging and as a believer and a naturalist, he's done what he can to make this a serious science and prove Darwin's theory."

"And you met this reverend?"

"He came in here with patrols. One was mine. He named the first valley where he found these fossils, Turtle Cove because of all the fossilized tortoise shells. There is more to it. Maybe someday I'll have time to look into it. Certainly not now."

"You are a lot more diverse than I expected," she said as she scanned the hills ahead.

"And you aren't the featherbrain, I might have thought."

She gave him one of those looks. "You monster. How dare you ever think that?"

"Beauty."

"You think I am beautiful?"

"You know you are."

"Well, if I was, would being beautiful mean I would have a small brain!"

"It can mean things came too easily, and you never need to work for what you have." He smiled and put up a defensive hand. "I already know I was wrong about that."

She shook her head. "Good thing you are on that horse, or I'd definitely give you a lesson in how tough I can be."

He laughed. "I don't doubt that. You already have given me that lesson. Hey, look, I think that is the trace we are looking for." In the distance, he could see various hills and mountains, but a mist was hiding their color. Later in the day, it was likely to be clearer. Good. No storm clouds. If they could get off the rim before nightfall, he knew a safe place for them to camp. They'd go into Watson in the morning, after first light.

When they reached the trail down, he felt uneasy at how much it might slide. "I need to check this out. Stay up here until I find out if it's going to hold."

"Wait! How do you find that out?"

"Just go down a ways. Blue is steady in such places. I don't know about your horse."

"Sammy."

"All right, Sammy. Let Blue and I check this out. Be right back."

She sat back on Sammy watching as Blue made his way down the loose rock and shale. She worried that he would slip, but the horse seemed surefooted. She was not so certain about hers.

The sound of a rattle and her awareness a rattlesnake was alongside the road and not happy came at the same moment that Sammy shied to the left and then reared up in fright. Belle realized she didn't have a secure seat, was going off and tucked to roll as she hit the ground. Her awareness that she had been too close to the edge came at the same moment she felt herself falling again and this time down the side of the cliff. She reached out trying to grab onto anything, but the rock was all loose. She rolled again and then stopped, shocked at how suddenly it had happened.

She got her hands under her and then looked to her left and saw open air. Carefully she levered herself to her knees. She had landed on a narrow shelf, maybe two feet wide. Very lucky. Below her, she saw the cliff was another hundred feet before it reached the valley floor, maybe more. There were other shelves, as narrow as this one. Would she be so fortunate as to land on one if she fell again? She took deep breaths to stop from panicking. Looking up, she saw nothing but a solid wall. She was safe for the moment but how would she get back up or down without getting killed?

"God, Belle," she heard Rand's voice from the rim. "Are you all right?"

"Not hurt," she called back trying to keep panic from showing in her voice. "I don't see how I can get off this shelf though."

"Don't move." She heard the sound of his boots moving across the top, almost instantly he was back. He looked over the edge. Just seeing his face stilled her panic. "That length of rope doesn't look long enough."

"Don't you fall," she said trying to smile.

He tossed the rope over the side. It was above her reach when she stood up as tall as she could.

"How far above you?" he asked, his voice calm and reassuring.

"Maybe eighteen inches." It could have been a mile from how impossible it was even on her tiptoes. "I could try to climb to it."

"No." The order was sharp and firm. "Stay right where you are, baby. Don't move. Let me see if I can get the end farther down."

She saw him then edging his torso over the rim and reaching down as far as he could as he lowered the rope. This time she could reach it. She hoped her hands weren't too slick with sweat to get a good grip. She wiped them on her pants. She would have to jump a little whether Rand liked it or not to get high enough to get both hands with a good grip.

In a moment, she was using one hand over another and her feet purchasing against the side to move up the rope. When she got to his hands, he said, "Climb up me now."

"I don't want to pull you over," she said trying to still her trembling.

"You won't," he said through gritted teeth. "Just do it."

Using his body, she clambered the rest of the way up to the rim and threw herself down with relief. In another moment, he wriggled his way back and was beside her. They were both breathing hard as they stared up at the sky.

"My God," he said finally before he levered himself up on one elbow and leaning over, kissed her hard and long. "You scared the living hell out of me," he whispered when he finally released her.

"Me too. It was a rattlesnake. Sammy evidently isn't dependable around snakes at least." She gave a little laugh.

He got to his feet and walked to the gelding that still looked uneasy, but at least he had not run off. Rand began moving the saddlebags and blanket from Sammy to the more reliable Blue. She added the rifle and scabbard. If Sammy was going to be unsure on the loose rock, they would not want to lose all the supplies they had before they could get down.

He turned then and said, "I could still take you to the ranch. It'd be safer."

"When will you get the idea I am not a delicate flower," she said with some exasperation. "Even you could have gone off a horse like I just did. I didn't hurt myself doing it."

"No, you did well. Regular woods woman," he said with a tired grin.

Obviously, considering the wounds on his chest, reaching for her had caused him a lot of pain, but he'd not said a word. "Are you all right?"

"I'll worry about that when we get down-- if you are determined to go down."

"I am." She was equally determined to stay with him as long as she could. Damn it, what would it take to convince this man that they belonged together?

Then she wondered if they did. She had never really understood what it would mean to be the wife of a military man when she was a girl. Now she knew. She had talked to Elizabeth Custer about the moving around she had done. Elizabeth had seemed to regard it as adventure to stay with George. Other military wives hadn't expressed the same feelings. They never had real homes as they constantly had to move, if they wanted to be near where their husbands were stationed. Some made their homes in a stable town, sometimes near family. They avoided moving, gave their children stability, but then they were rarely with their men.

There was another aspect. A cavalry officer faced danger as part of his career. A military wife had to live with waving good-bye as Garryowen was played on a flute and be the girl he left behind time and again. It took as tough of women as men. She had thought of herself as strong. Was she strong enough? This was so different than facing risk for herself.

And what about her own work? Well that she was not worried about. She had had enough of lying for a living. When this job was over, she would find something else to do. That still didn't answer the question. Or the even bigger one-- would Rand even want her as his wife? How would he feel when he found out about her ultimate lie?

"Assuming we don't run into another snake," Rand said as he distracted her from her musings and handed her the canteen to drink. "The trail down looks stable enough. I will go first leading your horse. You follow, and I want you to ride Blue. Trust him. He does fine on loose shale. His four feet will do better than your two with smooth boots."

"What about your boots and why are you going first?" she asked uneasily. The question of being a spouse would be moot if either of them didn't survive this. She knew how close to death she had just come. What if Sammy pushed him over, and he fell with no ledge to land on?

"Don't keep arguing with me, baby. I will go first, and we'll do this my way. I know you are good at being a spy. You saved my bacon thanks to that. But I am good at country like this. Trust my judgment."

She met his hard gaze and understood not only was he right, but that she did need to trust him in many ways. She was used to making all her own choices, but if she wanted this man, she'd have to make some adjustments just as she expected he would. "All right," she said finally with a small smile.

He'd called her baby twice now. She liked that endearment. It did a lot to soften her to the idea of letting him be the boss—at least in this.

The path down was at times wider, sometimes crumbly but the base seemed solid. She wanted to look around, as it was scenic and beautiful, like nothing she'd seen before. She felt compelled to keep her eye on Rand, as he led Sammy. Blue had a steady gait and managed the trail with ease. She kept about ten feet behind Rand. Although Sammy's hooves slid more than Blue's, he didn't panic. After two hours, they were off the cliff and past the worst of it.

Rand pulled the horses to a halt and had her switch back to Sammy. He handed her the canteen. As she drank, she looked around and for the first time could fully appreciate the beauty of this unusual place. There were eroded gullies with complex formations and pinnacles. The colors were mostly shades of blue. She was surrounded by blue.

At the floor of the canyon, a small stream meandered from what must have been a spring. The water in it was a whitish color.

"It's amazing. I've never seen anything like it," she said.

He pointed to the wall beside them and a bit of white. "Condon pointed out things like that. Look more closely." She leaned forward. The white shape, encased in rock, appeared to be a leg bone.

"More of the animal could be right behind that," he said. "Sometimes they find whole skeletons. This place was a graveyard of a sort. Possibly created by volcanic activity that caught animals unawares— one generation after another. Then this rock, its composition kept them as they were."

"Are there dinosaur fossils?"

"The theory is not. Oregon would have been under water that far back. You know this whole state carries the records of past life but it indicates a time of being a giant sea. This is all from the age of the mammals."

"You learned all of this from Mr. Condon?"

"The chance to actually see it. I was interested though in geology even as a child. This place is like a living history classroom."

"Have you camped here?"

"Not until tonight."

"If it wasn't for me, would you go onto Watson right away?"

He shook his head. "There is a hidden side canyon where we can stay until just light. It'll be safer. It's not just Forester and his men, you know. Early morning should get us to Watson without needing to fight our way."

A short distance down the canyon, he turned them. Another

stream ran from it, but it was of clear water. "Even a little grass if we are lucky." He patted Blue's neck. "Or if they are."

"I still worry that if it wasn't for me, you'd go on. I want you to think of me as one of your men and do what is right."

He dismounted and smiled as he lifted her from the saddle. "Baby, I have never traveled with a trooper braver than you. You are the remarkable one. This is just the smart place for us to spend the night."

"It is pretty." There was a stunted sort of tree that looked like a pine except its shape was more twisted. Under it was the grass, which he'd said they might find.

She was beginning to be aware of how sore her muscles were. She'd probably have some major bruises from the fall, but she was alive and on solid ground. That alone seemed a sort of miracle. Better yet, she was with Rand. They both could have been lying dead somewhere, but they weren't. They were vitally alive. Then she remembered his cut chest. She had to look to that. Her own hands had been scraped in her fall. Still, all in all, they were lucky, very lucky. She only hoped they could stay that way. So much lay ahead—none of it secure. But they had this moment. For now, it was enough.

CHAPTER 13

After giving them a good long drink, Rand unsaddled and tethered their horses by what grass there was. While he did that, Belle lit a small fire to brew coffee and heat up water for dried meat and vegetables. "I still have two biscuits left," she said pointing to the sack.

"Let's save them for breakfast. Bet you wish you were back in Chicago at one of those fancy restaurants ordering a sirloin steak." He smiled when she shook her head.

There was no place on this entire earth, where she more wanted to be. She was where she had dreamed of being for many years. She reached into her pack for the whiskey bottle.

"I need to get the grit out of your chest wound when you ground it in saving my life, and then, if there's any whiskey left, let's have some nips." She grinned. "Bet it will taste as good as the best in any fine restaurant."

He sighed with resignation. "I suppose you're right." He spread the blanket on the smoothest spot.

"Why don't you take off what's left of your shirt," she suggested. No point in getting alcohol on it."

He gave her a look but slid his shirt off his shoulders and put it alongside the blanket before he sat on it.

"Lie back, Rand. We wouldn't want the alcohol to spill on the blanket, now would we?" Before she knelt beside him, she laid the Henry at his right and took off her belt and holster to put it at the left.

"I am feeling a little vulnerable here," he said smiling with a look in his eyes she had never seen before.

"Really? I wouldn't want that." Of course, she would. She went to his feet and pulled off his boots and socks.

"Been awhile since a bath," he said with an apologetic tone-- as if she would care about the odor of healthy man. Her own wouldn't do with any close sniffs. Maybe a bath later would be in order, as this little creek seemed purer than the water below.

She wetted a cloth with the spring water and washed his wounds and then went onto the surrounding skin. She loved washing his body, wished a cloth was not between her and it. She remembered how it had felt to touch him, to run her fingers along the hard muscles.

"So far nothing has infected," she said as she worked. Although he had said nothing, she knew it must have hurt. She looked up and met his gaze.

"That's good." His voice sounded husky. She smiled and then looked back at his body. He was not unmoved by her touch.

"You could wash me too." She smiled as she began unbuttoning her shirt still kneeling beside him.

"Are you sure you know what you're doing," Rand said watching as the shirt slipped from her shoulders. She was wearing a thin chemise and she slid it down until her breasts hung free. Still kneeling above him, she met his gaze and saw the heat in his eyes.

"If I don't, you give me instruction," she said as she lowered herself beside him.

He put out his hands and lightly touched her breasts, then her nipples, causing them to tighten. Before she could say anything, he had pulled her on top of him and claimed her mouth with his. He pushed her lips apart and thrust his tongue within. This time she was ready for him and met his tongue with her own. As his hands moved over her body, she freely explored his. Determined he wouldn't dare turn back this time, she ran her hands down his belly to the buttons on his pants.

He groaned as she undid them, freeing his erection. "I want you naked, Rand," she said barely recognizing her voice. She pulled on the pants and soon had them off so that she could see him, all of him. He was such a beautiful man even with the new wounds. His erection jutted proudly in the air. He could not deny what his body wanted.

Before she could take off her own pants, he laid her back and began unfastening and then pulling everything from her. In moments, she was naked. Only his gaze touched her and yet she could feel him touching her everywhere. She moaned as he finally ran his fingers over her body, touching where no man ever had. She didn't need the touches to be aroused. She was so ready for him. She had been ready for ten years. She squirmed as she realized he wanted to pleasure but not enter her. She pushed him away.

He lay back with a smile. "Sorry. I went too far."

"You did?" With that, she straddled him and was over his erection before he could tell her no.

"I don't want to make you pregnant."

"This isn't just about you or what you want." With that, she took his erection in her hand and tried to direct to where she thought it should go. Never having done it, she knew she was probably clumsy.

With a growl, he pressed her over onto her back. Placing himself between her knees, he pushed her legs apart. His smile was hard-- his teeth clenched. If he still harbored doubts, she took them away by lifting her legs and bringing them together behind his buttocks. He thrust hard and entered her. He stopped when he reached the barrier he hadn't expected. She was ready for that and lifted her hips, driving herself up and taking him even deeper within.

His groan and his pulling out but then coming in even harder told her he would argue no more. For long moments, she tried to match his motions as she felt the sensations growing. Oh my God, what was that? She lost track of anything but his body and hers. The feelings when they exploded filled her body in a kaleidoscope of feelings as she cried out.

Not long after, she heard him let out a groan and she felt his convulsions. He turned to the side as he went back down to the blanket. When he would have withdrawn, she held him to her, not wanting to lose this moment she had waited for so long.

She had no idea how much time had passed when he cleared his throat. She met his level gaze.

"Do you want to tell me why?"

"Which thing?" she asked as he sat up.

"You know which thing."

"There was no Mr. Morgan. It was the only way I could work for the Pinkertons. Alan doesn't hire single women. So... with the war as it was, I made up a husband based on an unfortunate soldier who had been killed."

"Why didn't you tell me?"

"If you hadn't found out this way, I'd never have told you."

He shook his head with a little laugh. "You are a strange woman, Belle Stevens."

"Me? I'm a strange woman? What about you? You walked away ten years ago, and you never looked back."

"How do you know that?"

"You never came back."

"You weren't there. I wasn't in much of a position to do anything about you when I thought you were old enough. Then, if you will recall, a war came along."

"For you there is always a war."

He stood and walked to the spring, splashing water on his chest. She followed him and ran her hands over his naked body. She had dreamed of this day, of how it might be. It had been better than any dream. Even with all they faced, with the questions unanswered as to what kind of life they might manage together-- if there was to be a together, it still was better than anything she could have dreamed-- to be with him and now to feel his hands on her skin as they washed each other and made love again.

It was dark, with the moon high overhead, when she woke again and realized he was not beside her. He was sitting on the blanket staring into the darkness.

"Are you sorry?" she asked as she sat up.

"That we made love?"

"Yes."

"No, but maybe I should be. What if you got pregnant?"

"I am past old enough to be a mother. I love children. If I should be so blessed, I'd be glad. You don't want to be a father?"

"It's not that."

"What is it then?"

"It's my current situation. Even putting aside Forester, the Paiute, Shoshoni, and Arapaho situation is a long way from settled."

"How does that complicate things?"

"I want you to marry me. A chaplain is at our camp once in awhile. If he's not when we arrive, I can order him there, or we can go to Canyon City and find a justice of the peace. I want you to be my wife."

"Was that a question?"

"Of course."

"The answer is no."

"Why?" He turned then and she saw the hurt on his face.

"Because you don't want to marry me. You are just trying to do what is right."

"That's not so."

"It isn't? The way you said it sounded like it was. Besides if we wanted to be married, where would we live, what would we do?"

She didn't know why she was arguing with him. All she had wanted since she was seventeen was to be this man's wife. What was making it not work for her now?

"We can work that out." He rose, his naked body outlined by the moonlight. He was such a beautiful man in clothing but naked, he was like a sculpture and all that was masculine and strong. She desired him, but even more, she coveted him. "I want you to be my wife, Belle. And I don't want to take a chance on waiting until this is all settled."

"You're afraid you'll be killed." It was not a question.

"There is that, but it's not just that."

"Then we can wait until it is settled—at least with Forester. I don't need to tell you yes or no now."

"You want to go back East to Chicago and live in a fancy house." It also was not a question.

"Do you know me at all, Rand?"

"I have come to believe I do not."

She went to where she'd set down the whiskey bottle and took a sizeable slug, coughing before she handed it to him.

He laughed. 'You think this will settle anything?"

"No, but it sure warmed me up."

"Oh, I can do that." He took a swallow and then a second. "If you're going to get pregnant, we might as well make it worth our while."

She laughed as she took the bottle back and another drink. It was warming her. Well, that or something.

This time he took his time, playing with her and letting her play with him. He touched her places she had never imagined would be erotic. She was near to screaming when he finally came over her and joined them. Their climaxes came instantaneously.

When she woke again, the light was just coming up to the east. He rose when she did. They washed in the creek and then dressed without words.

"So what is the plan for today?" she asked and then barely resisting a laugh as she realized how mundane that question sounded. One any normal couple might ask, not those facing a life or death situation. She handed him one of the biscuits and nibbled on the other.

"Watson. Where I look to see if one of my men, most likely one of the lieutenants is shocked to see me." He smiled.

"Why a lieutenant?"

"It would not have to be but seems most likely if one of Forester's reasons for wanting me dead was to get control of the camp. They are the ones with the power to visit Canyon City when I was out on a patrol, also to be given information that an enlisted man would not have."

"I'll look then for shock."

He laughed. "They will be shocked enough to see such a beautiful woman with me."

"Then, you do think I am beautiful."

"God, baby, do you think I am blind?"

"I have thought that actually." She smiled at him as she wiped the biscuit crumbs from her mouth.

"Maybe a little where it came to you. I should have grabbed you right off the stage when I first saw you again."

"Nope."

"No?"

"You should have gone looking for me as soon as the war was over."

"And where would I have found you?"

She considered that. "I guess Texas not long after. There had been a lot of graft and this one small town in particular where some had been taking property and even hanging colored people."

"Carpetbaggers?"

She nodded. "And those already there who intended to profit from the war."

"I'd never have known to look for Mrs. Morgan. I assume you never told your parents about that identity."

"No. I hate lying. You might find that shocking, given the ones I've told you, but I really don't like it."

"It goes with being a spy."

"I intend to give that up once we see Forester put away."

"Why not give it up first and let me do the putting away. I will settle you at the John Day Ranch and come when I can."

"We'll talk about it after we get Jeremy and Jessica. By the way, how do you feel about adoption?"

His laugh this time was genuine. "Is this going to go with the territory?"

"Well, unless they have a relative to take them, someone who would love them, yes, it is."

"Where is their mother?" He walked over to the spring, squatted, and cupped water to drink. When she hadn't answered, he looked back to where she was sitting on a boulder.

"He said she was dead, but there was something Annie said that makes me wonder."

"Annie, the one who would like to kill me."

"She'll have to stand in line and then get past me first." When he smiled, she did too. "I have a feeling Annie knew something about Jessica's mother. Annie had worked for Bernice McDowell. Do you know her?"

"Not as a customer," he said with a laugh, "but yes, at the ranch the first time I visited. She wasn't there this last time though."

She thought about asking him if he had used prostitutes, but decided to put that off for the future. "Annie was working for her in Portland, before you killed her brother and the man who had been running things in Portland."

"I can't take credit for Grayson," he said with a crooked smile.

"Well, her brother then. She said she no longer felt safe in Portland. She headed for where she expected more money—Canyon City. She didn't directly tell me, but I think she knew Jessica and Jeremy's mother."

"Their mother was a whore?"

"I am not sure how Annie knew her. It sounds though as if she'd have been a woman to notice. From Annie's reaction, Jessica looks like her mother with fiery red hair."

"Bernice and Han Jei went to Baker City or maybe onto Boise."

"Annie hoped to find her—if she got out of Canyon City alive."

"This is getting complicated. Do you have a name, which we can trace, through your connections or mine?"

"I never heard their mother's name, but there must be birth certificates or something, maybe photos at the house. I can look after we find the plates, secure the children, and you arrest Forester."

"Where would you take the children while we work out the legality of having them?"

"To the ranch and my family. I think that's the only option, don't you?"

"And then?"

"I don't know—well other than I will quit the Pinkertons."

"Might you consider following a soldier around the country like Elizabeth Custer does?"

"I might if the right man asked in the right way—which has yet to happen."

"Uhmm, what exactly are you expecting?"

"Courtship perhaps."

He laughed. "I will have so much time for that with running around the country after the Snakes."

"There will be life after that, won't there?"

"To the Plains or maybe back to Arizona and Apache."

She had to think about that. Before she could respond, he had come to her and pulled her to her feet. "You will be my wife, and the rest we work out."

"Oh I will, will I!"

"Yes, you will. Do you want a big wedding or can we just do it at the camp if the chaplain is there?"

"I will not marry a man who thinks he's going to die and wants to secure the name of his child."

"Who might not yet exist."

Her smile broadened. "We can keep working on it."

"I don't want an illegitimate son or daughter."

"There are no illegitimate children." She sighed and started to turn back to the horses.

He grabbed her up in his arms and swung her around. "Marry me."

"That sounded like an order."

"Would that work?"

"No."

"All right. I give up—for now. But this is not settled."

As she mounted Sammy, she thought about why she was not eagerly saying yes. She had wanted this man for ten years. He was more desirable to her now than he had been when she was not much more than a girl. But she wanted him to want to live. She didn't want to marry him only to lose him. She wasn't eager to watch him riding off to one battle after another to the tune of Garryowen and where someday she saw him borne back to her only to be buried. Was she strong enough to be the wife of a career soldier? She had seen herself as a strong woman. However, to be the one waiting, that required a kind of strength she had yet to test.

As they rode down the canyon, they left behind the blue cliffs and came into a broader canyon with a river winding through it. The rocks were high on both sides. The valley floor was lush with grass and deciduous trees with their leaves beginning to turn golden.

"This is so lovely," she said, in love with the terrain.

"It is a magical place. Someday it'll be a good place to live."

"Not now?"

"Not without a fort around you. It will change though."

"I have never visited the Hardman Ranch. Is it pretty like this?"

"Different. The cliffs are still colored, not so intense. There are more pines, the river moves faster."

"Mama loves it."

"Why haven't you visited?"

"Well, Mama didn't go all that long ago. I was tied up in Texas, and I told you what I felt once I got this assignment."

"It's now called the John Day Ranch."

"Really? Jed Hardman gave it up."

He laughed. "You are joking, of course. Have you met him?"

She shook her head. "He must be special though to have gotten Raine to marry him."

"He is that. He runs the place like a Scottish laird, which your sister calls him teasingly." She noticed that as they rode, Rand constantly scanned the land ahead and now and again behind. It would take some time for her to adjust to the danger of just riding through this kind of country. Her projects had had the possibility of danger but not of being part of a war. Mostly it was gather evidence, hear what others said, and report back. Rand's was a whole other world.

"So why the name change?"

"He's setting it up to withstand whatever comes against him. Adam bought several sections to the west. They were trying to interest me in buying ten thousand acres up river."

"Why? What would you do with it?"

"What he is doing, I guess. Run cattle, log, grow fruit. Matt is building a home for their family in the main pasture. It's like a small community, well positioned to defend during the time that is necessary, later to make a good living for several families."

"But not you?"

"I didn't tell him no, but I can't do it right now. I have a job to finish."

She felt an inner excitement. Then she wondered did she want that kind of life any more than following the guidon? She liked big cities. Theater. Restaurants. But... "So you will decide after Forester?"

"Not just him. I want to do my part in ending the Snake War."

"Or get killed." She had gone from a surge of hope, to doubt, and finally to anger all in a moment. She could not believe all Rand stirred in her.

"It's not on my agenda," he said with the kind of cocky grin that was oh so familiar to her.

"So you'd park me somewhere and be off fighting battles where you could get killed."

She saw his expression change. "Baby, pull your hat down. I see a rider coming."

She was in the mood to fight with him but did what he asked. The rider passed with a brief scan and a casual wave.

"Did you know him?" Rand asked after they were well past.

"I haven't seen all of Forester's men, but he would fit the type."

After a few hundred feet, Rand said, "Time to pull our horses into this grove and see what he does."

"You think he'd come after us?"

"If he works for Forester, he'll either try to get word back or take a shot at us—at least one of us. To do that, he'll have to get in position. He won't expect us to be waiting when he tries."

"You are scaring me."

"Good. Now get a little further down behind me. You keep your Colt but give me the rifle this time."

She handed him the Henry and backed Sammy behind Blue. She pulled her Colt from the holster and waited, hoping that this was nothing. Hearing the sound of approaching hooves, it looked like he hadn't been wrong.

"Stop right there," she heard Rand say, "or take a bullet." He brought his horse into the road with his rifle pointed at the man.

"Howdy," the man said pulling his horse to a halt. "What's up, mister?"

"Forget something?"

"Yeah, my uh... Never mind."

"Take your gun out of the holster, use your other hand and hold it with your fingertips, before you drop it to the dust."

"Look, stranger, I don't know what..."

"Do it," Rand interrupted.

"This makes no sense. Why should I do it?"

"Because if you don't, I'll kill you."

"Why? You don't know me."

"You being an innocent stranger, you'll do what I say."

"What happens after that?" She could see the man was considering his odds.

"Two possibilities. You get taken to Camp Watson for questioning or you draw that gun and end up lying alongside this road until the coyotes come and eat your flesh.

The man made a low growl but threw his gun down. Rand came alongside the rider and pulled his Remington from its scabbard. "Nice new gun. Looks expensive. Where'd you get it?"

"None of your business."

"All right, you will be riding ahead of us, and I have a feeling you know right where Watson is."

"I didn't do nothing wrong." He glared at Rand.

"What's your name?"

"Smith."

Rand snorted. "Well, Mr. Smith, an innocent man won't be worried about answering some questions once we get there." He threw his leg over the pommel of the saddle and dismounted, without taking his rifle or eye off the man. Picking up the weapons, he shoved the revolver into his belt. He backed up to hand the extra rifle to Belle before he remounted. Belle was impressed that he did it all without for one moment taking his gaze from the stranger.

"Injuns along here. I'd be first in line," the man protested with more concern now than anger. "I could get killed. You got no reason to do this."

"You were heading north until you saw us. You turned around and headed back. In this country, given my recent experiences, that's enough reason. You work for Forester, don't you?"

"That's not against the law."

"We'll see about that."

"You sound scared of Forester."

"Should I be?"

The man looked then at Belle as she rode out of the small copse of trees. "I know ya, don't I?"

"Do you?"

"Seen ya in Canyon City. You worked for Forester. Guess you don't no more."

She could see, by the expression on his face as his look shifted from her to Rand and then away, he was lying. Even though there had only been moonlight that night, she was relatively sure now that she had seen him as one of those moving the rifle boxes out of the shed. It would explain the newer rifle Rand had handed her.

"I'll be asking the questions," Rand said. "Now ride ahead of us, no faster than I tell you, and if you try anything at all, it'll be easier leaving you here for the coyotes than taking you to Watson. Got it?"

The man growled but gigged his horse lightly in the side. He turned in the saddle to look at Belle. "You picked the wrong side, lady."

"Should I know you?"

He shrugged.

"You could get an easier time of it with the law," Rand said, "if you were willing to testify what you know."

"Or I could end up like you will—dead."

CHAPTER 14

Riding into Camp Watson, Belle saw men running out of the buildings. As Rand dismounted, they were around him with questions, their eyes scanning over her but politely asking nothing.

"Sergeant Smith, put this man in the guardhouse and secure him there."

"Yes sir." Salutes, men with curious eyes, and then she was ushered into a room at one end of a long building with a porch that stretched its length.

"These are my quarters," Rand said, "but will be yours until we leave."

"You can't stay with me, I suppose." She smiled back at him.

"It wouldn't do. This post has no women. The men would be bothered if I suddenly took a strange woman in my room." He smiled. "Of course, if you married me, you could be here for visits. If you say the word, I will send for the chaplain."

"We can discuss that later, but I don't know what has changed between us."

He gave her a hard look but nodded as he delved into a closet for a fresh shirt and jacket. He threw the ruined shirt on the floor as he dressed. "The bastard got my campaign hat," he growled as he pulled a cap from a shelf.

He turned when he was properly garbed and smiled at her perched on his bed. "I'll send a corporal with water for bathing. I need to question the man we ran into. Unless you want to be part of that."

"What would be best?"

"I don't know. The only way you can be there is if you identify yourself as an agent. Is it the right time for you to do that?"

She considered that as she took her hair down and twisted it back up in a tidier bun. "It might help. Sometimes the name Pinkerton scares people."

"What about Mrs. Morgan?"

"I'd rather keep the name and protect my family for now."

"Fine, then Mrs. Morgan, do you wish to come with me to see what this scum knows?"

She laughed. "You have already made up your mind who he is, haven't you?"

"I think he was there when Forester had me. Some of them were behind me, but the voice seems familiar. He told me that about another dead man as bragging rights. I should probably have shot him out there, but I hoped to get information. I still hope for that."

A knock at the door interrupted them. It was Lieutenant Murphy. "There was a letter for you from The Dalles," he said pointing to a missive on Rand's desk. "If it's not being presumptuous, where have you been, sir?" He looked curiously at Belle.

"Where is Lockwood?" Rand asked.

"He went to secure your prisoner."

Belle could see Rand didn't like that. "I asked the sergeant to do that."

"He said he could take care of it."

"Get over there on the double, and be sure he's not taking care of more than that."

Murphy gave him a probing look but hurried off.

"Lockwood could be my spy," Rand said as he buttoned his jacket and started for the door.

"You're not going to read the letter?"

"When I get back."

"I'll come too," she said.

Before they could get across the parade grounds, a shot rang out. Murphy had not yet made it to the guardhouse. He headed there on a run, as did Rand, with Belle not far behind. When they arrived, the man who had identified himself as Smith was dead on the floor. Lockwood was standing over him with a revolver still pointed at the body. He looked up as they entered the room.

"He had this," he said and pointed to a knife in Smith's limp right hand. "You missed it when you took his weapons." There was clear disapproval in his voice. "He tried to use it on me."

Rand nodded but said nothing. "Report back to me in an hour." He turned Belle, and they returned to his quarters.

"I didn't miss the knife, not one that size," Rand said when they were inside. "And Smith, or whatever his name is, was left handed."

"So your spy is Lockwood?"

"It would provide a reason to kill Smith before he could reveal anything. But that won't be proof. It could be a piece of it eventually. It also helps me to know who not to trust."

"You're frowning. What else?"

"Just Lockwood has had time here to interest others in the conspiracy. He might not be the only one. We are in a turbulent time and insurrections can seem quite appealing to the shortsighted or those looking for simple answers to complex problems."

She forced herself to look at him steadily when what she felt was fear for him. "So what must you do?"

"Right now? Read the letter from Colonel Schaeffer." He smiled as he went back to his desk. When he had perused it, he handed it to her. He rolled a cigarette while she read it. He took a long satisfying draw and waited for her response.

"Your father showed up in The Dalles and took the steamboat to Portland."

"Rat deserting the sinking ship as fast as possible."

"It seems there had been insufficient evidence to hold him."

"Not then."

"So will you try to have him arrested in Portland?"

"I will let Schaeffer decide that when I write him what happened and what I am doing next. I won't wait for a reply though before I head back to Canyon City."

"Today?"

"Tomorrow morning. I need a good night's sleep and so do you if you are determined to go with me."

"I am. Besides would I be safe here with a lieutenant who murders those who might get in his way?"

"Good point." He smiled at her again as he blew out the smoke. "When Lockwood and Murphy return, do you want them to know you are a Pinkerton?"

"It serves no real purpose now but then how do we explain me?" She grinned at him and liked the darkening of his eyes. Even more, she liked the desire she saw there. She had never had a lover. She found she very much liked the experience.

"That is a problem." He laughed. "Even more of one is when Adam sees you with me and decides to beat me to a pulp."

"He'd not do that."

"Oh he would... if he thought I was taking advantage of Martha's baby girl."

"Maybe he'll assume I am taking advantage of the handsome captain."

He smiled but ignored that. "In a few minutes my lieutenants will come through that door. You are the smart one. How do we handle you being with me?"

"How much information might your spy lieutenant actually have about what Forester did?"

"Assume all. It is safer to figure for the worst."

"Well, what if I was out for a ride and came across you injured? Of course, I had no idea how you'd been hurt, but helped you and then when you were well enough, we headed here first? Nothing about my being a Pinkerton since they aren't being actually interrogated."

"I like it. A beautiful angel came to my rescue."

"Nobody can prove otherwise. Give them no more information than you must. I'll watch their faces while you tell them."

When the officers entered Rand's quarters, both didn't try to hide their curiosity. "We were concerned about you, sir," Murphy said.

"It was a close one," Rand said. He ushered them to the seats in front of the desk. Belle was sitting in his only rocking chair.

Rand introduced them to her and then succinctly told the story of what had happened to him. "I was dumped in the hills with the assumption I would die there without succor," Rand finished. "My good fortune was that Mrs. Morgan had gone for a pleasure ride. She saw me and saved my life."

"That was fortunate," Murphy said with a smile.

Lockwood looked at Belle. "Did you see the men who did this?"

She shook her head. "I just saw Captain Phillips with his horse standing near him. To be honest, I thought he had fallen at first until I saw... Well evidence of other injuries incompatible with falling from a horse."

"A shocking experience. We are lucky you kept your head. Why did you not take the captain back to Canyon City?" Again, it was Lockwood with the questions.

"I was afraid moving him would make his injuries worse. Of course, also, he's a large man. How would I have gotten him on a horse? I needed to nurse him where I found him."

"Could you find that place again so we might track the scoundrels?" Lockwood asked.

She felt convinced he was Rand's spy. There was a wily expression in his eyes, and then the questions intended to trip her up. "I wish I could help you, gentlemen, but as I told the captain when he regained consciousness, I had gotten lost myself. I was fortunate to find him, or I could have wandered in the hills forever and died there. I should never have ridden out by myself. I was feckless in the ways of wilderness." She smiled as sweetly and innocently as she knew. "I enjoy riding so much that I lost track of where I was. I was an imprudent woman to ride off by myself."

She didn't look at Rand to see how this was going over with him. She was more interested in keeping her eyes on the two lieutenants. Murphy struck her as genuinely concerned for his captain and the experience he had endured. That didn't mean he was necessarily not the spy. Spies were good at lying. She was familiar with that.

"Mrs. Morgan and I were both fortunate," Rand said. "I will be allowing her to use my quarters, of course, while she is here. She will ride back with us tomorrow morning when I go to Canyon City and arrest William Forester."

"If you were injured, shouldn't you wait a bit for that?" Again, it was Lockwood. "I could go with Pat, and we'll arrest him."

"No, I will be leading this patrol Tell Perkins, Coleman, Manning and Sullivan to get their squads ready to ride in the morning. Murphy, you will stay here, and Lockwood, I want you go come with me. In the morning, I will be sending Muldoon and O'Toole to The Dalles with a letter. You are dismissed." They saluted and left the room, closing the door.

He turned back to her. "I would like to write Schaeffer all that you learned. With your permission."

"Of course." She wished for another of his fiery kisses. Not likely given the circumstances, especially since he did not want to sleep with her in his quarters. Damn what the soldiers thought, although she understood he could not afford to feel that way.

He smiled then and left his desk to pull her into his arms. "Will you dine with me, Mrs. Morgan? You must be famished. I know I am."

"I wish I had a dress to wear but... yes, I'd like that very much."

An hour and a half later, Rand escorted her back to his quarters. "Are you exhausted?" he asked as he closed the door.

"What did you have in mind?" She smiled with a provocative look that he had come to recognize and like a lot—except this time.

"Writing that report for Colonel Schaeffer; but if you would like to go to sleep, I can do it in the map house."

"I don't mind." She sat on his bed and watched him with those beautiful eyes and the soft shape of her lips, lips that were so kissable.

He took off his jacket and forced himself to stick to business. It took him half an hour to get down the facts, as he wanted them presented. The question of what the colonel would want to do about his father was up to him. He didn't sugarcoat his father's role in his near murder. Exactly how that would play in a court of law, given his father's proud reputation, he was unsure.

He had heard taps, and the post had gone dark before he folded the full report and sealed it into an envelope. He looked then to see that Belle had curled up on his bed, only having removed her boots.

Despite what he had told her, he was undecided about where he would sleep. He was not willing to leave her alone, not given the potential of not just Lockwood but maybe others under Forester's influence.

Although his lieutenants did not know the full extent of Belle's involvement in saving his life. Forester was likely to know and could have told anyone. How was he getting information to the traitor or traitors? Perhaps simple walks out at night to meet with a messenger. It wasn't as though the camp was a prison. The men were free to go beyond the log walls.

"Come here," she said in a voice not much above a whisper.

He rose and walked to the bed. "I need to find my own bed."

"You have one, although, it is a small bed." She reached up and pulled him down to sit on the edge. "There's so little room," she whispered as she bared his chest, pushing the shirt from his shoulders. The night air was cool, although considering it was mid-October, not as much as it could have been. His skin was quickly heated as she ran her fingers over his chest and then his shoulders. "Come to bed, Rand."

"How will that look?"

"Oh you want to ruin it by worrying about that?" she teased.

He cleared his throat as he thought about that. How much did he want to worry about it?

"There are no women at this post?" she asked.

He shook his head. "It's a small station, barely enough quarters for enlisted men and officers."

"Are the men married?"

"Some."

"Where are their wives?"

"Very few women follow the guidon like Libby."

"It's discouraged?"

"You once said you met her. Did you?"

"Yes." She pulled him down onto the bed to lie beside her. "I liked her. She is a woman of strong will."

He smiled against her hair as he kissed her. "You didn't bump noses, being you are a strong woman also?"

"No. She might've felt a tiny bit annoyed one night when he appeared to be flirting with me right in front of her. Then, he gave her one of those looks that told me he only did it to make her jealous and excite her, which apparently worked as they retired early that evening."

"He's a man who stirs emotions. Did he stir yours?"

She laughed. "I was already in love." Before he could say anything more, she pulled down his head and silenced any possible words with her lips.

"Your imaginary husband?" he teased when she gave him the chance.

"You were my imaginary husband."

Over an hour later, naked, they lay entwined, the blankets pulled over them. "You love the military life, don't you?" she asked as she nuzzled his neck.

"It's all I have ever known."

She blew on his skin before she kissed the junction of neck and shoulder. "There probably was more glory on the Plains, chance to win medals. Why did you come back to Oregon?"

"Last I had heard you were in New York City. Nowhere I'd be likely to be stationed. I didn't know your name even."

She smiled as she felt his kiss on her temple. "I always knew where you were."

"Ah, the spy network."

"There are many resources available to spies. I followed you through the Civil War."

"Then you were not too surprised when I came riding up at the Jamison's Station."

"Seeing you was still a shock to me."

She felt his smile against her forehead. "I didn't know you were here until I saw you. I did though know I liked this state. I had another option that would have meant Kansas. I preferred this one. It hasn't been easy though."

"Marauding Indians?"

"More government cutting back. Last winter I had to pay for enough food to get us through until spring without malnutrition."

"That's terrible."

"It's the aftermath of the war. Kansas might not have been better."

"This is a very small post, not even a fort."

"I like that part. I call my own shots to a point anyway. It was a good place to be. Anyway, up until I got asked to get evidence on Forester and then had to worry about this beautiful blonde, who had become a spy."

She laughed. "I guess we both chose dangerous careers."

"Dangerous and ones requiring following orders."

"That too. You must like the military life since you have done it so many years."

He thought of answers he could have given her, but he wasn't ready for that kind of revelation. "Some parts."

"I want you to stay with me tonight, Rand. I don't care what others think. For all they will know you could be sleeping on the floor anyway."

He had long ago made up his mind as to that. As long as he could be with her, he would.

With reveille, Rand quickly dressed. Sitting on the bed, he pulled on his boots. "You can sleep in a bit," he told the woman, whose blonde hair was spread across his pillow, and who he had made love to twice during the night. "I'll bring you breakfast in about an hour."

She smiled without comment and closed her eyes.

Outside, Corporal York was just stepping onto the porch.

"Find Muldoon and... Private Carmody," he ordered sending the man off. He trusted those two not to be in Forester's pay. He wasn't sure of almost anyone else.

Half an hour later, he had sent them with three others off with the letter for Schaeffer and returned to his quarters with a tray of two cups of coffee, hotcakes, and bacon. Pushing open the door with his knee, he saw Belle was dressed and pulling on her boots.

"I could have gone to the mess with you," she said as she twisted her hair into a bun. "I really could use a real bath though."

He smiled as he put the tray on the desk. "You are gorgeous, more than even that night at the ball."

"Is your vision not so good?" she asked with a laugh as she took a piece of the bacon.

"Good enough to recognize a beautiful woman."

"All right, enough of the blarney. Tell me what happens today." She took a sip of the coffee.

"We go to Canyon City as soon as we eat. I am taking four squads, which amounts to just under fifty men."

"Just to arrest Forester."

"And whoever tries to stop me. You and I, with one squad, will stop at his house and get the children and his counterfeiting plates, if they are still there—plus any weapons in that shed. The other three squads will go into Canyon City to his office, to the house where he held me, and arrest him if they find him—also anyone at that house as it seems to be part of their operation."

"He might get away."

He nodded as he rolled and lit a cigarette. "There is no easy way to do this. Nor any guarantees. The squad going into town will be my first sergeant. He's good. He knows the places to look."

"Are ten men enough to go to the house safely?"

"It depends on where Forester and his men are... I am taking Lockwood with me."

She jerked her head up. "You can't mean that."

"I can and will. I want him where I can watch him when we go into the house. You will deal with the children. I will go into that underground room with Lockwood."

"That's a terrible risk."

"Right now I have nothing I can use to accuse him. If we get Forester, I might, but as it stands, I need more."

"He killed once to hide secrets."

"What's your better plan?"

She frowned and gave him a look. "I don't have one." She also had begun to wonder if she would have a hard time convincing the children to come with her. They had to want to come, or she'd have to leave them. She did not want to leave them.

"How about the household staff? Are they apt to prove dangerous?" he asked as he grabbed a heavier jacket from his closet. He handed it to her "The weather outside looks as though it might turn cold and rain."

"What about you?"

"I'll be fine. I am mad at Forester over him taking my best hat though. Damn that man. It has gone through a lot of campaigns with me."

"And as to his staff," she said as she put on the coat. "There is a butler, who I have only heard called Jenks. He seemed polite and I can't say much more for him. He probably hasn't said more than a dozen words to me. The cook and maid is Sally Hensen. She is wonderful with the children or was. The driver, who I had contact with is named James Dunham. I don't know anything about him. None of them paid much mind to me; so maybe not anything more than household staff."

He belted his holster and revolver to his waist as he smoked.

"Shouldn't you contact the sheriff of Canyon City as soon as we get there?" she asked uneasy at the potential violence he might face— that they might face.

"What reason do you have to think their lawman is not on the payroll?" He took another long drag on the cigarette before he snuffed it out. "I met him once six months ago and he didn't strike me as being much help either way."

"All right." She knew he was right. She had no idea who would be safe or a help in Canyon City. There had been many people at that ball.

"Wear your gun," he said as he reached into the top of the closet for a black felt hat. She liked how it looked on him as he pulled it on and winked at her. She felt a shiver then of fear. Would either of them live through this day? The one consolation she had was last night and how wonderful that had been. She had to think positively-- it wasn't to be their last night.

William Forester walked into the Campbell house. "Josiah, get together a company. We are going for a trip."

"Right now?"

"Yes."

"Why?"

"Call it instinct." It was based on who had not returned, and on the fact that two of his men had ended up dead. There was no proof they had not been killed by Indians. If so, where was Phillips' body? Something had gone wrong.

If there was one thing Forester prided himself in it was his knowledge of men. He needed to get out of town for a few days but more than that, his men needed to see themselves as an avenging force. To the south, they were likely to run into some small tribes, women and children even better. The men needed to believe in his power. They needed action where they saw themselves with a victory and him as a leader they could trust.

The other thing he trusted in himself was his instinct to recognize trouble coming. If Phillips had survived, he would be coming. He wouldn't be alone. Any action his men got in town could be the end of his power. No, he needed a success, and he had a pretty good idea where he could get it.

"All right. Mr. Moriarty too?"

"No."

"He might not like that."

"He might not." He smirked. "Now go."

Jason followed him into the kitchen. "What are you doing here?" Forester asked him.

"I thought you'd want me to come where you are going."

"You could wait here and ambush your brother," he suggested. "Show me how valuable you are."

"Randall? You think he's coming here?" His voice sounded worried.

Forester sneered. "You don't appear to like that idea."

"It's nothing to me. I didn't do anything to him."

"No, it was all your father, wasn't it?"

"It was."

"He saw you there. He knows what you are doing, have been doing."

"I suppose."

"Jason, you are not stupid but you are also not worth a lot. You certainly aren't a man I'd want in a fight at my back."

The younger man flushed.

"You can yet prove your worth to me. You stay here. Hide in the woods. When you see your brother, shoot him. Shoot him dead with one clean shot to the head. When you do that, you will get your reward."

Jason frowned. "I am not that good a shot."

"Then you better be close." He laughed. "Don't let him see you as he won't let you get off a shot if he does. He knows who you are now."

"I haven't ever killed anyone."

Forester snorted. "Whatever you do now, it's not going to be with me—unless you prove you have some value. Time to earn your keep. Now get out of here. I have things to do. They are things men take care of."

When Jason left, Forester smiled. He didn't expect much from the young man. He had recently proven more annoying than pleasurable, but one never knew. Having several irons in the fire would benefit him. The one thing he didn't want is for Rand Phillips to stay alive. If his lieutenant failed him, then maybe Jason would take care of it. Either way, he was out of there, as he was certain of one thing. The captain would be coming.

CHAPTER 15

By riding hard, they were at Canyon City before dusk. Rand motioned for his men to divide. Sergeant Smith had his orders and headed for town. Lockwood seemed satisfied to be turning to the left and the Forester home. That squad, along with two packhorses, included Sergeant Coleman, who Rand had seen in battles and knew to be a good man in a conflict. As for the privates, Rand kept in mind that it was possible Forester had had more than one man at the post. He would watch his back.

At the house, he gestured for seven of his men to take one pack-horse and head to where the shed was. "Any guns or ammunition, take them."

On the porch, he didn't knock but slammed open the door with his boot, breaking it and sending it forward with a jolt that sent an older gentleman stumbling backward.

"Jenks," Belle said as she moved beside Rand. "Is Mr. Forester here?"

Jenks looked shocked but shook his head. "Out of town he said."

"Where are the children?"

Sally had come out of the kitchen, her face filled with alarm at the invasion. "What is this? Where you been, ma'am? Who are these folks?" She gestured toward the soldiers.

"I am Captain Philips, here to arrest William Forester," Rand said. "Do you know where he went?"

"No sir, no I don't." She began to shake.

"Where are the Forester children?" Rand asked with the tone that assumed he'd get answers.

"Upstairs," she said and then looked back at Belle. "You ain't gonna hurt them babies, are ya, ma'am?"

"Of course not." She looked back at Rand.

"Go talk to the children," he said as he turned to look at the parlor.

"Come with me, Sally," Belle said and headed up the stairs.

In the spacious and ornately decorated parlor, Rand saw the wooden panel Belle had described. It took only a moment to slide it open. "Corporal Jensen stay up here and keep watch. Lockwood, you come down with me." He grabbed a kerosene lamp and headed down the narrow stairs. He had every reason to expect Lockwood to give himself away if he'd been there before. At the bottom there was a big table, bookshelf and in the center of the room, a large press. He whistled as he realized the only way it could have been gotten there is with the house built around it.

He set the lamp on the table and looked for plates on the shelves. Except for the one in the press, they were all there, along with stacks of phony currency. Before he could tell Jensen to bring five men back to the house, he saw what was on the walls—men's coats, jackets, some military, including his own. He cursed as he realized Forester had set up a kind of trophy wall. Not for the first time he wished he had not been unconscious, with no idea what had been done to him while under Forester's power.

He heard a movement behind him, felt it was Lockwood wanting to get a better look. He realized then that one of the jackets was of a lieutenant. He stepped to one side to let his junior officer come closer when he felt a blinding pain in his shoulder.

Whirling at the attack, he landed a solid fist against Lockwood's jaw, ignored the knife jutting from his shoulder and the pain as he pounded him again before Lockwood, who had doubtless expected he had landed a killing wound, could retaliate. The lieutenant's fist collided with Rand's jaw but not enough to stop him from landing two more solid blows first to Lockwood's face and then his belly. The lieutenant fell back, landed hard, and lay still.

Rand reached up for the knife and pulled it from his flesh. It was a small knife with a long, narrow blade. There was little bleeding. It appeared to have not cut through a muscle, as he could still use his arm fully. He'd had worse. At the top of the stairs, Jensen yelled down. "You okay, Captain?"

"Get down here." He knelt by Lockwood and discovered the

reason he'd gone limp. The man had hit his head hard on the metal of the press. From the angle of his body, he likely had broken his neck and died instantly.

"What happened?" Jensen asked looking with shock at the body and then at Rand.

"Lockwood attacked me. Get the troopers back here as soon as they have the guns loaded. I want two of the plates and the printed money out of here and on the other packhorse as quickly as possible." He turned back to the press and with a hammer he did what he could to make sure it didn't print anything else. He turned to the plates and damaged all including the two he was taking. They'd print no more money.

Rand turned then to remove his jacket from the wall. He'd be damned if he'd leave it a trophy for a madman. On a nearby table was his campaign hat. With a grim smile, he took it.

His shoulder, although painful enough to make him aware, had bled little. He assessed it wasn't significant and pulled his heavier jacket over the lightweight one he was wearing. He looked again at the wall. Nine men's coats. Two had been military, one of those doubtless Lockwood. It looked as though Forester had been counting coup, not deaths but... "Damn to hell that bastard," he muttered under his breath.

Upstairs, Belle found the children both in Jeremy's room. "You left us," Jessica said with a cry as she ran and hugged Belle's legs.

"Just for a time. Now I want you to gather your things and come with me."

Jeremy sat on the bed, the stubborn expression she had expected on his face. "What if I don't want to go?" he asked mutinously.

"I want to go," Jessica said, tears running down her cheeks.

"Did their father say this was all right?" Sally asked with concern.

"No. Sally, you should come too."

"I have a job here."

"It's your choice." Belle turned back to Jeremy and squatted down. "Remember the things I taught you about the woods?"

He nodded with a frown.

"Well, the man who taught me, that man, who knows about tracking and woods better than any man I ever knew, he is where I want to take you for a while."

"Forever?" Jeremy asked still frowning.

"We will decide that later. For now, it's a camping trip. But you will like it. There are other children there, some your ages."

Jeremy now looked undecided.

"If you want to come back later, we will discuss that also. So what do you say?"

He nodded. She then set about packing bags for each child with basic clothing needs and a few toys for each.

"I have my compass," Jeremy said pulling it out of his pocket.

"Good, you can practice using it on this trip."

She quickly ran into what had been her room and threw a dress, skirt, blouse, and underwear into Jessica's bag. When she looked up at Sally, she saw the concern on her face. "I will take good care of them. You really should come though, Sally."

"On horseback?"

"I am afraid so."

"I can't ride."

Belle delved into her pocket and pulled out her money. She counted out five twenties. "Sally, if you are smart, you will take the stage out of Canyon City as soon as you can get a ticket."

"You are scaring me, ma'am."

Belle put the money in her hand and closed her fingers over the bills. The children watched her with big eyes. "There is reason for that. Get to The Dalles and wait there. I will work out something for your future."

"This is bad, ain't it?"

"Yes, it's bad. Jenks should go too."

"Who are you, Mrs. Morgan?"

"No time for that." She picked up the children's bags. "Downstairs."

Sally followed now with tears in her eyes. On the first floor Jenks was standing back against a wall, still look shocked as two soldiers came out of the parlor and onto the porch each carrying sacks.

"They were still there, then," she said to Rand as she saw him on the porch watching the securing of the packs. The sun was just starting to set.

"And the guns. Lockwood is dead.'

"What happened?" she asked trying to sound calmer than she felt at hearing that.

"He fell, hit his head, and broke his neck." He looked back at the children. He managed a smile for them but she saw it wasn't without effort. She also noted he was wearing a different jacket.

"You got yours back," she said. It was an inane comment, but she wanted him to meet her gaze. He didn't.

"Yes." He looked then at the two old people standing on the porch and looking forlorn. "I will see you both to The Dalles if you wish."

"What would we do there, sir?" Jenks asked.

"Better than what you will do here. This will soon not be a safe place for you," he said in that level tone she had heard him use before in tense situations. It was steadying in dangerous times when common sense said panic, but it never was what Rand did.

She heard the sound of a shot at the same instant Rand ducked and drew his gun. He had fired before she half realized what happened.

Quickly he stalked to the woods, gun drawn, but not firing again. She followed, running to keep up with his long stride. Only then, did she see the body and recognize it as Jason. Rand knelt and felt for a pulse.

"He's dead?" she asked although it was obvious. She saw the bullet hole in his brother's forehead.

Rand nodded and rose with a sigh.

"He tried to kill you." It wasn't a question.

"I heard the whine of the bullet. It was that close. I didn't even know it was him until I reacted." He looked pale.

"He would have fired again if you hadn't." She put her hand on his arm.

"I know."

Jensen had come to stand beside him. "What do you want me to do, sir?"

"Throw his body over a horse. We'll take it and Lockwood's with us."

At that moment, the rest of Rand's company rode up. "He wasn't in any of the places you told us to look," the sergeant said. "The Campbell home had nobody in or around it."

Rand rolled a cigarette. "It's too late to get back to Watson. We'll camp outside town tonight. We can take one more look around before we leave in the morning."

"Couldn't we stay in town?" Smith asked.

"No. Tomorrow, we'll leave together and split up when the road goes north. You will take three squads to Watson along with these two bodies, have them buried there. Secure the plates, rifles and ammunition. I'll write the basics of what happened for you to give Murphy. It will tell him to send word to Schaeffer in The Dalles. For now, have

Murphy keep the plates and guns at Watson until Schaeffer says otherwise."

"And you?"

"I will take Coleman and one squad to get the children and Mrs. Morgan somewhere safe." He took a long draw on his cigarette.

"Where are you taking them?" Smith asked.

Blowing out the smoke, Rand said, "Where they will be safe." He then looked back at the two on the porch. "You two need to leave."

"I'm scared, sir," Sally said.

"With good reason. You are not accountable for what your boss was doing in the basement. That is unless you knew about it." He gave them a stern look.

"No sir, never had no idea at all," Sally said and Jenks nodded. "I'm just worried about the wee ones." She looked at the two children now at Belle's side.

"They will be safe. You need to make yourself safe."

Belle handed Jenks the same amount of money that she had given Sally. "Be on the first stage for The Dalles." She handed him a slip of paper. "Contact this man and tell him the situation here."

Jenks looked at the note and then back at her before he nodded.

Rand turned back then, securing the packs. Belle could see he was angry and looked exhausted. They had to get away from this place. She untied Sammy's reins and moved him nearer the porch. "I can take Jessica with me but who will let Jeremy ride with them?" She looked at the soldiers who were now regarding the whole thing with curiosity.

"I'd be proud, ma'am," a private said and urged his horse forward. "My name is Otis Sichy, son."

"Is that all right, Rand?"

He nodded, but she knew nothing was all right from what he saw on his face. He had just killed his brother, and she could only guess how that hurt. His father had betrayed him and now his brother would have killed him had he not missed. This was no place to help him through this, to say anything reassuring.

She lifted Jeremy behind Private Sichy and then Jessica in front of her saddle before she stepped up, put her arms around her, and turned Sammy ready to move out with the troop.

Rand mounted Blue in one swift motion still smoking the cigarette. He waved his left arm in the air motioning for the troop to head out. A few miles out of town, they found a copse of trees alongside the river and made camp.

She wanted to comfort him, but her first priority had to be the vulnerable children. After they ate, and the camp quieted down, she watched for an opportunity. He had written his report on a single sheet of paper, then sat smoking and moodily staring into the dark. She gave up trying to think of how she could help him with his pain. She had to husband her own strength and fell asleep with a child on each side.

In the morning while they ate breakfast, Rand and two squads went back into Canyon City on the small hope that Forester might have returned. An hour later, they were all heading west. They rode as a company until late afternoon when they came to where their roads went separate ways.

Jessica had snuggled against her. The child was still upset. She wished she could reassure her, but she was uneasy herself. Did Rand blame himself for killing his brother and for Lockwood's death? He had come close to death again. She was unsure what was making him so tense and whether she could offer words that would help.

With fewer men to command, she hoped he and she could at least talk when they took a break, but he didn't take one until they were two hours up the road. Then it was to water the horses in the river and give the men a break to stretch their legs, eat something, and drink from their canteens.

Clearly, he was in a dark mood, as he stood off by himself smoking. If she had not had Jeremy and Jessica to reassure, she'd have gone to him. As it was, she was torn. The children needed reassurance, since their lives had been upended yet again. Fortunately, Private Sichy was talkative, and Jeremy was interested in hearing his stories.

Belle walked to where Rand was staring at the river. "Are you all right?" she asked.

"Fine."

"Something is bothering you."

"I didn't get Forester. That's not good."

"But you got the plates and guns."

"But not the reason they existed. It also likely did little to stop his plans for a rebellion. The probability is he had more phony money stashed elsewhere. We could not search the whole town."

"What happened to your lieutenant?"

He shook his head with a bitter smile. "I think something got revealed he didn't want known. He tried to kill me."

"Rand!" She guessed she had known.

"I hit him, and he fell backward, hit his head on the printing press.

Irony, you might say. I'd have preferred he stayed alive but." He shrugged and then winced.

"You pulled a muscle?" She saw now that what she had taken as stress was also pain.

"No. Likely to keep his secret from being revealed, he knifed me. It didn't amount to much but..."

She interrupted. "Are you insane? You were wounded and again ignored having it tended?"

"It wasn't anything."

"I'll be the judge of that." She pulled him to one of the large boulders along the river. "Sit. Do you have medical supplies with you?"

"Some."

"My God, do you have no sense of self-preservation?" She was furious as she worked to help him get the jackets and then shirt off his shoulder. The entry wound wasn't a large one. Her concern went to how deeply had it gone. "Can you move your arm freely?"

"Yes. It's nothing."

"Maybe if you had gotten it treated right away. You lost blood."

He shrugged and then winced. "Only some."

"Have you heard of infection and blood poisoning?" Her anger was coming out of fear.

"It's not infected, is it?"

She was furious. "Not if he used a sterile knife. What do you think?"

He glared up at her. "That was not funny."

"Neither is a man who would ignore a wound that is probably infected. Do you have any sense at all where it comes to yourself?"

"I am used to working when I have minor injuries." He bit off the words, now as angry as she was.

"But you did not have to this time." She felt like screaming at him but that would not do much good for either of them. "Sergeant Coleman," she said raising her voice to get his attention. "Can you bring me your troop's medical supplies? The captain is injured."

Jeremy and Jessica came over to see the extent of the wound. Jessica quickly moved away, but Jeremy was fascinated. "Does it hurt?"

"The captain has no sense of feeling," Belle snapped, "so he wouldn't know."

Rand glared at her but softened the expression before looking at the boy. "Yes, it hurts some if I think about it."

"Get used to it," she said under her breath as she looked through the bag Coleman handed her. "It'll hurt worse before it's done."

"What do you mean?"

"I mean your supplies are limited. A bottle of whiskey, some bandages, surgical tape but no poultices or anything to reach the infection that I am sure is beginning deep within the muscle."

"It'll be fine," he said with a grim smile. "And don't scare the children."

She gave a snort. "When you fall off your horse, you think that might scare them?"

"I don't fall off horses."

"You may well do that this time. How far are we from the ranch?" If she could get him to her mother soon enough, maybe this wouldn't be as bad as she feared. She had seen such wounds that appeared minor and instead killed people. She gritted her teeth.

"How can you tell it's infected?" She could see he didn't like that idea.

She pressed alongside the cut and he jerked away from her. "It's swollen and the pain is how." She poured the whiskey over the wound, but it wouldn't go deep enough now to reach where the infection was brewing. The only hope was her mother's herbal remedies. Even a doctor might not have been able to save him if this went as deep as she feared, and the infection grew from within.

"About forty miles. We can't do it today, not with the children and you."

"I could do it, and we can carry them when they fall asleep. The sooner I can get you to Mama, the better this will go. I have no real experience with wounds other than opening them as I did that one you got from the Indian attack. It though was shallow. This is not. I can't open it. We have to draw the poison out."

"Did you notice the clouds moving in?"

"Another reason to hurry."

"A reason to camp out tonight. The moon is already less full. A horse with a broken leg won't get us there any faster—not to mention the risk of the Paiutes or Shoshone hitting us. No, we cannot get there tonight. We'll find a safe place to camp though, protected as much as possible in case it does rain." His tone said he would brook no different outcome.

She stopped arguing. She was frightened for him, but maybe he was right. He wasn't, however, considering what was best for him. As always, his concerns were for others.

She tried to push the edges of the wound apart as much as possible, pressed on the area to push out blood and a clear liquid. She poured the alcohol again over the wound, feeling some satisfaction at his angry hiss. Using what she hoped was clean water from the river, she washed away the blood before she applied a bandage.

No longer trying to hide his discomfort, he shrugged back into his shirt and jacket.

"Where did you find the coat?" she asked as she sat on the other boulder.

"In the basement."

"Strange."

He nodded with a sardonic smile. "More than you know." Jeremy was watching them, and so he said, "I'll tell you the rest later."

The boy looked at him with curiosity. "You are a captain."

"How do you know that?" Rand took a sip of the whiskey that Belle handed to him.

"They called you captain."

He pointed to the bars on his shoulders. "These are epaulettes. The two silver bars at each end mean captain. When I was in the war, I had a colonel's rank and that had two gold stars."

"Why aren't you a colonel now? Did you do something bad?"

Rand smiled "It was what they did when the war was over. Just everybody, pretty much lost rank. I think there was some thought that there had been too many promotions due to pressure of war."

"Were you mad at them then?"

"No, when you are in the military, you take what comes. Fighting it just makes you mad for no gain."

Jeremy looked at Belle. "Are you in the military too?"

"No."

He sighed and walked back to where Sichy was teaching Jessica how to play a game involving lines, circles and crosses in the dust.

"They are nice children," Rand said.

"They deserved better parents. After what Annie said, now I am wondering about what really happened to their mother. Forester being who he is, what might he have done to a woman in his way?" When he sighed his agreement, she wished she could take him in her arms but that wasn't possible even if it wouldn't have hurt him.

"We aren't all as lucky as you," he said as he rolled another cigarette.

She smiled. "You're right."

"So you've forgiven me for not letting you tend this wound right away?"

She wished she could kiss him. "Only if you promise not to die from it. If you die from it, I will never forgive you."

He smiled faintly as he lit the cigarette. "I'll do my best."

She watched him smoke. Even if he survived this, and though she could see he was starting to flush from a fever, he probably would, many things could kill him. She had been a fool to fall in love with a man living such a hazardous life. She had done it though when she'd been too young to weigh the costs. Maybe she understood for the first time why he had pushed her away ten years earlier. Maybe she'd even forgive him for causing them to miss all those years. Maybe.

CHAPTER 16

After one more night camping just south of where the river was joined by the North Fork, Belle could see Rand was running a substantial fever, but there was little she could do about it. They had to get to her mother, and she had to hope she would know what to do.

The children were tired but excited when they finally were on the road that led to the ranch. Although she had read the descriptions, she was shocked when she finally saw it nestled in front of tall pines, a stream not far below and a rocky ridge framing it to the north. The house was more lodge than cabin. One other cabin was at the far end of a long meadow with a third in the process of being constructed.

From the house, a tall man, with wavy, golden brown hair resting on his shoulders, strode out. "Captain," the man she guessed had to be Jed Hardman strode forward, "what brings you here?"

She saw the moment he saw her and then the children. "What's going on?" He smiled then. "This can only be one person."

She dismounted and tiredly lifted Jessica down from the saddle. "How do you know that? You've never met me."

"Saw a photograph and heard descriptions. He gave out a whoop that brought two women running out. She had eyes for only one. Tears began to roll down her cheeks as she recognized her mother. How had she stayed away so long? Her mother was also crying as she ran forward.

"Belle, Lord in heaven, thank God for mercies. Belle." And she drew her into her arms.

Raine was also smiling and laughing as she hugged Belle next. Amy was coming out next with flour all over her hands but she also laughed as she saw her little sister. "Finally you got here," she said as she gave her a big hug and a little swat on the rear.

It was then that she saw the old man with a white beard and a smile that sent her heart racing. "St. Louis," she cried as she threw herself into his arms. She wasn't just glad to see him but remembered how he had saved Matt's life with his medicine. Her hope for Rand's survival increased. Surely, between him and her mother, they could deal with whatever was happening with his wound.

Jed was looking up now at the soldiers. Rand had not dismounted and looked exhausted. "What's wrong, son?" he asked as he stalked over to Rand's horse.

"Who is this?" Raine asked as Jessica and Jeremy stood now beside Belle. "Do you have children?"

"Can I explain after we get Rand inside? He's been hurt."

Jed had just reached Rand when he sank forward on his horse. Only willpower and determination had gotten him this far. "Captain," Coleman yelled as he got to his side and helped Jed lower him from the horse.

"It's all right," Rand said straightening. "Just blacked out a minute."

"What is wrong?" Martha turned from her daughter to study him.

"He was stabbed four days ago now. He didn't get any treatment to begin. He's running a fever."

"All right, get him in the kitchen." Her mother looked then at the children. "And who might you two be?"

"Jer and Jessica," Jeremy answered looking around with curiosity.

"We are glad to meet you," Raine said. "We have some children here just about your ages. Laura, Elizabeth, and Rufus are with Toddy having a lesson in science. Elijah is out with Adam and Matt to get a deer. Amy, could you take them into the extra room and help them get settled."

Private Sichy took their bags off the horse and went with them.

"I have to get back to Watson," Rand said as he walked slowly up to the house.

St. Louis shook his head. "From the looks of it, you're not going anywhere but to bed for a few days, Captain, and that if you're lucky."

"No time for that."

Sergeant Coleman walked alongside him and Belle realized that he was making sure his captain didn't end up falling on his face. Rand looked back at the men who had dismounted and were waiting for orders. "Set up a bivouac for tonight," he said.

"Maybe the barn would be smarter," Jed said. "Looks like rain." He had taken Rand's other side.

Rand's face looked confused. "All right. Yes, the barn."

"We had a big roast last night," Raine said. "You men are welcome to come into the kitchen and get something to eat before you do that. You look hungry." The men smiled with appreciation and relief when Rand nodded.

Inside the house, Martha directed Rand to be taken to a small room off the kitchen. Raine was busy cutting bread and slabs of roast beef. "Take your shirt off," Martha said. "It seems with all the injuries here, we needed a small apothecary."

When he started to remove his jackets, Belle's hands were there first. He felt tired enough that he didn't complain as she also pulled away the shirt. Her mother's lips pursed as she looked at the angry wound. "You were stabbed?"

He nodded stoically bracing himself for the examination.

"Lie on your stomach on the cot. St. Louis, see what you think while I get some hot water," she said as she went back into the kitchen.

Belle took his good arm as she helped him lie back on the cot.

"I am not helpless," he protested.

"Maybe I just like doing it," she said with a smile she forced, which she probably intended to be reassuring but only looked worried.

With a sigh, he lowered himself. It did feel good to be lying flat and for the moment when he had nothing that he had to do. Jed Hardman would take care of the horses, of the men. While he needed to get back to Watson as soon as possible, falling off his horse wouldn't get him there. He felt St. Louis' strong fingers probing around the wound.

"Not good," the old man said muttering to himself. "What kind of blade was it?"

"Narrow, long, I guess, but not a big knife. It didn't bleed much."

St. Louis sighed. "Worse kind when they go deep."

Martha returned with a kettle of hot water, cloths and a bowl. She looked at St. Louis for affirmation. "I was thinking that we'd apply heat to this first. The biggest problem with a knife wound is the instrument is not clean. Bullets are better," she said with a smile, "if you have a choice next time."

"I'll remember that."

"I brung some herbs with me, but I don't like the looks of this. Startin' to streak too," St. Louis said with a gruff sigh.

Belle looked up at him stricken.

"Just mean it'll take longer, that's all." The old man smiled at her. "I brought what I use for injuries. Problem being getting it down to the source of the problem." With that, he was gone.

Martha put a bowl of hot water on the stand by the cot and handed a cloth to Belle. "Wash around it. Then soak the cloth in the hot water. Form it into a pad. Put it over the wound and press down." She looked down at Rand. "This will be painful, but it will help your body fight this infection." She looked back then at Belle. "As soon as the cloth cools, put it back in the hot water. Just keep doing it until the water is no longer warm. St. Louis and I will make some poultices which hopefully will draw the infection to the surface." She disappeared again.

Belle perched on the cot beside him. "You do have a habit of getting hurt," she said as she worked. "I see other scars."

"Wars aren't particularly healthy. I was lucky at that. Ouch, that does hurt."

"Sorry."

"I only wrote the quickest of explanations for Murphy. I need to get a more complete report to Watson regarding what I found at Forester's house and how Lockwood and then General Phillip's son died. I am too shaky. Could you write it for me?"

She heard the pain in his voice at both the physical and emotional wounds, as he no longer called Jason his brother. "If you dictate it."

"Thank you."

She enjoyed running the cloth over the muscles on his back. They were long and powerful without being bulky. His skin had a golden tan, which meant he must sometimes work outdoors without a shirt. She would love to see that. In fact, she'd love to see the length of him lying on his stomach with no clothing. He had muscular and beautiful, if that was the right word for a man, buttocks. She smiled at her awareness that since it was her thoughts—she could call it whatever she wanted. Either way, it'd not be happening anytime soon.

It was good that Amy had taken Jessica and Jeremy under her wing. This had to be so distressing for the poor babies. When the other children returned from their lessons, that would help. Then she remembered Raine had a baby who should be six months old. This place was alive with new life. When they had ridden up, she had been surprised at how instantly she had taken to the rugged mountains, tall trees, and that beautiful river. She had never really liked it around Oregon City, which partially explained her wanting to leave—among other reasons.

This place though, it spoke to her soul. The wildness, the rock formations, and yes, even the possible danger. She had never sought a calm and peaceful life. When she left Pinkerton, where would she find the right place for her, the right job?

Absently she continued to stroke Rand's back as she replaced the compresses. His eyes were closed. She wondered how much he liked it here. He would probably never want to give up the military life. Was it one she could live? It didn't look like the wives generally did live it. They waited somewhere for the few short hours they could be with their men. They raised their children mostly by themselves-- if they were even blessed with offspring. The Custers had not been.

Her mother and St. Louis returned, this time with a small bowl. Belle left her place at the bed for her mother. "This will hurt at first," her mother warned. "Yell if it helps."

Rand gave a little laugh, but she saw how he tightened his muscles in preparation. When the hot poultice made contact, he sucked in a hard breath. When he could finally talk, he choked out, "A bit, huh?" When the poultice cooled, she repeated it.

"Now this last one we will leave in place by bandaging it loosely. We will though need to do this three more times if all goes well."

"If it doesn't?" he asked.

"St. Louis will have to open it. We won't if we don't have to though, but it may be the only way if you have a pocket of poison deep inside."

"He will be all right, won't he, Mama?" Belle asked. She tried to hide her fear.

"He needs rest, lots of liquids and I have something for the pain. A tea. I'll be right back with that and then he'll just need to sleep."

The tea was bitter, but he drank it all. Before she left, he said, "Mrs. Stone, would you be able to bring me some paper and pen. I need to send a message back to Watson if I really am not going to be fit to go myself."

"You could try, of course," Martha said. "I doubt you'd make it." She smiled then. "I'll be right back." When she returned with pen, ink and paper, Belle took it.

"I'll be writing this for him."

"Good." The curiosity in her mother's eyes was evident, but she asked nothing before she exited the room. There would be questions, of course. Belle was dreading that, but her family deserved the truth. She was tired of living with lies.

"I appreciate you doing this, Belle. So write what I tell you." He described the underground room's layout, the press and the plates, the stacks of phony currency. He stopped then and she looked over at him. "I am just trying to think how to phrase this. There were jackets on the wall. One of them was mine. Nine jackets and coats. Two military. One was that of a lieutenant."

Then it was her turn to frown. "That's very strange. On the wall?"

"Nailed to it."

"For what possible reason can you imagine?"

"Everything I can imagine I don't want to think about." He grimaced. "Probably better to leave that out for now." He went on to explain what he wanted her to write which was about Lockwood's attack with the knife and the fight. When he concluded, he said, "That should be enough. If you want to write your own message to Pinkerton, you can send it with this. The men will take both to the Watson, where I will request it be sent to Colonel Schaeffer and yours can go along."

She sighed. "You're right. I should do that." While she worked out how to phrase what she had learned, the important events relating to it, and her having the children, she decided to make this also her resignation. Folding the paper, she looked over to see Rand seemed to be asleep. She felt exhausted herself, but she could no longer put off explaining to her family how she had come to be here.

In the kitchen, Amy and her mother were peeling potatoes and making biscuit dough. Raine had her nursing baby in her arms. St. Louis was sitting at the table drinking coffee.

"He's a beautiful boy, Raine," she said as she sat at the table beside her.

"Jesse."

"Where are Jeremy and Jessica?"

"They were tired, and I put them on our bed for a nap, explaining we'd be right here when they woke," Amy said.

"How does Rand seem to feel?" her mother asked as she poured hot water into a teapot.

"He's not good at admitting to pain; so I don't honestly know."

"I am concerned about the wound." Her mother poured her daughters and herself a cup of tea after St. Louis shook his head.

"Knives can turn real ugly, 'specially if they don't bleed enough," St. Louis said, his tone as somber as Belle had heard.

"I was afraid of that." She tried not to think what those words meant. "I hoped you could do something though to heal him."

"It went deep and is at the least infected. If what we've done doesn't reach that infection, we'll have to open the wound with a sterile knife and hope we can get something far enough down." Her mother sighed.

Raine put her baby down and came back to take her own cup. She and Amy both looked expectantly at Belle. "We are surprised to see you come riding up here with the soldiers and children," Amy said finally. "No letters, no word."

"Sorry."

"You know I didn't mean it that way."

St. Louis stood. "You gals wanta talk this out by yoreselves?"

"Sit back down," Martha said. "You are family and whatever Belle tells us, you will hear sooner or later anyway."

"I understand how you must feel. And yes, St. Louis. I am happy you are here." She smiled at him. "Your wisdom is always appreciated. I just wondered if it would be better I tell you now or wait until everyone is here." At that, she heard the sounds of boots on the porch and a door was flung open.

"We're back," Jed's deep voice came from the door as he swooped up his wife in a hug. Matt was just behind him.

"Toddy is with the children," Adam said coming in the door from the main room. "Laura said she'll look in on Jessica and Jeremy if they wake. It should be fine for now. She is a born mother." He grinned.

When they all sat at the table, Belle tried to think how to explain her lies. She hated the idea of disappointing her mother. Before she could start, she heard the door open. Rand had no shirt on and leaned against the doorway with that crooked smile.

"I was in better shape the last time I saw you," he said smiling at Adam.

Adam laughed and went to him, giving him an affectionate pat on his good shoulder.

"You should be in bed," Belle said with the proprietary way a woman had for her man. She knew it and could not stop herself. If her family wondered about that too, well there was a lot more coming, for them to get angry about.

Rand moved to sit at the table. "I figured there'd be a few questions and heard the horses ride up. Hard to sleep even with that witch's brew." He grinned at Martha. "No offense meant."

"None taken," she said, "but you better sit down before you fall down."

"I will have to give my men their orders."

"You'd fall on your ass if you try," Adam said heading for the door almost before he quit talking. "Which ones do you want? I'll bring them to you."

"Corporal Jensen and Sergeant Coleman. And thanks." He sunk in a chair. Belle could resist no longer and felt of his forehead. "Your fever is higher."

"I'll be fine."

It seemed only moments when Adam was back with the two soldiers.

"You don't look good, Captain," Coleman said.

"I'm not. You'll have to go back to the camp without me. Leave in the morning at first light. I'll be back when I can ride."

"You want us to bring men back here?" Coleman asked.

Rand shook his head. "Just get back and keep the camp secure. Watch for trouble and not just the Indian kind. Belle, will you give them the letters."

When she handed them to Coleman, Rand said, "Tell Murphy, after he reads mine, that he is to get the other two to Colonel Schaeffer in The Dalles. He will know what to do with them."

"We will bring out food for your men when it's ready," Raine told them as they left.

"You sure you have the energy to explain this?" Adam asked Rand.

"Probably not, but you need to know. My concern for a conspiracy at my earlier visit turned out to be very real. Thanks to Belle, I did find the press, retrieved the plates, what printed money was there, and rifles Forester had been buying. I didn't get him though."

"And Belle's involvement in this was?" Jed asked with that piercing gaze, which she saw was so much a part of him.

"I am a Pinkerton agent or was," Belle said. "I was sent to investigate William Forester by posing as a governess." She looked over at her mother and expected to see more shock than she did.

"I did wonder," Martha said. "I must admit it wasn't on my probable list of what was leading to your traveling and the mystery as to where you lived, or why you didn't want me visiting."

"Most of the time I wasn't there."

"Why hadn't we heard you were in Canyon City?" Jed asked as he got up and moved to the counter, leaning back against it with his boots crossed in front of him. She could certainly see why Raine called him the laird.

"Actually I was there as Mrs. Morgan."

"You've been married and not told me?" her mother asked, for the first time with a hurt expression.

"I had lied to Alan. Alan does use women, but not young, single women. I made up a dead husband to get the job. But then, of course, lying is a way of life for a spy."

"I guess I understand." She saw her mother didn't. She would try to explain why she became a Pinkerton later-- if she even could.

"I didn't tell you I was in Canyon city because I had chosen that life. You had not. In the beginning, I had no clue that it went beyond counterfeiting, which was bad enough. By the time I knew how ruthless Mr. Forester was, I had no way to get word to you or even Alan. I didn't know who I could trust in Canyon City. I also could not afford to lose my cover as it might've meant my life... would have meant. And could have endangered you all. I didn't know about the broader conspiracy until Rand and I were able to talk."

"After she had saved my life at grave risk to her own."

"What happened?" Amy asked her own expression turning to worried more than annoyed.

"You tell them," Rand said.

Jed got up and went to the sideboard to bring out a bottle of whiskey. He turned to look at St. Louis and Matt. "I know Adam, Rand, and I could use one. How about you two?"

"Yeah," Matt said, while St. Louis shook his head but took a refill of his coffee cup from Martha.

As Rand sipped his whiskey, he felt the warmth through his body. He didn't expect the energy to last long, but it helped. He wished for a smoke. He didn't have the energy to go outside for one. He'd have to tough it out.

"My part in the first attack on Rand began when a woman I knew from the stagecoach ride down came to my door," Belle said.

"First?" Adam asked.

Belle nodded. "She told me that the captain was being brutalized. She was frightened for her own life and didn't like what she had seen. I gave her money to help her get out of town. I just hope she was able to do it.

"Because I had figured, from the time I realized what kind of man Forester was, that I might have to leave Canyon City fast, I had made some preparations. Realizing Rand was in trouble, I headed for the stable, got my horse and gear. Before I could go to the house, where she had said he was held. I saw three horses go past, heading north. One had a body draped over it. I made an assumption that it was Rand or his body." She swallowed and let out a breath. "I followed but at a distance enough to avoid being seen."

"My God, you were brave," Jed said with admiration in his voice.

"I wasn't thinking of anything then but that if he could be saved, I

had to stay with them and not be seen. I... I could not let him die."
Rand saw the effort she was making not to cry.

"They turned off the main road and onto a side road. Because
they had slowed down, I felt they were looking for a certain place. I
left Sammy, my horse, took my Henry and went on foot to avoid any
chance they would see me. I couldn't wait. I was afraid... Earlier I had
come across a man who had been murdered, his throat slit. I feared
they would do that to Rand if he wasn't already dead.

"When I got to where they had dismounted, I heard them talking
and one started toward Rand with a knife." She sucked in a breath. "I
shot and killed them both."

"That took real guts, lady," Adam said.

She managed a smile as she looked at him, Matt, and then St.
Louis. "Between you three and my father, I had good teachers.
Anyway, I did what I had to. When I got to him, Rand's pulse was
strong, but he was unconscious. I could only think I had to get him
away from there in case others came. I rigged a travois." She smiled
again at Adam. "I was paying attention to those lessons you
taught me."

His smile was tight. "You are a Stevens in all the ways that count

"When I got Rand to where I thought it would be safe, where
there was water, I started to treat his wounds. He'd been hit hard on
the head. More had been done to him." Again, she stopped and took a
breath. "He came to, and well that is when we learned what we had
each been doing."

"You are both lucky to be alive," Matt said. Rand knew the truth
of that. He tried to think if he'd left anything unsaid.

Martha sighed. "I don't have any words of wisdom right now
except... We need to get dinner ready." She rose and reached over to
feel of Rand's forehead. "Your fever is up. If it's not down by morning, we will have no choice but to open the wound."

He let out a breath.

"You should lie down, Rand," Belle said, worry in her voice. "Let
me apply the poultice again."

"Help him to the second bedroom beyond the great room," Raine
said to Jed as she headed for the stove. "He'll be more comfortable
there than in the treatment room."

"I am fine. I can walk there by myself," Rand said rising and
feeling a momentary faintness that he fought it back.

Adam went to his other side and he and Jed brooked no argument.
As the three of them walked into the great room, six sets of children's

eyes looked up from the game they had been playing with Toddy. "You okay, Captain?" Toddy asked as he rose.

"Fine. Just tired." He knew this was a lot more than tired. He wasn't just in pain at the site of the wound but felt sick and weak. His whole body ached. Blood poisoning. He'd seen it with others. Most of the time it was fatal.

CHAPTER 17

B elle had hoped to follow Rand but stopped when she saw the worry on Jeremy and Jessica's little faces. Jed and Adam would get Rand settled. She needed to reassure her charges. She had disrupted their lives, and they had every reason to wonder why. How much could small children understand of the situation?

She only knew her mother had come with her when she settled onto the long sofa. "So tell me your names?" her mother asked with that voice, which had reassured so many children. Belle hadn't seen her mother in nearly five years. She seemed to have changed little in not only her beauty, but her compassion for others.

"Jessica." The little girl looked on the verge of tears.

"Do you know we have a toy box?" her mother asked.

"I don't like toys anymore," Jeremy said with the surly look Belle now saw as his backup mode.

"Goodness. Not even when some are toy ships and soldiers?"

Jeremy's expression changed. "They have toy soldiers, like Captain Phillips?"

"Mostly these are from another war. Have you heard of Napoleon?"

Jeremy looked at Belle. "A French general?" he asked.

"Yes, that's the one. Well these soldiers look more like part of his army. They are made of metal, and you can set them up into various battle lines. Rufus and Elijah sometimes play with them."

He looked at the older boys. "They still play? My father said playing is for babies like Jessica."

"We just play different ways," Eli said with a smile.

Jeremy showed interest. "I could... uh look at how you do it. Are you two uh cousins?"

Eli grinned. "I'm his uncle."

Rufus gave a low growl. "And thinks he can boss me, but he can't."

"Why don't you boys show Jeremy the box in your room. I am thinking we need to set up the extra bed there. Would you mind sharing your room with him while he is here?"

"It'd be fine," Eli said.

"Eli has taken to sleeping here in the bunkroom with Rufus," Raine said. "It is kind of fun for them. There is another bed in there."

"All right, and my name is Jer... to my friends."

With that, the three boys were off.

"You can share Elizabeth and Laura's room, if you like, Jessica, or do you also have a nickname you prefer?"

The little girl's lower lip pursed out. "Jessica." She looked on the verge of tears.

"We'll show you the room," Laura said. "We'd like having you there. I have a doll you might like." She smiled with that motherly attitude she tended to have to all the younger ones.

In moments, they were gone leaving Toddy, Belle, and her mother sitting on the sofa. Belle felt near tears herself.

"Dinner is almost ready. Do you think Rand will want to eat?" Amy asked as she and St. Louis joined them.

"You won't like this much," St. Louis said, a somber expression on his face, "but can't wait to open that knife wound up. That fever, the swelling, his weakness, the boy has blood poisoning."

"That kills people," Belle said unable to stop the tears.

"It can, but it won't Rand." The confidence in her mother's voice helped Belle get hold of herself. "I already started steeping a concoction that will strengthen the body's humors. It's made of turmeric, garlic and honey. He will have to drink that every two hours. Then we'll use St. Louis' yarrow poultice. It's applied warm and draws out the poison, but, I am afraid, you're right, old friend. First, we have to open the wound as far down as we can safely go. I have had good results with using salt in a wound to draw out poisons, but a knife can go so deep that it's hard to get it down that far. This all is going to be very painful, and we have no opiates to ease it for him."

"He's a tough one," St. Louis said. "I saw it in his eyes. Even when he was just a youth and facing war with no fear."

"I remember the time you brought him to our cabin to take Adam with him south," Martha said.

"He's always had grit," the older man said. "He'll pull through, but it's gonna to be a hard week—for him and you." His gaze was on Belle. She wondered if he saw her as tough enough.

"I started a soup for him," Amy said. "After we eat, you can take it to him." She looked at Belle with a knowing expression in her eyes. "Do you remember on the wagon train, when Mama and St. Louis pulled Matt through what should have killed him? They will Rand. Come on, let's eat dinner before it dries up."

"I am not hungry," Belle said feeling something grabbing her stomach such as she had never felt. She'd been in dangerous situations, even when she saw Rand unconscious, she had felt fear, but this was worse. She'd had a taste of what life might be like with him and now she feared he would die.

"You love him, don't you?" her mother said and Belle realized she had been watching her.

"I don't know..." She could deny it no longer. "Oh yes, I do. Yes, I love him for all the good it can do."

"I should have seen it," her mother said.

"I did." Raine had entered the room when Belle had not seen her.

"How could you?" Belle asked now crying. "I wasn't here."

Raine smiled. "No, I saw it in him. It was a year ago right before Thanksgiving. He had come here after saving Jed's life in The Dalles. It was on his face when your name came up and he looked at the photograph of you. I knew it then."

"You didn't say anything," her mother said.

Raine shook her head. "Because I never dreamed Belle would feel the same." She smiled softly. "You have been such a run around, sister dear." She reached out and wiped away a tear. "I never imagined he had a chance with you."

When her mother handed her a handkerchief, Belle wiped her eyes. "I've loved him since I first met him in Oregon City, but he said I was too young. He left, and I thought... Well anyway it still seems impossible."

"Because you want to go back to the big city and be a Pinkerton?" Amy asked.

"No, not that." Belle sniffled. "I just don't know how I'd manage as the wife of a cavalry officer. I know a lot about what that life is like. I'd be always waiting somewhere for him." More tears. For a woman who had rarely cried, she was becoming a virtual fountain.

Her mother rose. "Why don't we keep him alive first, and then you can figure out the rest. I know it can seem complicated. It did for me with Adam, but it's amazing how often it ends up simple." She smiled, patted Belle's shoulder and with St. Louis at her side, headed for the kitchen.

Jed and Adam walked into the great room. "We got him down, but he's not looking good," Jed said. He looked then for the first time at the teary Belle. "Of course, with Martha and St. Louis here..."

"Where are the children?" Adam asked as he settled on the sofa.

"Getting adjusted to the change of two new ones. Laura is thrilled." Amy smiled. "She loves playing mama, and Jessica is more than ready to be mothered."

"You have raised wonderful children," Belle said almost instinctively touching her own belly. She had not had a period since she made love with Rand but that didn't mean she was pregnant. It hadn't been long and she had also had a lot of stress. For the first time she knew if she was pregnant, she'd be happy about it. She never had imagined wanting a child of her own.

She looked up and realized they were all looking at her. She managed a smile. "All right, I told Mama, Amy and Raine. I am in love with him."

Adam was the only one not smiling. "And how about him?"

"I don't know."

"He better hope he doesn't survive this if he doesn't do right by you," he said with a tone she'd never heard before.

She met his gaze levelly. "I am a grown woman, Adam. I will take care of this without you threatening him."

Jed laughed. "I think I could use another whiskey. This family is getting too complicated for a simple southern boy." He headed for the cabinet and poured a shot for himself and Adam.

Josh came in from the kitchen. "Supper is ready," he said. "Matt is taking it out to the troopers."

In moments, they had all gathered at the table where plates of boiled potatoes, roast beef, squash, and biscuits were heaped. Martha stood at the end and said a simple grace before they passed the food. As they ate, there was little talk but probably a lot of thinking. Belle didn't want to eat, but she hadn't eaten more than a few bites for two days. She forced herself to eat as much as she could.

"You said something about soup?" she asked looking at her mother.

"Yes." She rose and gave her a tray with two cups, one was a herbal concoction, bowl, spoon, and towel. There was no argument as to who should take it to Rand. "Tell him in about half an hour, we will be in there to... well do what we can to open that wound and get the healing started."

When Belle entered the bedroom, she saw a double bed, plain dresser, and Rand lying on his belly under covers to his waist and twisting restlessly. His eyes came open when she closed the door.

"I should get up," he muttered.

"You should stay right where you are. Mama will be here soon to treat your wound. In the meantime, can you sit up to eat?"

He gave her one of his looks but twisted and levered himself to a sitting position, propping his good shoulder against the headboard. "I'm not hungry though," he said in a surly tone. His brooding expression told her that he wasn't going to take well to being a patient.

"Drink the tea first. Mama said it will help your body fight this."

"What was in that?" he asked grimacing as he drank it all.

"She didn't say but if it's what I remember from being a child, most likely turmeric, honey and garlic." She grinned at his expression as she sat on the edge of his bed, holding the tray until he had finished the tea.

"You have to marry me now," he said as he unenthusiastically sipped at the chicken broth.

"I do?"

"We both know I might die from this. What if you are pregnant?"

"You won't die, and I don't want a deathbed wedding." She also wanted to hear him say he loved her. She had heard what Raine believed, but she wanted the words from Rand. His rejection of ten years earlier still stung. She knew nothing had been settled between them. They still hadn't resolved what kind of life they would have.

He set the soup down. "I don't want my son or daughter to be bastards."

"They won't be, and there is no baby."

"You know that for certain?"

"Well, not for certain. Look, my love, I am quite capable of raising a baby without a man around."

"God, you are stubborn. Think of the child."

"If I realize I am pregnant, and when you are better, we can discuss this again. But for now, no."

He swore but didn't argue as she helped him lie back down. He sucked in a breath to get control of the pain. "It seems I've done nothing but get injured since I saw you again. You must think I am useless."

She smoothed the hair back from his forehead. "I think you lead a dangerous life, but remember how my father was killed."

"Toppling a tree as I recall."

"Which split when it should not have. Life just is what it is."

"You would say that being a Pinkerton." She could see he worked for a smile.

"Well, it did condition me some to the idea of danger. I sent my resignation with the letter to Alan."

"You sure you don't want to keep on with it?" He clenched his jaw. There was so little she could do to help with the pain and it hurt her to see how he was suffering. She forced her mind from it.

"I am tired of living a lie. I will find something else."

"Marry me." He managed again that tired smile, and she loved him even more for the effort.

Before she could answer, Adam. St. Louis, and her mother entered the room. "You know what we have to do," Martha said. "It won't be much fun."

"Nothing much has been recently."

His gaze turned to Adam who was watching him with cold eyes. "You and I will talk when you're better," Adam said with none of the friendliness that had always been there.

"I figured as much."

"St. Louis is going to open the wound," Martha said as she brought thick towels to put under his shoulder and then roll on the mattress on each side of him. Belle moved out of the way.

"Adam," St. Louis said, "I need you to hold his shoulder down."

"I won't move."

"No man can guarantee that. Gonna hurt like blazes. First, the knife goes in and slowly finds the path the original knife took. Then me and Martha gonna press on the wound to get out all the pus. After that comes the hardest part."

Rand gave a little laugh as he looked up from the corner of his eye.

"I will have to pour very salty water in the wound," Martha said. "That will be agonizing, but salt is good for drawing out infection. The salt water can get where the sterile blade cannot."

He nodded. "All right."

Adam handed him a small stick. "Bite down on it."

"You'd rather not hear me scream," Rand said with an attempt to joke.

"I'll save that for later."

Belle realized Rand hadn't been wrong about her stepfather's attitude toward him if he saw him as not doing right by her.

"Rand asked me to marry him," she said with the words out of her mouth before she'd thought of how the pressure would now transfer from Rand to her, and that this wasn't the right time for such a discussion.

"Ah," her mother said. "And so, what did you say, dearling?"

"That I won't."

All three looked up at her and Rand took the stick from his mouth. "But she will." He put it back in, but before he laid his head down, he winked. The simple gesture made her again fight back tears.

"What can I do to help?" she asked as St. Louis took a long, thin blade from the tray. It looked lethal.

"Get on the other side of the bed and along with your ma, put all your weight on his other shoulder. I know you won't mean to move," he said looking down at Rand. "The body can sometimes react despite the mind."

Rand nodded. He tightened his muscles and bit down as hard as he could on the stick as he felt the knife enter his shoulder. "I gotta angle this slow like to feel where the blade went and get to that pocket o' poison," the old man said with a calming voice as he worked by feel and instinct.

It seemed forever as he strained every muscle to lie still. Finally, the blade slid out, he gave a groan of relief.

"Now we gotta express as much of the pus as possible. The more we can force out, the easier it is for your body to fight this," he said, his rough voice surprisingly soothingly as he began slowly pressing and then with more pressure. "At least, this won't be doin' more injury." He could hear the smile in his voice. "Just feel like it."

As the pressure and pain built, he bit back down on the wood. The pain was worse than the original attack had been. It seemed to go on forever.

"We got quite a bit out," St. Louis said taking a cloth and washing away a thick putrid fluid. "Not much longer now but one more step."

Martha had moved and poured a liquid onto the wound that soon turned into a burning agony. He sucked in a breath as again he bit down on the stick.

It was long moments or maybe it wasn't, he lost track of time, before a warm soothing substance was patted onto the wound, followed by tying a loose bandage around his shoulder to keep the poultice in place.

As the pain eased a little, he managed to say thanks.

"Wish I could say it was over, son, but may need to do it again. We need to get rid of those red streaks. There's more now than when we first saw the wound. Now, try to sleep for a bit. Rest will help yore body do its work."

"Want a whiskey?" Adam asked. "It might help."

He let out a breath. "Yeah."

"You need to rest too, Belle," Martha said.

"But..."

"No, little gal," St. Louis said. "You get sick and won't be doin' him no good." Belle sighed but left with them.

A few moments later, Adam returned with the glass and whiskey, Rand rolled onto his side and managed to get an elbow under him. Adam helped him to a sitting position.

"There is a pastor down at Monument. Comes in once in awhile. Want I should get him?"

Rand snorted. "I didn't get the impression that idea was going over well."

"What she wants and what is good for her are two different things. She's quite a woman but the most stubborn of the Stevens women, and that's going some."

"I know that. Of course, that stubbornness saved my life, so I can't find too much fault with it." He took a sip of the whiskey wishing again for a cigarette. By the time he was up to going outside to get one, maybe he'd have broken the habit—although as it stood, for what lay ahead of him, he needed the relief they gave him. For a while longer anyway.

"You love her?" Adam asked sitting back and looking relaxed, but Rand knew the question meant he was anything but.

"I've been in love with her since I met her ten years ago in Oregon City. I never told her how I felt because it seemed the wrong time. I left to get away from what I saw as a mistake for both of us."

"And now?"

He shook his head. "I've asked her several times to marry me. Demanded even, but I can't say this is still a good time. This Indian war isn't over. I have a feeling the situation with Forester isn't either. His children are here. If he figures that out, this could turn ugly for you all."

"How would he find out?"

"I was told there is one traitor at the fort, don't know who. Maybe more than one. The letters we sent might not have been smart given that. Might be smart if you and your family got out of here."

Adam considered that. "You know I won't run."

"I knew that. None of you will. He's got an excuse to come here now. They are though his children unless I can kill him. And, I wouldn't mind killing him if he gives me half a chance." Either the whiskey was going straight to his head or the wound was sapping more of his strength, but he began to feel drained.

Adam reached over and helped him lie back on his stomach. "Sleep for now. Tomorrow will take care of itself. It always does."

"Just one thing more." He had to get this out.

"I'm listening."

"Keep Belle safe. That man is a monster. Don't take anything for granted with him. He is likely to have figured out, one way or another, that she betrayed him. He shouldn't know she was a Pinkerton, unless he gets hold of that letter, but it won't matter, he's the kind to look for revenge."

"All right. I'll take that into account. I wish I could keep you safe too."

Rand looked up and saw the smile. The man didn't yet know that Belle could be pregnant. He might yet turn angry at Rand for taking what he had no right to. He didn't know how to make that right, not with Belle unwilling to marry him. Adam's friendship was the most important one he'd ever had. He wouldn't blame him if he couldn't forgive him when he understood all that had happened. He wasn't sure he could forgive himself. He should have been more responsible. Should have…

When he woke, Belle was in the chair alongside his bed. There was a lamp burning. "You should go to bed," he croaked.

She came to him, lifted his head, and put a glass of water to his lips. When he had drunk all he would, she lowered him. "I am supposed to change the poultice. How do you feel?"

"Like I got stabbed twice." He had to work for a smile, but it was worth the effort when she smiled back.

At least the changing of the poultice didn't hurt. It felt soothing. It could do little though for the pain that seemed to be in all his muscles. He understood what he was facing. He'd seen men with lesser wounds die. He had not been as naive about the risk from a knife attack as he had indicated. He had though been determined to get Belle to the ranch where she would be safe. Or as safe as anywhere would be until Forester was locked up or dead. Then he thought of a concern.

"Belle, in the morning, I need you to write another letter for me."

"To whom?"

"Colonel Schaeffer. Can your family get a letter to The Dalles through the mail?"

"I think so, but why?"

"We both sent our letters with Sergeant Coleman. What if he or Murphy is also part of Forester's organization? Or they got waylaid?"

She tightened her mouth as she considered that. "What can we do about it?"

"A test-- when we get word to Schaeffer... another way."

"All right, what shall I say?"

He was feeling fuzzy headed. The pain seemed to fill his body. He had to work to get his thoughts together. "Just write what we found, where the letters went and how they were sent. Where the plates should be. Although they are no longer... usable, no one but I know that. And about the guns. Explain and..." He tried to make his thoughts come together.

"All right. I will do it. Now stop worrying about it, Rand. Concentrate on you for once."

He was silent a moment. "Are the streaks still there?"

"Yes. You need to now think pleasant thoughts," she said. "You're scowling and that cannot help your body fight back."

"Tell me you'll marry me and that'll be a pleasant thought." He looked up and saw the frown on her face. "Belle, I want you to be my wife."

"For what life?"

"We can work that out later. We kind of jumped the gun with this anyway. Let's go the rest of the way and work out the life later."

"Can we talk about it when you are on your feet?"

"Do I have a choice?" Now he was wondering if there was another reason she was saying no. Maybe she didn't love the man he was. Sometimes dreams were so powerful that reality was a disappointment. Was that the situation with Belle?

She smoothed the hair back from his forehead. Then began to massage his back muscles, working them to ease the tension in them. She was good at it and despite the pain, he felt himself begin to relax. He was not happy he'd gotten no answer, but when he got on his feet, he would have one.

CHAPTER 18

Belle only left him to sleep after Raine came to take her place. They had agreed to take shifts and replace the poultices all night. She got up once in the middle of the night to take two hours and was replaced by Amy finally to sleep until morning.

When she woke, she badly needed a bath but that would have to wait if it was even possible. She thought then of the luxury of staying in one of Chicago's best hotels with hot water and a big tub. That kind of luxury was one of the things she did miss when living so far from civilization.

She debated putting on the dress she had retrieved when at Forester's home, the only dress she now had, but decided not to put on clean clothes over her dirty body. Dressed in the only other clothes she had, she went to check on Rand. He was sleeping, seemingly more soundly, but he was burning up with fever and the red streaks were beyond the bandage. She felt fear rush through her, the kind of fear she had never known. She would not lose him—but how could she hold him?

In the kitchen, her mother was slicing bacon strips. "I think he will be all right," she told her with that reassuring tone she had heard from her since childhood.

Belle poured herself a cup of coffee. "He is desperately sick."

"Yes, but he's a strong man and young. It all works in his favor."

"And you. You two will be the ones who save him if he lives."

"There is one more thing we can try if the red streaks don't start to recede in a few hours. St. Louis told me about it. Bread poultice."

"Bread?"

"Yes, I've not had reason to try it, but St. Louis said it works and nobody knows why. Evidently, you put a slice or two of dried bread over the wound, pour some water over it and then bandage it in place. I am not sure why, but he says that it fights deep infection, ones that are affecting the whole body. If it gets worse, we will have nothing to lose by giving it a try."

Belle stiffened. She couldn't think he could die. She had to concentrate on something else. The job. "I need to get a letter to The Dalles. How hard is that to do?"

"Of course, we don't have regular mail delivery out there, but a postal office is not too far away. Dayville. Is this an emergency?"

"Rand thinks it is."

"Write it, and then we'll ask how to get it there."

Raine came in with Jesse in her arms. "This was a long night."

"I appreciate your taking a turn with Rand," Belle said as Raine settled Jesse into a crib, handing him a rattle and a carved animal, which seemed to fascinate him if his cooing sounds were any indication.

"Since it appears he's going to be one of the family," Raine said, "it's important to get him healthy again." She smiled at Belle's look of uncertainty. "That is if you want him to be in the family."

"That's not decided."

"Oh that sounded like our Arabelle," Amy said as she entered catching the tail end of the conversation. "Never make things easy."

Another time Belle might have felt annoyed, but this time she had to agree. "What can I do to help with breakfast?" she asked rather than spit back a sharp response.

"Gathering the eggs would help," Raine said as she looked in the cupboard. "I think scrambled eggs might be good for Rand this morning."

"Where is the hen coop?" She liked that idea. Getting out of the house would be good for her nerves.

"I'll show you." Amy pulled on boots and a jacket and handed Belle a basket.

The coop had been built sturdily, which was essential, given all the varmints in the region. It had an equally impressive wire cage around the outside. "Matt dug the wire deep," Amy said as she showed her the door in the back. Inside they could access the egg boxes from a room that stored grain in tight barrels. One hen, unwilling to give up her egg, had to be pushed off. The rooster looked at them suspiciously.

"There are two dozen laying hens, half a dozen pullets, and four hens that Mama is saving for stewing. If more of us end up living here and as the children grow, we will need more."

"This is an impressive yield." She had two dozen full sized and one tiny one in her basket.

"When men work hard, they eat heartily. This place takes a lot to keep eight men fed as well as children growing up so fast."

"I can imagine. Well," she laughed. "I can't but will take your word for it."

"We process a lot of vegetables and now have several fruit trees beginning to produce. Mostly though we have bought the fruit from a farm down in Kimberly, beyond Monument."

"When I was in Canyon City, I studied the map to get an idea of where I'd have to go if I had to leave fast. I have a general idea of the country here."

"You have been quite the adventurer."

Belle looked over and saw only a smile on Amy's face. "There was a time you wanted adventure," Belle said as they put the feed out for the hens and then secured the door to head back to the kitchen.

"And I have lived one." Amy's smile widened. "It wasn't what I expected. I married this man, who had been my friend since as far back as I could remember. I adore him and find every moment with him exciting even in the mundane moments. It's about getting to know more about him through the stages of life, having children together— it's been an adventure such as I never dreamed."

"It's what most women want, I guess." Belle sighed as they stepped up on the porch.

Amy reached out to stop her. "Everyone has to find their own adventure, Belle. Maybe this place isn't it for you. Maybe it's not Rand. Don't let anyone push you into what isn't right for you."

Belle looked at her with surprise. "I thought you'd be the one most wanting me to marry Rand. Haven't you always said I was selfish?"

Amy laughed. "Did I say that? Well, maybe, baby sister, I am just as feisty as you are, and we butt heads. Might that be the case?"

Belle smiled and felt a sense of relief. "I would love it if we could be friends."

"We are sisters. Isn't that enough for you?" Amy giggled.

"Sisters you don't have a choice about. Friends though, those you choose. I always felt a little apart from you and Raine, being so much younger, but now it doesn't seem there is that difference."

"Put the egg basket down, sister," Amy ordered. When she did, Amy grabbed her in a hug. "Yes, we are friends. And I will love hearing about all your adventures."

Before Belle could respond, the door opened. "Eggs, please?" Raine said as she reached for the basket.

"Please tell the children, it's time to get up," Martha asked Belle, from where she was frying bacon.

Belle headed back down the hall and looked in on Rand before she went to the children's rooms. The girls were already whispering and so she opened the door without knocking. Jessica seemed enamored of whatever Laura was telling her. She looked up at Belle. "Samhain," she said. "That's what it is next week. Did you know that?"

"No, I did not. What does it mean?"

"It's when we play games and bob for apples, and something Uncle Jed called Puicini. It's kind of fortune telling. Do you think that's bad?"

Belle smiled. "Not at all. How do you play it?"

"You are blindfolded and then there are four saucers in front of you. They are moved around. The one you choose is what your next year will be full of."

"And the saucers are each?"

"Earth, water, beans, and money. I guess we all want money as not sure what the others would mean." Laura grinned. "Uncle Jed said they do this from where he came. It's a nighttime game. He said sometimes even with fireworks. I haven't yet gotten to do it but they said we will tomorrow night."

"It sounds like great fun especially the bobbing for apples."

"It might be pagan." Laura's face took on a worried expression.

"It doesn't sound like that," Belle said as she helped Jessica out of her nightgown and into a dress. "It sounds like it is nature oriented. Working the earth and it yielding all you wanted, would be like a garden. The water would be maybe a trip." She smiled as she considered other options. "Or enough rain to keep the land good. "Beans would be food, and of course, we know what money is, don't we."

"He said they sometimes decorate for it too. It's also about the ones who... went before us. Kind of, I think."

"Then even better."

"Except, he said sometimes there are ghost stories," Laura said. "That might be scary."

Now Elizabeth and Jessica looked worried. "What's a ghost?" Jessica asked.

Laura looked at Belle for help.

"Well ghost stories are just for fun. They are supposed to scare us but in a way that we know it's not real. So you get tingles up your spine." She reached over and tickled up Elizabeth's back. "And they can be about mysteries where nobody knows what really happened, and they tell stories to try and figure it out. Does your Uncle Jed have some ghost stories that he shares?" she asked trying to turn this back to Laura. She hoped she had said nothing to interfere with what Amy had been teaching.

"Uncle Jed said he would tell us one. One he had been told when he was a little boy. It has to be in the dark though. He said anyone could tell a ghost story if they wanted. Do you know any?"

Belle smiled remembering how she had admired her older sisters and wanted them to show interest in her. Now she had a niece. She had not thought how important a responsibility that was.

"Well, if I think of one, I'll definitely share it."

Laura, Elizabeth and Jessica smiled broadly.

"And I forgot," Belle said, "head to the kitchen. Breakfast is ready."

She knocked on the boys' room. When no one answered, she opened the door a crack. They had already gotten up.

She found a table in the great room and wrote the details of what she had found and what Rand had done. She sealed it into an envelope addressed to Colonel Schaeffer. She hoped Rand was worried for nothing, but there was no way to be sure. This letter would be a reasonable precaution.

Back in the kitchen, the children were gathered at one end of the long table. Jed Hardman was leaning back against a counter and sipping his coffee as he talked to Matt. Adam and St. Louis were at the table with the men she had been told were the Kalama brothers, Josh, Jed's half-brother, and Toddy. It was a crowded mix of laughter and talking with the women doing the serving of mounds of food.

"Belle," her mother said, "eat now, and then take a plate to Rand. Maybe he will eat today." The request left Belle with mixed emotions. While she wanted to bring Rand his food, she also didn't want the family to have too many expectations.

"I will take him breakfast," Adam said rising. "I'm done." Before anyone could argue with him, he was gone with a tray.

"I'll saddle the horses," Josh said as he headed out the door. "How many today?"

"Four should do it," Jed answered. "Won't take many of us to bring down the cattle in the north section. I want most of you to stay here."

"Why?" Josh asked.

"Just because."

Josh laughed and went out.

197

"Are you expecting trouble?" Raine asked as she heated up coffee for everyone.

"Not especially, sugar," Jed said, "but better safe than sorry. Isn't that a proverb or something?" He rolled and lit a cigarette. "I would like you two," he said looking at the Kalama brothers, "to check along the river for tracks. If you see strangers, fire off two quick rifle shots. Don't try to stop them. Just let me know. I won't be that far away."

"I need to get this letter posted," Belle said holding it out for Jed to see. "How will that be possible?"

He looked at her a moment and nodded. "All right. Joe and George can get it down to Dayville. Jack, you hang down by the river and keep an eye out for unwelcome visitors."

"So who is staying at the house?" Toddy asked as he helped himself to another hotcake.

"You, of course, and Adam. I will take Raine with me." He gave her the kind of smile that had Belle looking away. She saw what they had and knew her mother had that, had had it twice-- first with her father and now Adam. She had wanted it too. She might have the man now—if she was willing. Was she woman enough to claim that kind of partnership relationship?

Raine's smile was wide as she ran for her change of clothing.

"So she works with the cattle?" Belle asked Jed, sipping her coffee and trying to adjust to this crazy world.

"Good at it as I am. Fancy, her mare, has a real knack for getting the cattle moving. We'll take Ace. Deucy should stay here. She never got a feel for cattle. When she goes out, they drive her instead of her them." He grinned.

For the first time Belle was aware of two dogs who had come to alert when their names were mentioned. They were so well-behaved, that they'd not made their presence known.

"Pretty dogs," she said. She saw Jessica was uneasy with them.

"Cattle dogs. Or Ace is," Jed said. "Deucy likes children, doesn't she, Liz?" he asked Elizabeth.

"Sure does."

Raine came back in the kitchen this time wearing pants, boots, hat and a leather coat. "My God," Belle said with a laugh, "my sophisticated sister has turned into a cowboy."

"I love doing it, but I never dreamed I would either," Raine said and soon they were out the door. Belle walked to the window and watched them ride off. Raine was grace in the saddle, riding alongside her tall husband, with their dog ahead of them and Josh and Matt right behind.

"This is a very strange place," she said as she turned back to look at her mother who was smiling.

Toddy rose and said, "Time for lessons." The children followed him into the great room with Jessica and Jeremy seeming enthusiastic about the whole idea of schooling.

"The poor little mites," her mother said as she sat at the table with a cup of coffee. "It's easy to see how they have been thrust from pillar to post."

Belle nodded. "They grabbed my heart with how they had so little love. Their father, even before I knew the rest of him, he was cold to them. He used them. It's why I was afraid to leave them there."

"Well, I am glad you brought them. I don't know what we can do long term. Where is their mother?"

"That is the question." Belle heated up her coffee, adding a bit to her mother's cup. "He had indicated that she died. The children don't seem to know, but I met a woman on the stage down, Annie Jessup. She looked strangely at Jessica when I said the children's mother was dead. I tried to get more information from her, but she was afraid and only wanted out of Canyon City. She was looking for Bernice though. Maybe Bernice would know more."

"Last we knew, she was heading for Boise."

"Could we get word to her? There is a complication. Annie's brother was killed by Rand."

Her mother frowned. "How?"

"Saving Jed's life, according to Rand. Not that that would be much consolation to Annie. She wanted revenge for her brother's death. I wasn't sure I wanted her ever to know that Rand was the one who did it. Bernice would know, wouldn't she?"

"It wasn't a secret after they got back here. Do you think she was just talking?"

"Maybe. I didn't know her well, and then she seemed to be gone. I..."

Adam walked in with the tray, the food only partially eaten. "His fever is up. I don't like the look of this at all."

St. Louis had been silent at the table just listening. Now he said, "We need to try the bread poultice. Poisoned blood has to be fought more ways than what we've tried so far could do."

Martha nodded. Belle saw that she had put slices of bread on the top of the pie cupboard. They were well dried. Belle filled a bowl with water to wash him with and a glass to drink. "I could sure use a bath," she muttered as she thought about how cold the water would be."

"After we're finished, use the spring," her mother said, as she and St. Louis headed for the door. "It's what we do."

"Isn't that a little too invigorating?" She gave a little laugh.

Adam was right behind them. "It's a hot spring. We rocked up a tub and it's not bad. Of course, getting out is, as you said... invigorating." He smiled.

Rand woke in what he gauged to be late afternoon. His shoulder was sore but overall, he felt better than it had. When St. Louis had said they were trying a bread poultice, he'd had his doubts, but something seemed to be helping. He had been lying on his stomach but twisted onto his right side and then saw Belle sleeping in the chair.

He lay quietly to not disturb her. She was wearing a blue dress and was almost painfully beautiful. Her beauty though went beyond the physical. It was the sweetness in her face, strength in the set of her lips, and determination in her eyes. The man who won her for his wife would be a fortunate man. Years ago, he had had a chance to be that man. He hoped it wasn't too late.

"How do you feel?" she asked, her beautiful blue eyes filled with concern.

"I think better."

She moved off the chair and came to the bed. "Drink some water." She reached for the glass on the nightstand and then helped him to sit and lean back against her as she held the glass. He knew he was probably too shaky to hold it, but even if he could have, he was glad to have her arms around him, the feel of her body against his.

"I like your dress," he said when she set the glass down but didn't let go of him.

"I had stuffed it in a bag before we left the house with the children. I didn't have time to take much."

"Sorry you lost so much."

"They were just things."

The house was so quiet. "Where is everybody?"

"Jed. Raine, Josh, and Matt were bringing another of the herds closer to the house. I think it was for branding and castrating. I heard them ride in a few minutes ago. Adam is with the children and helping Toddy teach them. Before I came in here, they were talking of a nature lesson. Mama and Amy are fixing supper. St. Louis was out there talking with them. Think you might be hungry tonight?"

"For something." He smiled. He was definitely feeling better. "You smell sweet, good enough to eat."

She gave a little laugh. "Better than for the last few days. It turns out there is a hot spring just above the house. I had a delightful bath in it."

"I could use one too." He could only imagine how he must stink after the riding and then being so sick.

"I can give you another spit bath. I've bathed almost all of you the last three days."

"God, three days?" Experimentally, he rolled onto his back—not too bad.

"You were really sick, Rand. Mama said though this morning that the red streaks were gone. She thought you would be feeling better soon. She and St. Louis are miracle workers." She kissed his hair before she lowered him down and took her seat again in the chair.

"Sorry to be so much trouble." He felt angry with himself for letting any of it happen.

"It wasn't like you wanted to be put through so much misery," she said.

"I could have been smarter."

"Ah so you want to feel sorry for yourself. Well, then I guess you will have to do it."

He gave a laugh. "All right, maybe that is it."

"Men don't like being sick."

"How do you know so much about men?" His smile was teasing.

"Instinct... and I did have a father."

"I should get up and start..."

Before he could finish the sentence, she was back on the bed and had her hands on his chest. "Do you have any idea what we all went through keeping you alive?"

"I can guess."

"Only when Mama says it's all right do you get up if I have to have you tied to this bed."

He smiled then. Maybe the first time he'd genuinely felt like smiling in longer than he could remember. "I might not mind that if... you were going to think of things to keep me happy being there."

He heard the thumping of boots before the door opened.

"Hey, he's not looking too bad," Jed said. Matt and Adam were right behind him and echoed the opinion. "We can put him to work..."

Martha had followed. Her yelp stopped them. "In four or five days-- maybe. He stays in bed today. Tomorrow chairs. And then a little gentle walking around. Easy does it is the word for a while."

Rand smiled again. He'd not spend that long in bed or lying

around, but he liked that they were caring what happened to him. "Where are my clothes?" he asked with what he hoped didn't show too much interest.

Adam chuckled. "You will be getting those when Mama says it's a go."

"Damn."

"It's not that bad to stay in bed," Matt said with a crooked smile, "just hell is all."

"We'll bring you dinner in about fifteen minutes," Martha said as she left. Rand could hear her down the hall. "Who'd have thought bread poultice."

CHAPTER 19

It was two days later, and all the hell Matt had said, before Rand
got the all clear to wear his clothes and go for a walk outside. Still
Indian summer, it barely would require a jacket. St. Louis had
removed the bandaging and nodded approvingly. "Soak it a good long
time in the hot spring. Mineral water will be good for it," he said.
"Belle will take you there." Outside, Belle took his arm in a way that
was both supportive and affectionate. In her other hand, she carried
her Henry—per Jed's insistence.

He enjoyed the stretch of his legs as they headed toward the hill
behind the house. It was easy to see how much strength he had lost
after six days mostly on his back or sitting trying to concentrate on
reading when all he wanted to do was be active. It was going to take
time to build himself back up.

"I am surprised your mother let us go off alone," he said.

She laughed. "Why wouldn't she? I am the one without a job here
right now. Have you noticed they all have tasks that are part of getting
food or bringing in money for the family? I don't have one, so it's
logical for me to guard you at the spring."

"It's a private setting." The most alone they would be since they
had arrived. "And we're not married-- yet."

"It's not like we will be bathing in it together."

"We won't?"

"Silly, Rand, I am not a virgin anyway."

"I do have reason to know that."

She cast him a sideways glance. "You do."

"Do they know that?" He felt a little uneasy at that. They had been so good to him, and how would they feel if they knew he'd taken her without a wedding ring? He was more conventional than he had imagined.

"They have not asked. They're busy most of the day. I had no idea how much work there was to get food ready for the winter up here. St. Louis is helping Mama dry the last of the summer produce. And they've been bringing in cattle every day for branding and castrating."

"I was surprised when you told me that. That Raine helps with the cattle. It's not the usual thing for women."

"We aren't the usual women though, are we? I mean we ride astride. We take off on adventures. We go after the men we want." She laughed.

"You didn't go after me," he reminded her.

She gave a derogatory snort. "What do you call what I did when I was seventeen?"

"Too young."

The trail narrowed as they went above the barns. Just as they hit the woods, Rand heard the sound of hooves below. He turned in time to watch the herd being driven into the corral. The small cattle dog was nipping at noses and heels as the riders yipped and cut off any reluctant to enter the corral. The dust was heavy in the air as the last longhorn was pushed into the pen and the gate closed. He heard Raine laughing as she jumped off her horse and patted the dog on his head. Jed was heading for other gates as Josh began to build a fire. He had to admit, it looked like fun.

"Don't even think it," Belle said. "You are not remotely strong enough for that." She was right—for now. He let her turn him back toward the spring, but for the first time he realized he might actually like that kind of work.

The path wound up past some boulders until it entered a small glen. The pool ahead was almost turquoise with the light from the sun just penetrating the glade. Steam rose from one end.

"This is a beautiful place," he said.

"And you can indeed take a bath." She pointed to a portion walled off by rocks. "It makes it hotter." She pointed to the bar of soap hanging from an overhanging branch. "I'll keep guard and promise not to watch... too much."

"No towel?" he asked as he began unbuttoning his shirt and shedding it and jacket before he sat to pull off boots.

"Mama said air dry is better." She grinned as she turned away. "So when you have soaked, and your shoulder too, for as long as you can stand it, sit on that boulder and let the sun dry you."

"It's a pleasant day for late October but not that warm."

"It's the change of temperature that is good for your body and you. At least that's what she told me."

He stripped off his pants and then stepped into the water, surprised it was as warm as it was. "Volcanic?" he asked as he slowly lowered himself and then reclined back against a large boulder. His shoulder didn't hurt that much even touching the rock. Now all he had to do was regain his strength.

"I guess there are hot springs all over these hills."

"It feels good. You should join me." He said the words and regretted them immediately. How could he resist her, if she was in the water with him, and they were both naked? No matter what her intentions, he'd be trying to seduce her and seducing himself in the process. He wanted her, but he wanted her married to him the next time it happened between them. He could convince her. He would convince her before he had to ride off again. He hoped.

She turned then to look at him. He knew she would see nothing as he was submerged, but it heated him up just thinking she was watching. He recognized the expression in her eyes.

"Like what you see?" he asked as he moved enough out of the water to where it was just below his navel.

"You know I do." She smiled and looked down the trail. "Hey, Matt and Josh are coming."

"Wonderful," he said and sunk back in the water.

"Head on home, girlie," Matt said as he began removing his shirt. "We need a soak before we start branding. We'll guard him now."

Belle saw Rand's reluctant smile. She was feeling some of the same but she nodded and left. Matt had been her favorite since the wagon train west. Whatever he said, even calling her girlie, went over better than from anyone else.

Walking up onto the porch, she tried to put aside her feelings at seeing Rand beginning to take off his clothing, then watching him in the pool where she knew he was feeling well enough to want to tempt her. It wouldn't be hard. She also knew how much he wanted them married. She still was unsure if she was pregnant. Oddly being pregnant would make her less apt to marry him for fear he was being trapped.

In the kitchen, her mother was peeling potatoes. "You didn't leave him up there alone, did you?" she asked as she turned to meet Belle's gaze.

"Matt and Josh came." She slumped into a chair feeling a ton of conflicting emotions not to mention an upset stomach. Was this an early indicator of a baby on the way? It would be a complication at the least.

"Would you like some tea?" her mother asked as she sat across from her.

"What kind do you have?"

"I made some chamomile this summer which has a settling effect on the stomach."

She smiled as she looked up. How much did her mother know? "Sounds good. Is it safe?"

Her mother laughed. "Would I give it to my youngest daughter if it was not?" She went to the cupboard and put tea leaves into a small cloth bag before she poured boiling water over it.

"Well... No."

"Are you pregnant?" her mother asked as she sat back at the table with the pot and cups.

"I don't honestly know."

"Why are you saying no to marrying him? Do you hope to go back East, and he wouldn't want that life, or maybe you don't love him now that you could have him?"

"None of that. I do love him. It's just... who wants a man who rejected her and then only asks her to marry him to give his child a name?"

"Perhaps you should have thought of that before you made a child possible."

"Are you angry at me for lying to you about what I was doing and now because I don't know if marriage is the right thing?"

"You have to live your life for yourself, Belle, not what I want or don't. I can't know what is right for you. The only thing I can say is if you love that man, don't reject marrying him out of fear."

"Is that what I am—afraid?"

"Isn't it?" She poured the tea into her cup.

"Maybe." It was amazing, as she had known little fear when physical danger threatened. Now though, was she afraid?

"Belle, don't let it keep you from fully loving him if that's what you feel. You know since you were a child, you have been afraid of intimacy, and I don't mean sex but caring deeply for people and being accountable."

She had never thought of it that way. Maybe it was her problem.

Would that make her a terrible mother if she was pregnant? Could she truly give Rand what he deserved from a woman? She faced it squarely and needed to look within for the answers. Maybe when her father had died or even when Rand first rejected her, maybe she had protected herself to the point she had killed off a capacity for love. Or was it still there and just waiting for her to acknowledge it?

Rand debated whether he'd had all the soaking heat he could stand when Matt's voice disrupted his daydreaming. "What's the plan now?"

"For what?"

"For Forester."

He considered that as he met the shrewd gaze of the man, who in this family he knew least.

"I was hoping I'd hear from the colonel before I had to decide."

"What does he have to do with it?" Josh asked as he edged himself onto a rock and began the drying process.

"I sent him a letter after I sent off the one to the fort. I would like to know if the first one got to him."

"Somebody would dare destroy or divert it?" Matt asked.

"I don't know, but since I don't, if someone did, that message, including the one Belle sent, might have gone straight to Forester not to The Dalles."

"And you sent it anyway?" Matt's expression had darkened.

"When I did, I wasn't thinking clearly. I seemed to go in and out of being lucid. All I could think was I had to report what I knew. Only later did it dawn on me that if the traitor was Sergeant Coleman or Lieutenant Murphy, then it might not go where it was supposed to. In that case, the letter will be the test and tell me at least if one of those two are traitors."

"Then Forester might again have the plates?"

At that Rand smiled and levered himself from the water. The cool air felt good. "Not those anyway. They will look like workable until someone tries to use them. I had destroyed his press, but I figure he could have another. Maybe he also had plates elsewhere."

"What are the odds?"

Rand considered that. "I don't know." He met Matt's level gaze. This was a man to be an equal partner in a battle.

"Something's eating at you," Matt said as he continued to watch Rand with a knowing look.

"Why would you think that?" Rand asked as he felt his skin was dry enough to pull on pants.

"I don't think. I know."

"Something is. Two things."

"And they are?" Matt wasn't letting it go.

"Not any particular order. In Canyon City, I killed my brother. Maybe you can't understand what that means." He looked then at Josh. "Or maybe you can."

"Why did you kill him?" Josh asked. "That would make the difference."

"He took a shot at me. I heard the whine of the bullet by my head. I didn't even know it was him-- until I fired. It wouldn't have made a difference though if I had known." He let out a sigh.

Matt's smile was tight. "I know more about that than you might expect. I killed my brother also to save my own life. I know it's not easy because a man always thinks his brother will be his best friend, like Josh and Jed are, but it's not always that way."

"No." Rand shook his head. "It wasn't for me with Jason or my father for that matter. They both betrayed me. Nothing like the family I see up here."

"That might keep you from wanting a family?" Josh asked.

He had to think about that. "No. I know it can be otherwise. I left home early enough that it didn't scar me like it might have."

Matt's smile was hard. "Yes, it can do that. You said two things. The other is your father?"

Rand grimaced. "Yeah, that he would do to me what he did. I was kidnapped by Forester, turned into a victim." He hated even saying the word, but it was the truth. "He tortured me, but not all of what he did to me do I know as I got knocked out cold. I don't know if that might be impacting my thinking now. I've faced danger, been hurt, but never expected what happened. I don't seem able to get a handle on it."

"It does leave a scar that nobody else sees," Matt drawled, as he eased out of the water. He was tall, about Rand's height. Big boned, he was muscular, a powerful looking man. They were probably of an age.

"You speak from experience on that too." It wasn't a question.

"We are more alike than I knew."

Rand considered that. He needed to say it to someone. "Forester, the man who did this to me." He pointed to the fading scar around his nipple. "He had jackets nailed to his wall in the room where he kept the press and plates. Mine was one of them. There were others—all men's." Rand knew how much that knowledge had unsettled him. He wondered how Matt had read it so easily.

"Trophies," Matt said as Rand moved away from the pool and sat on a nearby boulder to pull on his socks and boots.

"So it would seem."

"And just not who he killed."

"You are instinctive about this."

"I grew up having to learn about this," Matt said without Rand asking. "It plays with a man's mind."

That was sure the hell the truth. "It does," he said trying to get a handle on himself now that he was feeling stronger.

"You do have to get past it."

He did know that.

Josh shook his head as he also got out of the water to dry off. "You two are confusing the hell out of me," he said. "Is there something out of this whole thing I need to understand?" His Georgia accent was even stronger than Jed's or even Matt's. Southerners is what they had in common. Raised in Virginia, Rand had some of that too in certain moods.

"Not if you're lucky," Matt said as he belted his cartridge belt to his waist.

"I have been thinking what to do about Forester. If the first letters never got to the colonel, then it means Forester knows where Belle and the children are. This place will be facing a possible attack by him."

"How many men has he got?" Josh asked as he also dressed.

"I don't know for sure. Maybe fifty. Maybe more. And of them, how many would be dedicated to the cause of insurrection? Questions and no answers. He held a ball and there were over one hundred people there. How many of those men were also partners in his plot? I wish I had the answer."

"Is it better to go after him or let him come for us?" Matt said contemplatively. "He'd have an excuse with those children. I'd turn over heaven and hell if someone took mine."

"From what I know, he's not your kind of father, but it would give him an excuse and maybe to bring in more men. How long before I am likely to get a response back from Schaeffer?"

"How long ago did you send it?" Josh asked as he sat next to them on a wooden bench Jed had made.

"Six days."

"I could ride down to Dayville tomorrow and see if there's anything there."

Rand felt annoyed with himself that he was not yet up to riding that far. His weakness was getting in the way of his responsibility.

"Interesting time for this kind of problem," Matt said with a small smile.

"What do you mean?"

"Tonight is a special night. The night of the dead—or so Jed has said. He promised the children some games and ghost stories. Samhain is what he said the Celts call it."

"Occult?" Rand asked rising and feeling better than he had in over a week.

"Maybe. Some believe it's when the veil between the other side and us is thinnest. Got anyone over there who might want to get at you?"

"Most likely a few," he admitted with a wry smile.

"In the South, it's innocent, a big event, games, with some fortunetelling going along with it," Josh said.

"I don't much want anybody telling me my future," Rand said as the three began to walk back down the trail.

"Bad news comes soon enough is my take on it," Matt said.

"It's just for fun," Josh protested. "The children like it."

"It helps if they don't know the reality of it," Rand said. He hadn't had much of a childhood. Maybe some games would be good for him —take away some seriousness. His belief in the other side though was pretty slim. Maybe that was good.

"If you had killed him, this would not be happening," Harold said with little sympathy as Forester paced the room.

"You are not helping. You are in this as deeply as I am and you know it. You were there when we tortured him."

"Slitting his throat before he was sent out to be found would not have left us with him still out there somewhere."

"It also would make obvious he was taken somewhere when already dead. He was hurt again. Maybe seriously."

Harold chuckled. "Do we?"

"You saw the message."

"I also saw Lockwood's dead body and the damaged plates. Whatever condition he is in, I would not count on it lasting."

"I need motivation to raise up my army."

Harold laughed again. "You mean your rabble, don't you?"

"Don't be so negative."

"I am being practical."

This time it was William's turn to laugh. "Oh yes, so practical when you took up with that whore."

Harold gave off a growl. "Do not besmirch my love."

"You have to be joking."

"I am only lucky to have Annie in my bed at night. She could have left Canyon City if I had not found a way to convince her to stay."

William sighed. "With a combination of bribery and using her own need for revenge."

"It's smarter than your plan. If she kills Phillips, we'll not be blamed."

"Well, she's not apt to get close to him either."

"You don't know that."

"I do. He won't trust a whore to be at the fort and no way would Hardman let one into his compound." Forester threw himself into his chair. "Phillips will only come here with troopers at his back. Lockwood was far more reliable than my other man in the camp."

"The other one got word to you regarding what happened."

"True but, Harold, he's a true believer. That's always risky."

"There is that. I think we should just get out of town and let this proposition go for now. We still have enough money for a while anyway."

Forester bit the tip off a cigar and lit it. He took a long, satisfying draw. "Cigars like this don't grow on trees, Harold. Your whore won't be with you long either if you don't have nice toys to satisfy her."

"All right. All right, but this all seems very risky." Moriarty scowled as he moved around the room restlessly.

"Given who you are sleeping with and the tricks all whores know, you should be in a lot better mood than you are." He smiled more broadly when Harold actually flushed.

"I am worried."

"Of course, you are always worried."

"Tell me the plan."

"My cook and butler failed me. There has to be a cost for that. Plus they are the only ones who could tell how they let the children just go with that traitor governess and the military."

"I take it they have to die."

"Sad but true. It provides the emotion needed for my ill-trained but fortunately gullible crew. Not only did the military kill them, but Phillips murdered his own brother. Heinous. With the right emotional rage, we will all head for the Hardman ranch and attack them."

Moriarty dropped into a chair. "Oh, that should go well. Hardman is a trained military officer. From what we have heard, he's got that ranch set up like a fort."

"You have a better idea?"

"You won't be with the militia?"

"Of course, I will. You too. I will leave my five best men here. Can't afford to have them accidentally killed. If it begins to look as though it won't work, I'll be back here and arouse the rabble for the deaths of our troops." He smiled

"I won't go."

"Why not?"

"It's not a bad plan but I am no good on a horse. You can do it better without me. I'll be here with those men and my Annie." For the first time, Moriarty smiled with what looked like genuine pleasure. "I think this might actually work." He rose and headed for the door.

"You don't want to be here when I murder my staff?"

Moriarty shook his head. "I prefer hearing about such second-hand." With that, he was gone.

CHAPTER 20

F or the first time since he had arrived, Rand had been able to eat with the family for dinner. Even better, the food, which included ham, baked potatoes, corn, and pumpkin pie, had tasted good. The children were beyond excited when plans were discussed for the evening celebration.

Belle had not met his gaze once, which made him wonder again if she had been disappointed in the reality of who he was. The man a girl admired at seventeen wasn't necessarily who she wanted almost ten years later. He had proven to be a less than apt protector. The fact that his feelings had only grown stronger didn't mean it was reciprocal. If it had been, she'd have accepted his proposal and they would already be married.

"Whiskey for the gentlemen in the great room," Jed drawled as he headed there. "Cigars also for any who want them. Children go to your room and come when we have everything ready."

Jack Grimes said he was too tired, after the day they had spent, and headed for bed.

Rand observed that Jeremy and Jessica seemed very much at ease with their new friends and the home. They were as excited at the promised evening as the Stone and Kane children. Raine went off to put their baby to bed while Belle, Amy and Martha cleaned up the kitchen.

In the great room, Rand settled on the sofa. St. Louis on the other end of it. When offered a cigar, he took it with pleasure. Someday he'd give up the habit but that was not today. "Good tobacco," he said as sniffed it before Jed lit both and then handed him a shot glass.

Matt came in with the big tub of water with Josh behind him bearing a basket of apples. "Ever bobbed for apples?" Jed asked Rand.

He shook his head. "Never heard of Samhain either. You superstitious, Hardman?"

Jed grinned. "A few times-- times like when a gun is pointing at me or a bear is facing me."

"Not sure that counts as superstition," Adam said as he fed wood into the fireplace to encourage the flames to grow higher.

Rand took a long draw on the cigar as he considered what he had to do next. He could not stay here much longer. "I will have to get back to the camp whether I hear from the colonel or not."

"You sure you're up to a long ride?" St. Louis asked. "You still look pale."

"Not yet but soon."

"What are you expecting from the colonel?" Adam asked as he sipped his whiskey but turned down the cigar. Rand repeated what he had told Matt.

"Smart to check that way," Jed said. "Mails here are unpredictable between Indian trouble and bandits. Good for Josh to find out if anything's come in."

"You understand you can expect trouble if the letters got diverted to Forester or I had a traitor at the fort, who relays what happened when the plates and guns arrived."

"I have been securing this place against trouble since I got here, but the truth of it is, we can't secure every acre and keep it functioning as a ranch."

"From what you said, Forester sounds crazy, touched in the head," Matt said. He stopped when he saw the children entering from the hall with Eli at their head.

"How soon before this shindig starts?" Eli asked with all the arrogance of a growing youth. Jeremy Forester looked uneasy at what he had heard but said nothing.

"Half an hour," Jed said. "Time to get Jesse settled, and the ladies in from the kitchen. Play in your room until we call you."

When they were again alone, Matt said, "You believe in ghosts, Jed?"

Jed blew out the smoke. "Mostly the kind that we have inside us."

"You ain't planning to scare my children are you?" Matt asked. "I have enough trouble keeping Rufus's imagination from running away with him."

"Nah, it won't be that kind of ghost story." Jed walked to the fireplace and stuck in another piece of wood as the women entered.

"Do you miss Georgia?" Rand asked him.

"I never wanted to live there. I think about my family, of course, but except for Josh, they are all dead now. I chose this life and never looked back."

"Would you like to visit there sometime?" Raine asked as she put her arms around his lean waist.

"No, sugar. I have all I could ever want right here." He smiled at her. The warmth in her eyes, as she returned his gaze, was what Rand had hoped to see in a woman who loved him. Raine was clearly a woman who belonged to a man and was proud to acknowledge it to the world. Belle, who had not come to sit beside him, appeared unwilling to be that woman. He had to suck it up and accept the truth of it. She had saved his life. Maybe that explained what she had given him out on the trail—emotion born of the trauma of surviving when one should have died.

"I appreciate ya opening yore home to an old-timer like me," St. Louis said.

"It's no favor," Jed said. "I knew that this place needed a family. I didn't expect Raine to bring them all to me, but she did." He grinned. "And wisdom from those who've lived a few years, that is of much value in my eyes."

"Not much how a lot sees it," St. Louis said with that probing look Rand had seen before in his eyes.

"It's how those in my family did," Jed drawled. "And how I do."

Amy went to get the children, who returned with large eyes. Rand watched as Jed taught them how to bob for apples and then play the traditional games. They were excited but clearly most eager for the ghost story that had been promised before bedtime.

"I hope they will sleep well after it," Martha said from where she had cuddled against Adam. Sleeping by the fireplace were the two dogs.

"If they don't," Raine said tweaking Jed's cheek, "we know who to blame."

"I heard these stories as a small one," the tall southerner drawled as he rose and began to lower the lamps until the room was barely lit. The moon outside was rising but it was a crescent that provided little light.

"The stories I was told come from the swamps and cypress forests of Georgia and the home of Two-Toed Tom." He moved around the room as he described a home where many generations had lived and where a ghost was determined to keep for himself.

"Do any of you know what a ghost looks like?" he asked with a smile as he scanned over the children.

"Ugly?" Rufus suggested.

"Like you maybe," Eli added with a grin as he gave his nephew a light punch on his arm. Rufus responded with a giggle.

"For those who have seen ghosts… or claimed they did," Jed said, "they don't agree. And most folks don't see them at all. They just see what they do when they break something or make noises intended to scare people."

His story took the side of the ghost. He created sympathy of the poor ghost who only wanted to keep his home from intruders. Rand saw it took the fear from it but not the excitement as the children listened with rapt attention. With the ghost's great disappointment in failing to scare anyone, the sorrow all fell upon the poor trapped ghost failing in his assigned task.

"And then one brave little girl confronted the ghost and made him show himself."

"Oh yeah, like it would be a girl," Rufus protested with a low growl.

"Did the ghost hurt her?" Laura asked, ignoring her brother's insult as she cuddled her little sister to her. Jessica had from the beginning sought comfort on Belle's lap.

"No, he was glad she saw him. He felt less lonely when she asked him what he needed. She told him they would not be scared; so he should do all that he needed to be happy. 'I just want someone to hear my story,' the ghost cried.

"'Let it be me,' she said as she then sat and listened as he told her of his life, how he had come to be where he was. After she heard it all, he smiled and vanished, never to be seen again."

"He should have killed someone," Rufus suggested. "What kind of ghost is that?"

"Killing isn't good," Jeremy disagreed. His face grew somber. "I wonder if my mother is a ghost."

"This is the time when the other side is very close to us," said Jed. "It is a time to ask for stories, ours or those from the other side."

"Now?" The little boy's expression grew worried.

"Are you sure this is a good idea?" Raine asked as she nudged Jed's shoulder.

"Of course, because we are all here to be together and make it not scary. What is your mother's name, Jeremy?"

Rand had little belief in another side and wondered if Jed did. The boy looked uneasy as he considered the request. "My father never told me. And I was pretty little when she left."

"What did she look like?" Belle asked tenderly brushing the hair back from Jessica's forehead.

"Like my sister. She had red hair. It was curly and pretty. She was beautiful."

Rand wondered if he could get more information on the missing mother when he got back to the fort. More likely, it would take his next trip to The Dalles and the telegraph to get to those who might have such records for the Foresters.

"Where did you live, Jer?" Rand asked remembering the preferred nickname.

"Virginia and then California."

"Well, let's see if any ghosts want to talk to us," Jed said as he took a seat at the dark end of the room.

"Being scared does not seem a good idea before bed," Raine again reminded him.

"It's not scary to talk to the other side," Jed corrected her. "They are like my story not scary. They just want us to listen."

"You sound like you believe in ghosts," Adam said with a skeptical tone.

"Of course. I am a southerner," Jed said with a smile. "Now let's just listen and when we listen, whatever we hear, we will tell each other. Deal?"

Rand had no real belief in anything, certainly not that his mother might try to reach out to him from across a mysterious divide. Still he didn't try to ruin Jed's celebration of Samhain. He glanced again at Belle as she comforted the little girl. She would make a loving mother. That thought gave him no pleasure. If she was pregnant, it was clear she would shut him away from their baby.

It was his own damned fault for making love to her before he had the right. If he could have, he'd have kicked himself. He ruined it for them both. Twice maybe. How would their life have been if they had married when she had wanted when she was so young?

He had been right back then though. He knew it. If she was rejecting him now, likely she would have eventually left him. What could the military offer a woman like her that she could not find better with another? He would work to be a friend to her, to support her as best he could for as long as he lived. He would do likewise for any child if one happened to be on its way.

When no one reported any sightings of ghosts, Jed brought out his guitar. "Some of these were African folk songs that I grew up hearing."

Jed's voice was on pitch, deep and soulful. He brought intensity and a deep meaning to each song. He concluded with one that Rand had heard during the war—Aura Lee. A song of a man in love with a golden haired woman. It might have been Belle.

Finally, Jed stopped and said, "When we sleep tonight, remember your dreams. In the morning be sure we all share them." With that, the children were taken off to bed by Belle and Amy. Raine, responding to the wail from their baby, left to feed him and then go to their own bedchamber. "I should also head for bed, Martha said. "Heaven likely is feeling very deserted. "She pulled on Adam's arm to head for their cabin.

With only Josh, Matt, Toddy, St. Louis, and Rand there, Jed lit a cigar and poured whiskey for those so inclined. Rand was. "When I came north, I saw folks didn't celebrate Samhain. I missed that until I finally had a family here."

"I grew up in Virginia," Rand said, "but never heard of it."

"We'll probably have a few children crying tonight," Matt said with a laugh. "And I spent some of my childhood in Georgia but heard of it but never had the family do anything like this. Of course, I didn't exactly have a family sort of family back then."

"It's not a bad thing to be aware of the other side," St. Louis said, and Toddy nodded approval. "The other *side* can be on our side."

Belle woke when it was barely light after a restless night, which had nothing to do with ghost stories. She was torn as to what to do about Rand. She found herself emotional and wanting to cry when she never cried. The longer this went, the more she believed she probably was pregnant.

She lay trying to decide what to do about it. The idea of trapping Rand into a marriage he had never wanted was abominable to her. Their having sex had been more her idea than his. She could stay at the ranch, but if she did that, the family would be taking on the responsibility she knew should be her own.

Everyone here had a job. What would be hers when she was pregnant? On the other hand, what would she do if she left and how to deal with a baby? She would have to get a job. To avoid Rand finding out and feeling obligated to her, she could not stay long at the ranch. All too soon, this would be obvious.

She had saved some money, which she could access in Portland.

Until she had the baby, she could work in a shop. She knew how to do that.

The knock at her door interrupted her musings. "Come in," she said and saw it was Raine.

"Is something wrong?" she asked as she sat up.

"I think so."

"It isn't Rand, is it?" She felt that fear, only connected to him, that seemed to fill her.

"It might be, but it's also you."

"What did I do this time?"

Raine came and sat on her bed. "You are not facing reality."

"Thanks for such a high opinion of me."

"Belle, I have seen it. You are pushing away a man who loves you and who you said you loved. Why?"

"It's not right between us."

Raine gave a disbelieving laugh. "And how did you come to that conclusion?"

"I won't trap a man into marrying me."

"And you somehow had the idea you are doing that to him?"

"I could."

"If I thought you didn't love each other, I'd stay out of this, but that is not the case. You are hurting yourself and him. Wake up, sweetheart."

Belle felt tears rolling down her cheeks. "He didn't want me before. He has never told me he loves me now."

"Men aren't always good at expressing their feelings, and you and he have had little time to spend talking about what either of you want. He asked you to marry him. More than once."

"I need to leave here and get far away."

"Oh my God, that is the most foolish thing you could do."

"Thanks." Belle found being annoyed helped staunch her tears. She got out of bed and began dressing.

"You are good at some things, but relationships have not been one of those. You are not too old to change."

"You are too used to bossing people around." At least some things never changed.

Raine smiled. "It's an older sister's job."

"You can't fix this."

"I think I can. I still have a home in Portland. Clem and Sally are there. Do you remember them?"

"Clem anyway, from the wagon train, right?"

"Yes, I also still have two businesses, which currently I have someone managing. I could let you live in the house and work in or run the businesses."

"And the condition?"

"Talk to him and tell him all that you feel. Do that and if this doesn't work out, then I will help you."

"I don't want to be rejected."

Raine smiled and shook her head. "It's obvious you are smart and brave about many things, but this is not one of them. You do not know what he'd like. Do you know what he's thinking right now?"

Belle sat back on the bed beside Raine. "Probably that he was smart to reject me before."

"Find out. And I have another question. What about Jessica and Jeremy?"

"I would like to take them with me, of course, but they are not my children. Doesn't that qualify as kidnapping?"

Raine grinned. "You already did that part. Why don't we talk to a lawyer and see what rights you might potentially have?"

"How would we do that?"

"I have a good man in Portland, who I have relied on. Jed has one in Canyon City. Why don't we talk to one of them and see what the legal situation is with their father on the run and no mother around."

"There is a possibility that she is not dead."

"Why do you think that?"

Belle told her about Annie and her background including anger at someone killing her brother. "The thing is, she was so odd about Jessica. I had the strangest feeling she recognized her from having known her mother. I couldn't get her to talk to me, but she was trying to reconnect with Bernice."

"All right, we can get word to Han Jei, but it will take time. If their mother is alive and left her children, they might not be much better off with her."

"Better than with him for sure. I would appreciate it if we can figure out how to get a letter to Bernice to get more information from her if Annie made it that far."

"What makes you think she wouldn't?"

"She had known Dylan Hoyt, maybe was even his lover." She remembered the note that said I love you and that key, might it have been to someone else's room—maybe Annie's. "If she was involved with Dylan, it might have been reason enough for Forester to have her killed to be sure she didn't reveal his secrets."

Raine rose. "Write your letter and let me see if Jed knows anyone who is heading east... and then I'll write the basics in a letter to his lawyer in Canyon City." She smiled down at Belle. "You do have a lot of complications in your life, little sister."

Belle sighed. "It has been worse." She looked up with a crooked grin.

"How?"

"I didn't have a big sister on my side." She rose then and took Raine into her arms. As the sisters hugged, Belle knew she would not absent herself ever again from her family as she had done. She needed them.

At the first trace of light, Rand rose, dressed in his outdoor gear, strapped a cartridge belt and revolver around his waist and went to the kitchen for a cup of coffee. He took his tobacco and papers outside and rolled a smoke. As he was dragging in the first welcome puff, Jed came out. "So what's the plan?" he asked looking pointedly at the gun.

"I need Blue. Is he in the lower pasture?"

"You up to riding?"

"I figure to find out." He smiled as he watched the big man through the smoke.

Jed rolled his own. "You clear this with Martha?"

"Did I have to?"

Jed laughed as he lit his cigarette. "Nah. Just wondered if I'd get in trouble with her or Belle."

"Did Josh already leave for Dayville?"

Jed nodded.

"Hope it's safe."

"Me too. Last time he killed three Indians. Be nice if he could get by this time without killing anybody." Jed grinned.

"In short he can take care of himself."

"And me too if required."

Rand stepped off the porch still smoking and headed for the corrals. When he saw his bay, he whistled and the gelding came right to him. "You been a good boy?" he asked rubbing the big head.

"He takes to you."

"And me him. Blue Dawn happens to be my horse."

"Not the army's?"

"I wanted a horse I could count on. Best bet for that is to buy your own. I take him with me whenever he's not been worn down by earlier patrols."

"Where are you taking him today?"

"Maybe up toward that patch of ground you showed me and were talking about me buying."

Jed smiled. "I'll go get my gun and us some biscuits. Need me to saddle him?" Rand gave him a look, and Jed laughed.

"While I throw one on Blue, want me to saddle your stallion too?" Rand asked. "I saw you working him the other day. The big black one with two white stockings, right?"

Jed chuckled. "Yep, Midas. If you can saddle him, you're a better man with a horse than I ever met." He ran for the house while Rand went up to the barn for his tack.

Blue eagerly followed Rand, making that the easy one. He felt some soreness and stiffness in his muscles as he threw the saddle over his back, but overall, it felt good, and he was encouraged.

Rand left Blue secured to the railing, grabbed a lasso, and went back to the horse corral. "Hey, Midas," he said whistling, "you're needed."

The stallion looked at him with interest but didn't move. Rand went over the fence. On the ground, he again gestured to the stallion. Two mares came but the stallion played coy. Before he could walk to him and try to throw a loop over his head, Jed, now armed, returned and handed Rand three strips of bacon. "Martha's up. She didn't say anything when I told her what we were doing."

"Midas is ignoring me. Want me to rope him for you?"

Jed chuckled again. "Oh, that'd go over well," he drawled. "He is loyal to me."

"A lot don't like riding stallions for their testy nature."

"I won't say he can't have one. I plan to breed him. For now, I keep him away from the mares when they are in heat, as I don't have time to raise colts. Right now they are all ignoring him."

Jed whistled, the stallion came, giving Rand a dismissive look.

Jed made quick work of saddling him. In half an hour, they were riding up the river.

"Your stallion is wanting to run," Rand observed.

"Your gelding have a good gait?"

"The best. Let's let them go." He leaned forward in the saddle and nudged him with his heels. Blue didn't need to be asked twice. Soon the horses were racing over the ground. Feeling the air in his face, the thunder of the hooves, and the big horse between his thighs was more healing for Rand than anything he'd had happen since he he'd been stabbed. Only one thing felt better under him, and the way she'd been treating him, that didn't look likely to happen anytime soon if ever.

A few miles and they slowed their mounts. Jed pointed out landmarks. "See what makes this place valuable," he said as they entered a big meadow. "Sub-irrigated." He pointed out the spring on the hill above the meadow. "That one is also heated some and artesian."

"So ranching it?"

"Or orchards, even grapes and of course, logging the hills. Timber is always needed in a growing community. This piece is ten thousand acres and dirt cheap since it's not in the area like Susanville where there is likely to be gold. When you settle the Indian trouble, its price will go up. Being on the North Fork is worth a lot for the water. The other plus is this elevation, lower than around it. It makes it a kind of banana belt for eastern Oregon. It gets rain too. Not much more a man could ask for in land."

"Other than no Indian trouble," Rand suggested.

"Other than that."

"I guess you'd know how to use the land having been raised on a plantation."

Jed nodded. "My daddy was good at business. He taught me a lot. His way though of handling women, that one I want to do different. What I saw didn't work real good" He laughed.

They stopped their horses and rolled cigarettes. Jed hooked his leg over the pommel of his saddle. Rand wondered if his body was up to that and found the stretch of muscles was good. He was on the mend. All but his heart.

"So what do you think?" Jed asked.

"About what?"

"This land. Do you want it?"

CHAPTER 21

When Belle entered the kitchen, her mother turned to watch her. "He went for a ride."

"Who?" But she knew and felt furious. "That was stupid," she said shaking her head at the offer of coffee.

"I could make you some oatmeal. How does that sound?"

She had never been an oatmeal person, but that sounded surprisingly good. She nodded. "Why did you let him go?" she asked.

"He didn't ask permission."

"He almost died. Surely he should not have gone riding so soon."

"Jed went with him."

"Oh that helps a lot."

"I actually think it's what he needed. The next step of healing. For an active man, he needed to start using his muscles again. It will be all right."

She accepted the cup of tea that her mother made. She hadn't had the severe morning sickness she knew some could get, or she might yet, but she was relatively sure she was pregnant. She felt annoyed with herself at letting it happen at the same time she felt excited at the idea of her own baby. It had not been part of her life plan, but it suddenly felt right. She wondered if it would be a boy or girl. Then she remembered her promise to talk to Rand and be honest. It was about the last thing she wanted to do.

Raine came in with Jesse and set him down in the corner, where he protested but quickly settled into moving blocks. For being not much more than an infant, his dexterity led to him being frustrated at the difference between his goals and his accomplishments. He didn't give up. "Where is everybody else?" Raine asked.

"Adam said they wouldn't go far, but he and St. Louis took Eli, Rufus and Jeremy into the woods to teach them about tracking and looking for signs. I have not yet seen the girls or Amy and Matt, but I think she wanted to get some work done on the inside of their home and discuss what was needed with him. They may have taken the girls with them."

Raine took the bacon and a cup of coffee. "Does it bother you to see me eat or drink this?" she asked.

"Why would it?"

"Just wondered."

"Did you talk to Jed about the lawyer?" she asked smiling at her knowledge that Raine was probing for information regarding morning sickness. Well, if she told anybody, it'd be Rand. Besides, maybe she wasn't pregnant. Maybe it was just a false alarm. Women had such, or so she had been told.

"He left too early."

"Talk to a lawyer regarding what?" their mother asked as she sat down to join them.

"Jeremy and Jessica," Belle answered. "I can't keep them forever without finding out if there is a way to do it legally."

"They are very nice children, and you'd like to keep them?"

"Of course. I certainly don't want them going back to their father. I need to know if their mother is still alive. That could influence a possible adoption. Of course. I want what is best for them. I don't know if there are other family members who would have first rights."

"They like it here," her mother said sipping her coffee.

"I know."

"I need to make bread today," Martha said rising to go back to the counter. "You girls can take turns kneading the dough. Remember how you used to do that?"

"I'd like that," Belle said.

"How do you like this place?" Raine asked as she sipped coffee.

"What's not to like. It's so beautiful and filled with a strange energy. I don't know what it is, but it's very special."

"So you will stay?"

"There is a lot to consider. Could I really help here?"

"You know you could."

Martha went to the stove and dished Belle out a bowl of oatmeal.

"That smells good. Is there enough for me too?" Raine asked.

In moments they were eating. "Where do you get the milk?" Belle asked between bites.

"A small dairy down in Monument," Raine said. "We send Jack down once a week with the large milk jugs, and store it in the cold spring on the other side of the house. It keeps long enough. We make our own butter too, sour cream with what doesn't keep, but with growing children, that's not a lot. I have been thinking about giving cheese a try."

"You have become quite the ranch wife," Belle said shaking her head.

"That surprises you?"

"I thought of you as a business woman, and you did theater. Don't you miss all of that?"

"I could do theater if I wanted, but no, I don't miss it. I had that life. I liked it, but now I have this one. I like it too."

"She even shot a grizzly," Martha said.

"You killed a bear?" Now that surprised her more than the domesticity.

"Jed might have killed it first. He split its head open with an axe, but I did shoot it." She smiled proudly.

"Grizzlies live around here? I heard the wolves but never thought of grizzlies."

"Generally if they are around, Jed does shoot them. It's sad as they are magnificent animals, but they pick off the calves. A black bear isn't so willing to go up against a horned mama cow, but a grizzly will. So, not many left in this area except for now and again one traveling through."

"I've never seen one but have heard of them. Jed is a powerful looking man for sure, but why did he take an axe to it? Seems too close to be safe."

"It was about to attack me and Bernice in the hot springs pool. He did it to save our lives."

"What a brave thing to do. Quite a man."

She heard the door open and the sound of boots accompanied by Jed's laugh. "He is, if you mean me."

When she turned to look, she saw Rand behind him. He looked happier and more relaxed than she had seen him maybe ever. She hoped her talk with him would not take that away.

Before she could suggest they go for a walk, Jed walked to the window. "Josh is back." His voice sounded concerned.

"He can't have already gotten down and back," Rand said as they went outside and down to the barns.

In moments, they were back. "He didn't have to go all the way," Jed explained. "He met Gage on the way up, and he had our mail." He began sorting through it and handed Rand his letter. Belle studied his face as he read it.

When he looked up, his expression was the one she had seen when he was prepared for battle. "He didn't get the letters." His gaze met hers. "Neither of them."

"So Forester knows why I was there."

"If Coleman or Murphy weren't killed in getting it, one or both of them are traitors." His expression was troubled. When he saw her studying him, he said, "Both were men I had trusted more than anyone on the post. Makes me question my judgment as well as be disappointed."

"So he knows we have the children. What do you think Forester will do about that?" Jed asked looking at Belle.

"Do you think I did wrong to take them?" Belle asked.

Jed shook his head. "Not a chance. No way should you have left them with a man like that. Who knows how he'd have used them. The question is will he come up here after them?"

"Not based on love," she said regretting her words when she saw St. Louis, Adam, and the children entering the kitchen from the great room. Jeremy looked at her with the hard expression she had seen often on his face—especially when it involved his parent.

"You talking about our father?" he asked.

Rand nodded. "I guess what Belle said is no surprise to you."

Jeremy nodded. "He just uses us. If he could use us, he would do that."

"Not everybody gets a father who is that great," Rand said with a tight smile. "Sometime you, Matt, and I will have a talk about that, but for now, we need to have an adult confab. You boys could go over to Amy and Matt's home and bring the girls back here for Toddy's teaching today, what do you think?"

Eli nodded and led Jeremy and Rufus off.

"What are you thinking?" Jed asked as he poured himself a cup of coffee.

"That I'd like one too." When they were both sipping their coffee, Rand said, "I think Jeremy hit on it. He would use the children as an excuse if he wants to not only take you out as a power, but also get revenge for his lost plates."

"If there are traitors at the fort, maybe he has the plates again."

"He won't be using any of those," Rand said with a smirk.

"That won't make him happy," Jed snickered.

"Considering all he tried to do and did to me, probably including getting my weak brother to take a shot at me, his happiness is no concern of mine. I will leave for the post in half an hour." He looked then at Belle. "I need to talk to you."

"You can't be serious? You nearly died. You need longer to recuperate."

He took her arm and led her out the door. "Is it too cold for you?" he asked as they stood on the porch.

She shook her head but wrapped her arms around herself. He took off his jacket and put it over her shoulders. "I need to go. I hope you can see that."

"And when you fall off your horse, who will drag you back on."

He laughed. "I took a trial run this morning. I'll be all right. If I feel I can't make it in a day, I'll camp part way. I need to get to the post and deal with the traitor. Then I can deal with Forester."

He saw she didn't understand. It didn't matter. He had a duty to perform. Forester could not be allowed free rein to run havoc over others. Rand didn't want revenge. He wanted the man taken out of power.

"I want something from you before I go, Belle."

"What?" Her tone was resentful.

"I want you to promise to be here when I get back. I am worried about what Forester might do and not just to you but the children. Stay, keep them safe, and give me a chance to make my case to you when I return—and I will return."

"In ten years?"

His smile softened. He turned her and lifted her chin. "You know better." He bent then and claimed her lips. The kiss deepened as he thrust his tongue into her mouth. When her arms came around him, he tightened his hold. When he finally released her, they were both breathing hard. "We have things to settle," he said and had to clear his throat. "Promise you will give us the chance to do that."

"I'll wait. I've waited ten years. I guess a few months won't matter." Her expression said they would.

"It won't be that long. I will resolve the issue of the traitor, get together a company, and go back to Canyon City. I don't see Forester as the kind of man who can live out in the woods. Somebody will know where he is if he isn't back there causing trouble."

"I still think you should heal longer."

He smiled and brushed his lips on her forehead. "Me too, but there isn't time. Forester has to be neutralized. A man like that can't be left to run free."

"You could be killed."

"I won't argue with you about this. It is what I have to do." After what he experienced with Forester's machinations, he wasn't about to be trapped again. He'd been through several wars. He had confidence he could handle this. "To do that though, I need to know you are safe and waiting here for me."

"I will be here."

He put his arm around her and walked her back into the kitchen. He looked at Jed, St. Louis, and Adam who were sitting at the table sipping coffee. "I don't have to tell you to look after her. I also don't have to tell you to be ready for anything. I do not know what to expect from Forester or Moriarty."

"Who is he?"

"To be honest, I don't know his whole role, but I have every reason to believe he is an equal in this. If they show up here, they won't come to talk. If they did, it'd be lies. Most likely though they will come and hit hard hoping to surprise you."

"You want me to come with you?" Adam offered.

"No. I want you to be right here. I can take care of out there if I don't have to worry about what's here."

"That is such a typical thing to hear a man say," Belle said, not hiding her irritation.

Rand laughed. "It is, isn't it!" He kissed her on the forehead. "I will be back." With that, he was out the door.

A moment later, she saw him riding his horse faster than she felt safe as he headed for the crossing of the North Fork. She let out a sigh and sat at the table.

"He's right, you know," Adam said. "He has a job and nobody can really help him do it even if I'd also like to."

She realized then the truth of that. Adam had loved Rand for as long as she had. Longer as they had bonded in the Rogue Country. "I know," she admitted.

"We have to make some plans for this place," Jed said. "Let's have a confab in say an hour and figure out how we prepare for what might be as well as get the branding and castrating done."

"Aren't you going to order everybody?" Belle asked feeling in a surly mood.

Jed snorted. "I could if you think I should, but it'd work better if we talk it over as a family with all opinions considered. I'll go over to Matt and Amy's house and suggest they come back. Toddy should have the kids in class; so we can talk this out and hopefully come up with a plan that works."

"I'm sorry," she said reluctantly. "I was being rude."

"You apologized," Raine said with amazement in her voice.

Belle looked at her, at first not understanding before she realized what she said. "I apologize when needed," she said defensively. "Just it's rarely needed." With that, she laughed, and they all laughed with her.

An hour later, except for Jack, who headed down to Monument for the week's supply of milk, and Toddy who had the children in the great room, the adults gathered in the kitchen around the table.

Jed laid out the concern and the possible complications. "I built the fence below the house to fend off an Indian attack. It will protect the ones behind it from rifle shots if they don't stick their head up too often." He grinned. "It should work for the possibility of a militia showing up here."

"You think that will happen?" Matt asked from where he sat at the other end with one boot on the chair beside him.

"It could. From what I know of men like him, Forester manipulates and uses people. He may try to inspire his followers to attack us to get back his children who had been kidnapped. He will use what he needs in order to rile up his force."

Josh went to the pump and filled a glass of water. "But we have the cattle to brand and castrate, or do we let them go loose now after gathering them?"

"I think we can do the work if we have some of us at the barricades. And that could include any woman who can handle a rifle."

Martha smiled as she absently rubbed Adam's shoulder. "That means all of us then."

"It does."

"I don't like it, of course," Adam said, "but you are right."

"We'll work up a schedule," Jed said. "Anyone who wants to take a turn with the cattle is welcome. Josh and I will get the job done as fast as we can, but we'll keep them corralled afterward."

'Why?" St. Louis asked.

"Just might be a good idea."

Belle saw that he had a reason but wasn't about to reveal it. "When we finish with this part, I need to talk to Jer and Jessica," she said. "I want to see what they want."

"Excellent idea," Amy said. "You could use the great room, and I'll take the others outside for a few calisthenics."

After the children had run outside, Belle settled Jessica and Jeremy beside her on the big sofa.

"Is something wrong?" Jeremy asked.

"I want to explain a little about what I am thinking. You can tell that things are happening."

"I saw the captain ride off. Did he leave us?" Jeremy said with the kind of hard expression on his face that a child should not have.

"No, he had a duty to perform, something he had promised to do." She wondered how much children could understand and what would make this better for them. "So much happened since we left Canyon City, and I have had little time to sit and talk with you."

"You want to leave us now?" Jessica asked with a worried expression. Again, it upset Belle how children so young would have learned to think that way.

"No, I do not. I want to know though what you want. We took you from Canyon City because it wasn't going to be safe there. I had little time to explain what I wanted, but first I would like to know what you would want. It must be hard for you to understand all of this."

"What's to understand?" Jeremy asked. "You want to get rid of us too."

Only the truth would deal with this. "No, I'd like to adopt you."

Jeremy looked stunned. "Adopt? Like make us your family?"

"Exactly. It is what I want, but I may not be able to do it. I have to find out what we can do legally, and there is the consideration of your father and mother. Even though your father has done bad things, he might still have legal rights to you."

"I don't care," Jeremy said with tears running down his cheeks. "I'd like to be part of this family and be adopted by you."

Jessica nodded. "I want you to be my mother."

"Then I will talk to a lawyer about it. I will do everything I can to make it happen."

"But our father might try to stop you," Jeremy said with those eyes that were too knowing for a nine year old.

She nodded. "And I do need to find out if your mother is still alive. You don't really know she died, do you?"

Jeremy shook his head. "No... but I did remember her name. I didn't want to tell you."

She smiled. "That would help if you tell me."

"It was Mary. MaryAnn, I think."

She hugged them both to her. "All right, I will do what I can to find her and get permission for you to live with me or even, if she is alive, for her to come and live with us all. So why don't you go outside and play with the others."

She rose but before she could go back to the kitchen, Jeremy ran to her and grabbed her with a big hug. "I love you," he said and then ran out. Jessica gave her a hug with the same words and then they were gone.

In the kitchen, she relayed what the children had said. "Good," Martha said, "this is going to work well. I feel it in my bones."

"Fortune telling added to your witch's brews?" Amy asked teasingly.

"You might say so." She smiled and set out to punch down the bread and shape it into loaves.

Half an hour later Jack Grimes came into the kitchen with the cans of milk. "Russ Adamson said he's riding to Boise in the morning. "He said if anybody got a letter to go east, he'd take it when he comes by."

"Oh my," Belle said as he went out the door.

"What is the problem?" Raine asked from where she had begun to brown chunks of beef for a stew.

"Maybe I am reluctant to have the children's mother be found. What if she wants the children?"

"She might," Amy said, "is that all that's worrying you?"

"What if it triggers Annie coming here to get revenge? She had a gun on the stagecoach when we were attacked, and she wasn't hesitant about firing it."

"You think she'd try to bushwhack Rand?"

"It had occurred to me."

The four women sat at the table and considered. "Maybe it was all talk," her mother suggested.

"It could be. She said her brother sent her money and his not having that anymore as well as the local waterfront boss—Russell Grayson being killed—forced her out."

"Oh, two grudges," Raine said as she sucked in a breath. "She could blame Jed for that one."

"Maybe I am being too imaginative. Besides, I guess it's possible Bernice would tell her anyway, but would it even come up until Bernice got the letter asking about a MaryAnn, possibly Forester, if she didn't change her name, with flaming red, curly hair?"

"Do you have a choice?" Amy asked.

She shook her head. "You're right. Just Rand has been through so much these last months. I don't want him in more danger than his job takes him."

"It might be Annie never got to Bernice," her mother suggested in her usual level tone. "It also might be they already have talked about it. Bernice knew the truth of what happened. She was living here then and heard the whole story. Annie might know how it happened and has let it go."

"Well, there is no choice," Belle said and rose. "The children have to come first."

CHAPTER 22

R and rode into the fort tired but feeling satisfied at making the
ride with only two rests along the way. He was almost physically
back, to where he had been. All right, he admitted, only to himself, he
wasn't, but he would be.

He dismounted and responded to the corporal's salute as York told
him he was relieved to see him.

"Thanks. Ask Sergeant Coleman and Lieutenant Murphy to come
to my quarters in half an hour," Rand led Blue into the corral. "You
are the best, big boy," he said to the gelding as he unsaddled him and
gave him a good brushing before putting him in a stall with hay.

When he got to his quarters, the sergeant and lieutenant were
waiting.

"You could have asked one of the men to take care of your horse,"
Murphy said as he followed Rand inside.

Rand took his jacket off and put it on the hook, collected the
makings for a cigarette before he sat on the front of his desk. He had
already taken the strap off his gun to make it easy to access. "I could
have, but I like Blue to be loyal to me. Loyalty is important. Sit in the
chairs, gentlemen." He watched the two men as he rolled a cigarette
and lit it. Let them stew. Most likely only one was worried.

"Sergeant Coleman," he said after his first satisfying draw on the
cigarette, "do you recall my sending a letter with you which was to go
to Colonel Schaeffer?"

"Yes, sir. I was to give it to Lieutenant Murphy. Which I did."

Murphy shook his head. "I got no such letter."

Rand smiled as he smoked. Not a surprise that the traitor would lie. It still came down to which one. He met their gazes again. "So one of you is lying."

"Corporal Wilder saw me give it to him," Sergeant Coleman said.

Rand raised his voice. "Corporal come in here."

Jensen came in. "Yes sir."

"Get Wilder."

"No need," Murphy said slumping in his chair. "I got the letter."

"Jensen, stay by the door. So now, Murphy, explain." When he saw Murphy reach toward his gun, he reached out and slammed it from his hand. "Jensen put the lieutenant in irons."

In moments, Murphy was handcuffed and pushed back into his chair. "Now explain."

"Got nothing to say."

"You and Lockwood were in this together."

"You have no proof."

"I have the fact that an important report did not reach Schaeffer." He sat back on the desk smoking. "I have another that too much information got through to Forester and others in his gang. I have enough to hang you, and you know it."

"Do it then. I believe in the cause. The government is corrupt. We need a new one."

Rand shook his head. "You are a fool, Pat. Jensen, take him to the guardhouse."

"And what do you want me to do, sir?" Coleman asked.

"In the morning put together a company. I want Sergeants Manning, Sullivan, and you. I'll be leaving Smith here in charge until we can get two new lieutenants down here. For now I need sleep."

"Yes sir."

When he was alone, Rand blew out the light and undressed. Naked he collapsed onto his bed but kept his gun under his pillow. He had no reason to think there were more traitors but at this point, anything was possible.

He felt frustrated that a good man, as he had always known Murphy to be, had been waylaid by a phony cause led by a man who knew how to inspire as well as to torture. Rand understood what he had to do next, but he didn't like any part of it. So many that fell in with someone like Forester were like Murphy, not personally greedy but naïvely patriotic and easily manipulated. It didn't mean they couldn't kill just as effectively.

He fought to keep himself from thinking of Belle, but her image filled his thoughts. He remembered her as a girl and then as the beautiful woman that she had become. If she accepted him as her husband, what life would she want? He knew what he wanted, but he might have to give that up if he intended to hold her. And hold her, he would. If she had loved him once, she would again.

When he woke at Reveille, he changed his immediate plan. The tap at the door came when he was dressed, armed and ready to go. "Do you wish breakfast here or in the mess, Captain?" Corporal Muldoon asked.

"Mess but I have something to attend to first. Come with me, Jim."

He walked across the parade grounds to the guardhouse where he was greeted by Private Sichy.

"I need to talk to Murphy. You two wait outside." He entered the room where at one end there were two iron cages, one occupied. He sat on the bench and looked at the man lying on the cot watching him.

"You ruined your career and life, Pat," he said. "Want to tell me why."

"I told you why. This country is going to hell in a handbasket. The president is corrupt. Congress worse. What they done to the South is criminal."

"I see." He rolled a cigarette. "And you figure someone like William Forester can fix that."

"The Colonel has ideas."

Rand gave a short laugh before he took his first drag on the cigarette. "How well do you know him, Pat?"

"Well enough to know he can inspire people and he will make this a better country—at least the part he controls."

"So not so much an insurrection as another civil war, and this one taking the Northwest out of the Union?"

Murphy sat up and ran his fingers through his hair. "Something like that."

"And it was worth hanging for?"

"Hanging? I haven't done anything that would justify that."

"Yes, you have. You are a traitor. I was nearly killed thanks to Forester's plotting that you were helping by carrying information to him. I don't think you know Forester all that well... Or do you?"

"What'd that mean?"

"Tell me what you know about the man you call a colonel."

"He's a great strategist. He cares about little people. He'd never do what you did in the name of your country."

"What did I do?"

"Steal his children and murder his cook and butler."

Rand had to work to school his features. "And how did you learn I did that?"

Murphy buried his head in his hands. "You killed Lockwood to keep it all quiet."

"And who told you all of this?"

"We have a network, of course. I'll be a captain in his army when we claim this land and all east of the mountains in Oregon for now. We can do a better job killing the savages than you ever did. When people see how we govern, the rest of Oregon will fall into place along with Washington. It'll be our own country and a damn sight better than what is coming out from back East, the lousy, sniveling carpet-baggers."

"I don't have time to argue with you, Pat," Rand said rising. "I am sorry for what you believe."

"You think you'll catch him," Murphy said with a smirk.

Rand sat back down and took a calming draw on the cigarette. "What do you know that I should know?"

"Nothing."

"Do you know how I'd get information from you if I was the man you admire so much, a man who takes a title he never earned, never served in any military. Did you know that?"

"Don't have to serve to know how to lead."

Rand shook his head. "No rules either as to how you'd lead or get information. Do you know how Forester gets it?"

"What are you talking about?"

Rand put the cigarette between his lips. "Using torture and murder. Forester has many games he enjoys, when he has someone weak. Did he do any of that to you?"

"He wouldn't do that."

"Tell me why he nails jackets to a wall as trophies?"

"That's not the colonel."

"That is the colonel. The part of him you don't meet until you are weak or under his power."

"But then..."

"We didn't tell you the whole truth regarding what happened under your colonel because at that point, we didn't need you to know. Dylan Hoyt was an agent for the military investigating the counterfeiting and purchasing of arms that Forester was doing. Hoyt was murdered, his throat cut but only after he'd been tortured."

"But the colonel... he let you go?"

"Hardly." He opened his shirt to show Pat the scars. "Here's what your hero likes to do. I'd been hit too hard to satisfy more of his savage pleasures. He thought he was sending me out with two of his men to be tied to a tree with my throat cut so it would look like the Paiutes did it. Pinkerton though had also sent an agent to investigate Forester. That agent saved my life."

"And then Mrs. Morgan found you?" Now Murphy was looking disturbed.

"Mrs. Morgan was in Canyon City working for Pinkerton. She is the one who found the counterfeiting plates and the arms he'd been amassing."

"But the children and the household staff that you murdered."

Rand shook his head. "I had a squad with me. Do you think I could have murdered them and kept it secret?"

"You murdered your brother." Pat was beginning to sound desperate.

"When I came to the house for the children, to get them away from a sadistic bastard, to make those counterfeiting plates worthless, my brother tried to shoot me from where he'd been hiding. His shot missed. Mine did not. You have been duped, Pat. Ruined your life and for a lie. I didn't kill his staff. Obviously, Forester did when he found the children gone. We only took Jeremy and Jessica with us to keep them safe.

"Belle came to love those children and after she'd seen what Forester did to me, what someone else had told her he does to anyone under his control, she couldn't stand seeing the children left there. My bet is if they had been there, they'd have also been murdered as part of his plotting and then leaving evidence to implicate me or Jed Hardman. Forester knew Hardman would stand against him. He takes out anyone strong who is against him."

"God." Murphy sunk his head again in his hands. "I can't believe this."

"I did not kill Lockwood either. He saw the jackets on the wall. My guess is one of them was his, which since Lockwood wasn't dead means he had been Forester's lover. Lockwood stabbed me but missed a killing blow. We fought, and he fell, hitting his head. I wanted him alive, not dead."

Murphy let out a sigh. "How can I know what to believe?"

"You think I'd cut myself like the marks you saw?" He buttoned his shirt and tucked it back in. "You have been played, Pat. I am sorry for you as you ruined your life, but worse, you've done real damage to a lot of innocent people also." He rose and headed for the door.

"Where are you going?" Murphy asked.

"To arrest the leaders, Forester and Moriarty and anyone with them."

"Wait."

Rand turned. "For what?"

"They won't be in Canyon City."

Rand felt as though his heart stopped. He knew but asked anyway. "Where will he be?"

"Getting his children."

"How many men?"

"Fifty last I heard. I am sorry, Captain. I didn't know."

Rand ran for the door. "Have the bugler blow To Arms," he yelled to Sichy. "I want Squad B, C, D, and F fully armed and on horseback in ten minutes. Supplies enough for a week out."

He saw Sergeant Smith running toward him. "You will be in charge here with A and E. No patrols, secure the fort from any possible attack. No wood gathering." Just in case, this also was a trick. He couldn't afford to wait. He headed for the corrals. Blue had had a night's rest. It would have to be enough for both of them as they would have to ride hard and fast.

Rising from the supper table, Jed said, "Josh, Jack, and Matt come with me to the corrals and let's finish up the last forty head; so tomorrow we don't have to go back."

The three rose. "You don't need me?" Adam asked as Belle helped her mother and sisters clear the table.

"Stay with the house. I have an uneasy feeling about this. Not sure what it is, but St. Louis, Raine, and Martha, how about you take turns at the barricades until I get back, and I'll take the night watch."

"You think someone needs to be there all the time?" Amy asked as the children watched with big eyes.

Jed stopped. "How about taking the children into the great room, Toddy. Weren't you starting to read them *Tanglewood Tales?*"

Toddy rose. "I was."

The children still looked uneasy. Only Eli gave Jed one of those looks that said he knew what was up.

"All right, I want someone with a gun here in the house." He looked at Belle. "Are you armed?"

She smiled and patted the specially made pocket in the dress she has selected when she left the Forester home. "Yes."

"Then two armed. Toddy is a lousy shot. He will stay with the children if there is an attack." He smiled. "I hope I am worried for nothing, but we need to be prepared in case I am not. I will finish with the cattle in the small pen as quickly as I can."

"I should change," Belle said running from the room. Her dress did have a pocket for a gun but she wanted to be wearing her pants, a coat, and her revolver with more stopping power. She felt some of what Jed did. Something wasn't right.

When she came back through the great room, she carried her Henry. She smiled as she heard Toddy reading, with great drama, the story of the giant Antaeus and the pygmies. She loved all of Hawthorne's stories, and another day she would have loved staying to listen. Now she felt a need to reconnoiter around the house and see where entry might be made if someone was not coming the front way.

At the barricades, her mother and St. Louis were sitting, four rifles between them, drinking tea. "Jed did a good job on this," Belle observed as she saw the thickness of logs with slotted portals to shoot through.

"You think they'll come at us like a trained army?" St. Louis asked.

"I don't really know," Belle said. "In the Civil War, it wasn't unusual to have half the force come directly forward but others from the side when it was possible to cut around. Forester was never a soldier but he likely studied the battles."

"You sound like you were a soldier, Belle," her mother said.

"Well, I was working for Alan through much of the War. I have seen a few battles, not from the thick of the battle but observing with the generals. Most of them didn't ride at the head of their troops—except a few like Custer, Pickett, or Stonewall." She expected that if Forester was to be with the men attacking the ranch, he would do the same—stay away from the line of fire.

"You ever know Custer?" St. Louis asked. "Hear a lot of stories about him."

"Not well, but I have met him. We can talk about it later. I need to go on around the house. I wanted to familiarize myself with the approaches. Remember, stay back from those portals if shooting starts."

"Other than when we are firing," her mother said with a smile. Belle observed they had boxes of cartridges alongside their rifles. They were ready.

By the time Belle had made her away around the lodge, she felt confident in the way Jed had cleared any covering underbrush. Anyone approaching the house would have to do it in the open with one exception—to the northeast and the hot spring creek. It also flowed past the barns, which meant Jed would be aware of what moved that way.

She walked back into the house to the great room where Toddy was concluding the story. Since it was her favorite part, she sat to listen.

"Some writers say, that Hercules gathered up the whole race of Pygmies in his lion's skin, and carried them home to Greece, for the children of King Eurystheus to play with. But this is a mistake. He left them, one and all, within their own territory, where, for aught I can tell, their descendants are alive to the present day, building their little houses, cultivating their little fields, spanking their little children, waging their little warfare with the cranes, doing their little business, whatever it may be, and reading their little histories of ancient times. In those histories, perhaps, it stands recorded, that, a great many centuries ago, the valiant Pygmies avenged the death of the Giant Antaeus by scaring away the mighty Hercules."

He closed the book. "So you see, might doesn't always make right and sometimes the small can vanquish the powerful by their wits and standing together."

"It doesn't really work that way," Jeremy said with his mouth set in that stubborn line.

"Oh really," Toddy said, "and you know this why?"

"You couldn't beat Jed in a fight."

Toddy grinned. "But I would not try."

"See."

"When I see someone powerful like Jed, someone who is also mighty of spirit, I connect myself to them. They become my friend."

"Even if they were a bad person?" Jeremy was clearly thinking deeply.

"No, not then. Then I would stay away from them or get someone mighty like say Captain Phillips on my side, and he'd take care of them."

"He almost died," Jeremy said. She saw in his eyes how important this was to him and why he was unwilling to give up the argument.

"His power though overcame that."

"With help."

"Which is the point of the story," Amy, who had also been listening, said. "We all need help and that's not a bad thing."

"Except it doesn't come."

"Sometimes... and sometimes it does."

Belle heard the sound of two sharp shots. "Toddy take the children into the kitchen please. Time for a snack." The walls were thickest there. Amy followed and grabbed a rifle from the rack. She was brave in a pinch and from the look on her face, she knew this was one. Knowing how she felt at the idea of Rand in danger, she could only imagine the emotions Amy was suppressing as Matt was out at the corrals.

"Toddy, would you serve the children pie?"

Adam came out from the backroom with his rifle. Amy looked then at Belle. "Jesse is asleep in the crib in here, but if this gets noisy, you will have to hold him... one of you." She then ran outside to the barricade.

Belle saw men riding across the pasture toward the house. At first she thought not as many as they had expected, then she saw there were two bunches, coming from opposite sides of the pasture. The women were holding fire and waiting until they got closer.

She was as surprised as the attackers must have been when a herd of long-horned cattle came galloping toward them. Jed and Matt were riding at their rear, both bareback and firing their rifles. The cattle were in a full out stampede.

Belle forced her attention back to the house as she heard a barrage of bullets, no idea from where any were coming. The likeliest location for an attempt to enter the house would come from those men to the right, who could circle the barricades.

Adam, after checking on the barricades, returned to the kitchen. They propped the door open as they waited for the expected home assault. He gestured to Toddy, who moved the children into the treatment room alongside the kitchen. Other than Jeremy and Jessica, the children had been trained for their roles in any attack. They showed no fear. Although tears were running down Jessica's cheeks, she did as ordered and stayed with Toddy.

She brought her rifle to her shoulder when she heard running feet. She shot the man on the left, saw him fall, as Adam took out the one on the other side. The third raised his gun but then turned to run. Adam stalked past Belle.

"Stop right there or die where you are," he yelled. There were more shots and then silence in the house with shots still heard outside.

She looked then to see more riders had entered the pasture with a trumpet blast and more firing. These wore blue coats. She smiled. To the rescue again, she thought as she ran through the house. Before she could get to the other end of the great room, she heard a scream from Raine. "Mama!"

Adam turned white as he ran out the front door to the barricades. Belle looked and saw her mother slumped against the wall, holding her bleeding arm and smiling. "Just a scratch," she said as St. Louis ripped open her sleeve to deal with the injury. So like her mother to think first of reassuring others. Belle knew if she ended up half the woman her mother was, she'd have her work cut out for her.

This job though was not done. She would bet everything she had that Forester had stayed out of the fighting and was waiting, with a small crew, where he expected to be safe, where a general would have waited, a command position, where he could run like a rat now. She was not going to let him get away this time.

CHAPTER 23

As the men in the militia, looking stunned, began throwing down their weapons, Rand saw Forester wasn't with them. He hadn't expected he would be. He rode past his troopers with orders to take their weapons and secure the prisoners while he spurred Blue toward where Forester would be, as a man who always let others do his fighting.

He saw the running horses before he got to the ridge and spurred his tired gelding, into a gallop. Receiving the burst of speed that only a trained warhorse could deliver. He smiled grimly as he cut off the exit path and saw Forester and those with him recognize their situation.

Although Forester had raised his gun, Rand didn't slow. He lowered himself over Blue and rode straight for him. He turned Blue at the last second as he launched himself on the cur.

The force of his leap took Forester from his saddle, he landed with him and rolled. When Forester coughed and tried to rise, Rand landed a fist squarely in his face as he used his other hand to twist the gun from his grip. Forester tried to fight back but Rand had his chance to do what he'd not been able to the night he'd been taken. He landed five solid blows before he finally let Forester collapse to the ground.

"Stay right where you are and don't make a move," he heard Belle's yell and managed a tired smile. There was another shot and he saw her Henry pointed at the other men. Slowly they put their hands in the air.

Rand yanked the barely conscious Forester to his feet.

"You three get off your horses," he ordered.

"We didn't do nothing," one man said as Sichy and York rode up.

"Put these men in cuffs. Then make sure the other men are sitting on the ground and unarmed in the open space below the house." When Muldoon would have taken Forester, he said, "No, leave him for now." He turned then toward Belle who was standing with her rifle crooked in her arms.

"You save my hide again?" he asked as smiling he walked to her.

"It's a rough job but somebody has to do it," she said with an answering smile. "Of course, I am not sure they intended to shoot you. More just to escape."

"Either way, good work, Mrs. Morgan." When he would have kissed her, Jed rode up.

"Looks like a clean sweep. The men below gave up without much of a fight. There is something a little strange about this."

"Too easy?" Rand asked thinking the same thing. He turned then to look at the still stunned Forester.

"Whatcha figurin' to do with him?" Jed gestured to Forester, his Georgia accent stronger as Rand had heard before when he had been in battle.

Forester stared at the two as he regained his voice but without the imperious tone more familiar to Rand. "Take off these chains. You can't do anything with me."

"You want to bet?" Rand asked, tempted to hit him again.

"Mama got shot," Belle said, as she turned and ran back to the house.

"Luckily just a flesh wound," Jed told Rand. "Not that you can convince her daughters, son, or Adam of that."

Rand patted Blue on the neck as he considered the still stunned looking Forester. "Any other casualties?" he asked.

"Five of theirs killed, two in the house. The rest crumbled under the longhorn stampede and the cavalry showing up. What are you going to do with them?"

"I am thinking." He turned back to Forester. "Where is Moriarty?"

Recovering enough to smirk, Forester just looked at him.

"I could use your methods to get the answer."

Forester smiled. "But you can't, can you?"

Rand let out a breath. The miscreant was right. He couldn't. Rand had already pushed his body beyond exhaustion, but he had one more thing to do. He looked back at Jed whose own smile was making Forester look a little less sure of himself.

"He can't," Jed said, "but I could. Want me to?"

"No, but it's tempting," Rand said with a laugh. "I will need to talk to those who were stupid enough to follow this bastard. What comes next may go easier if they understand the fools they have been. Will you take Blue to your corral?"

Jed nodded as Rand pushed Forester in front of him up to the house. At the porch, he ordered two of his men to stay on each side of Forester, before he stepped onto the porch. He let gaze roam over the men now sitting on the ground and looking uneasy at their situation.

"You are all under arrest, but I want you to understand the lies that brought you here. You were told children had been kidnapped and their caregivers ruthlessly murdered. You were told you were fighting for a just cause with a leader who would lead a new nation in a way you could be proud."

He pointed to Forester who now stood mute. "You followed this man and believed his lies. You bought them because you wanted to think there was a better way. Some of you wanted to be part of a better way. Some maybe only hoped to profit from someone like William Forester who murdered his staff to get you to believe his cause was just.

"The courts will determine the worth of each of your individual cases, but I want you to understand something very important for the next time you are led by someone who has charisma but no honor. This nation was founded by organized leadership. Yes, the country did fight to free itself from Great Britain, but it did so under a Declaration of Independence and quickly a Constitution, not written at one man's behest but by the new government. When we fought the War between the States, it was to keep order, to keep a government elected by the people. It was no one man leading others and creating anarchy, which is what William Forester was attempting to do by spreading phony money, by arming Indians."

He saw the disbelief on some of the faces.

"Yes, the arms he brought have found their way into the hands of hostiles. Some of those guns may have murdered a friend or relative of yours. Chaos is how someone like Forester gets his power. He brought you here with lies. I did not order the murder of Lieutenant Lockwood or Sally Hensen and Jenks."

He heard a hiss from Belle, who he realized for the first time was standing behind him. He wished he had had time to tell her first although there was no way to soften such a blow.

"I offered his all too loyal but mistaken servants an opportunity to be taken somewhere safe. They stayed with the home because of possible loyalty, or they feared losing their jobs. They also did not fully understand the sort of man for whom they worked.

"At Camp Watson, Lieutenant Murphy told me about the lies you were told regarding their deaths. We did not kidnap the Forester children but rather took them into protective custody until we could secure their safety. Yes, they are here. Courts of law will determine where they live, but it is a court of law that should do that. I cannot prove this, but believe that Forester convinced my own brother to try and kill me. He shot first.

"This all tells you the kind of man William Forester is. He is a man who would have run away if he could have. This is a man who kills when someone is weak. He tortures." He opened his shirt and pointed to the scars around his nipple and on his chest. "What kind of man does this kind of thing? I will tell you, the sort that abuses and lies for only one reason-- his own power." He buttoned his shirt.

"I do not know how long you will each spend in prison for your part in this conspiracy, but when you come out, I hope you will look beyond showy words, remember the price your forefathers paid for this land, the blood that was spilled to give men freedom and the right to vote. Voting is how we make changes, not through violent means. For all who hoped you joined this man with some hope of making a better world, I guarantee that was not what William Forester wanted with his corrupt and perverted view of life.

"All right. You will sleep in the meadow with armed guards ordered to shoot any man who attempts to leave. Through the cold night, you will have time to think about what you've done. You will then walk back to Watson and be taken in chains in a wagon to The Dalles, or you can make a run for it and take your chances on the marksmanship of my men. You still have a choice regarding your actions. Not the outcome."

Rand looked for Sichy. "Chain this one with the others. That is all."

It was the longest speech Rand had ever given, and he felt totally spent. For the first time he wondered how his body had held up through what he had demanded of it. When he turned back to the lodge, Jed was at his side. "You will stay in your room tonight, of course," he said with that drawl that made Rand smile despite his exhaustion.

"I appreciate that." He thought then of the missing Moriarty, but even more what Jed had said. This had been too easy. These men weren't trained military in any sense. What had Forester hoped to gain here? "I'd like to talk to everyone later."

Inside the kitchen, Rand saw Martha sitting in a chair and complaining that everyone was making too much of this as they flitted around her. Adam still looked pale. "I thought the barricade would keep you safe," he repeated. Clearly, he was able to deal with danger to himself but not his wife.

Eli was standing with the other children. "Next time, I man the barricades and Mama mans the kitchen," he said in that stern eleven year old voice.

Martha laughed. "When I am ready to let you tell me what to do, I will let you know," she said. "It was just a fluke that the bullet got through and I think it might have bounced off the wall because of how it hit me with so little force."

"She *would* still be giving orders," Belle said with a little laugh, which Rand saw she was forcing.

"Do you want something to eat, Captain?" Toddy asked as he heated back up what they had had for supper.

"No, but anything you can offer my men would be appreciated. We rode like the devil to get here."

"And thank God you did," Raine said. "It might have ended very differently otherwise. There were so many of them."

Rand slumped into a chair wishing for a smoke.

"Want me to roll you one?" Jed asked.

Rand smiled tiredly. "I can manage and thanks." When he lit it, he took a satisfying draw. "It's been a long day." And for him, it wasn't over. He had to talk to Belle, but he felt so tired, he wasn't sure his mind was capable of putting together the arguments needed to convince her to be his wife.

St. Louis was pouring himself a cup of coffee. "Never seen the like of it. Cattle stampede on one side and cavalry riding up from the other." He chuckled.

"My men got a surprise with that one too," Rand said as he smoked.

"I didn't expect you'd be coming," Jed said as he leaned back against the counter, boots crossed in front of him. "I knew though how irritated the cattle were at having been corralled. They are half-wild at best. They seemed our best chance to throw the militia off-guard."

Rand laughed. "They were that."

"So what now, Captain?" Belle asked. She was sitting at the opposite end of the table and studying him.

She would ask that question. He gave her the easy answer. "I will get these men back to the fort, as I said with them walking all the way. Then I will have them taken in wagons to The Dalles, where a court can deal with them."

"And that includes Forester?" Adam asked from where he sat beside Martha, rubbing her neck.

"I'll question him again, but he won't start trying to bargain for his life until he knows there is no hope. He's not there yet."

"What do you mean?" Belle asked.

"And how did you find out he was heading here?" St. Louis asked.

"When I got to the fort, I got Murphy to admit he was also a believer in Forester's cause. I convinced him of Forester's nature and he told me the plan." He took another drag on his cigarette. "It might help some with his court martial. It's a real shame how even good people can be duped by someone like Forester just because he's a smooth talker."

"You did a pretty good talk yourself, Captain," Toddy said as he took a helping of the warmed up stew. "I wouldn't mind writing that down." He grinned.

"You do that," Rand said. He had something else to work through but felt incapable of getting there mentally. "I am sorry, but I really need to lie down." He fought back a wave of weakness. He felt Belle's arms come around his waist. There was nothing he wanted more.

With his boots off and both of them lying on the bed he had used when at the home before, she asked, "Now what else is going on?"

"Jed figured it out. This was too easy. Forester didn't just want the children back or even to take this house. He may not have even hoped for that."

"What did he want?" She paled.

"I can't think it through right now, but you be thinking of what is most likely. I need to sleep. When I wake up, we need to have a confab." He saw her worried expression but was too exhausted to do more than close his eyes and instantly fall asleep.

It was almost dark when he woke, aware Belle was sleeping beside him. He truly had slept like the dead if he hadn't been aware she had stayed with him. "How do you feel?" she asked as she ran her fingers along his chest, stopping at the buttons.

He grinned. "Like I would rather be doing that but better not. This isn't over."

"I figured that's what you were saying."

He sat up and pulled on his boots. "You should come with me. I want to talk to the others regarding what comes next."

She nodded and followed him to the kitchen where the family, minus Martha, Toddy, and the children, were sitting drinking coffee.

"How you feeling, Captain?" St. Louis asked handing him a cup.

"Like I can use that." He sat at the table with Belle settling next to him. "I don't know how much you have already figured out," he said smiling. As much as he was used to giving orders, he saw how it was with this family and felt a relief that it was so. It was far better being part of a group that he could trust than dispensing orders unsure who might be a traitor.

"Nothing much," Josh said. "Toddy went with Martha, Jack, and the children to their cabin. They could do with playing with a cat and the dogs without worrying about what happened or might yet."

Adam was sitting with one booted foot on the chair rail next to him. "Jed told us what you and he agreed. It's not over."

"It won't be until we have the ringleaders. Moriarty is one of them and not sure about Campbell but he wasn't here either and he let his house be used as a place for murder and torture."

"Any idea about what happened to Miranda?" Belle asked worry in her voice.

"No, but we will find out if she made it to The Dalles," Rand said. "If she went beyond, where would she go?"

"She used to live in Oregon City."

"Miranda Campbell, right?" Adam said. "I knew her back then. She ran a small cafe. Best coffee and cinnamon rolls in Oregon... in a cafe at least." He grinned. "Your mama makes a mean cinnamon roll. I never met her husband though."

"He was usually gone," she said. "Off trying to find gold or something that would get him rich with no work. I guess he thought he found it here."

"So Moriarty, Campbell and who else?" Rand rolled a cigarette.

"I didn't see that James Dunham was here, but I don't know that he is part of any plot," Belle said. "He was just his driver."

"The question I have is what percentage of Canyon City would be sympathetic to Forester and Moriarty's kind of causes?" Rand asked.

"It's hard to say," Jed said lighting a cigar. "Most though are likely just there for the gold. The Chinese aren't going to be in it. They just want to stay out of trouble. As likely as not, they can be victims of those kinds of militias."

"You didn't feel that the attack this morning was intended to accomplish much here, you said," Rand said watching Jed through the smoke.

"You've seen military attacks. This was sloppy. They weren't really trained, way too quick to surrender. I don't think they had much idea what they were getting into. These weren't military men or those who fought in the war, not in my opinion."

"I think you're right."

"What are you going to do?" Adam asked with that thoughtful expression Rand had seen so often on his face.

"Go with my patrol with the prisoners as far as the junction. While they go onto the fort, I will take two platoons and head for Canyon City to get Moriarty and whoever else is with him."

"That sounds too dangerous," Belle said, not bothering to hide the worry in her voice.

"They won't be expecting us right away. As soon as Moriarty figures out what happened here, he'll be gone."

"How will you find him?" she asked.

"You will tell me the address." He smiled and looked into her beautiful eyes. "You can't tell me you don't know it."

"I do, all right, but I don't want you to do this."

"You want it over with, don't you?"

"You know I do."

"Then I have to do this. We need this past us for any safe future, here at the ranch of elsewhere. Moriarty might try to start this all again somewhere else. He is as guilty as Forester—for all we know, even more. Forester might be the one out front and Moriarty the real brains."

She nodded. "I should go too then."

He smiled and brushed her cheek with his finger. "No, you should not. I need you to be here, safe. You wouldn't help me this time. You'd just distract me."

She gave a humph but didn't argue, which surprised him but also relieved him.

"I'll go with you," Jed said. "When are you leaving?"

"You can't do that," Rand said. "You have to keep this place safe."

Jed laughed. "It's set up for easy defense, but there isn't much chance more of the Canyon City toughs will show up here. We won't be gone that long anyway."

Adam reached for Rand's cigarette and took a long draw. "I'll go too."

"Why?" Rand asked shaking his head. He didn't want any of these men risking their lives for him. "What would Martha say?"

Adam handed back the cigarette. "She and I already talked about it. I figured what you'd be doing. I am not letting our best chance to get Belle married off get killed." He laughed at Belle's look of annoyance.

Rand felt a warm glow at their support-- even as he hadn't wanted either to come. They were backup he'd never had. It was surprising but satisfying to find it was there for him now where his family never had been.

"You should all stay here," he said trying one last time to keep them safe.

"Waste your breath all you want," Jed said. "At first light, we will be riding with you."

After having made love, Rand and Belle slept without words. It was only as the moon was going down that she said, "I really wish you wouldn't do this."

"But you know I have to, my little warrior."

She did know that. She also knew she could not go with him. There was more and more probability that she was pregnant. She didn't feel a need to avoid the ride but instead the danger. She would not risk the baby—if there was one. Strangely, she realized she had taken on a responsibility that went beyond her own life. She hadn't told him and would not until he returned. He didn't need more pressure. She had to believe he would return.

"You will be here when I get back, won't you?" he asked as he put his arm around her to draw her against him.

"I wouldn't go off without knowing you are all right."

"Damn it, Belle, I want you to be my wife. You keep putting me off."

"I'm not the one running off." That irritated her. "Ever for that matter," she added.

"We are not going to argue." He kissed her temple.

"Fine."

He chuckled. "When I get back, we will talk. Agreed?"

"Wait a few days, rest up, and we can talk now." She knew he wouldn't agree, but she almost liked arguing with him, at least when she knew he was right, and it was more play than a fight.

"I can't wait on this, and when I make my case for you marrying me, I need my wits about me."

"Your case huh?"

"Oh yes." He ran his hand over her breast, teasing the nipple. He didn't have time to do this and he pulled it back. "And I have a good one, I think."

"Any hints?"

"When I get back."

Rand, you are wearing yourself thin."

"I'll take a break soon. Winter is a slow time for us."

He needed it now. She saw how tired he was, how unwilling though to let go. "All right, but when we talk, I promise nothing."

"I would not ask you to. Just wait." When she started to get up with him, he said, "No, I want to carry you just like this in my memory, your golden hair spread across the pillow, one beautiful breast peeking out from the blanket." He dressed quickly and then came back, put one knee on the bed and leaned down for a last kiss. Her arms went around his neck pulling her to him.

When he rose, he laughed. "Just like this. Hold that pose." With a wink, he was gone.

A full day later, Rand, Jed and Adam turned toward Canyon City with two squads. They had ridden ahead of the prisoners who were with two squads under his two most reliable sergeants, Smith and Manning. They would go to Watson, load the exhausted prisoners into wagons and take them to The Dalles along with a letter he sent for Schaeffer laying out a full report. He had Sergeants Perkins and Coleman with him. He had no reason to believe any of them had become traitors, but he supposed that would be tested, as it had been with Lockwood—in Canyon City.

"You have a plan?" Adam asked as the three of them rode abreast down the road.

"Roughly-- not get killed."

Jed chuckled. "I heard that one suggested before."

"It's the best one," Adam said, "but other than that."

"We will have to camp tonight and go in tomorrow morning early. There is a good spot off the road about eight miles out of Canyon City."

"Good idea," Jed said nodding approvingly. "Tired horses and men won't win us any battles."

"Not when we have a choice. I don't think Moriarty will be panicking yet. He could still believe Forester succeeded."

"If that was ever the plan," added Jed.

"If," Rand agreed.

Two hours later, they had set up their camp, eaten the rations they brought and were smoking and reclining around the small campfire. Six of the men were playing cards.

"You ever take up poker?" Adam asked Rand. "I don't remember you playing it."

"My life has been enough of a gamble," Rand said taking a last draw on his cigarette before throwing the butt into the small fire.

"You do have a way of finding danger," Jed said smoking his cigar.

"I do, do I?" Rand asked with a laugh. "I wasn't the one nearly got killed in The Dalles."

"Other than Montgomery and Graham," Adam said.

"Other than." He laughed as he rolled another cigarette. No point in saving the tobacco. He might not be around to smoke it another day.

"You a fatalist, Rand?" Jed asked watching him through the smoke.

"What makes you ask?"

"A theory that a lot of men who came out of the War are."

"I suppose that makes sense. It might not seem like it, but I think positive. I expect to make it through any battle. In my personal life, with Belle, I am less certain."

"She still holding your feet to the fire?" Adam asked taking the cigarette from Rand and drawing on it.

"She is."

Jed chuckled. "You get the frosting before the cake there?"

"What? That didn't make any sense."

"Something my wife told his," Adam said with a laugh. When Rand handed him the makings, he rolled his own cigarette. "The gist of it is you build the relationship first and then you have sex. It works better."

"You believe that?" Rand asked trying to decide if it made sense.

"Of course not, I'm a man." The three of them laughed as they shook their heads and smoked.

"Where is Moriarty's home?" Jed asked. "Do we all go there first?"

"Assuming no gunmen are waiting for us on the road in, yep," Rand answered. "Unless you have a better idea."

"Not me. I like taking off the head of the snake first."

"You folks are just full of sayings," Rand said with another laugh. Overhead, the moon was just rising over the rimrock. It was slowly filling back out from its crescent.

"So we just knock on his door?" Adam asked.

"Unless we kick it in first. I did that with Forester's home but can't say it gained anything except scaring his help."

"Back to your problem with my stepdaughter. I don't think kicking it in would do much to get you Belle either," Adam said watching the glow of his cigarette.

"No, she won't take to being pushed." Jed agreed. "Stevens

women are tough, loyal to the core, but you don't order them around and get anywhere with it."

"I've tried begging."

Adam laughed. "I can't see you begging."

"Well, not like I'd do it with witnesses." Rand chuckled. "It didn't work either. I think I have to make it more attractive to her. And that might require leaving the military."

"You know I'd like you to do that," Adam said. "But I don't want you angry with her later for it."

"I wouldn't do it if I couldn't let go freely. I am kind of sick of it and frankly that piece of land Jed showed me looked pretty tempting."

"I already started the purchase of it for you," Jed said with a crooked grin when Rand looked over at him.

"You are the laird!"

"Man's got to think positive if he wants anything. I saw how you looked at it. I knew you wanted it, but it might take you awhile to decide. If you don't want to work it right away, I can manage it for a few years, maybe more now that I have a son."

"It's a ways off for him being old enough," Rand said. He wasn't displeased at what Jed had done. He had wanted it. The only question was how soon could he manage it.

"It is. Anyway don't feel pressured on it." Jed laughed.

"No, I wouldn't... of course, assuming we all walk away tomorrow." It was his turn for a laugh. Maybe he was more fatalistic than he thought.

"We will," Adam said, "and I hope you do let the damned military fight their own wars. Sounds like it'll be a few years before the John Day Ranch is immune to battles anyway."

"Back to tomorrow. I'll send one squad to the Campbell house in case Josiah is there. We'll take the other with us and get Moriarty. If we're lucky, we'll have it all secured in time to have breakfast at one of the cafes in town. Know any good ones?"

"I haven't even been there. Too busy getting our cabin built."

"Jesse's cafe used to be good if it's still there," Jed said.

"Something to look forward to then," Rand said as he lay flat, determined he would sleep well.

"Afterward..." Jed added and then the camp was quiet.

CHAPTER 24

"How do you live with this?" Belle asked Raine as the two of them sat in front of the fire in the great room.

"This wonderful ranch and the land here?" Raine asked with a smile.

"You know what I meant."

"All right, yes, I do. It's just who he is. If I want him, what is my choice?" She reached down and petted Deucy who was curled at her feet.

"What if he was killed, and you had to raise Jesse alone? Would it still be your choice."

Raine shook her head. "Belle, Belle, you do have a way about you. I am actually kind of glad you haven't changed though." She smiled. "And I will answer that question because I know you have a reason."

"Don't if you wish I'd never asked it."

"I have naturally thought it. Of course, I don't want to think he could be killed. Jed is my life, my everything, the man I never expected to find. But, if he were killed and never came back to me, I'd still be glad we had what we did. It's been very good with him, better than I ever imagined. I'd be so grateful I had Jesse if that was all I had left of him."

"I can see how he treats you, like a partner, not a slave."

"At one time I didn't understand how that could be."

Belle sighed and looked into the flames. "I have tried to put myself in the place of Libby Custer and imagine following Rand from post to post, knowing that what we are facing tonight is happening over and over again until he either retires or is killed. It is an hard life for a woman."

"There are options though, to stay one place, keep the home fires burning and then be there when he returns."

Belle nodded. "The wife of a career soldier."

"You don't think you are strong enough to live it?"

"I might not be." She sucked in a breath. What was her choice either? "I do love him."

"I know. And you are having his baby, aren't you?"

"It seems most likely, but how did you know? I am not very far along, not showing. He didn't notice before he left."

"It's the glow you have, and how you changed what you eat in the morning."

"I didn't think it would happen. I thought it was a safe time."

Raine smiled. "Those tend to be pretty uncertain especially with all you have been through."

"Apparently."

"Do you mind?"

"No, I might've thought I would, but I don't. I'll be glad but just more glad if he comes back."

"And what answer will you have for him when he returns? He will ask you again."

"You know the answer to that too, don't you?"

Raine smile and rose. "I need to go to bed. But yes, I do know." She reached down and hugged Belle before she climbed the stairs to her room with Deucy right behind her.

Belle sat for another hour before she went to her own bed. As she undressed, she thought over where he was. She wished she had given him her answer before he left. When she got under the sheet and covers, she could still smell his masculine scent. She took his pillow and put it under her head. Tears wetted it before she finally fell into a restless sleep.

Riding into Canyon City, Rand felt confident with no doubts this would work out as they had planned. He divided off from Perkins squad and took Coleman's with him. At the home he had been told would be Moriarty's, he, Jed and Adam dismounted and he left the squad on horseback with three at the back and the rest out front to make sure no one made it out of the house and away.

Knocking on the door, Adam went around the house while Jed stood back. With no immediate response, he knocked again

"Hold your horses," a male voice said. He'd only heard Moriarty's voice once, at the Campbell home, but he was sure it was him.

When the door was flung open, Moriarty stepped back as Rand prodded him into the room with the barrel of his revolver. "I guess you know how things went," Rand said to the robed man.

"What are you talking about?"

"You know that too."

Shockingly Moriarty smiled. "Do you mind if I dress before we talk?"

"If I go with you." Jed behind him, he followed the man into his bedroom where he watched him pull clothes from the back of a chair.

"You have no reason to arrest me, of course," Moriarty said as he began to dress.

It was then that Rand realized from the pillows that two people had slept in that bed. "If you come out of that closet, I won't kill your friend," he said his gun still pointed at Moriarty."

"Maybe I don't care all that much about him." A woman emerged from the wardrobe, her derringer pointing at Rand.

"Do I know you?" he asked but didn't change where his weapon was pointed.

"You should. We met briefly at the stage stop. I am Annie Jessup. I know you shot my brother in the back."

"Makes this interesting."

"Even more so," Jed came through the door but he wasn't holding a gun. His hands were out at his side. "I am why Bill Jessup was shot."

Rand saw Annie's expression turn less certain. "What are you talking about?" she asked, but she hadn't moved the barrel of her weapon. Still pointed at Rand's belly, it was a small gun, but it certainly could kill. In his belly, death might take awhile, but it would be just as definite an end. If Adam had made it around back, he'd be at the window.

"Your brother decided to kill me, Miss Jessup," Jed said. "He was mad that he'd quit the ranch, that I wouldn't rehire him, that his crooked dealings for Graham were finished. He was behind me, no way for me to get at my own gun. He had me dead to rights."

"Billy wouldn't shoot anyone in the back," she said. "But that one did."

Rand could almost see her finger tightening on the trigger.

"Sweetheart," Moriarty said, "don't do it. They will hang you. What that one said is true. I heard the story."

"They made it up to cover themselves." She was crying but hadn't released the gun. Rand considered jumping her but someone was likely to get shot that way. He didn't want it being himself or Jed.

"Sometimes men do shoot someone in the back," Rand said. "I did it to save Jed's life. I still think about it, wish there'd been another way. There wasn't that night."

"Bill was wanting blood and he was going to have it," Jed said. "He knew he had no chance against me face to face. He wanted me to suffer, worry before he did it, or he'd have killed me right away."

Moriarty moved then to put himself between Rand and the weapon. "Annie, they have to have arrested William or killed him."

"Arrested," Rand said.

"There are troopers outside."

"A squad at the back and front." He had heard movement beyond the window. Adam had made it there.

"He deserves to die," she said, but she put the gun on a dresser and her hands over her face.

Adam pushed open the window and stepped through. "Wise choice, Moriarty," he said, his revolver still in his hand.

"Nobody wants to kill anybody," Rand told Annie as he put cuffs on Moriarty's wrists. "Well, with a few exceptions."

Moriarty smiled. "Yes, there are exceptions. A man like me can sometimes choose a poor partner and end up wishing he'd done otherwise when he finds out all of what that means."

"This was all Forester?" Rand asked.

Moriarty smiled. "Is anything ever that simple?"

Rand turned him and sent him outside before him. On the road, he saw that his men had two other men in cuffs. If this went well at the Campbell house, it would be about as good as possible.

"What about her?" Moriarty asked as he gestured with his chin back at Annie standing on the porch.

"No charges that I know of."

Moriarty smiled. "Good. Annie," he said looking at her, "there is some money in the dresser. Use it to get a start."

She was openly crying. "I want to go with you."

"Where I'm going, that's not possible but thank you, my dear. You gave me some of the happiest moments of my life."

Annie looked then again at Rand. "I don't know if I could have killed you."

"Before, we go, I have a question for you. Belle needs to know if you know Jessica and Jeremy's mother."

"Why?" Her expression had turned sullen.

"She wants to adopt them unless she can find their mother."

"She'd do that?" Her mouth dropped open.

"She has come to love them."

More tears ran down Annie's cheeks. "Their mother is dead. She... had left him when she knew she was sick, not long after Jessica was born. Bernice took her in. You know prostitutes are often more caring than others-- for those at the bottom." She raised her brows and gave him a defiant look

"I don't try to figure people out," Rand said. "I hope you can find a better life than what you had."

"I doubt it."

Jed, who had mounted his horse, said, "It's always a choice."

Annie snorted her disbelief but only watched as they rode off.

When they got to the Campbell house, Josiah Campbell was also in cuffs and a heavyset woman stood in the door, bruises on her face and more tears running down her cheeks.

"You were supposed to have left town, Miranda," he said as he dismounted.

"I tried but Josiah got to me first." She pursed her lips together. "I guess now he won't be stopping me."

"Might not be a bad place to live now," Rand said as he remounted. "I hear you are a good cook. Always need those."

"Where'd you..." And then she looked beyond him to Adam on his horse. "You."

"Yep. I remembered your cinnamon rolls, Miranda." He smiled.

Jed nudged his stallion forward. "I might suggest if you want a start here, that there is a woman back at 12 Main Street, she could use a start too."

"Annie?" Rand asked.

He nodded. "It makes it a choice for her... either way."

Miranda smiled for the first time. "I do have a start. The money Belle gave me."

"I owe you my life," Rand said. "I won't forget it. Goodbye." With that, he turned Blue onto the street and toward the fort. They were going with five prisoners and so they stopped at the livery stable and picked up a wagon with two horses to carry them.

As he rode out of town, he thought how lucky it had all gone down. Nobody killed. More prisoners, one who might be helpful in putting Forester away for a long time if not leading to his hanging. He'd have to testify as to Moriarty's assistance at the last, something he knew Moriarty had counted on when he did what he did. Or had he really loved Annie? Who knew?

"So what's the plan now?" Jed asked as he came up alongside him.

"You head back to the ranch. I go to the fort and take care of the details. Tell Belle, I'll be back in less than a week, and she better have a wedding dress picked out.

Jed laughed. "I might tell her you'll be back in less than a week, but the last part of that, you have to deliver for yourself."

Rand joined in the laughter. For the first time in longer than he remembered, he felt good. Even better, he had a home to go to when this was all over. He didn't remember the last time for that. It was a good feeling.

It was almost a week later with snow lightly falling, Rand came riding back to the Hardman ranch. He was confident that Belle would have waited, but if she had not, he had arranged for a long break, until after Christmas before he would return to Watson. He would go after her.

From the house, the children came running out onto the porch as he rode Blue down to the corrals. Jed came from the barn. "So you made it back."

"Is she still here?"

"Of course," she said following Jed out. "I was just learning how he puts a shoe on a horse's hoof."

"And why would you need that?" he asked swinging down from the saddle.

"You never know when information will come in handy." She was wearing her boy's pants and had that cocky smile that he had come to love.

He ignored Jed and pulled her into his arms. "Now we need that talk."

"You don't want to say hello to everyone first?" Jed asked with a teasing grin.

"After the talk."

Jed laughed and walked toward the house.

"All right," Rand said, "I'd like to do this more romantically, take time, court you properly, and make you happy with it but this is how it's going to end anyway." He got down on one knee. "Will you marry me, Belle Stevens Morgan?"

She smiled at him. "Leaving off the Morgan. I have a question."

"Shoot."

"Why?"

"Because I love you and can't imagine life without you. I want to live with you until we are both old."

"Or one of us dies given your lifestyle."

"So my lifestyle is an issue?" He rose and pulled her back into the barn to lower her to a tack box.

"It's not an easy one for women."

"Did you really retire from Pinkerton?"

She nodded. "I did."

"So what life do you want now?"

"What are my options?"

He laughed. "You are certainly a stubborn woman. Let me take care of Blue and I'll be back with my answer."

He made short work of taking off Blue's saddle and releasing him into the horse corral. Then he came back to where she had not moved from the box.

"I will be your kept man if you wish it. I will move east with you if that's where you want to go."

"I don't have any great love of the East."

"Where then would you like our life to be?"

"I don't have a plan."

"Well, then let me suggest one."

"I am listening."

"It's simple. There is a short and long range. If it agrees with your desires, in the long range, I buy the ten thousand acres adjoining Jed's ranch, and we live on it. We build a home, raise crops, have children, and grow old there. How does that fit with your plan?"

She pulled him down to sit on the tack box and opened his jacket. "Kind of cold for that," he said gesturing toward the snow falling.

"I am thinking right now of very short range." In a moment, she had pulled his shirt open and moved down to his belt.

"You don't have any questions?"

"Not at the moment." She had his chest bared to her touch and lips before she removed his cartridge belt and went on to undo the first button on his pants.

"Out here?" he asked trying to put a scandalized sound to his voice when all he felt was raging desire and heat.

She slowly opened all the buttons on his pants where his erection sprang free.

"It seems you do have an opinion," she said as she knelt and took his tip into her mouth.

It had been too long for such games if he hoped to satisfy her. He lifted her up and began undoing her buttons. In a few moments, she had pushed off her boots and he'd slid off the pants. He lifted her over him. They came together in a white-hot heat as she lifted and thrust down on him. When she muffled her scream against his shoulder, he felt his own release.

It was long moments before he could talk and even longer before he could adjust his clothing as she pulled back on hers. Surprisingly or maybe not, they were neither one cold. He held her on his lap, cradled in his arms.

"So what day do we get married?"

"The sooner the better," she whispered against his neck. "And... I like the option you offered of living here." He felt her smile against his skin. "Are you sure though?"

"I am. Jed said he already started arranging for the purchase. I have mostly banked what I've made in the military and had a small inheritance from my mother. Land prices are low. We will have to start with a little smaller house than Raine and Jed's." He grinned. "But it won't have to be a shack either." He could see the wheels turning and hoped she wasn't thinking of reasons to change her mind.

"Will you ever want your father part of our life?"

He hadn't expected that question. "No. I don't hate him but he wouldn't make our lives better, not with his bitterness."

"Will he go to prison?"

He shook his head. "I suspect he had a small part in their organization. He can claim duress. If he testifies against Forester and Moriarty, he's likely to avoid prison."

"Can you really let go what he did?"

He smiled and kissed her forehead. "I suppose there'll be times I'll wish it could have been otherwise, but your family became the only real family I had from many years ago. I am just fortunate to get them along with the love of my life."

She smiled at that.

"There is a short range-- six more months in the military. I want to do what I can to end this uprising. I sent word to the colonel that as of May 20th, when my enlistment is up, I won't re-sign."

"Did he reply?"

"He congratulated me."

"You don't have to do this. I have had time to think about it, how it would be. I will follow the guidon if that's what you want."

He was surprised. "I thought you'd not consider that."

"If it is what it took to make you happy."

"It's not. The spring campaign will be my last. I want to be here for my children, not off somewhere. I find I like the idea of ranching, maybe growing grapes, even making wine. The challenges will be different, but they appeal to me."

"So, we get that chaplain of yours up here, as soon as you can do it."

"Good or if there is a little church nearby, maybe a traveling preacher. I want you my wife as soon as can be. I have a month off. We could take a little trip if you'd like, then start setting the foundation for our home, wherever you want it; and in the meantime, start making babies," he said feeling a contentment that he'd never known.

"Do you mind if we already did that?"

"You mean Jeremy and Jessica? I am delighted. They told you what Annie said."

"Yes, and we also got a letter from Bernice. She knew her as MaryAnn Foster, but the description left no doubt who she was. She died three years ago. When she left him, she had consumption and that's why she didn't take her children-- even knowing what he was. She had no family to go to. There won't be any impediment to adopting them, but that's not what I meant."

He lifted her up where he could meet her gaze. "Ours?"

She smiled.

"When?"

"Probably our first time and I'd say... oh about the middle of July or thereabouts."

He laughed then. "My god, I waited a long time for you, but it was worth it."

She gave an exasperated snort. "You waited?" She laughed with him.

"So shall we go in and tell them to plan a wedding?" He kissed her again as he rose.

"They already know, and Mama's been making the dress. It's about time you make me an honest woman."

He laughed. "Seems to me that's the other way around."

"Well maybe." Arm in arm, they walked to the house.

Inside the kitchen, the family had gathered and was waiting.

"Well, she finally said yes," Rand said as he accepted a shot glass of whiskey from Jed.

She groaned. "I finally said yes, huh! When was the first time this subject came up."

"You would hold a grudge," he said pulling her to his side.

"If you think you can win this one, boy, you are going to have a lot of lessons ahead for you," Adam said with a chuckle.

"You all need to quit teasing him," Martha said. "And you can either call me Ma or Martha. Either would be fine."

His warm glow was growing. "I like Ma," he said as she used her good arm to pull him into a hug. "Never had a mother to use it on." He looked then at the two children who were standing a bit apart. "And what about you two?" he asked kneeling down to their level. "You ready for a grandma?"

Jeremy smiled broadly. "You really do want us?"

"Hey," he said with a laugh. "It's a package deal. If I want you, I have to take her." He felt the nudge in his ribs with her knee. It was the big smile from Jessica, which had him feeling the most warmth. As much as he loved the idea of being part of this big family, helping this ranch become a place to provide food and a life for them all, he loved even more that he would have his own family, a chance to raise children and do right what his father had failed in doing.

An hour later, Jed, Adam, Matt, St. Louis, and Rand sat on the sofas in the great room, while the women got the supper ready. The children had gone to one of the rooms to play. "And what about the trials?" Jed asked sipping his whiskey.

"I got word before I left the fort that they arrested my father trying to board a steamer. I think he's more of a material witness than anything else. He is a broken man."

"And Forester and Moriarty?" Adam asked.

"Moriarty will get off light after the help he was not only with naming names, but testifying against Forester for several murders we didn't even know about. It's possible he was the real brains behind the counterfeiting operation but it won't be proven."

"So what comes next?" Matt asked. He wasn't drinking a whiskey but instead had a cup of coffee.

"I can be here until after Christmas; then will have to be part of the spring campaign. My enlistment isn't up until the end of May, but then I'll be back. Not a bad time to start a cabin."

Jed laughed. "Oh, we'll be starting it long before then. Matt's roof is on, and it only takes finishing it inside. We'll get your walls up as soon as you figure out where you want the cabin."

"Did you have a preference?" he asked knowing he did.

"Well, you said ten more years before this trouble with the hostiles is past. I was thinking it'd be best, close to us. How about to the other side of this house, above Adam and Matt's? Keep us all together, but I am willing to start it over on your piece of land if it's what you'd rather."

Rand shook his head. "No, what I'd rather is right here. That little piece would be a good place. Windows that can look toward the mountains."

Jed slapped his back. "Then it'll be done with enough rooms for three children—and more." He grinned.

Standing with the men looking into the fire, watching as Adam fed another log, Rand felt a satisfaction that he'd never expected to know. He'd never known men he had trusted so much. His own brother hadn't been worth much or maybe he'd never had a chance; but now he had men near him who felt more real than brothers could ever have been.

When Belle came in to tell them food was on the table, he held back from the others heading for the kitchen. "Just one more thing," he said.

"Is it a problem?"

"No, it's just I want to thank you for waiting for me."

"Well, I didn't exactly stand around doing that."

"No, but in the way that mattered most, you waited. And even though it might not look like it, I did too." He bent then and kissed her lips. He knew a truth that he felt lucky to have learned in the most meaningful way.

The best things in life were worth waiting for.

Oregon Historicals
Book 1 Round the Bend
Book 2 Where Dreams Go
Book 3 Going Home

Find all Rain Trueax books at
Romanceswithanedge.blogspot.com

www.ingramcontent.com/pod-product-compliance
Lightning Source LLC
Chambersburg PA
CBHW071130170626
46809CB00002B/555